Praise for *The Lost Heir*

"Rivera Sun is an amazing author. The way she threads the principles of nonviolence into the fabric of her novels is a beautiful experience. It is an education that everyone in the world needs - now more than ever." - **Heart Phoenix, River Phoenix Center for Peacebuilding**

"Rivera Sun deserves an international audience and I hope she gets it." - **Amber French, Editorial Advisor, International Center on Nonviolent Conflict**

"Five stars. It's *Harry Potter* with a contemporary message." - **Gayle Morrow, retired Y/A Librarian**

"In this book Rivera Sun pulls off an impressive feat, creating an original exciting story that deftly teaches ways to create a world that works for all. Thank you, Rivera Sun, for another outstanding contribution to the field of nonviolence through this series!" - **Kit Miller, Executive Director, M.K. Gandhi Institute for Nonviolence**

"I highly recommend gathering the children around you and reading *The Way Between* and *The Lost Heir* so everyone can enjoy and embrace these masterfully-told, exciting adventures." - **Scotty Bruer, Founder of PeaceNow**

"I highly recommend this novel to adults and children alike. You will be inspired by Ari Ara!" - **Angela Parker, Mother and Board Member of the Social Justice Center of Marin**

"During times when so many of us, especially the young, are still figuring out how to make this planet more just and livable, this book couldn't have come at a better time." - **Patrick Hiller, War Prevention Initiative**

"Ms. Sun has created a world filled with all the adventure and fun of mystics, martial arts, and magic contained in *The Hobbit*, *The Ring Trilogy*, and the *Harry Potter* series but with deeper messages. There are not enough superlatives to describe this series!" - **Brenda Duffy, Retired Teacher**

"The strong emphasis on seeing the power of nonviolence in practical use sets this young adult novel apart. The story is remarkably animated - it stays with you!" - **Chris Nelson, Chico Peace & Justice Radio**

"Rivera Sun has once again made the practice and methods of strategic nonviolence clearly accessible and understandable to both adults and youth in an entertaining and exciting story. *The Lost Heir* is both sobering and uplifting, and a "must read" for fans of fantasy and science fiction." - **Michael Colvin, Oregon Fellowship of Reconciliation**

"Rivera Sun's creativity, wisdom, insight and joyful nonviolent activism for all ages fills me with awe and hope. If we were all to read her books the way we have read Harry Potter's, we would be well on our way to sending a different message to our children." - **Veronica Pelicaric, Pace e Bene/Campaign Nonviolence**

"So good! This is exactly the kind of book I like to read and I really loved the message. It is already making me see things in a different way." - **Beth Preston, Third Grade Teacher**

"The reader is swept up in the story and his or her imagination is ignited by the author's beautifully descriptive use of language." - **Casey Dorman, Editor of *The Lost Coast Review***

"Nonviolence is rediscovering our true selves, so in a way, we are all Lost Heirs. Don't just give this book to someone, read it with them." - **Stephanie Van Hook, Executive Director, Metta Center for Nonviolence**

The Lost Heir

- An Unruly Royal, an Urchin Queen, and a Quest for Justice -

The Lost Heir

Copyright © 2019 by Rivera Sun

Rising Sun Press Works
P.O. Box 1751, El Prado, NM 87529
www.riverasun.com

Library of Congress Control Number:
2018962454

ISBN 978-1-948016-01-8 (paperback)
978-1-948016-06-3 (hardback)
978-1-948016-02-5 (ebook)
Sun, Rivera 1982-
The Lost Heir

For Maja Bengtson
for believing in this story years ago.

Other Works
by Rivera Sun

Novels, Books & Poetry

The Way Between

The Lost Heir

The Adventures of Alaren

The Dandelion Insurrection

The Roots of Resistance

Billionaire Buddha

Steam Drills, Treadmills, and Shooting Stars

Rebel Song

Skylandia: Farm Poetry From Maine

The Dandelion Insurrection Study Guide

Freedom Stories: volume one

The Imagine-a-nation of Lala Child

RISING SUN PRESS WORKS

A Community Published Book Supported By

Rivera Sun's novels are launched into the world with the generous support of a broad community of readers and supporters. Thank you to the following individuals, families, and professionals for their kind generosity:

Brian Cummings
Nancy Audette
Gloria Sirrine Switzer
Judith and Gino Schiavone
Caroline C.
Burt Kempner
Martin Dahlborg
Chuck Gregory
Sunshine Jones
Charles Johnson
Maja Bengtson
Noel Wetzel
Gail and Ken Kailing
Karen Lane
Beverly Campbell
Jeralita Costa
Donna Price
Robin Wildman
Hilda J. Richey
Barbara Van Kerkhove
Natasha Léger
DeLores H. Cook
Romaldo, Carol, Luigi & Loki
The Peace Professionals, LLC
Rosa Zubizarreta
Sally and Mark Kane
Genevieve Emerson
Deborah Cooper & Ava and Zoe Gorky
Chuck Collins

A Community Published Book Supported By

Cindy Reinhardt
Jake Donaldson
Marada Cook
Ryan, Eli, Ivyn, Arty Redmond
Glenn and Darien Cratty
Judy and Chris Pinney
Joni LeViness
Mikaela Moore
Jaige, Adam, and Aubrey
Amanda, Pete, Solas & Caulder
Monarda, Oakin, Grous, Bamboo
John Mazzola
Elyssa Marie Serrilli & Amanda Marie Stein
annie kelley, multifaith peaceweaver
Gerry Henkel
Sofia Rose Wolman
Elizabeth Cooper
David Geitgey Sierralupe
Jaimie Ritchie
Wim Laven
Jem McGuire
Rev. Silvia A. Brandon Pérez
Elizabeth Carroll
Sarah Bunting & Isaac Devenny
Leslie A. Donovan
David Cutler
Pamela Twining and Annabelle & Jasmine Ploutz
Lynn and Chris Wadelton
Sean Patrick Duffy
Sarah Day Hanson

. . . and many more.

The Lost Heir

by

Rivera Sun

Table of Contents

Table of Contents

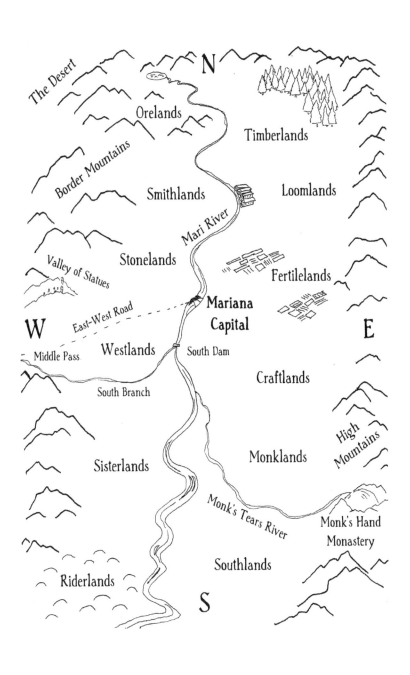

CHAPTER ONE

. . . . .

The Lost Heir

Ari Ara swung her leg over the window ledge and peered down the high stone wall of the House of Marin. She was about to break a dozen rules and frankly didn't care. If she couldn't sneeze without offending somebody in Mariana Capital, then she might as well have a little fun while she was at it. In the three weeks since she'd arrived, she hadn't been out of the House of Marin once. Instead, she'd been cooped up in her quarters enduring a mind-numbingly dull crash course in conduct and manners. Her tutors were a set of stodgy old toads whose disapproving frowns curved across their faces like the gargoyles glaring from the spouts of the rain gutters. After the first, tedious welcoming reception - where she'd apparently shocked the nobles by breaking every single law of etiquette ever invented - the Great Lady Brinelle had postponed all other events until the Lost Heir learned to behave in accordance with her newly-discovered rank as a double royal.

Sitting on the window ledge of her luxurious quarters, the long-lost daughter of the late Queen Alinore of Mariana and the Desert King Tahkan Shirar snorted in exasperation. It was hard to follow rules if you didn't know they existed! She'd like to see the pampered nobles get thrown into the High Mountains without any guidance . . . they'd realize quick as lightning that there was more to know in life than which fork went with the salad!

Ari Ara felt like the caged bear cub the villagers had trapped: constantly on display, poked at by everybody, and roaring with frustration as they tried to train the wild out of her. She'd been scrubbed red and raw, fussed over until she wanted to scream, scolded until her head hurt, and kept indoors until she thought she'd go mad with boredom.

Meanwhile, just over the rooftops, the siren song of Mariana Capital called to her. If she leaned out the windows far enough, she could catch the smells of roasting nuts, fresh-caught fish, and ladies' perfumes as the aromas wafted on the breezes. She could hear the vendors' songs as they hawked their wares and glimpse the tops of people's heads as they passed down the road.

Mariana Capital rose like a crown atop a large island in the middle of the vast Mari River, packed shore-to-shore with houses and shops. Three bridges spanned the narrow East Channel while the wide East-West Bridge crossed the bulk of the river on the far side of the island. Riding into the city on her first day, she'd gaped at the crowds of people and craned her neck to stare at the towers and tiled roofs climbing the crest of the river island. She'd ogled at the enormous houses along Marin's Way, but all she'd seen since the moment they'd turned into the courtyard of the House of Marin was the insides of rooms. The Great Lady said she could only go into the city with an official escort and that couldn't be arranged for weeks.

The constraints of her new life rasped against her like a cat's tongue until a blister of resentment and a searing itch of curiosity rose inside her. She'd never been forbidden to go places before. As an orphan, no one had cared where she'd roamed across the black cliffs and deep forests of the High Mountains. Each day, the rolling tones of the Great Bell in the top of the University Tower called to her, and secretly, she promised she would come.

Which was why, on this fine and foggy morning, Ari Ara was sneaking out to see the city. She'd risen before first light, slipped on her old training clothes, thrown the hood of her black Fanten cloak over her conspicuous red hair, and climbed out the window. Honestly! She wasn't some Capital noblegirl who'd slept in fluffy beds all her life. She had run wild across the mountains as a child, fended for herself as a Fanten shepherdess, and been an apprentice in the rigorous trainings of the Way Between under the stern watch of the Great Warrior Shulen. She could take care of herself!

Ari Ara stretched her fingers out. Slick moisture coated the surfaces of the stones. River mist veiled everything in sweeps of white and shadowy grays. The building bent slightly with the curve of the island and a long stone ledge extended the length of the wall. Ari Ara tested the cracks in the old mortar between the granite blocks. She grinned. Easier than chasing yearling lambs down from the cliffs! She slid her toes onto the narrow ledge and began picking her way carefully along the length of the building. The mist shivered as the first touch of dawn light rose over the distant mountains. The fog condensed and hunkered down thickly over the city. She could hardly see her hand, let alone the river below or the guards on the parapet at the top of the house.

Perfect, Ari Ara thought with a grin. This type of weather made everyone sleep in . . . and after last night's festivities, even the maids would be sound asleep until mid-morning. She, on the other hand, was wide-awake, since she - and her deplorable manners - hadn't been allowed to attend. Her absence had set off wild speculation among the guests that the Lost Heir was as stark raving mad as her father, the Desert King. Several nobles had even tried to sneak into her quarters to find out the truth, but the guards turned them away.

Ari Ara concentrated as she stretched over a tricky section around a stone carving. Her wiry muscles tensed. Her grip slid over a slippery spot. A sheen of sweat beaded her brow. Once past the statue, she quickly reached the corner of the house and picked her way down the drainpipe to the narrow alley below. She wiped her damp and grimy hands on the sides of her pants and pulled her Fanten cloak tighter around her shoulders.

While the nobles slept, the city stirred. The clang of dawn bells and clank of kettles echoed hollowly in the streets. Shrouds of mist walked up and down the cobblestone roads. Figures loomed alarmingly then vanished in the cloak of gray. Murmurs of voices ran through the alleys and bounced off stone walls. Ari Ara quickened her pace through the tangle of alleys that curved like the coiled river dragons on the emblem of the House of Marin.

She rounded a corner and toppled out onto what could only be Merchant's Way. A grin burst across her face at the sight of the street she'd heard so much about, but never seen. Here, it was rumored, you could find everything from ripe tomatoes in midwinter to your true love on summer solstice. Merchants traveled by lamplight to reach the street before dawn. The haggling and trading started at first light and rose loud enough by noon to be heard on the distant west bank of the river valley. Pushcarts and horse-drawn wagons packed the edges of the market road. Heaps of merchandise piled up on tables, crates, and blankets. Already, cooks jostled shoulders trying to find the freshest produce of the day. Servants shouting out orders to sellers for cases of herbs, flapping hens in crates, baskets of eggs, and bundles of onions. Ari Ara edged her way through them, eyes wide.

"Lookin' fer something?" a street urchin bellowed, clutching a woman's arm. "The maze of the market's fixed in me mind! I'll find anything you want, lady!"

The woman shook the urchin off and swept onward. The market shifted each day; there was no order to the awnings, tents, and tables except the whims of merchants and the friendships between flower sellers who pulled up carts next to each other to gossip and share a pot of tea. A potter spread out his shelves next to a carpet seller; an apple grower sat next to a book-and-bauble vender; brand new wares were placed beside antique and salvaged goods; pipes and tobacco were sold near herbal teas for lung health. The humble (shoe polish and sealing wax) stood by the exotic (singing birds and eels in glass tubs). Above the street, rows of shops opened on top of stone steps. Watermarks from the spring floodwaters marked the foundations. Flower baskets hung in the windows. Banners declaring the shops' specials hung from hooks beside the doors.

Ari Ara wove through the teeming crowd, listening to snippets of conversations between serving maids, snatches of sharp bargains being haggled by farmers over the price of turnips, bantering exchanges between odds-and-ends merchants who swapped and gambled on what the vagaries of the day would bring to the cart. Round women waved handkerchiefs to get each other's attention. Small scruffy boys whistled through their fingers. Market girls with baskets poised on their heads flirted with young warriors on their way to the Training Yards.

Suddenly, as she rounded the next bend of Merchant's Way, a hand grabbed her arm, locking like a vise around her wrist.

"What are you doing out without your blue mark, eh?" a huge smith growled at her.

"Huh? What?" she stammered, scrambling to figure out what he meant.

The smith snatched up a strip of blue fabric from the rags stall next to him and tied it around her wrist. The rag merchant, a dour woman with a pinched face, stared coldly at her, skinny arms crossed over her flat chest.

"Don't let me catch you roaming about markless again," the smith scolded gruffly, muttering about thieving desert demons as he shoved her down the street.

"Those water workers are more trouble than they're worth," the rag woman grumbled to the smith. "It's madness to have so many Desert People here in Mariana. After all the wars we've had with them, they're likely to rise up and rip our throats out in the night."

"Ah, but the nobles are raking in a fortune on their work," the smith answered with a shrug.

Ari Ara wanted to protest that she wasn't a water worker - whatever that was - but then they'd demand to know her true identity, and she couldn't reveal that! Instead, she slid out of sight among the crowd, rattled by the encounter. Ahead of her, she spotted a coat marked by a blue slash of fabric sewn in a diagonal across the back. The tall, thin man walked behind a rotund, white-aproned chef who was making choice selections of fresh-foraged mushrooms and spring herbs. The water worker carried an enormous pack into which the day's purchases of berries, bread, fish, and cream were loaded. Ari Ara stared shamelessly, a thrill of recognition searing through her at the bronzed skin and almond eyes of the man. Her heartbeat quickened at her first actual sight of her father's Desert People outside of a stiffly formal greeting to the ambassador on the first night. Feeling her gaze, the thin man turned, shooting her a quick flash of a smile and a stern look accompanied by a jerk of his head to tell her to get on her way.

"Best not to dawdle, young one," he murmured. "Water workers like us can't be caught idle."

Ari Ara started after him, trying to follow the blue slash, but she stumbled into a passel of old women arguing over who got the plumpest duck and lost sight of him. As she circled around the women, Ari Ara saw other water workers with the blue mark, all Desert People, all carrying loads and running errands with haste.

A ripple of motion behind her made her duck. A Marianan street urchin sailed past, rifling her hair with a hand swipe that had been intended to knock her across the back of her head. The ragged child kicked the next water worker and knocked the parcels out of a third man's arms.

"If you want something delivered in one piece, it's best to use an urchin!" the boy hollered, racing away as the desert man muttered a curse under his breath.

Up and down the Merchant's Way, roving packs of urchins - city orphans who refused to live in orphanages - darted through the crowded street like minnows in a stream, carrying messages for coin and delivering packages. They idled by the booths and shops, waiting for customers to come out then offering to carry parcels back to homes. They sidled up to merchants and asked if they needed pick-ups or deliveries made. They bought candies at a markdown and carried the maker's branded trays up and down the streets, selling and sampling, and pointing people back to the maker's stall. And, Ari Ara noted, they picked pockets, swiped apples from carts, and nabbed chestnuts off trays with nimble fingers.

They plagued the Desert People like hordes of biting flies,

pinching and kicking the water workers as they hurtled past. They even snatched bundles and tossed them back and forth like balls while the frantic blue-slashed water workers scrambled to stop them. Twice, urchins tried to trip Ari Ara, but she was too quick. She leapt over the outstretched legs and strode purposefully onward - the spitting image of a young errand-running water worker - all the while trying to sort out how the Desert People wound up as servants to their enemies.

And why did the urchins hold such a hard grudge against them? she thought, dodging a rotten apple chucked at her head.

A congested tangle of the crowd carried her between rows of houses and out onto a wide plaza. Like most of Mariana Capital, the open space bent irregularly. The northern row of shops stretched longer than the south, the eastside shops wider still, and the west side held no shops at all, only a long line of statues. Ari Ara crossed the foot-worn cobblestones toward it.

The tallest statues loomed like giants as she drew close. They were stacked in a wide row, one in front of the other, sometimes five or six deep. Numbering in the hundreds, they stood like a still and silent crowd watching the foot traffic on the plaza. Each was carved out of stone; some granite, others marble. A few were hewn from the black rock of the High Mountains, and she couldn't imagine how they moved the huge slabs of stone so far. She spotted smaller statues, too, even a collection the size of her hand. From the weather marks and styles of dress, she guessed that they had been carved one-by-one and added over time. Small offerings lay at the feet of some; others stood unadorned. In the center stood three tall statues of the famous brothers - Marin, Shirar, and Alaren - caught for all eternity in the historic moment of dispute that had founded the two countries of Mariana and the Desert. The torn halves of the Map of the World lay in Alaren's hands, the slice of the Border

Mountains at his feet. Marin and Shirar glared fiercely at each other, swords in hand. A dozen small ledges were carved into Marin's pedestal, each festooned with flowers, candles, and offerings. Shirar and Alaren's feet were bare.

"I'll come back," Ari Ara promised to the forlorn statues, "and bring something for you both."

"Don't bother," grumbled an accented voice behind her.

She whirled and saw a young water worker staring up at Shirar.

"We leave offerings to our ancestor, but those urchins steal them," he explained.

The boy spat onto the ground near Marin's base.

"What's between you and the urch - " she started to ask, but an angry voice interrupted her.

"Wipe that up," an urchin commanded, grabbing the desert youth by the shirt. "Your spit isn't fit to scrub our sewers."

Ari Ara stiffened. He had no right to scoff at anyone else's grime! The urchin was as filthy as an untended statue. Rips in his trousers showed his grubby knees. His feet were black with dirt. His jacket was a collection of patches, all of which had seen better days.

"The urchins' thievery of offerings is a greater insult to your ancestor than my spit!" the water worker shouted back. "Marin would be ashamed of you! Even if he hated his brother, ancestor spirits are ancestor spirits. You shouldn't disrespect them."

Ari Ara saw the urchin's fist clench. As his arm drew back, she darted between them, knocking the blow aside with a move from her training in the Way Between.

"Fight!" someone hollered.

A crowd of urchins, shoppers, and merchants gathered. A handful of water workers raced over, ready to help the youth. Ari Ara spun to stop the desert boy from launching himself at the urchin youth. She twisted him to the left. Then she whirled and sent the urchin rolling across the flagstones to the right.

"Stop!" she shouted, but the jeers and cheers of the two factions drowned out her words.

She ducked under the urchin's punch and grabbed his arm, pulling him off-balance and to the side. The desert boy charged after him, so she leapt and caught him by the waist, dropping to the ground to use her weight to bring him down.

"That's no water worker!" someone shouted, recognizing the girl. "That's the Lost Heir!"

Ari Ara cursed under her breath as she knocked aside another blow. The Way Between was the most controversial and fascinating subject in the Capital besides the Lost Heir. The Way Between, or *Azar* in Old Tongue, was neither fight nor flight, but everything possible in between. It was a way of changing danger to mutual safety, bringing the thrust of violence to a halt without causing further harm. She and her mentor, the Great Warrior Shulen, had finally convinced the Great Lady to let them start holding public trainings . . . she hoped she wasn't ruining that opportunity.

"Stop!" she hollered, sliding between the two and holding out her hands.

The boy clenched his fist; she slid in front of him and stared him down. The urchin shifted to spring, she pivoted to thwart him.

"Quit yer brawlin'," a voice ordered in a snap of command that froze all the urchins in place. From the sidelines, a dark-haired urchin girl swaggered out of the crowd. She was skinny as a ragged yarn string and close to Ari Ara in age. Her hair was braided in hundreds of strands, some wrapped around with colorful cloth and threaded with glass beads. Her blouse was as white as any shop girl's, but her breeches bore a patchwork quilt of fabrics, cut in a style that defied and mocked convention. A bulging pouch hung from her leather belt. Crimson stockings rose to her knees. A vest of stitched strips of cloth was buttoned with a row of strange, odd-shaped buttons, no two alike.

"Who are you?" Ari Ara asked.

"Rill – short for Everill," the girl replied with a proud toss of her head. "I'm a Capital urchin. A first-class South End river dog at yer service."

A rash of snickers and chortles erupted from the urchins, making Ari Ara suspect this girl was more than just any old street urchin. The girl winked and a slip of a grin flashed across her foxlike features. Her eyes flicked up and down Ari Ara, taking her measure.

"If you're really the Lost Heir, give me your blessing," she demanded, reaching out her dirty fingertips in an appeal to the fabled Protector of Orphans.

Ari Ara blinked in surprise. All orphans invoked the Lost Heir as a special saint and protector, calling out in times of sorrow and need. Until this moment, Ari Ara hadn't realized she had stepped into the very legend she'd prayed to as a child. A flash of unguarded honesty shot across the urchin's features. Ari Ara recognized the expression; the intense yearning in Rill's face was like holding a mirror up to her own. A hush fell over the crowd.

"I don't really have any magic powers," Ari Ara confessed.

"Yer the *Lost Heir,*" Rill objected. "You've got all the powers in the world!"

"Not until I'm officially confirmed," Ari Ara admitted with a sigh, remembering the tedious lecture she'd received on the year-long waiting period before the nobles validated her claim to the throne, "but I can promise to look out for my fellow orphans with any power that I have."

She reached out a hand, unconsciously imitating the handclasp of warriors, indicating loyalty and unbreakable oaths. Rill sucked in her bony cheeks and spat into her own palm. Shocked cries broke out around them, but Ari Ara didn't hesitate. She spat into her own hand and reached for Rill's. The urchin snatched her hand back with a challenging gleam in her eye.

"Do you mean it? All we get from nobles is lies and empty claims," she complained.

"I'm not a noble – or wasn't until recently – and my word is as good as yours," Ari Ara shot back as the hot bite of her temper flared.

"Prove it to me, then. Grant me a boon," Rill demanded.

"If it is in my power," Ari Ara cautioned.

"I hear yer bringing the Way Between back to the warriors. Let the urchins study it, too."

Surprise shot through the crowd of Marianans at the request. Everyone knew that the Great Warrior Shulen and the young Mariana Champion Emir Miresh had vowed to return the nearly extinct art of the Way Between to the warriors. No one had considered opening those trainings to ordinary citizens and street urchins . . . until now.

In a voice only Ari Ara could hear, Rill begged.

"We urchins is kicked down and beaten by anyone bigger'n us - and that's everyone. Offer us yer strength, Protector of Orphans, your magic as it may be, in the form of the Way Between."

"Done," Ari Ara declared, slapping her palm into Rill's hand.

The girl's eyes lit up with excitement. She lifted her fist above her head in victory and a rippling cheer burst out loud enough to make bystanders flinch. From every direction, the call was returned from the pint-sized lungs of children. The urchins' scrawny arms waved vigorously in the air. Ari Ara's eyes narrowed, realizing that Rill's request had been calculated and executed with all the skillful maneuvering of a war strategist.

"Who are you, really?" Ari Ara demanded to know.

Rill leaned in close and spoke in a breathless whisper.

"As you are to all Marianans, so I am to the street urchins of the Capital. The name's Everill Riverdon, known to some as the Urchin Queen. We are now in yer debt and at yer service."

"Rill!" an urchin boy hollered from a lookout point on one of the statues. "The Watch is coming!"

CHAPTER TWO

. . . . .

Urchins Nest

In a move worthy of a master of Azar, Rill dove through the crowd and vanished. The urchins slid into the side alleys. No keener to be caught by the Capital Watch than the others, Ari Ara bolted between a pair of stout washerwomen and wriggled through a huddle of merchants to race after the urchins into the maze of streets.

She lost the urchins at a crossroads and slowed to catch her breath. The fog lifted over the rooftops of the city. Morning light streamed between the buildings. She had run into the Dressiers District that sat in the heart of the island. The Houses of Dress sat along the street like a row of snobby women forced to share a bench, pretending to ignore one another while stealing envious looks at each other's fashions. Bolts of cloth hung off hooks. Window displays brimmed with color. Shops burst their seams with the latest fashions. Beneath her feet, Ari Ara could feel the stones shuddering with the churnings of the waterworks that tapped into the ever-present power of the river and powered the machinery inside the workhouses of the Dressiers District.

Ari Ara slid into the quieter residential streets of shop girls and tailors. Only the nobles used carriages, and here the thoroughfares narrowed. None spread wider than an oxcart and some stretched just big enough for a person to squeeze between the buildings. Peddlers shoved small pushcarts toward the plaza, yelling at Ari Ara when the tightness of an alley forced her to climb up and over their wares. Servants trudged to work in the noblehouses in the expensive end of the city. Riverboat sailors and laborers veered to the west side to look for a day's work on the docks. The second stories of houses overhung the bottom floors. Walkways connected balconies, porches, and rooftops. Laundry hung damply from window to window. Voices clattered in kitchens. Smoke rolled out of chimneys. Ari Ara narrowly missed a drenching from a wayward toss of dirty bathwater into the guttered grates in the street. Rattling waterworks lifted drinking water through shuddering pipes up to third-floor apartments. Clanging mechanics powered creaking fans that circulated air through the rundown buildings.

The Southenders were every shade of poor . . . and the deeper she walked into the maze of alleys, the poorer they got. People slept in the streets and built precarious shelters of blankets and old shipping crates. Men pulled caps low over brows and huddled in doorways. Tired women leaned thin elbows on windowsills and stared blankly as babies pulled at their breasts.

A few times, a shiver of unease rippled through her. She sensed eyes tracking her, eyeing the blue scrap of fabric on her wrist. On those occasions, she used the Way Between to slip out of view or borrowed from the skills of the elusive forest-dwelling Fanten women who had raised her and vanished into the alleyways. Eventually, she untied the rag and pulled the hood of her Fanten cloak tighter over her hair.

She hit a dead end. Then another. Frustrated, she backtracked and wound up in a walled courtyard at the end of a street. Panic gripped her. She wondered if she were lost. Then she caught a glimpse of the sun between the rooftops and the four directions reoriented in her mind. She studied the wall blocking her way, stepped back several paces, churned into a run, leapt high, and propelled herself on top of the wall with a heft of her wiry arms. Teetering for a moment, she stilled the momentum of her leap and peered beyond in astonishment.

A massive tree towered over the southern-most tip of the island, round as a house and taller than any of the buildings. It was a Great Tree with the same red bark and thick, curving limbs as the ones she'd grown up under in the Fanten Forest in the High Mountains.

This must be one of the original Mother Trees, Ari Ara thought in awe, remembering stories she'd heard as a small child.

Hammocks hung like spider webs in the boughs. Around the tree, a breathlessly rickety concoction of ledges, ladders, and platform roosts lined the backs of the nearby houses. In the nest-like nooks, bundles of blankets and small heaps of belongings piled up. Urchins clambered up and down ladders at breakneck speeds. Chatter and whistles and hollers raised a small din. A few curious eyes landed on Ari Ara as she froze half-crouched on the top of the wall. Slowly, she straightened to standing and a whistle of an alert rang out. Silence fell instantly. Urchins whipped into crouches. Heads spun toward her. Sleeves rolled back. Fists balled up. Ari Ara tensed to bolt.

Midway up the tree, a familiar, narrow fox-face bolted upright, swinging her legs over the side of her hammock and staring down.

"Well, well, look who followed us home," Rill remarked in a tone of disbelief. "Stand down, urchins."

A scatter of protests broke out.

"I said, stand down you ruddy lot of insubordinates!" Rill hollered.

"But she - "

"I don't care if she stole your mother's fingernails, you're not laying a finger on the Lost Heir."

A round of startled gasps swept the ledges and platforms. Heads poked up over hammock edges. A crowd gathered beneath the wall, whispering and pointing. Reluctantly, the drawn slingshots loosened and the hands on belt knives lowered. Rill tossed a knotted rope out of her hammock and climbed down faster than a tree rat. Ari Ara stayed perched on the wall with all the wariness of a wild deer in a High Mountain meadow, ready to leap away in an instant. Rill studied her from the ground then scaled the wall.

"Welcome to Urchins Nest, Highness," Rill said with a mocking half-bow. "How do you like our roost?"

She gestured to the scaffolding of tiny shacks and ledges.

"Impressive," Ari Ara replied honestly.

"What brings you chasin' us down here to the Urchins Nest?" Rill asked as she paced the length of the wall, lithe as an alley cat and twice as suspicious. "Couldn't have been the fresh air."

They wrinkled their noses as a waft of sewage and rotten eggs swept by.

"Curiosity," she answered with a shrug, not wanting to confess that she was lost. "Why'd you run off? Scared of the Watch?"

Rill's smile glinted sharp.

"What do y'think, river dogs?" she called out in a voice that reached the furthest parts of the Nest. "Is yer Urchin Queen scared of anything?"

A holler of laughter rang out at the notion. Everill smugly raised an eyebrow at Ari Ara.

"Not scared, just stretching our legs. The Capital Watch is always trying to catch us, see? Evading them is our favorite form of exercise," she told Ari Ara. "They get a bit of coin each time they manage to snatchety-snatch us urchins off to the monks and the sisters like the other orphans."

Ari Ara grinned. She'd evaded capture by the warrior monks when they tried to send her to the sisters, too. She'd had no more interest in following the sisters' rules than any urchin would.

"The Watch tries to demolish the Urchins Nest about once a year," Rill went on. "They never can catch us, though, and we rebuild. There's some of us orphans who loves our freedom more'n square meals and a cozy bed."

Suddenly, the thin girl's face pinched in thought.

"How'd you get here?" she demanded to know.

Ari Ara tilted her head.

"Same as anybody . . . I walked."

"Past the Thieves' Den and the Swords-For-Hire and every unscrupulous troublemaker this side of the Border Mountains?" Rill exclaimed. She snorted with disgust. "Ain't a Southender left worthy of the name. *Someone* ought to have kidnapped you for ransom by now."

"I'm hard to catch," Ari Ara retorted with a touch of pride. "And I've a knack for disappearing when I need to."

Rill flashed her an approving grin.

"You'd fit right in at the Urchins Nest!"

"Better'n at the House of Marin, I'm sure," Ari Ara sighed, though in truth, her days as a High Mountain shepherdess were as distant from the tangles of the South End as they were from the refinement of the North End.

19

Rill laughed so hard she nearly fell off the wall, slapping her knee and holding her chest. The urchins howled with her, calling out, "Truth!" and "Right you are!"

"Why don't you show me the Nest?" Ari Ara dared to suggest.

"Mayhaps I will, mayhaps I won't," she replied evasively, making a show of studying her fingernails. "The Lost Heir can't order the Urchin Queen around."

Howls of laughter applauded her words. Ari Ara caught Rill's defiant glare and grinned back.

"You're in charge of this lot, then?" Ari Ara asked.

Rill shrugged.

"More or less - though generally less," she remarked with a lopsided grin. "We sort ourselves out, s'long as no one breaks the Urchin's Code."

"What's that?" Ari Ara asked.

Rill eyed her thoughtfully.

"Give me your word you won't talk to the Watch and I'll give you a tour of our Nest as I answer that question."

Ari Ara promised. She'd lived on the edge of hunger and danger for the sake of freedom, too. She knew the precarious feeling of carving out a living amidst challenges and she'd no sooner snitch on the urchins than tell the wolves where the Fanten's lambs were hidden in the slopes of the mountains.

Rill hopped down from the wall. Ari Ara followed. Eyes trailed her every step from the ring of scaffolding and roosts. As they wove through the odds and ends scattered around the base of the Nest, Rill explained that the Urchin's Code was older than time and urchins, but it wasn't complicated: don't snitch to the Watch. Look after anyone littler than you. Don't steal from a fellow urchin. Don't hoard riches at another urchin's expense. And tithe to the Stew Pot.

She gestured to the makeshift kitchen with turned-over crates and half-barrels for chairs. A pair of urchin twins glanced up as they chopped piles of vegetables and tossed them into a simmering pot.

"Urchins' Stew," Rill said proudly. "It's my duty to make sure it's set to boil each day."

"Smells good," Ari Ara replied. "What's the recipe?"

"Whatever we've got at hand," Rill answered with a chuckle. "No two days are ever the same, not in life nor in the Urchins' Stew."

The Urchin Queen swaggered through the motley treasures of her domain. Her duties were to uphold the Urchin's Code, preside over disputes, settle quarrels, and collect the tithes that filled the Stew Pot. At Ari Ara's surprised look, she shook her head.

"Thought we thieved it all, did you?"

"Well, I - " Ari Ara spluttered in embarrassment, thinking of the pickpocketing she had seen earlier.

"You'd only be half wrong," the thin girl sighed. "There's some that nab, but we don't encourage it. Causes more trouble than it's worth and sets the Watch on our tails. An urchin's got honest work on this island - or we used to, anyway."

Her face darkened with anger and a cloud of worry.

"Water workers?" Ari Ara guessed, drawing from what she'd seen.

Rill nodded.

"Thrice-blasted desert demons are putting us out of work," she complained. "They trade their labor for water, see? They come here and the water is allowed through the South Dam through the Middle Pass into their drylands."

An urchin, Rill explained, once held the honorable profession of errand runner, package deliverer, odd-and-ends finder, day laborer, and an extra hand for whatever the merchants, artisans, and nobles needed. But now, the unpaid water workers did much of that work and the urchins were turning into nothing but ribs and bones.

"See that lot?" she grumbled, pointing to the urchins in the roosts above. "Time was, the Nest'd be empty at this hour of day. No lag-a-beds here. We worked in all the noblehouses, the merchant shops, the river docks, and most of all, in the Houses of Dress. Used to be a good way to learn an honorable trade. Oft-times, if we did well, we'd win an apprenticeship in the Dressiers District after a season or two, leading to a good profession as we grew older."

The water workers had ended all that. The first year of the Water Exchange, as it was called, the Houses of Dress had snatched up the free labor, competitively driving down their prices as a hot fashion for fine handiwork swept the island. The dressiers put hundreds of water workers to the tasks of embroidering and beadwork. Soon, the noblehouses added water workers to their household staff. Now, the Desert People ran errands and picked up packages, making pre-arrangements with the merchants.

"No apprenticeships, fewer and fewer coin tasks," Rill complained grimly, "if this keeps up, we'll be turned into plain old thieves and beggars just to survive. As it is, I lost twenty good urchins last winter to the sisters. The urchin's life was just getting too hard for 'em."

They came to the base of the Mother Tree. Under the lowest spreading branches, a patchwork of roof planks sheltered a ring of benches and a wooden throne that Rill flung her limbs across, draping a skinny leg over the armrest. Ari Ara looked around, fascinated. Beyond the throne, on a pair of shelves built against the base of the tree, piles of altar offerings - trinkets and charms, stubs of candles and the dust of incense sticks - sent prayers out to the protective spirit of the tree.

"I thought only the Fanten respected the Great Trees," Ari Ara mentioned.

Rill craned her head around.

"Years ago, a Fanten lady, Rhianne was her name, came down from the High Mountains. She came all the way across the city to pay her respects to the Mother Tree, as she called it. She told us that if we wanted to stay on the tree's good side, we had to pay proper respects to her."

Rill stopped, looking sheepish. She scratched the back of her neck as her face flushed.

"Silly, I know," she added quickly.

"I don't think so," Ari Ara answered. Rhianne was the daughter of the Fanten Grandmother that had raised her; she knew from her upbringing that the trees were more than just wood and needles. Ari Ara moved closer to the Mother Tree and placed her hand on the bark. When a tingle ran through her palm, she leaned her forehead on the trunk, whispering to the tree in Fanten Tongue. The branches overhead stirred, though the wind was still. Rill's eyes grew wide.

"She likes you," Ari Ara told the urchin, relaying the sense of fondness she had picked up. The Fanten lived in the feet of their Great Trees. Ari Ara had once seen a quarrelsome Fanten woman be driven out by her family's tree, made to sleep in the open until she made amends. The trees sent nightmares if you angered them.

"I bet she sends you good dreams," she told Rill.

"The *tree* does that?" Rill gasped.

Ari Ara nodded. Rill confessed that she'd had a number of prophetic dreams since hanging her hammock in the Mother Tree. She'd seen herself challenging the previous Urchin King four years ago, though she was tiny and he was nearly grown.

"The Mother Tree must have wanted you," Ari Ara said. The trees chose the Fanten leaders, it was said, though she'd never seen a choosing.

Rill shook her head.

"We vote on who's to be queen or king," she explained. "I called out the previous king for breaking the Urchin's Code and the others supported my claim."

Ari Ara lifted her eyebrows, but didn't argue. It wasn't her place to share the secrets of the Great Trees. If the Mother Tree wanted the urchins to believe they voted Everill Riverdon to be their leader, she wouldn't tell them the tree had ways of swaying people's hearts. Marianans always scoffed at Fanten tales, anyway.

"Want a view of the island?" Rill offered with a hint of a dare, pointing to the rising branches.

Ari Ara nodded. Rill hopped off her throne and swung up onto a thick bough. They climbed high up into the smallest branches. Here, the Mother Tree swayed in the slightest wind. The roofs of the Capital were far below. The city pulsed, alive in the heartbeat of her inhabitants. The breath of her daily bustle strained the corset of the docks and spilled out over the bridges. Houses overhung the stone embankments. The current coursed strongly on the west side and even swifter in the narrow channel on the east. Wharves extended into the churning waters, thronged with all manner of vessels. Ferrymen ported boatloads back and forth across the river with metered regularity. The farmlands spread out like a patchwork quilt, up and down the valley. Clouds masked the distant High Mountains.

"Do you miss your home?" Rill asked softly, catching her gazing in the direction of Monk's Hand Monastery.

Ari Ara nodded, suddenly unable to speak. Rill said nothing more, but let her wrestle with the flood of emotions, standing on the other side of the tree trunk in companionable silence. After a spell, Everill Riverdon made an offer that astonished even her.

"If you need it, we'd hang a hammock for you," she murmured with a slight shrug.

It was a wild offer, ridiculous for an urchin to offer the Lost Heir. But Everill Riverdon had one ear bent to the rumor-river and she knew the whispers that crisscrossed the city. She suspected that copper-haired girl's life was no easier than it had been before despite the feather beds and fancy dresses.

The Great Bell in the top of the University Tower began to toll. Ari Ara startled and groaned.

"Oh no! I'll never get back before they notice I'm gone!" she cried, climbing down the tree branches.

"You will if you use the Urchin's Way," Rill called out. "Follow me!"

A bough hung over the rooftops. Everill ran out along it and dropped down to the tiled peak. Ari Ara didn't hesitate; she ran after the Urchin Queen. She raced across the flat ridgeline, leapt the gap between buildings, and dropped off the far end of the next. Ari Ara sprinted a pace behind, reeled at the edge, and then saw the second story porch just below. She leapt, landing in a crouch next to Rill. They climbed over the rail onto the next apartment's porch. From there, they hopped onto a bridge between family complexes and scaled the wooden steps on the opposite house back up to the roof.

Rill shouted back encouragement. Ari Ara saved her breath and concentration for keeping up with the urchin's breakneck speed. Glimpses of the streets three stories below flashed by her eyes, but the heights were less than the High Mountains' black jagged pinnacles. She whipped up and down the tiled roofs fearlessly. Her leather boots gripped well enough, better than Rill's worn shoes, and once, Ari Ara grabbed the other girl's forearm as she slipped and hauled her back over the ridgeline.

"Thanks," Rill murmured. Then she took off again, dropping onto a flat roof above a guild shop and sliding down the gutter to access a bridge between second story porches. Ari Ara barreled down the wooden balcony behind her. They clambered up another ladder and sprinted over the next block of flat roofs. The black tiles of the House of Marin's roofline came into view.

"Beyond that balcony, there's a gutter pole smooth enough to slide down. Take a left into the side street and you'll be in the alley off the kitchen," Rill directed.

"Thanks," Ari Ara said, truly grateful. "See you on the training sands, then? Unless you're scared to come?"

"Urchin's Honor, I'll be there," Rill promised. "No Lost Heir of Mariana calls me a coward!"

Then she winked and ran, nimble as a cat, back across the rooftops.

CHAPTER THREE

. . . . .

Azar!

"Azar!"

Ari Ara dove sideways and rolled to her feet. Grains of sand stuck to her weathered trousers. A ragged rope belted her worn tunic. Unruly curls of red hair escaped her braid like an exploding bird's nest. Dust powdered her bronze skin and clung to her bare feet. She was filthy, disheveled, and utterly happy.

The tension of minding her manners and watching her tongue lifted like river fog on a hot spring morning. She leapt into the demonstration match of the Way Between with the enthusiasm of a fish jumping free of the net and escaping into a swift-flowing river. As she spun and dove, she had no time to think about the way her tutors had mocked her table manners as *fit only for shepherds and savages*, insulting the Fanten people. She ducked under a swinging kick and leapt toward her opponent, catching him off-balance and toppling him to the ground.

"Yield?" she challenged, gasping for breath and laughing at the same time.

A grin twitched on Emir Miresh's lips.

"Never," answered the youth. The sixteen-year-old Mariana Champion was a lithe, black-haired warrior with a quiet intensity born of a lifetime of duty and discipline. Five years older than Ari Ara, he had served as a guard to the royal family of the House of Marin since boyhood and won the annual Spring Trials for years. Emir's fine-boned features were marked by sharp focus and seriousness. The gentleness in his brown eyes showed hints of his good nature and loyal heart. A smile curled across his features at the challenge of the match. He flung her off and gave chase so fast she yelped as she dodged.

"Get him, Ari Ara!" a youth called out, his golden curls gleaming like a crown in the slanting light of the sun.

"Where's your loyalty, Korin?!" Emir hollered back.

"Torn," the noble youth answered, drawing laughter from the warriors as his newfound cousin forced his lifelong friend to backpedal. "It's smart to stay in favor with my cousin; she is the young queen, after all."

Technically, she was his second cousin - they shared a royal great-grandmother - but since only they and the Great Lady Brinelle remained of the House of Marin, custom allowed the use of the simpler terms of cousin, aunt, and niece.

"See if I ever save your neck again," Emir shot back.

Korin smiled, not worried in the slightest. Emir Miresh had been oath-sworn to protect him since they were eight years old.

"I'll take Ari Ara as my personal guard if she wins this match," he called back to tease Emir.

"Learn Azar and save yourself, cousin!" she hollered to him, a smile lifting her lips at Korin's teasing. He was a light-hearted youth who lolled about the Capital like a favored puppy, adored by everyone and taken seriously by no one.

Around them, bemused chuckles rose onto the dawn air. The Training Yards filled most of the North End of the island.

Sections of traditional practice sands flanked the wide drilling area in the center. The grounds teemed with warriors, some limbering up taut muscles in the dawn coolness, others already set to drills and formation practices. Warrior monks crouched on their heels watching the youths' match. These quiet men with shaved heads and gray robes had come down the winding trails from the High Mountains along with Ari Ara.

A set of warriors on break turned to watch. One crossed the Training Yards, waving to his friends to come with him. In moments, other practices halted and a rumbling stream of warriors drew close. Instructors threaded to the front and crouched low so their trainees could watch. The renowned cohort of women warriors approached. New recruits and grizzled warriors alike parted in deference to let them bear witness. The guards on the ramparts that flanked the Training Yards peered over the edge to get a good view.

A collective sigh of relief slipped out of the warriors; whoever, whatever else the Lost Heir from the High Mountains might be, she spoke the language of the body: muscles, sweat, conflict, courage. She stood equal to Emir Miresh, who had outshone all others in the Spring Trials. Her way, Azar, was strange, but compelling; it was obviously a powerful defense. The warriors exchanged quick, knowing glances. Here was a royal heir who could pull her weight in a tight spot, a girl that could defend herself against a nearly full-grown youth. The cheers grew louder, rising on the air of the quiet morning as the warriors applauded each close shave and narrow escape. Ari Ara's hairpins slipped free and warriors vied to pull them from the sands, tokens of luck from the Lost Heir.

Among the gathered was Everill Riverdon. The small urchin had slipped in late and wriggled her way to the front of the trainees. Her brilliant red shirt was tucked into a wide, iridescent gold and green woven belt. Her weathered pants boasted a number of patches, all different patterns, brazenly stitched in place with an array of threads, each brighter than the last. Boots clung to her skinny calves, bound with scarlet ties. A matching band of cloth wrapped around her head.

As she watched the demonstration match, Rill's jaw dropped. She'd seen Ari Ara disrupt that street fight on the plaza, but to watch her fend off the famous warrior Emir Miresh raised her esteem for the red-haired girl. Rill let out a low, impressed whistle. If *that* was any indication of what the Way Between could do, she'd personally rouse every urchin in the Nest before daybreak and send them marching along the Urchin's Way to the Training Yards tomorrow. Nobody'd lay a finger on her pack if they learned this!

To the side of the open sands, the Great Warrior Shulen called a halt and ordered those watching to standing. Everill glared fiercely around her, practically bristling as the members of the Capital Watch whispered and pointed at her. The Urchin Queen ranked high on their list of troublemakers. Before they could act, Ari Ara raced across the sands to the girl.

"You came!" she cried.

Everill nodded.

"And I'll stay, so long as no one throws me out."

"They wouldn't dare," Ari Ara answered. She'd expressly told them that the Urchin Queen was her guest, but she shot the Watch a nervous look before muttering, "Just stick by me."

Everill threw her arm over the heir's shoulders and grinned toothily as the warriors tensed.

"Made it back alright, then?" she asked in a hushed voice.

Ari Ara grinned and nodded. She'd slipped in the kitchen door and up to her rooms with none the wiser for her excursion.

As he stalked to the center of the Training Yards, Shulen

cast an askance glance at the pair and hid a smile. The dark-haired urchin brimming with street arrogance reminded him strongly of a certain shepherdess on the first day they had met in the High Mountains.

Trust Ari Ara to find the most disreputable child in the Capital to befriend, Shulen thought wryly, suspecting there was some truth to the wild rumors he'd heard that the Lost Heir had appeared on the plaza. He decided not to share his suspicions. He'd objected to the Great Lady's plan to turn Ari Ara into a proper noblegirl before letting her see the city. Shulen had wrestled with the girl's stubborn, rebellious streak long enough to not only know it, but love it. The harder the Great Lady tried to squeeze that girl into the cage of propriety, the harder Ari Ara would fight to get out. He kept close watch on his apprentice, hoping Mariana Capital wouldn't snuff all the fire and light out of her. Shulen glanced at Rill and chuckled. So far, it hadn't. Shulen put his reflections aside and stepped into the center of the training sands. He held his hands aloft. Silence fell instantly.

Ari Ara watched the old warrior proudly. Shulen had long held the respect of the warriors, prowling the yards like a gray-haired, silver tiger. Shulen had trained all but the oldest warriors, commanded most of them in battle, fought shoulder-to-shoulder with them, and spoken at the funerals of their comrades. He could beat any of the warriors and stood coolly confident even against the ferocious strength of Emir Miresh. In a few more years, the scales of strength would tip in the youth's favor, but time would also season Shulen's cunning edge. In the Way Between, that counted more than muscles.

"As you saw in this demonstration match," Shulen explained to the group in his stern and steady voice, "the Way Between stands in contrast to *Attar*, the Warrior's Way, and

Anar, the Gentle Way. While all three forms can be followed by anyone, Marianans and the Desert People have chosen to focus on Attar. The forest-dwelling Fanten have followed Anar. The followers of the Way Between are few, but growing in numbers every day."

He nodded to Emir and Ari Ara, his first apprentices, then to Korin and the warrior monks to acknowledge their commitment to the Way Between.

"The Way Between is an art unto itself. It is not," he warned the rest of the new trainees in a stern tone, "simply a way to win a fight. It is not a set of tricks to make you more skilled at Attar, the Warrior's Way. To master Azar, you must unlearn the ways of Attar. Violence is like a double-headed axe, circling in a vicious cycle that hurts the one who wields it, even if they pick it up for justice or defense. Azar breaks the deadly cycle and offers another way to resolve our disputes."

As Shulen spoke about the broader uses of the Way Between, Rill looked around with sharp curiosity, studying the reactions of the warriors. From what she had heard, many people found it difficult to believe in a non-martial art that could defend and protect without striking a blow in retaliation. Rill lived with one ear to the ground and the other hinged to the endless currents of the rumor-river. Skeptics across the island muttered that it was a conspiracy to weaken the warriors and that Shulen was in league with the desert demons. Such sentiments made few in-roads with the warriors who had fought alongside Shulen, but throughout the nation, tongues waggled and suspicions grew like weeds. Rill shook her head over such nonsense. She could see, plain as day, that the old warrior was a man of loyalty and unflinching integrity.

"Today, you will learn the physical form of the Way Between, how to use strength and skill to turn aside an attack, slow an assault, and stop violence from causing harm, but," Shulen's tone dropped into a warning, "this is only the beginning of Azar. It is said that Alaren could stop whole armies with a single word."

Ari Ara knew from reading the tales in the *Stories of the Third Brother* that legends were rooted in surprising truths. In this instance, Alaren had stopped Marin from launching a war by speaking the name of a lake where Shirar had once saved Marin from drowning. It seemed to Ari Ara that wars stopped and started, stalled and advanced a thousand times a day. Each person made choices that either worked toward peace or led to war. She looked across the Training Yards of Mariana Capital. Hundreds of heads turned in Shulen's direction, the faces of the warriors rapt with attention. On this dawn morning as the river fog lifted off the water, the sands were packed with people taking a step toward peace.

The battlefield is one step further from reality today, Ari Ara thought with proud satisfaction.

"The Way Between is not for cowards," Shulen cautioned. "We do not learn to de-escalate violence only to ignore the causes that led people to launch an attack. A follower of Azar will work with others to find and address underlying problems. Otherwise, we'll be flinging attackers away forever."

Just like in Attar, Ari Ara added silently.

Shulen called for the trainees to partner up and begin an exercise, one person trying to tap his opponent, the other trying to evade. Then, the pair was to switch roles without warning. It was one of the beginning training exercises in Azar, and as the orderly sands burst into chaos and motion, Ari Ara tried not to laugh. The serious warriors looked like a pack of village children playing Catch the King as they dodged their partner and collided with each other.

"C'mon Ari Ara, show them how it's done," Emir urged, tapping her on the shoulder with a laugh and darting out of reach. As Shulen had been trying to instruct the others, they switched from chaser to tapper without warning, keeping each other fluid in mind as well as body.

Next to them, one of the women warriors sought out the Urchin Queen with a wry smile. They exchanged a handclasp. The street urchins called the renowned woman the Phoenix, first for her beauty and second for the number of close calls with death that she had risen from.

"Well, well," the muscled woman commented, studying the yarn-string urchin. "Aren't you a daring imp, coming to this hotbed of Capital Watch, Royal Guard, and warrior?"

Everill shrugged. Urchins faced daily adversity in the forms of hunger, cold, crooks, swindlers, and the Watch. It was a hard life, but she wouldn't trade it for anything.

"All in a day's work for an urchin," she remarked. "We drink danger instead of tea; it's cheaper and wakes you up just as fast."

"I remember," the woman remarked dryly as Shulen called out the instructions. "I was an urchin once."

Rill nodded. They sang of the Phoenix in the urchins' ancestor song, along with all the other lowly urchins who rose through the ranks of trades, arts, and warriors.

"You ought to train as a warrior," the Phoenix recommended to the girl. "You've the courage for it."

"Mayhap I will," Rill answered as they circled to begin the exercise, "if I could train only in Azar."

"Not a fighter, then?" the Phoenix queried.

"Not a killer," she said, lifting her gaze to where Ari Ara was circling Emir Miresh, "but I wouldn't mind being a bit like her."

They watched the redheaded girl whip out of the young warrior's reach.

"Me neither," the older woman confessed with a laugh.

Then they saved their breath for the practice.

* * *

Sand spun underfoot. Ari Ara dodged Emir's lunge. Titters of laughter rose behind her, but she couldn't afford a glance, not right now. The rising sun dazzled her eyes, blazing through the lifting river fog, half-blinding her as Emir held his position, back to the sun. She tried to circle, turning him to the side as she searched for an opening through which to topple him.

Another flurry of women's voices - girl's giggles, Ari Ara thought - came from behind her. She ducked through the space Emir left under his elbow and glanced -

Thud!

His leg snaked out and swept her off her feet. Cursing under her breath, she smacked the training sands with her palm. On the sidelines, a pack of noblegirls floated in swaths of pale pink and lilac gauzes, fluttering from one bench to the next, whispering and giggling behind their fans.

"Focus!" she heard Shulen bark. The tips of her ears burned bright red.

Emir's sturdy, calloused hand stretched into her line of vision as he apologized for tripping her up.

"Sorry about that - I thought you'd jump," he said.

"Not your fault," she grumbled, taking his hand and letting him haul her up to standing. "I lost focus."

He clapped her on the back. A smile flickered across his face as he noticed the scowling glare she shot toward the sidelines.

"What are they doing here?" she muttered. The noblegirls clearly weren't here to practice, but what other purpose could they have at the Training Yards at this hour of the morning? As a rule, the young nobles partied long into the night and rose late in the mornings.

"Gawking," Emir replied in an amused tone.

"At what?" she grumbled.

Emir lifted an inky eyebrow.

"This may come as a shock," he told her, "but I'm considered rather good-looking."

Ari Ara rolled her eyes. She'd seen some of the maids collapsing in swoons of fluttering eyelashes when Emir entered a room.

"Too bad your charms don't seem to work on warriors," she shot back. "It'd be useful if you could make our enemies faint in heaps of adoration."

"Are you talking or practicing?" Shulen thundered from the other end of the sands, glaring at them from the midst of the lesson he was giving to a group of new trainees.

The girls laughed again, this time obviously mocking her.

"How do you put up with them?" she groaned to Emir in a low tone.

"Years of practice," he confessed. The year he'd shot up a whole hand in a growth spurt, changing from a skinny boy to a young teenager, Shulen had drilled him on ignoring such distractions. He flushed, remembering the night the old warrior had mock-kidnapped Korin while Emir was busy blushing from a Marianan lady's flirtations.

"Just pretend they're geese," he offered to Ari Ara.

The girl grinned - that wasn't hard to imagine! They returned to the practice, working with determined focus until Shulen called an end to the session. Across the yard, the trainees shook hands with their partners and began to disperse. Ari Ara eyed the gossiping noblegirls, but they were still huddled on the bench like a flock of geese, fluttering their fans and whispering between bouts of giggles.

"How'd you like your first day?" Emir called out to Rill as she neared. Emir had watched the Urchin Queen through the training and the girl showed an affinity for the Way Between. Her lifetime of ducking out of trouble and slipping the grip of the Watch was excellent training for Azar.

"Not bad," the urchin answered, eyeing the young warrior warily.

"I look forward to partnering with the Urchin Queen some time," Emir said politely.

Rill yelped.

"Knock my head off and the urchins'll pick your pockets clean for the rest of your life," she swore, backing up a pace.

"I wouldn't dream of it," Emir assured her.

He shook hands with a strangely quiet Rill. As he left, she squeaked in a low tone.

"I just shook hands with the Mariana Champion," she breathed with an awestruck laugh.

"Oh, please don't become one of those simpering girls who lose their wits over him," Ari Ara groaned.

"Not me," Rill promised, "but you don't understand, he's a legend. He's - he's - he's famous. We come to the annual Spring Trials just to watch him take down one grizzled warrior after another."

"Do they hold the Trials here, then?" Ari Ara asked, looking around the Training Yards, imagining them filled with young hopefuls and battle-hardened old fighters alike, pitting their skills against each other in the annual tests.

"Yes," Rill enthused, gesturing around with enthusiasm,

"they put up stands along the sides and the whole Capital crams in to watch the matches."

A wave of lavender perfume swept over them. Ari Ara gagged as the cloying scent collided with the pungent aroma of hard-working warriors. The noblegirls had approached along the edge of the sands, holding embroidered handkerchiefs over their noses and fanning the air as they walked. A tall brunette eyed the sweaty, disheveled pair of younger girls with a scowl of distaste. Gold clasps pinned back her dark hair. Her dress was trimmed with shining silver strands and showed her curves. Her features were beautiful, but coldness shadowed her eyes. She drew near and stared down her nose.

"You smell like a pack of warriors . . . or pigs," she drawled, waving her fan at Ari Ara and Rill as the noblegirls giggled behind their handkerchiefs. "But, I suppose that's to be expected from a pair of guttersnipes like you."

"That's the future queen you're insulting, Varina," Rill pointed out.

"That's *Lady* Varina to you," she snapped, "and I don't see any heir . . . all I see is a filthy little imposter."

Ari Ara sucked in her breath to snap back, but Rill beat her to it, walking closer in an insolent saunter of a walk, yawning in disdain.

"She's no imposter," she sniffed back, matching the noblegirl's haughty tone, "but I'd rather have a muck-rolled guttersnipe on the throne than a simpering pile of steaming horse dung like you."

The young noble tried to slap the urchin, but Rill ducked out of the way and toppled the taller girl onto the dirt by slamming into her legs with what looked like a fall.

"Oops," she smirked, "slipped."

The young lady's face turned livid purple as she struggled to her feet and brushed the dust off her fine skirts. The rest of her pack of friends shrieked and screeched at Ari Ara and Rill. The Urchin Queen rolled out of the way of Varina's kick and leapt up. Ari Ara grabbed Rill's arm and dragged her toward the side door of the House of Marin. They wove through the corridors, headed for the kitchen entrance on the opposite side of the rambling house where Rill could slip out unseen.

"You really shouldn't make more enemies than you already have," she chided the impetuous street urchin.

Rill made a face.

"Neither should you, but that one's got her hate-filled eye on you. Sometimes, it's best to knock 'em off balance before they smack you in the face."

"You didn't have to call her a pile of horse dung," Ari Ara pointed out.

Rill shrugged her skinny shoulders.

"That was Varina de Thorn and *horse dung* is a compliment compared to what she's really like. The House of Thorn is a rotten pack of greedy dock rats. Paid the Watch to roust the Nest two years back, wanted to cut down the Mother Tree and clean out the South End. I think they was intending to build Thorn Way on a scale to rival Marin's Way up here."

Rill's pinched face grew dark with dislike. Two urchins had been killed in the brutal eviction and she'd mustered every urchin in the Capital to carry their dead bodies past the House of Thorn to the House of Marin, demanding justice and the restoration of their rightful home in the Urchins Nest. She'd stirred up mayhem 'til the demands were met, too. The unrest still sent shudders down people's spines at the slightest mention.

"Nowadays," Rill said, "none of us'll so much as sell a bob of thread nor fetch a message for that noblehouse. I've been waiting years for the chance to spit an honest insult in her face."

Rill hopped ahead of Ari Ara and walked backwards down the hall, a calculating look on her fox-features.

"You'd best watch your back," Rill warned. "She's got a vendetta out against you and people that oppose the House of Thorn have a strange way of disappearing. Find out what evidence she's got for calling you an imposter - it's a bold claim to make if she's got nothing but her stinking hot air to back up those nasty words."

Rill stilled, putting a hand up to halt Ari Ara's reply. Voices and footsteps traveled up the hall. Korin dashed around the corner and skidded to a halt next to them.

"Mum's on a rampage," he warned, grabbing Ari Ara's arm, "you'd best hide."

CHAPTER FOUR

. . . . .

The House of Marin

Korin hustled them down the corridor. Around the next bend, he opened a wall panel hidden behind a hanging tapestry and revealed a passageway. Korin shoved them in and shut the panel. Ari Ara pressed her spine to the back wall. Rill's nails dug painfully into her shoulder. Korin lifted a finger to his lips. The trio held their breaths as the click of heels and swish of skirts approached. Brinelle's voice growled something about locking her son and niece in a tower for a decade. She turned down the next hall and only the sound of their hammering hearts remained.

"What'd you do this time?" Ari Ara asked Korin.

"Nothing, of course, but the chief steward seems upset about why Marin's armor is getting a piggyback on his great-grandson's statue," he confessed as a smile of mischief crossed his lips. "What'd you do?"

"Too much to remember," Ari Ara admitted with a sigh, "but Rill knocked over Varina de Thorn in the Training Yards just now."

"Well done," Korin remarked with a chortle.

41

He tossed his curls out of his eyes and studied Rill curiously, proffering his hand to shake as he introduced himself.

"Everill Riverdon, Urchin Queen," Rill replied, cheekily holding out her hand palm-down in the manner of monarchs.

"Delighted," Korin laughed, gallantly kissing the back of her hand and lifting an eyebrow. "Your reputation - for trouble, anyway - precedes you, Your Majesty. I've been hoping to meet you for years."

"Your cousin kindly invited us urchins to join the Azar practices," Rill confided with a wink.

"Did you really?" Korin remarked, looking at Ari Ara as a delighted grin spread across his face. "Great work, cousin. You've just brokered an alliance between the royal House of Marin and the Capital's most notorious band of troublemakers! I can't wait to hear what my dear ole Mum will say about that."

"Hopefully nothing," Ari Ara muttered.

Korin gestured for the girls to creep down the winding passageway that curled between the rooms. They squeezed through a narrow door that opened into an empty reception room. Korin tweaked the nose of a statue and the door shut seamlessly.

"That's our great-great-whatever," Korin told them, patting the statue's head, "and from all I've heard, she's much nicer dead than alive."

At their curious looks, he explained that the bust was the work of Marinmara, the disgraced firstborn great-great-granddaughter of Marin who abdicated the throne to pursue stone carving. Her parents disowned her in outrage and she packed up her tools and headed north to the stone quarries, founding the House of Mara in the Stonelands. Korin tapped on the nose of the pinched face and told them that after disowning her, Marinmara's royal mother had smashed all of the sculptress' early statues except for this one, which a maid saved by tossing down a latrine.

"It was lost for a thousand years. Then the sewer clogged and out came this lady, covered in slime." Korin's eyes shown with wicked mirth. "This bust is of Marinmara's mother. I imagine she had that disgusted expression before she spent a millennium in the sewer."

Rill let out a startled exclamation.

"There's a spot in the Under Way - the passages through the sewers and waterworks - that's called the Queen's Throne," she blurted out, "and I never could sort out why . . . but now I'm reckonin' that's where the statue was pulled out!"

"Did you know," Korin said to Rill with a calculating look in his eye, "that it's traditional for visiting monarchs to receive a tour of the House of Marin? Of course, Tahkan Shirar, being an enemy of the state at the time of his first arrival, was not offered such privileges. You, however, are more than welcome to be my guest, provided we trade some state secrets along the way."

"Such as?" Rill asked suspiciously.

"Showing me the entrances and routes through the Under Way," Korin replied swiftly.

Rill pondered that, then nodded at the fair trade: a tour for a tour.

"You two are going to get me into trouble," Ari Ara grumbled, planting her fists on her hips.

"No, I'm not," Korin insisted, "everyone thinks you'll be bathing and dressing and breakfasting for the next twenty minutes, at least. It'll be fine. Trust me."

She didn't, but Rill nudged her in the ribs and mouthed: *you owe me.* The Urchin Queen had shown the Lost Heir her domain; it was only fair to return the courtesy. When Korin promised to show them every secret passage and hidden staircase he knew, her curiosity got the better of her good sense and she agreed.

Brushing the dust off his tunic, Korin turned and posed like an orator.

"What you are about to hear," he proclaimed, "is the true history of the House of Marin – sordid and scandalous – that I have uncovered from the dust of obscurity with great effort and high peril."

Ari Ara grinned. If it was sordid history, she could perfectly imagine that peril – the Great Lady Brinelle would string her son up by his curls for his blasphemy.

"The hidden history of the illustrious House of Marin is a set of secrets so dangerous," Korin claimed, "that Emir Miresh would have to kill me, except that he's sworn an oath to protect me."

Ari Ara rolled her eyes at the nonsense, but Rill's eyes widened; she'd believe anything about Emir Miresh.

"We start with the dragon's lair . . . Mum's study!" Korin said with a flourish, guiding them through a pair of double doors to a chamber lined with books. A desk heaped with documents and scrolls sat in front of a large window. A pile of letters threatened to topple off the corner.

"This, of course, is the famous Map of the World," he commented, pointing to a framed map that hung above the double doors. Rill stared in awe, thinking of all the folktales she'd heard about that very map! It looked older than time, crumbling at the edges, the ink barely visible in some places. Two torn slits ran down either side of the Border Mountains where Marin and Shirar – arguing as usual – had slashed angrily at the map held up by Alaren as he tried to tell them that the world was big enough for both of them. In a swift pair of slices, the swords of the brothers had split the world. Marin took the eastern half in Alaren's left hand. Shirar grabbed the western half in Alaren's right hand. Alaren was supposed to take the sliver of the Border Mountains that had fallen at his feet, but he rejected the scheme, bitterly and accurately predicting that it would lead the brothers to war. He spent his life trying to "restore the whole world".

"That map," Korin said reverently, "is the start of Mariana."

"And the beginning of all the wars," Ari Ara muttered.

Korin threw her a startled look, but then nodded. She was right, though he'd never thought of it that way before.

The sprawling architecture of the House of Marin stood three stories tall and covered a quarter of the width of the North End. Every inch of the building held a treasure trove of old stories embedded in frescos, statues, paintings, furniture, hidden passages, and oddities. The original residence – built by Marin himself – had been expanded and remodeled by every generation in a hodgepodge of styles both stately and ridiculous. The official rooms that welcomed nobles and guests reeked of dignity, but the private corridors and quarters contained odd half steps, strangely-sized doors, and bizarrely-placed columns. Ari Ara found it reassuring. It bore testimony to the visions and foibles of real people, and reminded her that her relatives were the sort that enlivened family reunions, not just the heroes that did great deeds and were written about in history books. It made her feel that she might belong among these Marins who demanded skylights on the second floor, necessitating a hole in the third floor drawing room.

Years ago, Korin had grown tired of his mother telling him that he was failing to measure up to his illustrious ancestors . . . so he set out to find the non-illustrious ones. In the side margins and footnotes of the records, Korin discovered an astounding and colorful history of younger sisters and brothers, crazy firstborns who abdicated, inventor-cousins and artistic in-laws. As Ari Ara and Rill followed him down the winding corridors, he regaled them with the scandals, legends, and wild stories that he'd uncovered.

"Nice to know your family is as crazy as the rest of us," Rill commented.

"Crazier," Korin admitted with a smile.

A gash in the main hall marked the spot where Marin's grandson had saved his father's life when his nephew tried to assassinate him. A secret corridor between the library and an underground meeting room had led to infamous conspiracies and numerous affairs. Korin pointed out the exact spot where the mad brother of a king had danced all night until he dropped dead in exhaustion. He claimed the worn spot in the marble would enchant anyone who stepped on it. Rill gave it wide berth. He showed them the room - now used to store chamber pots - where the Cannibal Queen had devoured some of Shirar's descendants. When Ari Ara exclaimed that he was making it up, Korin responded that he'd caught a water worker singing in there to appease the ghosts. In the next room, the sword of Marin hung on the wall, polished until it glinted.

"Terribly heavy thing," Korin told Ari Ara with a groan, wincing at the memory. "I hope you never have to carry it. Mother told me I'd have to lift weights if I ever wanted to pick it up."

"If you've never held it, how do you know it's heavy?" Ari Ara asked.

"Better not to ask," Korin told her with a guilty grin, "then you never have to lie to my mother."

He led them through a stately dining room and said it used to be a war council room, but their great-grandmother abandoned it, claiming that Alaren's ghost was haunting it, trying to stop the war.

"I bet he did," Ari Ara muttered, well familiar with the legends about Alaren's ghostly escapades.

They finished with a spiral staircase used by the servants that threaded down from the eaves to the kitchen. Korin snatched a bread roll and tossed it to Rill as they showed her out through the side alley. Rill shoved it in her pocket, winked at the open-mouthed guard by the kitchen door, and whistled an urchin's tune as she strolled into the bustle of the island city's winding stone streets.

She ambled down Marin's Way with her ears tuned to the gurgle of the rumor-river's gossip and idle talk. If you listened long enough, Rill believed, the city confessed all of her secrets. She'd saved her skin more than once by paying attention to the currents of gossip. She'd just turned down the side alley that ran between two noblehouses when a pair of voices fell out of the window like a sack of bricks.

"They'd let that girl get away with murder," Rill heard the cultured tones of a noblegirl say. She lingered, leaning against the wall, pretending to tie her shoe. This girl had been one of the handkerchief-fluttering lackeys tailing along with Varina de Thorn, and Rill suspected she knew exactly who would speak next.

Varina's scoffing laugh rose and confirmed her suspicions.

"Someone will get away with murder before the year's out, but it's not going to be her."

"Surely you're not saying - "

" - I'm not saying anything, just that there are nobles who love this nation too much to let an imposter be confirmed as heir."

Rill snorted silently and rubbed her fingers together. What

Varina meant was that there were nobles who loved their war profits too much to let a follower of the Way Between gain both thrones and ensure peace. The noblegirls' nasty laughter rose as they moved away from the window. A shiver ran down Rill's spine. She was tempted to go to the Great Lady with what she had overheard, but decided against it. Those stuffed-shirt nobles would think she was making it up out of spite. Rill stalked down the alley, crossing her arms over her chest and bristling with distrust.

"Best to wait and let my river dogs sniff around," she cautioned herself. If she found evidence that the Thorns were up to mischief, she'd have a better chance of being believed.

Everill Riverdon, Urchin Queen, top of the Capital Watch's list of troublemakers, sighed and shook her head. It was a real blow to her reputation to help out a member of the House of Marin, but the Lost Heir had done her a good turn, letting the urchins study the Way Between. The Urchin's Code demanded that she pay it back in full.

I hope I don't regret this, Rill thought silently as she turned in the direction of the Urchins Nest, already plotting out which urchin eyes-and-ears to put to work. But, with an enemy like Varina de Thorn, ·Ari Ara was going to need all the help she could get.

CHAPTER FIVE

· · · · ·

Nobles Academy

"Where in the name of Marin have you been?"

The voice cracked like cold water over them.

Brinelle.

Ari Ara and Korin froze on the same horrified breath. Slowly, they pivoted to face the tall, imposing woman who had just rounded the corner of the hall. She stalked through the morning light that streamed in the row of windows, aflame in gold and strong as steel. Her mouth scowled in a thin line of displeasure. The slightest hint of silver strands threaded her mahogany hair. She was neither slender nor stout, but solid, brimming with sheer presence. Her jacket fit like a glove; her gloves curled like second skin. Her boots gleamed with polish, the sides adorned with fine leatherwork in the shape of river dragons.

"Morning, Mum," Korin called out cheerfully.

"Korin," she replied in a tone of exasperation, "what have I told you about the proper manner of greeting – "

"My Lady-Mother," Korin finished with a wrinkled look of disgust and a lazy bow.

"None of your impudence," she answered reprovingly.

Ari Ara eyed the formidable Great Lady cautiously. Before she had met her Lady-Aunt (as she was instructed to call Brinelle), Korin had told her so many stories of his overbearing, insufferable, domineering mother that Ari Ara had expected the Great Lady to be a large-bosomed, lace-ridden, stuffy old matriarch of Marianan society, rigid with etiquette. Instead, she discovered her Lady-Aunt was a powerful, sharp-witted woman ready to ride onto the battlefield and straight into the chronicles of Marianan history.

"Did the Lost Heir perhaps forget that she was to join the ambassadors from the Stonelands this morning?" she reminded Ari Ara, turning her fierce gaze on the girl.

The Great Lady's glare was rumored to have stopped an army in its tracks and Ari Ara gulped. She'd remembered the meeting as soon as her Lady-Aunt had mentioned it.

"No . . . I went to Azar practice instead," she confessed.

"Ari Ara of the High Mountains, you may enjoy brawling like a commoner, but – "

"I was *not* brawling," Ari Ara shot back, remembering keenly the time Shulen had scolded her for such acts.

" – you are not to let it interfere with your other duties," Brinelle chastised her, "and I'd rather you practiced in private sessions with Shulen instead of out in the Training Yards with all the warriors gawking."

"We all stand in the same Trials," Ari Ara retorted, quoting the phrase that made commoners and nobles equal in the annual tests of warriors.

"Nonsense!" Brinelle snapped. "There is no call for you to stand Trial at all."

"Why not, Mum?" Korin chimed in, obviously enjoying the conflict. "I had to stand Trials last year and have Emir run circles around me. Might as well let her stand – if only to give him a taste of his own medicine!"

The look Brinelle shot her son could have cracked windowpanes, but he merely smiled back, undaunted.

"Ari Ara ought to train with the rest. It'll inspire them to work hard," Korin suggested. "Otherwise, their queen'll be saving them instead of the other way around."

Brinelle scowled and switched the subject, questioning Ari Ara sharply about the presence of the so-called Urchin Queen in the Training Yards this morning and the strange reports she'd heard that the Lost Heir had been spotted scuffling on the plaza.

"That's ridiculous," Korin cut in. "Nothing but fanciful tales made up by idle tongues. I know for a fact she was here that day because she was annoying me with her endless questions."

Brinelle sniffed, suspicious of her son's ready excuse, but a bell tolled the hour and she threw up her hands at the passing time.

"Go get cleaned up and meet me for breakfast in my quarters," she told the pair. "If the Lost Heir is so eager to meet people and make friends, then perhaps it's time for her to go to the Nobles Academy along with her cousin and try to make a good impression among her peers."

Ari Ara gulped, thinking of Varina. Her Lady-Aunt had told her over and over that having the Mark of Peace, the hidden symbol of the Lost Heir, inked between her shoulder blades wasn't enough to claim the throne. To have her royal blood recognized, she had to impress the heads of the other twelve noblehouses and win their votes of confidence at an official confirmation hearing within one year of her arrival at the House of Marin. Ari Ara frankly thought she had gone from Lost Heir to Lost Cause. Even the Great Lady had doubts. On the first day she'd met Brinelle, Ari Ara had seen her Lady-Aunt's dismay as she'd stood with a pounding heart in the formidable regent's study. Brinelle's eyes had raked over her, weighed her on an invisible scale, and found her lacking. She could still remember the disappointment in her aunt's voice.

"*That's her?*" Brinelle had exclaimed, her tone as flat as a sledgehammer on a cold anvil.

Korin had burst out laughing at the look on his mother's face. Ari Ara flushed to the tips of her ears, but she lifted her chin defiantly.

"Yes, here she is, the long-lost double royal heir," Korin had announced, stifling a grin, "the daughter of Aunt Alinore and the Desert King."

"Leave him out of it," the Great Lady retorted, scowling at the mention of her long-standing enemy, Tahkan Shirar.

Brinelle's fierce gaze had studied the lines of Ari Ara's cheekbones and the shape of her skull, seeking out the indications of her royal lineage in the bend of her nose, the shape of her lips, the size of her earlobes. She rose from her chair and circled Ari Ara. She tugged the back of the girl's tunic down with a disdainful finger to check the authenticity of the Mark of Peace inked into the skin between her shoulders, noted the interlocking half circles of sand dunes and water waves, and sighed.

Any minute now, Ari Ara had thought sourly, *she'll pull back my lips to inspect my teeth.*

By Marianan standards, Ari Ara was short for her eleven years, a compact creature, wiry with lean muscle, skin bronzed by sun and roughened by wind. Her brazenly red hair – so much like her father's, Brinelle noted in disappointment – curled fiercely as it escaped the twists of her loosened braid. Her fists perched on her hips. Her chin jutted forward with defiance.

Her head lifted with stubborn pride. Her blue-gray eyes flashed with anger at the inspection.

"You take after your father," Brinelle commented archly, though, truth be told, she saw a great deal of Alinore in the girl. Her cousin's eyes stared back at her as if measuring all the years and hard decisions Brinelle had been forced to make. The look unsettled the Great Lady and an edge of brusqueness snapped in her tone.

"I suppose you'll have to do," she added with an air of disappointment.

Ari Ara stiffened. Behind her, she heard Shulen's warning cough. Brinelle met her hotly defiant glare with cool amusement. The girl would more than suffice; with proper training, the fearlessness and bold confidence with which the impudent imp was eyeing her could be molded into a suitable temperament for a royal heir. If tempered correctly, she would be unstoppable. The Great Lady intended to be the hard whetstone upon which the sharp blade of this young queen was honed. Sparks would fly between them, but in the end, the girl possessed the proper elements – pride, defiance, courage, strength – that could be forged into the steel of a queen.

Weeks after that initial interview, Ari Ara still sensed the Great Lady's piercing gaze measuring her up and finding her lacking. She washed and changed as swiftly as possible, and soon sat stiff and uncomfortable in Brinelle's private rooms. The low table was laden with fresh bread, sweet fruit, jams, butter, and tea, none of which she dared eat for fear of dropping strawberry jam on the cream blouse or dragging the embroidered cuff of her short, black jacket in the butter dish. Beneath the tablecloth, she smoothed the creases out of her long tailored skirt and wriggled her toes in the heeled shoes, trying not to think about the strange box of a hat pinned to her upswept hair. She felt like a trussed pig about to be thrown over a hearth spit. She'd faced full-grown warriors on the training sands with less nervousness.

The young nobles attended a private academy just a few doors down on Marin's Way. There, they studied politics, trade, command, ethics, history, mathematics, and a long list of other subjects that daunted her. Lunch was served on twenty-piece place settings and rank was observed. Korin had told her a slew of outrageous stories about the young nobles, inventing most of them on the spot simply to see her horrified reaction - at least, that's what she hoped. All of this left her with the impression that the young nobles were such a stifling and vicious den of gossipy vipers that, over brunch, she dredged up the courage to ask Brinelle if she could simply be her apprentice - a prospect scarcely any less daunting.

Brinelle arched her eyebrows and refused, turning instead to scold Korin for flipping his butter knife in imitation of a blade juggler.

"The Academy structure will be good for you," Brinelle replied to Ari Ara. "After all, I hear your education was informal and . . . irregular."

Ari Ara swallowed. A blush climbed her cheeks. She'd only learned to read last winter. Her earliest education had been in the dances and ways of the reclusive Fanten. Until this year, the subjects of High Mountain thunderstorms and shepherding had replaced reading and writing. Even now, her brushstrokes remained shaky and her reading slow. She could speak Fanten Tongue as well as Marianan, but she suspected that skill wouldn't be prized in the Capital. Brinelle asked her if she'd ever studied the Four Arts, and Ari Ara was saved from answering when Korin dropped the butter knife into his mother's teacup.

"Yes, the Academy is the proper place for you," Brinelle concluded as a maid hurried to clean up the spill.

Shulen, who was standing discretely by the door, cleared his throat and muttered something about throwing her to the wolves.

The Great Lady eyed him sharply.

"I'll assign Emir to guard her at the Academy," Brinelle stated.

From the look on Shulen's face, Ari Ara doubted Emir's warrior skills would help her survive this kind of wolf pack.

"You don't have to send Emir," Korin groaned. "The Academy's as secure as a fort. The noble youths only bring guards because it's fashionable. The Headmistress said it's getting ridiculous. Last fall, Varina's mother staged a kidnapping and ransom attempt to show how wealthy and important they think they are."

"Staged?" Brinelle asked piercingly. "How do you know it wasn't real?"

"Her guard said so when Emir asked why he hadn't been sacked for the breach in security," Korin answered, tossing a pitted cherry into his mouth.

Brinelle and Shulen exchanged looks of concern and exasperation.

"Ancestors, Mum," Korin swore in a sigh, "Isa de Barre's only a few years older than Ari Ara and her mother lets her come without a guard."

"Lady de Barre may be the most important southern noble, but her heir is *not* the potential ruler of two nations, Korin," his mother replied, shaking her head. "It will look like we don't value our heir if we assign anyone but the best to guard her."

"Don't make me use Emir's Champion's Boon," the youth threatened sullenly, staring moodily into his teacup.

Brinelle nearly dropped her fork.

"Korin! The Boon is not meant to be used for anything so petty as this."

"What's the Champion's Boon?" Ari Ara asked, speaking up for the first time.

Shulen explained the old tradition: the winner of the annual Spring Trials was granted a boon from the House of Marin. Usually the Champion requested support for the warriors or an act of kindness toward the orphans. It did not have to be announced at the Spring Trials; it was customary to think it over, as Emir was doing, and to discuss it privately with the Great Lady before formally making the request.

"Because it's mandatory that we fulfill it," Brinelle put in. "So, it's good form for the Champion to make sure his Boon doesn't bankrupt us."

"Mum," Korin pleaded, looking beseechingly at the Great Lady, "couldn't Emir just accompany us from gate to gate if you're truly concerned? It's only about a hundred paces from our house. If neither Isa nor us shows up with guards, it'll break the fashion for sure."

Brinelle lifted her eyebrows.

"I suppose it might work," she drawled, looking thoughtful. "Little Isa's quite the trendsetter, I've heard."

"*Little* Isa is just turned fifteen, Mother, and you'd best watch out. When she sneezes, half the noblegirls copy the way her nose wrinkles," Korin commented.

After brunch, Ari Ara fidgeted with the strange hat on her head as they crossed the cobblestone street toward the imposing gates of the Nobles Academy. She scuffed the ground and tried to muster enthusiasm for the day ahead. She could see packs of young nobles clustered in the entrance hall. She'd met some of them at the first welcoming reception, but she'd met hundreds of people that night; including the ambassadors, the heads of important industries, and the leaders of the monks and sisters' spiritual orders. She hoped at least one or two of the young nobles' names would come back to her.

The nobleboys wore the same tailored jackets and shirts with turned-up collars that Korin wore. Ari Ara eyed their comfortable trousers enviously. The girls all wore skirts or dresses without exception. At least she had been spared the trend toward fluffy volumes of pastels. A few willowy girls looked like one good puff of wind could blow them away. Ari Ara didn't want anyone to think she could be pushed around that easily. If she had her druthers, she'd have marched in here like Shulen in a plain tunic and sturdy pants. If not for Korin's arm thrown over her shoulders, Ari Ara would have bolted like a skittish lamb.

"Don't worry," Korin jollied her as they passed through the gold-leafed double doors into the entrance hall. "If anyone slights you - "

"I'll just ignore it as beneath my notice," Ari Ara promised with a sigh, reciting what Brinelle had told her.

"Until we get 'em on the training sands," Korin added cheerfully. "Then you can dump them on their heads."

"Boys," said a girl, sighing in disgust and turning toward them. "You think everything - oh hello, *you're* not a boy."

Ari Ara closed her mouth just in time to avoid Korin's elbow nudge. An impeccably attired young woman dropped a perfect curtsy of a greeting, poised and elegant as a swan. Feeling about as graceful as a goose in comparison, Ari Ara nodded in return – Brinelle had already informed her that a queen (even potential queens) never curtsied. The young lady stood with casual elegance, draping one arm over the bannister of the stairs and tucking the other across her hip. Her clean-cut black skirt matched her short jacket and the deeper rose of the trim set off the blushing pink of her paler blouse. Pearls pinned back her honey wheat hair and she wore a box hat that made Ari Ara realize it was supposed to look like a tiara instead of the miniature cake that was stuck on top of her own head. From looks on the faces around her, Ari Ara gathered this girl was probably everything a noblegirl was supposed to be – and everything Ari Ara was not.

Her feet probably aren't screeching curses louder than the pig herder's lazy sow, Ari Ara grumbled silently, annoyed at the shoes she'd been forced to wear. In the High Mountains this time of year, she'd be running barefoot across the black rocks and wouldn't cram her feet back into boots until autumn.

A smile transformed the young woman's face. All at once, Ari Ara put a name to the young woman: Isa de Barre, Heir to the Southlands. She'd met her at the welcoming reception on her first night in Mariana Capital. Right after Ari Ara had slurped her soup and shocked the room into dead silence, Isa had winked at her from the opposite side of the table, rolling her eyes at the nonsense of the nobles.

"I've *so* hoped to speak with you," Isa de Barre remarked with a gleam of interest lighting up her eyes. "I've been hearing the most astonishing stories about you. Is it true you fought off a wolf bare-handed?"

Ari Ara choked.

"No," she replied, "it wasn't – "

"Oh," Isa cut in with a sigh of disappointment, "I knew it couldn't be true – "

"It wasn't just one, it was a whole pack of them trying to eat the lambs," Ari Ara corrected.

The circle of girls closest to them let loose a shriek of delighted horror that turned heads.

"Ancestors!" Isa swore, placing her hand over her heart. She glanced around and then conspiratorially murmured, "Is it true that you were raised on dew and magic?"

Ari Ara laughed out loud.

"No. Are they really saying that?"

Isa nodded, her face alive with merriment.

"They're also saying that the Fanten taught you to fly on the wind and ride the mists," she admitted. "And, now I know this next rumor can't possibly be true – you're such a slip of a girl – it's just silly – "

"Spit it out," Ari Ara told her.

A delicate blush climbed Isa's cheeks.

"Well, I heard a rumor that you bested Emir Miresh in a match. That's not true, is it?"

"It is."

A ripple of gasps revealed eavesdroppers as the young nobles abandoned the pretense of their other conversations and stared at the pair. Isa's mouth fell open in a perfect oval of surprise.

"Surely, you're teasing me," she objected.

Ari Ara shrugged.

"Ask Emir," Korin suggested so mischievously that Isa decided it must be true.

"I will," she promised. "I'll do just that. I'd love to see his expression."

Isa shot the wiry, red-haired girl an admiring glance. At that, the rest of the noble youths stopped staring at Ari Ara like an odd beast and crept closer. They'd met her at the reception, of course, but the formal setting required a certain decorum and the questions they longed to ask couldn't be uttered under the close scrutiny of the older nobles. One girl's tentative question broke the silence and a hailstorm of queries assailed her. The wide-eyed girls asked if she remembered her mother, how she survived in the High Mountains, and did the Fanten wear clothes? The gawking boys wanted to know if Shulen really was as tough as he looked, how she beat Emir Miresh, and would she show them Azar right now?

"Not in those lovely clothes," Isa shot back, coming to Ari Ara's rescue, "and honestly, use your brains before you ask. Of course the Fanten wear clothes - it's *cold* in the High Mountains. You already know Shulen's tough as river rock, and if you want to know how she beat Emir, ask him, not that he's likely to tell you the secret."

A ripple of nudges and murmurs broke out as an older girl walked through the front door, accompanied by a muscular guard. Ari Ara silently groaned as she recognized the young noble.

"You may remember Lady Varina of the House of Thorn, Heir to the Orelands of the North," Isa began, politely introducing the two girls. "And this is - "

"Oh, I know who she is," Varina replied, her voice a cross between a purr and a sneer. "She's the girl who *thinks* she's our new queen."

A round of gasps and a squeak of dismay shot out from the group. Varina fluttered her black eyelashes and lifted a hand to her mouth.

"Oh dear," she said with a smirk, "I didn't mean it that way. Of course, the confirmation hearing will set all the disturbing rumors straight."

"What do you mean?" Isa asked bluntly, her eyes hard.

"Darling little Isa, you know as well as I that some - we won't name them - are saying that she's an imposter, that the Mark of Peace was put on as a fake by those savage Fanten."

"They're not savage," Ari Ara shot back angrily.

Varina widened her eyes.

"I'm sure they did their best, dear girl, but isn't it true that you slept in caves?"

"Yes, but - "

"And that you were left alone to fend for yourself as a very young child?"

"I had the sheep to - "

"Hardly substitutes for real parents," Varina said in a tone reeking of condescension. "And they couldn't exactly give you a proper education. You only just learned to read this winter, isn't that right?"

Someone tittered.

Ari Ara's ears burned with fury.

"But don't worry, little shepherd-girl," Varina sneered. "You're among civilized people now. We know you haven't any manners, education, or class. If you last long enough, we'll show you what's what."

She laughed in a coldness that could crack crystal. Others joined in. Ari Ara's cheeks flamed. Her mind raced for a response. She'd dealt with bullies before. It was simpler when she could just flip them with the Way Between, but much as she'd like to send Varina flying bustle over bosom as Rill had done, she doubted it'd go over well.

A hand fell on her shoulder.

"I rather like my new *cousin*," Korin told Varina in a light voice loud enough for the whole room to hear his endorsement in the emphasis. "She's fresh and unusual. We nobles are an inbred lot, and our old antics are getting rather dull."

"Your lordship's affection," she purred, "for your ... cousin ... is evident. And just as well, for you know the old saying: *a queen without her nobles is like a dressmaker without cloth.*"

Varina stared at Ari Ara with hard eyes. Then she turned in

a fluid motion and left. Ari Ara shivered at the ominous threat in her words.

Korin leaned over.

"Don't let the viper get to you," he whispered to her. "Hone up your verbal Azar. You're going to need it with this lot."

He gave her shoulder an encouraging squeeze, winked at Isa, and glared at the rest of the nobles, just daring anyone else to insult his cousin.

CHAPTER SIX

. . . . .

The Art of Dress

A bell tolled from the rooftop of the Nobles Academy. The youths scattered and rushed to their classrooms. Korin and Isa took Ari Ara by the shoulders and steered her upstairs. An undercurrent of murmurs, whispers, and nudges trailed them down the hall. The Academy boasted tall ceilings, but, like many buildings in the Capital, the design was intended to conserve floor space. Ari Ara saw the problem Korin had mentioned: the narrow classrooms, built for no more than twelve to twenty nobles, were crowded by the extra guards.

"You should see the older girls," Korin commented, holding the door open as they entered their classroom. "They pick young guards for their handsome features and then spend half the class making eyes at them."

"Mother said if I let my marks fall like my cousins' did," Isa whispered, "she'd yank me out of here and stick me with a toothless old tutor."

To Ari Ara's relief, Varina wasn't in their first class, but Korin warned that she'd be in their group for the Art of Trade the next morning.

"She's dense as wood at it and prickly as a hedgehog if you try to help her," Korin sighed. "But she's terrifyingly good at the Art of Politics, so be glad she isn't in the afternoon group with us this year."

Classes were taught with mixed ages and abilities, encouraging students to assist one another, cementing strong relationships among the children and heirs of the thirteen noblehouses.

"Plus," Korin explained as they sat down, "it solves the problem of erratic attendance as the nobles jolt back and forth from their estates to the Capital."

Unlike Scholar Monk's crowded, battered classroom for the orphans at Monk's Hand Monastery, this classroom was ringed with plush, padded benches in concentric circles. Fine curtains draped elegantly along tall windows. A bookcase with intricate woodwork held rare, old volumes. Ari Ara was nearly the youngest in the room; she spotted one skinny boy who looked small enough to be ten, but all the rest of the nobles at the Academy loomed large, towering over her.

The students rose respectfully when the professor entered. The short, curvaceous woman waved for them to be seated. Chestnut hair swept up in a twisting style, not one strand out of place. Her rich blue jacket matched her tailored skirt and the frothy neckline of her white blouse spilled like the crest of a wave between the lapels.

"When she isn't teaching us, she runs a much-respected, independent House of Dress," Isa whispered to Ari Ara.

The woman offered a brief word of welcome to Ari Ara as her eyes flicked across the girl from head to toe, weighing her up in a glance. She began the morning's instruction by asking the students to explain the Four Arts for the Lost Heir's benefit.

"I doubt she's needed to know them before now," she remarked, calling upon a mousy-haired girl with thick spectacles to begin.

"The Art of Trade," the noblegirl recited promptly, "covers skillful approaches to managing economy, resources, and finances."

"The Art of Politics teaches about law and power," a suave, clever youth answered next.

"The Art of War shows nobles the mastery of warriors, strategy, and battle," a stocky boy stated next.

"And," the Mistress concluded, pausing dramatically, "the most important for a noble to master is the Art of Dress."

Ari Ara caught her giggle just in time. Not one smile cracked on the others' faces. Even Korin looked serious. She snuck a glance at Isa, but the Capital girl hadn't so much as blinked at the ridiculous statement.

"I'm sorry, but did you say the *Art of Dress?*" Ari Ara repeated. "As in . . . clothes?"

"Precisely," the woman responded, pursing her burgundy lips together and furrowing her brow as if surprised by the question. "The Art of Dress is far more than simply clothes, however. The wardrobe of the House of Marin, for example, determines the fate of the nation."

Ari Ara burst out laughing.

The Mistress struggled to muffle her annoyance and wound up looking like a stork that had swallowed a snapping turtle.

"It is no laughing matter," she told Ari Ara reprovingly. "Crowns have been won or lost depending on what the king or queen wears to the dinner table. Who can explain this to the Lost Heir?"

Hands shot in the air.

"Style is the politics of culture," a student answered eagerly, "setting the mood and tone for the nation, reflecting times of abundance or scarcity; extravagance or frugality; innovation or conformity."

The Mistress opened the floor for a discussion and the young nobles - girls and boys alike - leapt in. Fashion was the political language of the Capital. Station, class, profession: one's dress revealed - or concealed - everything. Shop girls and seamstresses vied for seniority and advancement by the cut of their skirt or the arc of a neckline. While the boldest and brightest dyes were reserved by expense - and prohibition - for the nobles, the women and men of the Houses of Dress used the nuances of tailored hems, cuffs, and collars to turn traditional black skirts and ivory blouses into stunning displays of subtlety. Quality counted more than quantity among them. A shop girl might remake the remnant of a lady's dress into an accent streaking across a scalloped waistband. An antique fabric unearthed from an old chest might be discarded by a noblewoman, but treasured by the seamstress who tailored it into the edge of her underskirt and walked with a hitch in her step to proudly expose it.

Ari Ara listened in astonishment and finally decided the young nobles weren't pulling her leg when the boys jumped into a heated debate about the three Great Trade Crises caused by fabric speculation after the adaptation of the waterwheel triggered the industrial boom of the Loomlands two hundred years ago.

Korin related a historical example of how their great-grandfather had nearly lost the throne - and his life - amidst an embittered dressiers' feud when warring Mistresses of Dress had caused economic crashes. The twelve times great-grandson of Marin had won a war because his dressiers put trousers in style instead of full skirts and saved the fabric for the army. His great-granddaughter had lost a military campaign because poorly made uniforms had demoralized her troops.

"If you don't stay on the dressiers' good side," Korin cautioned Ari Ara in an undertone, "they'll lengthen the skirts when there's a cloth shortage and the nation will call for your head on a platter."

Ari Ara thought back over her excursion into the city. From the poorest street urchin to the wealthiest merchant, each and every one of the river island's inhabitants had been dressed to the heights of fashion and the limits of their pocketbooks. She'd seen shop girls flirting with craftsmen in finely-tailored tunics. Mistresses swept down the street wearing broad hats bedecked with enormous feathers. Women's skirts had flashed double layers of chartreuse and cerulean as they walked; golden underskirts swished beneath scarlet trims. Merchants' long coats had swirled behind them like peacock tails, flashing bright designs from within the darker folds.

And the more money a person had to spend on fashion, the more expressive his or her fashion became. Curtsying noblewomen lifted their first and second skirts to reveal a flash of Mariana blue to indicate loyalty to the throne. Fans fluttered with messages decipherable only between individuals - and wildly speculated upon by everyone else. Embroidered trims announced betrothals as one family's motif entwined with another's. A house's rising fortune was flaunted in expensive textiles. The subtlest details spoke volumes.

"Like Ari Ara's - I mean, the Young Queen's - dress at the reception on her first night here," Isa put in eagerly. "It was brilliant. It stated that she is both her mother and her father's heir, that she holds the Fanten in high regard for their kindness to her, and that she bears the Mark of Peace proudly. It also said that she will not bend to anyone simply to conform."

Ari Ara stared at Isa. Had she truly said all that? She'd just wanted to be comfortable. She remembered the day clearly. A maid had come to help her dress for the formal welcoming reception.

"I don't need help dressing," Ari Ara had objected indignantly.

The woman had lifted up a cautionary hand.

"Wait until you see these dresses," she warned.

Hours later, standing in the dressing room of her quarters, bound stiff as a suit of armor, unable to bend, breathe, or move anything but her arms, Ari Ara had flapped her hands in horror. The elaborate concoction created by the House of Marin's Mistress of Dress contained so many wires, stays, and petticoats that she could set the hem on the floor and lift her feet up underneath.

"I won't," Ari Ara flatly refused. "I *can't.*"

"You can . . . you must," the maid pleaded.

"I'll pass out," she promised darkly.

"No, you won't. All the ladies wear these. You don't see the Great Lady fainting, do you?" the woman pointed out.

"I'll go mad," Ari Ara threatened. "I'll tear it off in the middle of the reception."

"Oh, you wouldn't!" the maid exclaimed.

"I can't wear this thing. I'll trip on these shoes and crash to the floor."

The maid wrung her hands. That seemed likely. She'd had to force the girl to practice the tiny steps of the Capital ladies.

"Isn't there *anything* else I can wear?" Ari Ara demanded. She felt like one of the villagers' giant Feast Day puppets.

"You have to wear a gown," the maid explained, "and they're all this awkward and uncomfortable."

Not all of them, Ari Ara thought. Her eyes darted to the

small bundle of belongings that had descended the High Mountains with her. She knew one dress that flowed like water and moved like wind.

When the Lost Heir stepped into the Main Hall that evening, she wore her mother's shining dress made of a white silk so rare it had taken a hundred years of cultivation for the Desert King to collect enough to offer it as a love-gift to his wife. Woven in a Marianan pattern that shimmered like a fish in water and sewn in the Fanten's open-backed style, it was a dress of legend, unique in all the world. Ari Ara had kept one of the other dress' full petticoats to bring a swirl of motion to the gold-embroidered edges of the white gown. To add a touch of formality, she kept the pair of long brilliant blue gloves the Mistress of Dress had originally selected.

As she stepped down the curving staircase, the nobles in the Main Hall had erupted in applause. They showered the Mistress of Dress with compliments on the brilliance of using Queen Alinore's dress, the one that had revealed the Mark of Peace between the girl's shoulder blades. The Mistress blinked. A stiff smile spread over her lips. She took in the compliments, noted the Great Lady's bemused expression, and decided that taking credit for an unexpected success was more profitable than throwing a tantrum over her rejected design.

"It was an ingenious masterstroke by the House of Marin," agreed the Academy's Art of Dress instructor, flashing an approving smile around the Art of Dress classroom and thanking Isa for the example.

The rest of the morning's conversation navigated the dizzying landscape of loyalties and intrigue, wealth and war, style and law, industry and culture. They analyzed the nobles' ensembles of the past week, reading volumes from the wordless language of seams and sashes, hems and hats. They discussed the significance of the ladies' trend toward darker shades of purple and the lords' increasing preference for pastels. By the time the bell rang for lunch break, Ari Ara's mind whirled.

"Each of you shall hand in an essay on the themes of today's conversation," the Mistress told the students, "and the political reasons for the growing interest in ruffled seams. Class dismissed."

Ari Ara rose with the others, shaking her head in astonishment. She hadn't known what to expect when she came down from the High Mountains, but writing essays on the significance of buttonholes wasn't it.

"What do ruffled seams have to do with politics?" she groaned to Korin later as Emir escorted them back to the House of Marin. She'd paid close attention in the afternoon course on the Art of Politics, but she still couldn't figure it out.

"Water workers," Korin hinted. "Because of the Water Exchange that trades water for workers, there are two thousand of them in the Loomlands factories and over a thousand on this river island, hundreds in the Dressiers District alone. With that much cheap labor, fancy ruffles and tedious handiwork can come back in style as the price drops."

"That's awful," Ari Ara blurted out.

"Tell me about it," Korin sighed. "It looks idiotic."

Ari Ara shook her head and spun to grip Emir's elbow.

"Couldn't you use your Champion's Boon to end the Water Exchange?"

Emir moved so fast she nearly tripped over him, holding a finger up to his lips. Korin froze and gave her a shocked look.

"*Don't* ever say that again," her cousin hissed. "Are you mad? You'll get us all killed."

There had been several attempts to end the Water Exchange, Korin told her, clearly nervous even mentioning it.

Each one ended in disaster – assassinations, disappearances, scandals, and imprisonments by the nobles for inciting uprisings.

"Even Mum is afraid to oppose the Water Exchange," Korin confided. "Someone tried to kill her two years ago when she introduced an abolition bill into the Assembly of Nobles."

Ari Ara had difficulty imagining the formidable Great Lady intimidated by any threat, but Korin assured her that the water workers were a dangerous subject in Mariana Capital.

"Why?" Ari Ara asked, frowning.

"Well, money, of course," he answered in a worldly tone.

The water workers ensured vast profits for the nobles. Over a quarter of the Marianan economy tied to them in some manner or another. The wealth of the nobles surged to unprecedented heights, raking in profits from goods made by unpaid fingers and services provided by unwaged hands. These nobles defended the Water Exchange vehemently.

"You'll see the water workers touch in everything," Korin confided, "but especially in clothing and fashion. It's practically impossible to get around the Capital without running into water workers' labor."

"I'm still going to find a way to end the Water Exchange," she vowed.

"Trust me on this," her cousin urged, "leave the water workers well alone. Mum would have stopped it already if it could have been done. But it can't, so don't drag Emir's Boon into something dangerous like this, trying for the impossible."

Ari Ara set her chin. Nothing was impossible. There was always a Way Between.

CHAPTER SEVEN

. . . . .

The Hawk Keeper and the Seamstress

Unless under siege, the heavy doors of the gates of the House of Marin stood open during the day. Two expressionless guards flanked the sides like a pair of stone statues. They nodded to Emir Miresh as Ari Ara and Korin entered the courtyard. People thronged the open area. A carriage stood by the imposing marble steps that led into the House of Marin. The horses pawed the flagstones, striking ringing drumbeats with their hard iron shoes. In the corner by the servants' alley, a huddle of blue-slashed water workers silently endured the chief steward's inspection.

"New water workers," Korin murmured, peering curiously at the group. "Hopefully, there's a Hawk Keeper among them. Mum's been complaining ever since the last one broke his contract and returned to the Desert."

The Great Lady didn't employ many water workers around the House of Marin, the curly-haired youth explained to Ari Ara, but she made an exception for Hawk Keepers. The water workers were generally regarded as lazy and inept, but certain skills among the Desert People were highly prized, most notably the Hawk Keepers. Both nations used messenger hawks by the hundreds, sending them winging north and south, east and west, over the mountains and farmlands, through the wide river valley and the arid desert lands. Despite the best efforts of centuries of Marianan spies, the art and skills of the Desert Hawk Keepers had remained secret.

"We've Hawk Keepers of our own, of course," Korin boasted with a chagrined twist of his lips, "but they're nothing compared to the Desert People. I don't want to call it magic, but there's simply no other word for their uncanny ability to communicate with the birds."

Korin explained that a water worker with the ability to train and handle messenger hawks could earn enough water rights to support many families. Ari Ara wondered why the previous Hawk Keeper had quit. She wished the fellow had stayed, if only to help her chase down Nightfast, the black hawk her father had sent to her. She was told there was a special whistle that would call him down from the sky, but she didn't know it yet. She was stuck waving her letters to the Desert King in the air trying to get the attention of the black speck wheeling overhead. She had written to Tahkan Shirar during her second week at the House of Marin, telling him her impressions of the Capital, and asking him about her mother, the desert, his culture . . . curiosity burned like fire in her veins and the questions she most longed to ask were orphan's fears and longings, questions she didn't quite dare put on paper to her newfound father like: *Who are you? When will we meet? Will you like me?*

"Look," Korin whispered excitedly, pointing at a blue-slashed woman, "that's Mahteni Duktar! She's the most highly sought-after desert seamstress in Mariana Capital. Her work is worth a whole village's water. Mum must have paid a fortune to end her contract elsewhere. Bet you anything she'll be working on your wardrobe."

Ari Ara eyed the woman curiously. She wore a pale muslin dress covered by a black overcoat and an apron laden with tiny pockets, each bulging with the tools of the seamstress' trade: pins, measuring cord, scissors, thread, buttons. A bright blue slash had been sewn to the back of her jacket and across the front of her apron. A similar band of cloth tied back the tight curls of her copper hair.

The water worker standing beside Mahteni glanced up, sensing Ari Ara's gaze. She felt a sharp intensity in his look. Her footsteps slowed. The black-haired, bearded man stood amidst the huddle of new water workers listening to the chief steward's lecture with quiet dignity.

"Ari Ara," the Great Lady called, turning away from a hunched old woman near the front steps and gesturing for the girl to join them. "Come and greet the Lady of the Timberlands."

Ari Ara reluctantly tore her eyes away from the water workers and walked over. The ancient, wrinkled old burlap sack of a lace-encrusted matriarch thrust her beady eyes and beak nose in her face like a nosy crow. Her paper-thin lips pursed into a salted prune of disapproval.

"She takes after her father," the old woman sniffed with rasping disdain. "Atrocious hair; it should be dyed immediately. As for her appalling complexion, well, lightening cream would work wonders."

"No."

The word shot out of her mouth before she could stop it, every fiber in her body tensing against the scorn of the matriarch.

"No?" the bejeweled and withered woman snapped. The word was simply not spoken to one of her rank and station, even by this upstart of a girl.

75

"You can't hide the Desert in me," Ari Ara retorted hotly. "I'm no more ashamed to be my father's daughter than my mother's."

Shocked silence struck. All eyes leapt to the Lady of the Timberlands, expecting the fall of her wrath. Then a man's voice lifted in the sound of a hawk's cry piercing the wind. Heads whirled. A second cry joined the first, echoing from the top of the marble steps. A third hawk's call sounded from the cluster of water workers.

"The Desert People are attacking!" someone cried out in alarm.

Warriors tensed. Hands reached for swords.

"Stop!"

Shulen's command broke through the commotion, freezing everyone in place as he stalked across the stones of the courtyard.

"That is the Honor Cry of the Desert," he explained in a firm tone. "You know it only as a battle cry because that is the only place Marianans hear it, but it has many meanings . . . as perhaps one of those who lifted it will explain."

He scanned the faces of the newly-arrived water workers. A look of incredulous shock whipped across his features. He masked it swiftly, turning toward the copper-haired seamstress as she wrung the edges of her apron in her white knuckles.

"Mahteni Duktar," he barked sharply, "what is the meaning of this?"

The woman held her eyes downcast as she respectfully dipped a curtsy. When she looked up, her green eyes sought and held Ari Ara's.

"The Honor Cry is an ancient praise of our people," she answered, her voice trembling, but bold against the fear and anger of the Marianans. "We could not help it, sir. When the

Young Queen stood up for her father's people, how could we not raise it for her?"

Her smile stretched her bronze skin across the taut frame of her cheekbones. The Lady of the Timberlands gave a small growl of displeasure, but Brinelle merely waved her hand with a bemused expression.

"You are forgiven," the Great Lady stated magnanimously, "though you would be wise to refrain from such displays in the future."

"Yes, Lady," the desert woman answered softly.

The tension ran out of the yard in a whoosh. The new water workers hastily leapt to their assigned tasks. The guards returned to their duties. The Great Lady shot Ari Ara a warning look and escorted the old Timberlands matriarch into the hall. Korin grabbed Ari Ara's arm and hauled her up the steps, laughing.

"Never a dull moment with you, cousin. Go freshen up and remember, we'll have to deal with the Old Bat of the Timberlands at dinner tonight."

He wrinkled his nose and took off.

When she returned to her quarters, a black-winged hawk sat on the ledge of the open window. She crossed the room at a run, crooning to Nightfast as he ruffled his chest feathers. She untied the small scroll as the black hawk extended his leg. Ari Ara snatched the crispy, fried meat strips off the tray of food laid out on the table and gave them to the bird. He screeched softly, ruffling his feathers in the warmth of the sun. Ari Ara slid onto the low bench by the window and unrolled the message.

Daughter, I am told the Capital welcomes you with her open and powerful arms. She is a sly and beautiful city, rich with secrets and dangers. Walk carefully, but fearlessly.

Ari Ara smiled. Tahkan Shirar wrote with a decisive hand in bold characters that never hesitated on the parchment. He wrote of his astonishment at her early life, and included words of praise for the Fanten.

I have met few of their kind, for the mist-loving people rarely venture into our arid lands, but Shulen's great love, the Fanten woman Rhianne, impressed us all with her integrity and courage. Those two values are highly prized by our people.

Ari Ara gazed thoughtfully out the window to where the mountains rose in the far distance. She had seen Rhianne's ghost in the forest once, a beautiful and gentle woman who had been murdered during the Battle of Shulen's Stand. She pictured Shulen and Rhianne as the Desert King must have known them: young, in love, surrounded by treachery and dangers as they accompanied Queen Alinore. In those days, before the War of Retribution, Tahkan Shirar and Shulen had met as friends, not enemies. The death of Alinore and the disappearance of the heir had embittered everyone. How long does a blood-drenched battlefield lie fallow before life dares to emerge again? The war had cemented animosity in place for a decade . . . until now. Her appearance as the heir had given everyone hope - when it wasn't causing controversy. Ari Ara winced at the thought and returned to the letter.

We are a people of a great many legends and powerful myths that walk among us, Tahkan wrote. *You may find, Ari Ara Shirar, that your story grows far taller than you. No doubt, you will catch up to your legend in due time.*

Ari Ara Shirar. She mouthed the name, startled to realize she had a surname – two, actually. After a decade of merely being Ari Ara of the High Mountains, denoted by place instead of parentage, she could now use the two most famous last names of all: Ari Ara de Marin en Shirar. She laughed, wondering if the order would flip to Shirar en Marin when she was in the Desert.

The hawk nuzzled her hair with his beak, hoping for more of her food. Ari Ara rose and brought back the tray, feeding the bird while picking at the fruit. She ate absently with one hand and held the scroll open on the bench with the other, reading.

You asked in your letter to know more of your mother. Many in Mariana can tell you her story, so I will speak of the qualities the Marianans cannot see. When she first came to the Desert, Alinore met the glare of the fierce sun fearlessly, confident of the depths of the Mari River's spirit running in her veins. She moved like water and laughed like a stream, and it seemed to my parched eyes that life rose in her footsteps. I, who have known all ten words for thirst, would have crawled miles on my belly to find her. Before she came, I was content with my cracked lips and endless heat, but one sight of Alinore with her river-water eyes and I was filled with yearning. She promised the revival of all things green and growing. She unlocked the South Dam and for a few years the old fields of our Deep Sands Valley grew verdant. With her death, the dam was closed and water was sold to us only at unbearable costs.

He meant the Water Exchange, Ari Ara realized. The cost of the water was the lives of his people.

The handle on the door turned. She shoved the letter under the seat cushion.

"Toulukh!"

Mahteni Duktar's startled exclamation burst from the doorway. The hawk launched off the window and flew onto the woman's arm. She carefully held a set of garments away from his talons.

"You know him?" Ari Ara cried in surprise.

Mahteni's bronze skin darkened with a flustered blush.

"No, no – I mean, not personally – everyone knows the

Desert King's messenger hawk. Begging your pardon, I didn't mean to barge in. The Mistress of Dress sent me. I'm to deliver these clothes and take your measurements; the Mistress claims you've grown a full hand this week alone."

Mahteni awkwardly dipped a curtsy, trying to maintain her balance with the hawk on her arm.

"Go on you, off. The King sent you to her, silly," Mahteni chided, shaking the bird.

"What did you call him?" Ari Ara asked, leaping up and holding out her arm to let the hawk come to her.

"Toulukh, it's his name in our language. They call him Nightfast here, loyal and swift, dark as the black sky. He is a legend in my homeland."

"I've heard everything is a legend there," Ari Ara commented, thinking of the letter.

Mahteni chuckled.

"In many ways, yes. Rain is a legend. Baths are a legend. Green is a legend."

"Do you know the summoning cry for hawks?" Ari Ara asked.

"Yes, and if you'll put the hawk down and let me take your measurements, I'll have time to teach it to you before I have to leave."

"It would be handy if he came when I called," Ari Ara said, trying to get the bird to step off her arm onto the window ledge.

"If you keep feeding him your meals," Mahteni replied knowingly, eyeing her tray, "he won't just come . . . he'll bring you a fish to keep you from starving."

Mahteni tapped the window ledge making a clicking sound. Nightfast cocked his head at her and obediently hopped off Ari Ara's arm.

"Thanks," Ari Ara said.

"There is no need to thank a lowly water worker," Mahteni reminded her.

Ari Ara gave her a strange look.

"What is it?" Mahteni asked.

A flush climbed the girl's cheeks.

"S-sorry," she stammered. "I just – I just learned about the water workers."

Mahteni looked up with an odd expression.

"You don't object to being served by one, do you?"

"Why would I?" Ari Ara answered in confusion.

The woman's eyebrows drew together.

"Many people do," she answered with a slight flush of anger. "We are seen as dangerous and lazy."

"How can you stand it?" Ari Ara asked quietly.

"Because we must." Mahteni spoke the words as bald fact, a weary expression twisting her strong features. She rubbed a weathered hand over her eyes and stared up at the sky in an appeal to the ancestors.

"Stand quietly and listen closely, for it is best not to be heard speaking truthfully about this."

Ari Ara nodded. Mahteni asked her to hold out her arms. She circled the girl's waist with the cord, noting lengths in her mind. A desert woman needed no written notes to affix details to memory; an oral tradition such as hers took pride in their sharp minds.

"Officially," Mahteni explained, "we are called water workers, but when our servitude is not by choice, but by desperate necessity, then is that not slavery? What option is there between drought, death, or servitude?"

Mahteni spun the girl around to measure the width of her collarbone. She spoke in a voice that was soft and melodic, yet an edge of harshness clung to her hard truths.

"Here, the water flows day and night in rivers, mists, and rain. You will find it hard to imagine my home, a land so dry the air cracks in invisible lines. Our language has ten words for thirst. A branch of the Mari River used to flow freely through the Border Mountains into the Deep Sands Valley, but during the War of Retribution, the Marianans blocked the dam and made us pay for the water. We are a humble people, Young Queen, not given to great possessions. After several years of tithing, we had nothing left to give, and our children's first words became *beku, ongla,* and *saak,* the words for cracking thirst, delirium thirst, and kill-me-now thirst."

The Marianans struck a cruel bargain: a year of work for a year of water, one life for each family's survival. Despairing families drew straws, young sons rotated years of servitude, daughters like Mahteni gave up marriage and her own life for the survival of her sisters and brothers. Some were bartered into trades, laboring for craftsmen, particularly in the mills and factories of the Loomlands region. Others sweated as stevedores on the docks of Mari River – a dangerous place for Desert People since they often could not swim.

"I had skill in sewing," Mahteni explained, "and made my way to the Houses of Dress in Mariana Capital. Now, I have been brought here to work on your wardrobe."

Ari Ara struggled with the double weight of shame and sorrow. Her blood boiled in her veins, churning crosswise at the knowledge that one of her people would do this to the other. She pushed free of the measuring cord and spun toward the door.

"I'm going to speak to Brinelle," she cried. "This isn't right."

"Wait!" Mahteni hissed in alarm, snatching at the back of the girl's blouse. "Please, show some caution. All is hung like a spider's web in Mariana Capital. Speak for us, yes; nothing would make my heart happier, but stop and think before you do! The Great Lady will refuse – she has been appealed to many times - and what power do you have at present? None, not until the Assembly of Nobles confirms you as the rightful heir."

"But it's not right!" she repeated angrily.

"Then bide your time, learn quick, and when the day comes, free us and send the water back to the lands that yearn for it," Mahteni said in a breath of a voice, her eyes darting around nervously. "But be careful. You are used to honest dealings and you will find little of that in the Capital."

Ari Ara scowled. She'd seen her share of secrets in Monk's Hand, too.

A rap on the door startled them both. Mahteni opened it, gasped, and threw an alarmed glance over her shoulder at Ari Ara. Then she stepped through the doorway and slammed the door behind her. The muffled sounds of a hushed argument filtered through the wood.

"What are you doing here?" Mahteni hissed.

"I am the new Hawk Keeper. The steward ordered me to fetch the hawk in the heir's room," the man's voice replied with a low laugh.

"That is not what I meant," Mahteni snapped back. "When I saw you in the yard, my heart nearly dropped stone dead in my chest! How could you lift the Honor Cry in front of all those people like that?"

"Oh, how could I not?" the man's voice replied, rippling with humor. "That girl has the spirit of our people!"

"Recklessness is not the same thing as spirit," Mahteni shot back.

"You've been in the river fog too long," he retorted. "You have forgotten the hot temper of your blood."

"You'd best forget it, too – "

"She'll make the Desert King proud!"

"Because he's as reckless as she is!" Mahteni fumed. "Go now before someone sees you here."

"Let me talk to her – "

"No, you fool, are you out of your mind?"

"I'll report you to our king," the man threatened with a teasing note.

"Our king should know better than to listen to your nonsense over my caution," Mahteni hissed back.

"Do not deny me this, Mahteni," the man said in a rumble of command crossed with a hint of pleading.

A silence fell. At last, Mahteni opened the door and glanced in. Ari Ara caught sight of a flicker of fear in the seamstress' eyes. The man's hand, scarred from old wounds, touched the woman's shoulder. Tears brimmed in her eyes. Her narrow fingers darted up like birds to alight on his. Then she stepped back from the door and allowed him to enter.

The light behind him perched on his shoulder like a hawk, edging his beard in gold, hiding his face in shadow. The man slid through the door and shifted into view. He was tall and lean; his skin pulled tight over muscle and bone, except by the eyes where time had softened the lines into deep creases. His nose bent like Mahteni's, but his hair and beard were black as ink. His tunic bore the emblem of a hawk and leather traces wrapped his armband.

"Greetings, Ari Ara of the High Mountains," the man said formally, an odd catch in his voice. "I - we - have waited a long time to meet you."

"It was very brave of you to lift the Honor Cry," Ari Ara told him.

"It was foolhardy, that's what it was," Mahteni answered with a frown.

The man chuckled and ignored her scolding tone.

"What you did was courageous," he said approvingly, "standing up to the lady on behalf of our blood."

"It's true," Ari Ara shrugged. "They can't hide the Desert in me."

"No," he acknowledged with a wry grin, eyeing her red hair, "they certainly cannot."

He held out his arm and Nightfast winged to him from the window, screeching gently in affection.

"So, you are the new Hawk Keeper?" Ari Ara asked.

"Yes," he answered. "I will bring you the messages your father wishes you to receive, should this rascal of a bird not deliver them directly as instructed."

"What is your name?" she asked.

"Here they call me, Malak," the man said.

"Are you called by other names in other places?" Ari Ara asked with cautious curiosity.

"Yes, many," Malak answered. "It is common among our people to use names like the layers of an onion. The outer skin is the toughest, meant to withstand the pokes and jabs of the world. The inner name is the sweetest, reserved for those who get to know you best."

Ari Ara thought it would be impolite to ask what his inner name was, so she asked a different question.

"Does it have a meaning, *Malak*?"

"Yes," he replied gravely, his eyes never leaving hers, "it means *Eyes of the King*. I am his servant."

Mahteni rolled her eyes, but a hint of a smile crossed her lips.

"Then what are you doing here?" Ari Ara demanded to know.

"Meeting his daughter, watching over her, and going where

he cannot," Malak responded in a hushed voice as Mahteni craned her neck to make sure no one heard.

A silence fell. Ari Ara shuffled her feet as he stared at her.

"What are you looking at?" she asked, a sudden shyness flushing through her limbs.

"You," Malak answered honestly, a shine of tears in his eyes as he touched his fingers to his forehead and flicked them to the wind in blessing. Remembering his duty as *Eyes of the King*, he memorized her face, noting the subtle qualities the king had yearned to know about his daughter: the courage and sensitivity in her eyes, the bravado and sincerity in her manner of being, the tensile strength running through her limbs, the fleeting lines of childhood in her frame. A sense of sorrow swept over him as he thought of how eleven - nearly twelve - years of the girl's life had passed. Time had robbed the king of his greatest treasure: the swiftly vanishing years of his daughter's childhood. All too soon, a young woman would be emerging in the awkward shell of adolescence.

"You look like your mother," the Hawk Keeper told her.

"I do?" Ari Ara echoed in surprise. "Everyone says I look like my father."

"Perhaps they did not see her with the dry eyes of our desert," he answered, "but I see Queen Alinore's river-water eyes in the face of her daughter."

"Thank you," Ari Ara replied, moved by his words.

The strange, black-bearded man spoke again, hesitantly this time.

"If you should ever need anything . . . if you are ever in danger or feel afraid or need help from your father, come to me – "

"Malak!" Mahteni scolded him with a warning tone.

He held the girl's eyes.

"I am very serious," he vowed. "I may be only a lowly water worker, a Hawk Keeper to the House of Marin, but I would do anything to help you."

"Um, thanks," Ari Ara answered, hoping she wouldn't need to take him up on the strange offer. Brinelle might be a formidable dragon, but she wasn't dangerous . . . was she?

Rivera Sun

CHAPTER EIGHT

. . . . .

Urchin's Rags

The days turned into weeks and the weeks stacked up into the bricks of months. The summer thunderstorms cooled the burning edges of the days. The nights began to taste of cold and twice she caught the scent of the High Mountains riding the cold fronts down into the valley. Ari Ara treasured every minute she could spend in the fresh air - which is why, on the second week before fall equinox, she was grumpily mumbling under her breath about Academy instructors who gave out homework during the last few glorious days of good weather. The afternoon bustled along like a satisfied cloth merchant, round and resplendent, content with its crisp edges and bright sunshine. The sweetened scent of ripe grains swayed in the cheerful breeze. It was a shame to squander such a day on schoolwork, but Ari Ara, Isa, and Korin were stuck indoors in the stuffy Dressier's Loft under the roof eaves of the House of Marin, slogging through an Art of Dress assignment due the next day.

The language of style still evaded Ari Ara's comprehension, but she could sense it murmuring and whispering on every street corner and sitting room - grand or humble - in the island city. Isa tried to teach her the basic principles, but the Art of Dress was built on ever-changing rules. As soon as Ari Ara grasped one subtlety, it changed with the season's tastes. No matter how hard she tried, the Art of Dress baffled her. It was like listening to a conversation in a foreign tongue laden with double meanings, innuendos, backstory, symbolism, and metaphor. Isa and Korin would collapse into laughter at her interpretations so frequently that she began to use her whispered asides as comic relief during the long formal evenings of receptions, banquets, and ceremonies that she was required to attend along with the other two.

Secretly, Isa and Korin shared a strange relief in their young friend's inability to read the silent language. Ari Ara missed the snubs and slights, challenges and sneering offenses thrown at her from the faction of nobles who disliked the would-be heir. They mocked her wardrobe, particularly when she began wearing trousers instead of skirts to the Nobles Academy. After a month of resigned discomfort, she had confessed to Mahteni how much she detested the tight-waisted skirt and tucked-in blouse. A few days later, Mahteni entered her quarters with a broad grin and soft green garments hanging over her arm.

Ari Ara approached warily, but there were no stays or supports. Instead, she was delighted to discover that it was a pair of loose trousers.

"The Mistress of Dress and I are at daggers over this, but the Great Lady took my side," Mahteni confessed. "She says a girl who runs circles around Emir Miresh needs legroom more than tailored skirts."

Ari Ara cheered, but by the end of the week, Korin and Isa had noticed the pushback from the other nobles. Varina's circle refused to wear trousers, underhandedly telling younger girls that when they grew up, they'd leave behind the vulgarity of showing their legs like the Lost Heir. Isa refused to let Varina get away with such snobbery. Along with a handful of other noblegirls, she started wearing trousers, too, popularizing a new, rebellious countercultural fashion that the Academy's Headmistress would have banned if the Lost Heir wasn't wearing it.

"They slouch through the halls like a pack of desert demons," she complained to the Great Lady in a breathless rant.

Brinelle listened attentively then told Ari Ara not to slouch. If she was to determine style, she must be bold and proud, Brinelle told the girl. The Great Lady, like young Isa, was painfully aware of the factions among the nobles. She calculated the changing alliances each day, delaying and stalling the confirmation hearing as she watched for the winds of allegiance to turn in Ari Ara's favor. Many of the nobles walked the thin line of neutrality on the issue of the Lost Heir. Until she knew which way they'd vote, Brinelle would not risk them withholding their support.

In the eaves of the Dressier's Loft, Ari Ara covered her yawn, half-stupefied with boredom. She glanced longingly at Emir and Rill who were perched on one of the broad window ledges waiting for the rest of them to finish, enjoying the breeze and talking about Azar. The two had struck up a friendship during practices and, with Korin's admiration for the notorious troublemaker, it wasn't long before Everill Riverdon became a regular - if disreputable - visitor to the House of Marin.

Rill had kept her urchins glued to Varina de Thorn's heels, but she hadn't caught wind of any threats to the Lost Heir beyond the noblegirl's attempts to undermine her using fashion.

Rill didn't consider those dangerous . . . not until they involved poisoned rings or arsenic-laced hatbands.

Ari Ara sighed enviously as Rill and Emir laughed over something. Not for the first time, she wished she were an urchin, free to spend her days doing anything she wanted, able to swing out that window, scale the roof, and go running across the ridgepoles in search of adventures more interesting than deciding if pairing tangerine paisley with a maroon-puce plaid was an act of treason or just an eyesore.

"You can't put a Southern swayback corset with that Northern widestripe skirt," Isa was arguing with Korin. "It's so vulgar, you'd start a civil war."

"It's a peace offering," Korin protested.

Isa's pert button nose wrinkled, unconvinced. A pile of cloth swatches and heaps of parchment cluttered the cutting table. Ari Ara lifted the ink sketches and tried not to moan. They'd never finish the assignment, not with Isa and Korin arguing over the placement of every buttonhole. Ari Ara covered her eyes with one hand and plunged her other into the pile of swatches, pulling out a strip at random.

"How about this?" she suggested, holding up a rich, tight-woven blue.

The other two groaned and shook their heads. Ari Ara let out an exasperated sigh and gave up. She tromped over to the windowsill and plopped down beside Rill.

"I'll never make sense of it," she complained, waving the swatch. "What's wrong with this?"

"Nothing," Emir answered, "if you're a warrior."

Ari Ara squinted at the sample and eyed Emir's tunic. It was the same. She snorted and tossed the swatch in the air. Rill's quick fingers darted out and snatched it.

"Can I have this?" she asked.

Ari Ara nodded - there were plenty of those in the bins, trimmed off the warrior's uniforms.

"Thanks," Rill replied with a flash of a grin. "Mayhaps, I'll tell the urchins I snipped it off the back of Shulen's tunic when he weren't lookin'."

"He's always looking," Emir countered loyally, "and his tunic is a darker gray."

"Alright then, I'll say it's from your tunic," Rill amended, undaunted.

She pulled a small leather pouch out of her pocket and took out a needle, tiny scissors, and a length of bright red thread. Her thin, nimble fingers flew as she stitched the swatch to the worn spot in the knee of her trousers. The others watched her curiously. At last, noticing their silence, she glanced up.

"What? Haven't you ever seen an urchin rag-stitch afore? You don't think the Dressiers make these for us, do you?"

She lifted up the flap of her bright vest, a dizzying collection of multi-colored bits and scraps.

"Got this last week," she noted, pointing to a scarlet patch, "but it's a bit thin-worn and dull as yet."

"Dull?" Emir laughed. "Only to an urchin's eyes."

"Those're the ones that matter to me," Rill answered implacably. "You can tell a lot by an urchin's rags. I've got a coat back at the Nest that's got a bit of silk from the Urchin King afore me, and a patch he got from the Queen afore him, and so on back through time. There's not many coats like that one in the Nest; tells the whole history of urchining, it does."

She laughed at their expressions.

"Nobles aren't the only ones with an Art of Dress . . . only ours is a sight different. You can't buy an urchin's rags and you can't sell 'em neither. You've got to earn 'em, make 'em, and give 'em."

Every favor or kindness offered from one urchin to another was thanked with a rag-gift. A scrap of fabric, a strip of cloth, or a button was given for small good turns. Larger favors were returned with a coat, shirt, or even a pair of boots. Certain items like the King and Queen's Coat were passed down by position. The chief cook's apron held layers of flour dust from a decade ago between its patched fabrics. Wealthier inhabitants of Mariana Capital might cut off a piece of a fine coat lining on the spot and give it to an urchin in lieu of coin. If a scuffle broke out between urchins, the winner would cut off a strip of the loser's shirt and sew it onto their vest. A demanding urchin's task for a well-known noble or a university professor might yield a piece of fabric that forever told the story of the deed. And every urchin had a vest upon which the patches of their life story hung like medals of honor. Scraps of baby blankets and remnants of their lost parents' clothing were stitched on the underside of the left hand flap, close to the heart.

"On the King and Queen's Coat," Rill explained, "there's gifts from nearly every Queen of Mariana in the past hundred years. The oldest scraps are much-prized."

Ari Ara leaned over and picked up another scrap from the remnants bin.

"What about this?"

Rill scrunched up her face.

"Too new. Urchins aren't wearing nothing from the Loomlands these days."

"Why on earth not?" Emir questioned in surprise.

"Water workers," Rill said, spitting out the window. "Taking our apprenticeship spots, they are. We won't wear the work of their grimy hands."

"The rest of Mariana is," Emir pointed out.

Rill shrugged. Since when did urchins care what the rest of Mariana did?

"Better get back to work," Emir urged Ari Ara as Korin gestured to her to quit slacking.

"We'll help," Rill offered. "It'll go faster."

Ari Ara looked skeptical.

"I could dump Korin in the scrap barrel every time he argues with Isa," Emir offered.

Rill marched into the argument and demanded to know which they wanted more: high marks on the assignment or a day on the river? It was warm enough to swim off the North End and she'd bet her next meal Isa could wrangle the Great Lady's permission.

That broke the stalemate over plaids and paisleys. Isa and Korin split the men and women, setting Rill and Emir to work for each team. Since Ari Ara's suggestions were good only for humor, she was sent to find the swatches of cloth that each pair needed. Searching the length of the loft, Ari Ara ran her fingers down the bolts of cloth that lined the shelves built into the short eaves. At the far end of the massive room, a wall of windows sectioned off the Mistress of Dress' workroom. Ari Ara spotted Mahteni and another seamstress tacking a seam on a dress that had to be for Brinelle - no one else would rank that size of a ruffled skirt, nor the cost of that deep blue satin. Ari Ara ducked behind the cutting table and crept closer to get a better look, hoping she wouldn't be expected to wear a shorter version of that boat of a dress. As she neared, she could hear the two women chatting.

"You've heard the gutter streams," the second woman, a seamstress named Maggie, reminded the desert woman archly, undulating her hand to indicate the whispers of gossip that flooded the crooked alleys of the South End of the city and formed the darker strands of the rumor-river. "With that Azar-thingy and the Monk's Hand rebellion - "

Ari Ara choked. She'd known the nobles were not pleased about the monastery switching to training in the Way Between. They'd cut off funding when the monks chose self-reliance instead of meekly crawling back to Attar. But to call it a rebellion? That was a typical over-the-top Capital reaction.

"There's some that's saying Shulen's conspiring to put a Fanten pawn on the throne."

"Who told you that?" Mahteni asked, frowning.

"Some of the maids at the House of Thorn," she confessed. "They're saying she's an imposter."

"Hope floats like leaves in a storm wash," Mahteni answered with a derisive snort. "She's the image of her father, red hair and all."

"He's welcome to her," the older woman sniffed.

"Don't tempt him," Mahteni warned in a low hush of a voice. "Tahkan Shirar sends the Great Lady messages each week, requesting his daughter's presence."

"Well, he can't have her," Maggie stated contradictorily.

Rose blotches of anger flushed on the bronze cheeks of Mahteni's face. Her hands clenched as she struggled to control her outburst.

"And anyway, why would Shulen bother with a scheme like that?" Mahteni asked in a skeptical tone. "He's never been one for intrigues and political sleights of hand."

Maggie shrugged her plump shoulders.

"The current's running crossways on that," she confessed, telling Mahteni that some thought he was trying to start a war with the Desert while others claimed the outrageous: that he was trying to stop future wars from brewing.

"One of his warrior monks from the monastery told the

captain of the Watch that Shulen was ready to come back to the Capital, heir or none, and risk treason to stop the brewing War of Reclamation. Now, that's nonsense, of course. Our Great Warrior would never do such a thing!" Maggie declared boisterously. "He fights where and when he's told to."

Ari Ara rolled her eyes. Shulen *had* been planning to try to stop the threat of war; she'd overheard him saying so to the Head Monk last spring.

"But, all's I can tell you is that Shulen's loyalty has been questioned and not just by the gossips in the gutter streams," Maggie went on.

Ari Ara gritted her teeth. There was no secret conspiracy to put Azar on the throne. She bore the Mark of Peace, and so the two nations were stuck with her commitment to the Way Between. *People are so stupid*, she thought silently. Both she and Shulen would be happier if she could have just stayed his apprentice. Neither of them had asked for the headache of her royal blood.

"The little thing best watch out," Maggie said in a hushed tone.

Mahteni looked up sharply. Her eyes flicked toward the door. Ari Ara held her breath.

"Why's that?" Mahteni asked carefully.

"Our Mistress of Dress is one of them what thinks she's a fake - oh, she wouldn't breathe a word of that here, but I heard her grumbling about it on the first day the girl arrived in the Capital. Oooh, she was in a temper about Queen Alinore's dress, I'll tell you, only she never let on that it wasn't her idea."

Maggie fanned her neckline with her hand as she studied the fall of the collar. Then she shook her head and tore out the last stitches to do over.

"She'll be sabotaging that girl with every stitch, I swear, and more's a pity, 'cause she's a charming little thing all-in-all. The warriors like her, I hear tell, and my brother says the common folk have taken a shine to her well enough to get into tavern brawls over whether she's fake or real."

"The Mistress of Dress won't be undermining Ari Ara," Mahteni said firmly. "The Great Lady's said we're to do our better-than-best for the girl."

Maggie shook her head, doubtful. Mahteni rose and lifted a bolt of silver silk inlaid with blue and gold threads. Maggie gasped and dropped her needle. The desert woman told her quietly that if the Great Lady's command was not enough, the Desert King himself had sent his blessing and acceptance of the girl in the form of the finest fabrics the Desert People created.

"And there will be more of them," Mahteni vowed, "every time she wears a garment made with desert silk, our king promises to send another shipment. The Mistress of Dress is no fool. She'll turn the Capital style on its ear and rake in a fortune with this exclusive look. No other noblehouse will have these patterns and fabrics."

Mahteni smiled grimly. The Mistress of Dress may not *like* the High Mountain girl, but she wouldn't back down from the most profitable and extraordinary season of her life. If the girl turned out to be a fake, it was no skin off the Mistress of Dress' back. She had commanded Mahteni to oversee the girl's wardrobe, taking nominal credit for every success while positioning the water worker to bear the brunt of any failures. Mahteni knew this with the hard-eyed clarity born of six years in Mariana Capital. It was a risk she was willing to take to have the opportunity of a lifetime for herself, for Tahkan Shirar's heir, for the water workers, and for all her people.

The girl's bold words on the day they had met had planted a seed of an idea in Mahteni's mind. It grew in her thoughts over the summer as she observed her king's daughter. She began to add desert embellishments to the Lost Heir's wardrobe; nothing obvious at first, a silk cuff lining, a style of collar, a set of copper bracelets; just enough of a touch to set the water workers whispering throughout the city. Every day, Ari Ara wore a sign of the Desert. Every day, the water workers took heart. Every day, Mahteni wove a message of hope into the girl's clothes and reminded her people silently: *she is ours, too; she is a daughter of the desert as much as the riverlands.*

Mahteni said nothing of her mission. She simply and quietly stitched silk into trims and desert styles into garments. The Desert King's gift of silks made her task easier as it convinced the Mistress of Dress to allow her greater leeway.

Ari Ara crept away silently and returned to her task, but the overheard conversation stuck with her. As Korin and Isa finished the Art of Dress assignment - with Rill's surprisingly astute suggestions - she began to understand how clothes could be a politics of style. It wasn't about fashionable buttonhole placements and hemlines, it was about the jobs, wages, lives, and livelihoods hidden inside the garments: Rill and the urchins refusing to wear fabric made by water workers, the Desert King sending silks to show his people supported her claim as heir, and the way the fashion for ruffled seams was made possible by the cheap labor of the water workers.

Ari Ara mulled on these notions for days, noticing how Mahteni added subtle accents to her clothing and keeping track of what the other nobles said about such designs. She could tell who wanted peace and who loathed anything related to the Desert.

One morning, as Mahteni snipped an extra length of silk from the cuff of the jacket she was fitting on the girl, Ari Ara caught the fluttering scrap.

"Hold still," Mahteni urged over the pin in her mouth.

"Can I have this scrap?" she asked, pulling it thoughtfully through her fingers.

"What for?" Mahteni answered, pinning the fabric in place.

"I want to give it to Rill. Did you know the urchins won't wear water worker-made fabrics from the Loomlands?"

Mahteni glanced up, surprise flashing in her green eyes.

"They won't?"

She'd heard the urchins sought antique or vintage cloth scraps from the dressiers' shops, but she hadn't understood why they wanted the older fabrics.

Ari Ara shook her head and slid the silk through her fingers.

"They're mad that the water workers are being used for positions that ought to be theirs by apprenticeship."

Mahteni sat back with a startled expression.

"I hadn't thought of that," she admitted. Her auburn eyebrows drew together as she leaned in and began to pin the edge of the cuff into place.

"I want to take some scraps to Rill," Ari Ara explained, "and ask her if the urchins would wear them in support of ending the Water Exchange."

Mahteni thought silently for a long moment, then she spoke with determination.

"Tell the Urchin Queen that if her urchins will speak up for the end of the Water Exchange *and* the return of the water to the Desert, I'll see to it that they have the trims and pieces of every fabric the Desert King sends for you."

"Really?!" Ari Ara cried in delight.

"Not whole bolts, mind," Mahteni warned her. "The Mistress of Dress gets those, but anything I can pocket from your wardrobe, they can have."

She motioned for the girl to stop hopping around like an over-excited baby goat. She'd be turning twelve in a few short weeks, and if she was old enough to try to bring about the end of the Water Exchange, she was certainly old enough to hold still for five minutes.

Mahteni Duktar frowned over the pins in her mouth, ducking her head to hide her expression from the girl. The Desert King had delicate schemes set like slow-heating kettles over the thirteen noblelands of Mariana. She'd best contact him swiftly . . . his daughter was about to throw a few logs on the fire and bring his plans to a boil!

CHAPTER NINE

· · · · ·

Urchins' Feast

"No, absolutely not."

Brinelle continued reading a draft bill, not bothering to look up at the girl's preposterous request. A breeze carried the cool edge of autumn into the study through the open window and ruffled the papers on the desk. Brinelle slammed a paperweight on top of them.

That morning, Rill had jogged across the training sands and grabbed Ari Ara's elbow, her fingers cold with the bite of frost in the air, her cheeks burning bright red with the exertion of the practice. The urchins now came in packs to trainings, colorful as autumn leaves as they leapt into the exercises. Close by, a group of them laughed as they replayed their best moves from the training session. Rill pulled Ari Ara away from their prying ears as she tugged her jacket back on over her goose bumps. The two girls had been huddled in whispered conversations over the desert silks for weeks; Rill liked the idea, but needed time to work on the other urchins one by one . . . the concept of being allies to the water workers was a thick pill to swallow, even if it was good for them.

"I've got most of 'em seeing sense and the rest'll come around. Now, I hear you're havin' a birthday soon," she remarked with a casualness that didn't quite cover her excitement, "and I was thinking you could present the silks at the Urchins' Feast."

"The what?" Ari Ara asked.

Rill's mouth dropped open.

"Surely you know?"

Every year on the birthday of the Lost Heir, while the nobles prayed to find the child and mourned the death of Queen Alinore, the urchins threw an enormous festival in the streets.

"Drives the nobles batty, it does," Rill commented cheerfully, "but we figured the best way to draw the Lost Heir out of hiding was to throw a giant party. Any child with half a brain would come, right?"

The second year, the orphans had joined in, some sneaking out of the orphanages, others let out by sympathetic monks and sisters. The third year, some of the working parents had put out cookies and small cakes on their doorsteps, along with warm winter clothes. From that, a tradition had erupted.

"It's a grand festival, everyone in the city joins in now," Rill told her. "Clothes and treats on every doorstep. This year, it'll be wild with you actually here in the city, found and all!"

Rill stopped and looked slyly at Ari Ara.

"Me and some of the others, we've got a bet, though. They says you won't be allowed to join in, and I told them to stuff their ignorance under a sewer grate . . . of course you'd be dancing in the street with us - how could you not? We've been throwing you a party for longer'n some of us has been alive."

Plus, Rill added, *they were friends, weren't they?*

"I told Rill I would go," Ari Ara spluttered to Brinelle.

"Well, let that be a lesson to you in not making promises that you're not sure you can keep," Brinelle replied coolly, lifting up the addendum to the bill and frowning at it.

Ari Ara argued that the orphans and urchins had a special love for the Lost Heir. It would reflect poorly on the House of Marin if she didn't appear.

"You'll be spending the day receiving orphans from all over Mariana who have studied diligently and worked hard all year for the honor of meeting you," Brinelle pointed out, striking a line off the bill and jotting a note on the side.

Ari Ara bit back a sharp retort about being used as a prize to reward favorites and pets. If she could visit *all* the orphans in Mariana, she would. She knew from personal experience that the most scolded and punished orphans were also the most devout believers in the beneficent powers of the Lost Heir. All orphans of unknown parentage daydreamed about being the Lost Heir and everyone else prayed to the semi-mythical figure. *She* certainly had, given how often she'd wound up in trouble.

"An orphan," she told Brinelle in the most respectful tone she could muster, "does not look at the Lost Heir as a reward for good behavior. She cries out to the Lost Heir to help her when life gets tough. She dreams of the Lost Heir appearing and telling her everything is going to be all right. The Lost Heir comes to an orphan as he's crying with loneliness and tells him his parents loved him!"

She went on, explaining to this rich and powerful woman who had never scrubbed a cold floor on knees that poked through ragged clothes that the Lost Heir's legend was a special guardian to the children. She had a responsibility to appear in the streets on the night of the Urchins' Feast. Brinelle straightened her spine and took off the spectacles she'd just begun to use while reading the dense and detailed paperwork from the Assembly of Nobles. This morning, she'd plucked a gray hair from her temple. She looked at the nearly twelve-year-old girl standing in front of her desk, blue-gray eyes flashing with temper, pointed little chin stuck stubbornly up in the air, and suddenly, the Great Lady felt old.

"Did I just hear you say the word, *responsibility*?" she asked the girl, appearing both severe and surprised.

Ari Ara nodded, hoping Brinelle had heard more than that. The Great Lady pinched the bridge of her nose, thinking.

"What did Shulen say?" Brinelle asked her knowingly.

Ari Ara's body slumped. She crossed her arms over her chest.

"He said it was risky and dangerous," she muttered.

She'd argued with Shulen for an hour. He told her she'd have to be escorted by guards. She refused; you couldn't bring the Royal Guard or the Capital Watch to an urchins' gathering - they'd take off running. Shulen shook his head, his answer was no. Ari Ara told him huffily that she'd take it up with Brinelle.

"Fish will fly before she lets you go," Shulen predicted.

"I'm sorry," Brinelle replied, sounding genuinely regretful, "but my answer must be the same as Shulen's. Someone might try to kidnap or kill you."

"As if you'd care," Ari Ara muttered under her breath, a shine of hot tears hitting her eyes.

Brinelle put down her work.

"You may find this hard to believe, but I would be *very* upset if you were harmed," she told the girl, secretly appalled that Ari Ara thought her heart was made of such callous stone.

"Why? You and Korin could rule, just as you've always planned," Ari Ara spat out, staring at the floor, kicking the leg of the desk.

A sword blade of anger swung through Brinelle. She took a deep breath and wrestled it down.

"Ari Ara," she said carefully, trying to not lash the girl with her irritation, "my *plan* was to advise my sensitive and skilled cousin Alinore as she ruled. My *plan* was to grow old with my husband. My *plan* was to find Alinore's child and put him or her on the throne so that *my* child could be free of the burden that I have been forced to bear for the past decade."

Ari Ara started to protest. Brinelle slammed her palm on the desk. Ari Ara flinched.

"Don't interrupt," Brinelle snapped. "I have carried this nation on my back, largely alone and often unsupported, for twelve long and difficult years. I swore I would find you and put you where you belong, and that includes keeping you alive!"

Her voice dropped into an icy edge of warning.

"So, no, you may not go to the Urchins' Feast. You may not realize this yet, but with power comes danger: you may have enemies lurking among the populace. Ancestors forbid they should knife you, shoot you with an arrow from the rooftops, hire an urchin to poison you, kidnap you and drop you in the Mari River tied to a stone, or any other number of other ghastly murders - "

"They'd have to catch me first," Ari Ara muttered, spinning on her heel and stalking out the door.

Brinelle watched her storm away. A faint smile crossed her lips at the girl's last defiant comment. In a quiet voice, she finished her thought.

" - because, believe it or not, Ari Ara of the High Mountains, I've grown rather fond of you for all your temper and rule-breaking."

* * *

On the evening of Queen Alinore's death and the birthday of the Lost Heir, Ari Ara sat quietly by her window, watching the moonlight turn the East Channel silver. The ceremonies of the day had been long and largely tedious. Tradition held that the Young Queen gave gifts to others on her birthday and she had spent the day handing out a staggering amount of objects. She sat through a dawn vigil at the temple, honoring her mother's spirit. She received a long line of nervously smug orphans - the kind of perfectly-behaved snots she had scoffed at (and secretly envied) during her short and tumultuous stint at the monastery in Monk's Hand. At the dinner party with all the nobles, Varina had skimmed within a knife's edge of accusing her of killing Queen Alinore either by being born or by being part of a plot to steal the throne. The only good part of the evening was when Korin dumped his cake down the front of Varina's dress and apologized for mistaking it for a wastebasket.

As the House of Marin slowly quieted, a great clamor of celebration rose in the streets of Mariana Capital. When the glow of light from the window in Brinelle's study dimmed, Ari Ara pulled her oldest training clothes out of her bundle of Monk's Hand belongings and slipped them on. She'd grown, she realized in surprise. Her wrists stuck out of the cuffs. The worn knees of her pants puckered several inches above her kneecaps. A sense of time and change hit her suddenly. She shook out the folds of her black Fanten wool cloak with its treasured single line of silver elder ewe yarn, smelling the last traces of the scent of the forests and the clear, cold waters of the High Mountains. They'd be gone by morning, the danker air of the river threading into the wool. She inhaled the clear scents one last time, then flung her cloak over her shoulders. The hood hid her bright hair and would make her black against the night. She plumped the pillows under the covers in case a maid peeked in and left a note explaining where she was going. Just in case they did discover her gone, she didn't want anyone to panic and accuse the urchins of kidnapping her.

Ari Ara threw a stuffed, but light satchel over her shoulder and leaned out the window. The east wall of the House of Marin gleamed in the moonlight. Across the river, the silver-green fields swayed. Below, the stone walls stretched straight down into the murky depths of the East Channel. Pressing her belly flat to the wall, she slid her fingers into the cracks and inched toward the end of the house. After a breathless moment when a chunk of granite broke free under her grip, she reached the corner of the building and descended swiftly. She leapt the last few feet and landed in the alley as lightly as a cat.

Emir stepped out of the shadows.

Ari Ara sighed. She should have known.

"The Great Lady and Shulen send their regards," Emir remarked dryly. "They're not stupid, you know. They figured you'd do something like this."

"You can't stop me," Ari Ara bristled.

"I'm not here to stop you, silly," Emir shot back. "I'm here to go with you."

"What?!" she exclaimed.

Emir told her he'd called in an old debt.

"The Champion's Boon?" Ari Ara gasped.

Emir nodded. He'd been thinking about it for weeks and finally requested that the Great Lady allow the Lost Heir to join the Urchins' Feast. It was a gift beyond measure to the poorest inhabitants of the Capital: the urchins and orphans who had sacrificed parents to the War of Retribution and spent long hours of their short lives praying to the legend of the Lost Heir. He understood - even if Brinelle and Shulen did not - how important this was to Everill Riverdon and the other children.

"But - but - to use the Boon," Ari Ara stammered, honored and amazed, awed by the generosity of her friend.

Emir shrugged.

"It was the least I could do . . . and really, it's better this way. Thanks to your notorious bad temper, the entire Capital is talking about how you're not going. It cuts the chances of an assassination attempt in half."

"Just in half?"

Emir nodded, then grinned cheerfully.

"Don't worry. I'm sworn to throw myself in front of knives aimed at you. If anything happens, you'll have the rest of your life to regret causing my death."

"Thanks," Ari Ara groaned. "You don't really think we'll be attacked, do you?"

"No, and neither does Shulen or you'd be back in the House of Marin already."

"Things were simpler when I was a nobody," she complained.

"That's what Shulen says, too," Emir informed her. "He said he wished he could just chuck your hot head in the river like he used to when you were just his apprentice."

Ari Ara laughed. Emir pulled the hood of his cloak over his long hair. Then he pointed to her satchel and asked what was inside.

"A gift for the urchins," Ari Ara answered simply.

She strode swiftly down the alley before they could be stopped. The streets of Mariana Capital made her gasp in wonder. Emir grinned as she gaped like a wide-mouthed riverfish. Candles had been stuck into carved stone boxes. The doorsteps glowed in every direction. White banners painted with the circle of the Mark of Peace hung from the windows, balconies, and bridges. The black brushstrokes of desert sand

and river-water waves rippled in the night breeze. Throngs of children ran through the streets. Every stoop in the Capital was laden with trays of cookies and small cakes. She spotted a door cracking open as a hand extended, replacing an empty platter with a full one. Strips of vintage cloths - gifts for the urchins - adorned the railings. Tied bundles had been placed on the windowsills. On the top step of a flight of stone stairs, an urchin bowed his fiddle in a wild jig. Children laid down gifts on the steps at his feet to keep him playing through the night.

Ari Ara and Emir ran through the alleys, passing through games of Catch the King and foot races and whirl-in-the-wind. It seemed every turn revealed another musician: pipers whistling out crazy reels, drummers pounding cans and bottles in a cacophony of improvised rhythms, bands of singers bellowing out popular melodies. A pickle organ had even been wheeled out from a tavern to blast its plink-plunkety tunes into the night.

"How will we ever find Rill?" she hollered to Emir over the noise.

"Try the plaza," an urchin girl yelled back, spinning around when she heard the question.

They shouted thanks and made their way through the street party. The plaza blazed from the bright lanterns hung from the upper stories of the shops. Long ropes stretched into a web across the open space of the square. Buttons on thin thread had been tied to the ropes. Urchins leapt, snatching the round shapes and snapping the threads. Every yank set the rest of the buttons bobbing and the other urchins yelped as they missed their mark. Older urchins put younger ones on their shoulders and jumped so that even the smallest could win a button.

Rill was perched on the ancestor statue of Marin, cheering on the button-leapers and blowing on a loud horn whenever someone succeeded, setting off whoops and hollers throughout the plaza. She spotted them under their cloaks and teased Emir as they neared.

"You're a well-built urchin," she joked. "Ever think of trying for the Royal Guard?"

"We've brought a gift," Ari Ara said, holding out the sack.

"Put that away. Yer doorstep's already the talk of the Capital - or didn't you see?" Rill answered. "Orphans and urchins are coming back from yer gates with the history of Mariana in antique bands of cloth - the Great Lady must have emptied the museum for us!"

Ari Ara scanned the impromptu armbands wound around Rill's upper arm. One of the patterns looked familiar and she realized that she'd seen it in a portrait of Brinelle's mother.

"That was nice of her," Ari Ara exclaimed, delighted and impressed by the Great Lady's thoughtfulness.

"So keep your scraps, urchin," Rill told her grandly. "Tithe's been made by the House of Marin."

"Oh, you'll want this," Ari Ara answered. "It's from the other side of the family."

She held out the satchel and flipped open the top flap. Inside were scraps and pieces of the beautiful silks the Desert King had sent. Each had been rolled up, folded carefully, and bound with a second bit of cloth to make beautiful gifts for the urchins.

"Urchins' Ancestors!" yelped a girl sitting on the statue of Alaren next to Rill, looking down in shock. "Is that what I think it is?"

"Desert silk, the finest, straight from Tahkan Shirar," Ari Ara announced in a loud voice that froze the urchins in their tracks.

"What's he want?" one lad asked, suspicious.

"Same as us," Rill called out. "The end of the Water Exchange, and the return of his people and water. This sack is a gift in the spirit of solidarity. He wants his people to come home. We want our honest work back."

Rill took a scrap from the bag and had Ari Ara tie it around her upper arm next to the fabric from the House of Marin.

"Tell the Desert King that the Urchin Queen thanks him," she stated grandly, lifting her arm in the air.

A cheer rose up. The urchins dove for the silks and began tying them onto their arms. A fiddle struck up a familiar jig. A joyful burst of recognition surged through the urchins and orphans. Rill's toothy grin bloomed. She slung the precious satchel of cloth over Marin's sword and ordered another urchin to hand the silks out fairly. Then she pulled Ari Ara into the fray as Emir dove after them.

"Bet you've never seen an Urchin's Reel," Rill hollered in her ear. "Try to keep up and don't worry about the steps - there aren't any!"

Ari Ara let out a whoop of delight. There wasn't a dance invented that a Fanten-raised girl didn't love. At the Academy, she'd had to learn the stiff court dances of the nobles, partnering with Korin to practice the stately steps, but in her opinion, a dance designed to keep extravagant head ornaments in place didn't stir the blood and spirit like a real dance should.

As a second fiddle picked up the counter melody, the plaza began to writhe with motion. Orphans clapped and joined in with the lyrics - a shocking and humorous account of urchins' evasions of the Watch. Urchins leapt and hopped, spun and spiraled in a staggeringly chaotic eruption of sheer revelry. Emir kicked out a tap-step from his hills in the north, laughing at Ari Ara's startled look - he hadn't always been a warrior, he told her - but his eyes remained watchful.

Rill danced with abandon, throwing her arms high in the air and clapping along with the tune. Ari Ara joined her, setting off a cheerful match of such wild gyrations and astonishing leaps that a space cleared around them. As the second tune snuck in on the heels of the first, the pair didn't miss a beat. The fiddlers charged onwards, and the two girls strove to out-whirl each other. There wasn't a move either could try that the other wouldn't attempt. Emir stepped back into the ring of clapping children and heard the astonished gasp leap out of the throat of a newly arrived young orphan.

"It's her! The Lost Heir!"

Cheers, whistles, and trills broke out. Smaller children were hoisted up on shoulders to watch. Urchins stood precariously on the stone heads and arms of the ancestor statues. The older children's eyes shone with emotion. The younger ones hopped in place with uncontainable excitement at the magic of the night.

Emir swallowed down the lump in his throat as he watched the glow rising on the children's faces. He had seen many things in his sixteen years of life. He had seen the fiercest dedication of discipline under Shulen's training. He had witnessed a massacre of women and children. He had stopped assassins from killing his best friend. He had beaten warriors decades older than him. He had observed the schemes of the nobles and the extravagances of the wealthy. He had seen dire poverty, famine, and plagues. As a child, he had cried over the battlefields of war.

On the night of the Urchins' Feast, he saw the best of humanity shining like candlelight in the faces of the children. Joy brimmed in their eyes. Trust and faith returned to their hearts. Hope revived in the spirits of small children who had known much hardship in their young lives. A glow of wonder gleamed in faces of youths who had almost stopped believing in miracles.

Yet, a miracle had happened tonight: the Lost Heir had appeared. She was here, dancing, laughing, a child as they were; the lost one, found; returned to those who had held a celebration in her honor year after year, even while the grown-ups warred, mourned, and despaired.

Emir Miresh had risen to fame as the youngest Mariana Champion in a hundred years. He had been awarded honors and medals for his defense of Korin. He had been told many times that his life's achievements would outstrip even Shulen's.

Standing in a circle of clapping, cheering children, Emir Miresh knew that no matter what else he did in his life, his choice to use the Champion's Boon to bring the Lost Heir to the Urchins' Feast would be the greatest victory of all.

CHAPTER TEN

. . . . .

Alinore and Rhianne

Hours later, exhausted and happy to her bones, Ari Ara slipped through the side gate of the House of Marin with Emir. Her feet hurt from dancing. Her cheeks ached from laughing. The sound of the fiddle hummed in her limbs. The melodies of the music jumbled into a medley in her mind, along with two words shouted over and over by the urchins and orphans: *Happy birthday!*

The first well-wisher had been Rill, hollering it loud enough to cut through the cheers and turn them into a chorus of chanting. The fiddlers wove the raucous chants into a song as she struggled to hold back tears of emotion, overwhelmed. The Fanten didn't celebrate birthdays for the child, but rather birthing days for the mother. At the monastery, no one had asked about her birthday . . . and she wouldn't have known what to tell them anyway since she'd never known the exact date of her birth. Even earlier this day, her duties as potential heir had dampened the fun she might have felt on her first birthday celebration.

"Thank you for everything, Emir," she breathed fervently.

"You're welcome," he answered. "We apprentices of Shulen have to look out for each other."

The black-haired youth smiled and hugged her shoulders. A chill slip of wind ran through the empty courtyard. Ari Ara tugged the edges of her black Fanten cloak tighter around her frame. The sliver of moon emerged like a silver scythe between the autumn clouds. At the door of the House of Marin, a member of the guard nodded to them, his eyes sliding toward a glowing window near the training sands. Emir followed the man's gaze.

"Shulen's still awake," he noted.

"Probably worrying," Ari Ara sighed.

Emir shook his head.

"Don't forget how much he lost on this night."

Ari Ara flushed. She had forgotten. The heavy, mournful ceremonies earlier that day had focused on the death of Queen Alinore, but Shulen's wife and child had been murdered on the same day by the mercenaries seeking the queen and unborn heir.

"I'll stop by and let him know we're back," she promised, thanking Emir again and giving him a shove toward bed.

She crossed the flagstones toward the lit window. The shutters had been left open and the curtain flung back so Shulen could see them arrive. The glowing lamp illuminated his room while the black night cloaked her, so she peered in. Shulen's quarters in the Capital were as sparse and tidy as at Monk's Hand Monastery. His lacquered trunk sat in the corner. A row of books lined a small shelf. His battle armor hung on the wall. A soft blue rug covered the polished wood floor. A propped-open door revealed a room with a sleeping mat. A fire blazed in the main room, and Shulen sat near it with -

Malak.

Ari Ara blinked in surprise. The Desert Hawk Keeper and Shulen conversed in low tones, slouching in the manner of long-standing familiarity. The dark, angular man leaned forward on his elbows and shook his head at whatever Shulen had just suggested. The candlelight carved his bronzed features into a mask of intensity. He rose and, to her alarm, crossed to the window. She ducked down, leaning flat against the wall and holding her breath.

"I'm letting in some fresh air," she heard Malak say.

"Just mind your words, the yard has ears," Shulen cautioned.

"There's no one out there," Malak answered, his voice muffled as he returned to the table.

"There are enough rumors circulating this island already," Shulen grumbled.

"Ah yes," Malak agreed in a tone that rasped with dry irony, "I've heard that you're putting an imposter on the throne and that the desert demons you're in league with will be rising up any day."

"Nonsense, all of it," Shulen dismissed.

"Not all of it," Malak answered with a chuckle, "but even without the rumors, I doubt those nobles will confirm her."

Ari Ara blinked under the window, stung by the confession.

"It's sheer obstinacy," Shulen grumbled. "Everyone can see she's the spitting image of Alinore and - "

" - Tahkan, yes," Malak interrupted, "and that's exactly why the nobles won't confirm her. They'd never put his real daughter on the throne. That's why we have to be prepared to get her out of Mariana."

Ari Ara's jaw dropped.

"You can't just whisk her away," Shulen cautioned in a hushed tone. "The Marianans will accuse you of kidnapping her."

"She is ours!" Malak retorted hotly. "If Brinelle had listened to Tahkan's message, she would be in the Desert now."

"There's no point in trying to catch the river once it's past," Shulen answered calmly.

"Maybe the water workers should put credence to those rumors and rise up . . . just to teach them a lesson," the Hawk Keeper threatened.

"Don't unravel all the work your people have done in Mariana all these years," Shulen warned him. "If you must act, use the Way Between, not violence. Even if you take her to the Desert, she is still the daughter of Alinore as well."

A stony silence met his words. Shulen sighed.

"It's late," he said to the Hawk Keeper. "You should rest."

"Neither of us will shut an eye until she's back," Malak refuted, shrugging his wiry shoulders.

Shulen grunted in agreement.

"Let's go up on the wall and keep watch for her," he suggested.

Ari Ara heard the sound of a chair being shoved back. Before she could be caught eavesdropping, she rolled to standing and lunged to knock on the door. Her heart thundered in her chest and her mind spun with what she had just overheard . . . an uprising? The Desert People stealing her away? She scrubbed her face with her palms to wipe away the shocked expression hanging on her features.

Shulen answered the door with a worried scowl.

"I'm back," she said, squinting in the light and trying to look like she'd only just arrived. "Emir said to stop by and tell you. Thank you for letting me go, and . . . is that Malak?"

She blinked in a show of innocent surprise as the man appeared, hovering over Shulen's shoulder. His green-gray eyes scanned the courtyard behind her.

"Let her in, Shulen. The light draws attention," Malak suggested softly.

Ari Ara scooted through the doorway as they stepped back. Shulen shut the door and latched the window.

"What are you two doing?" she asked, hoping they'd include her in their confidences.

The two men exchanged long looks. Shulen shook his head slightly. Ari Ara bit back her groan. She knew that look; her mentor wouldn't tell her anything.

"We've been catching up on old times and painful memories," Malak answered when Shulen's silence grew too long. "The Great Warrior and I knew each other before the war, in happier times. I joined him tonight to keep vigil for the lives lost on this night."

She noticed the altar set on the mantle above the crackling fire. Bright autumn leaves had been laid out over a piece of fine desert silk. A portrait of two women leaned against the wall. A row of candles flickered in front of the frame. The wax pooled as the wicks burned low. Light flickered in gasps, sending the shadows darting about the room. Each one, Malak explained, had been lit in memory of the departed as he and Shulen passed the night.

"Is that my mother?" she asked, pointing to the painting.

"Yes, and Rhianne," the men answered on the same breath.

The Fanten Grandmother's daughter stood beside a tall young Alinore. Ari Ara realized that the beautiful white dress that fell to her ankles had been designed to reach her mother's knees. Rhianne, sleek and black-haired like all the Fanten, reached only to her friend's shoulder, petite as a child with a gleam of humor and secrets in her dark eyes. Alinore hovered on the verge of a smile. A long dark brown braid hung over her shoulder. The two stood on a ridge, one looking eastward, the other gazing westward. Alinore shaded her eyes with her hand. Rhianne pointed to something behind them. A burning sunset lowered over dunes and black mountains.

"*Looking forward, looking back,*
two friends of the east,
came to the lands of the west.
There they met love and started life.
Where they walked,
the water flowed,
and green grass grew in their footsteps," Malak sang.

For a moment, Ari Ara saw the women treading across the sands, flowers and birds following in their wake. Then a dry wind rode the desert man's sorrow and swept the images away, leaving only the scouring sands. Tears stung her eyes.

"Come," Shulen urged, "light a candle for your mother, and join us in remembering something beautiful or true about her."

He handed Ari Ara a small wax candle.

"I don't remember her," she confessed in a quiet voice. "She slipped into the Black Ancestor River even as I rode its crosscurrents into this world. I'm sorry."

She turned to give the candle back, but Shulen caught her hand.

"She loved you, even if she barely saw you - and the Fanten Grandmother says she did, holding you for a moment before she slipped away. Your coming was anticipated and celebrated by all of us: Tahkan Shirar, Alinore de Marin, Rhianne, and myself. We hoped for a girl who would be a friend for our daughter, but it was not to be."

Shulen's eyes deepened with sorrow. Ari Ara lit the wick from the flickering flame of the candle on the end of the row. The light blazed. The wax glowed. Another small gleam rose up to illuminate the portrait.

"Will you tell me the stories of these other candles?" she asked the two men.

They exchanged startled looks. Then Malak smiled.

"If not us, then who, Shulen?" he murmured before turning to Alinore's daughter. "I will tell you what I know, and more than that, I will sing our desert songs about her so you will see through the eyes of our ballads."

Shulen nodded. He pulled a third chair over and gestured for her to join them as he swung the blackened kettle over the fire for a fresh pot of tea. The embers on the hearth gleamed blue-black and hissing orange. Malak tossed a fresh log on. The wood crackled. A shower of sparks leapt up. The dark-bearded man stared at the hungry threads of flames. The steam entwined its pale fingers through the silver-gray smoke rising from the wood. Silence settled on the room like a frost, etched with unspoken words. Ari Ara shifted on the chair, sensing the ancestor spirits gathering on the chill edges of the night. The row of candles shivered. She thought she sensed the weightless touch of a spirit's hand upon her head. Malak closed his eyes in his carved face and drew breath.

He began to sing a haunting and eerie tune. The scales of the desert songs wove in forgotten half-notes and chords the riverlands had ignored for centuries. The melodies played the harp strings of Ari Ara's heart so evocatively that they snuck like thieves through the dark night and robbed the breath from her chest. She blinked as a shape moved on the air. Shulen noticed her widening eyes and nodded, pointing to an image that flickered in the corner as Malak sung the first words of a saga ballad and the shifting desert sands rose visible. Ari Ara gasped in startled wonder. The story in the songs came into sight, full of flickering colors like the embers of a dying fire. Figures strode out of the darkness for a flash of a second then dimmed as a new image emerged. Her mother rose, young and beautiful, on the day she had first met the Desert King. Ari Ara's heart clenched in a tight knot as unnamable emotions swept through her wiry frame, rattling her to the bones.

One ballad threaded into the next in a never-ending saga, sung masterfully by Malak. He lifted the melodies with great humility and reverence, as if he felt blessed to have the songs play the instrument of his voice. Ari Ara stared at him, awed by the sweeping mastery of the Hawk Keeper's singing. His voice was not the pitched perfection of the songstresses that performed at Brinelle's evening receptions. It was an expressive, utterly human voice, laden with subtlety and humor, rich with emotion, captivatingly expressive, as if Malak had seen into the soul of humanity and drunk the water of life, itself.

By dawn, Ari Ara had seen visions of her mother journeying to the desert, falling in love, and marrying. She'd witnessed the beauty of her two peoples coming together in peace. She saw Shulen, too, whose hair had been as copper as hers, not gray as it was now, and Rhianne, strange and different in her Fanten ways amidst the nobility of Mariana and the fiercely proud Desert People. She saw Shulen's child, the one who had died along with her mother at the Battle of Shulen's Stand. The girl was laughing in the arms of her parents. Ari Ara's shirt grew damp with tears, yet her heart rose with the sun. She understood, at long last, the beauty and the truth of their lives, not just the sorrow and grief of their loss.

"A person who is remembered in Desert Song is never lost," Malak said quietly as they bid her farewell. "We of the Desert have little in the ways of the material world, but we have riches of the spirit few here can even imagine. Go now, Daughter of Our King, sleep, and dream in the songs of your mother."

CHAPTER ELEVEN

. . . . .

The Women's Song

Three nights later, the portrait rose in her dreams. Alinore stretched out her soft hands. Rhianne stood with sadly smiling eyes behind her. The two women stepped through the wooden frame like a doorway. Ari Ara's dream-body ran to them.

"Come," they said together, each taking one of her hands.

They led her up the black ancestor river, past the three brothers - Marin, Shirar, and Alaren - back and back through time, telling her not to let go of their hands or she would fall. The river wound through a forest of Great Trees. The darkness throbbed with Fanten drumming. She saw the Fanten Grandmother dreamwalking among them, dancing an ancient dance of crones and ghosts, dry leaves and turning seasons. Ancestor spirits turned as she passed with Alinore and Rhianne. One by one the grandmothers asked:

"Ari Ara means *not this, not that*. Who are you, really?"

The spirits - Fanten, Marianan, and Desert - tugged her in different directions until her fingers slipped from Alinore's. Rhianne cried out with fear as she broke her grasp and suddenly, she was falling, falling through time.

She tumbled for an eternity, spinning; mad with fear and a soundless scream. Rhianne, a dreamwalker like all the Fanten, dove after her, eyes wild and desperate. The Fanten Grandmother followed on her heels, alarmed and pale. Ari Ara saw the houses of Mariana Capital rise up beneath her. The tangle of streets thickened and she thought that she would hit the ground - the real ground, in her own time - and it would kill her. In desperation, she called to Alaren. From a distance, she saw the ancestor spirit turn and dive through time, his hand reaching closer and closer as the ground raced up, closer and closer. At the last moment, he shoved her out of the dream -

- and she woke up, stunned breathless against her pillow, covered in sweat; wet, sticky blood between her legs. From the dream realms, she heard the Fanten Grandmother's laughter.

"Welcome to womanhood, little one," the old woman said, not entirely unkindly.

Then her voice vanished, leaving Ari Ara alone with her heart in her throat.

She sat for a moment, panicked, as the rising sun touched the edges of the shutters. Then she scrambled off the fine sheets, flushing at the thought of staining them and wondering what to do. She knew about the women's blood, of course; the Fanten had told her all about it. She just didn't know how the Mariana Capital ladies handled it. She'd rather leap into an ice-cold river than ask Shulen - or, ancestors forbid, Emir or Korin. Rill didn't blush at anything, but she was far across the city. Isa was houses away, and there was no way, not in a thousand years, that she wanted to ask Brinelle about this. The Fanten women used a special moss for their cycles, burying it in the roots of the oldest tree to repay the gift of life and shelter. Here she didn't even have an old rag - even the wash towels gleamed pristine white.

She shoved one between her legs anyway and stuck her head out the door.

"Um, if Mahteni is awake, would you please ask her to come?" she blushingly requested the expressionless man who served - in rotation with others - as a servant and guard. *Her jailor,* she'd testily thought more than once, but today she was glad to send him marching down the hall so she wouldn't have to waddle across the marbles tiles in search of Mahteni's advice.

The woman arrived as dawn crept in the windows. She laughed gently as Ari Ara blurted out her problem, then brought the women's rags she'd need. Ari Ara reached for them - she had Azar practice in a few moments - but Mahteni pulled away.

"You cannot have them without a proper ceremony of becoming," she said firmly. "Send word to Shulen that you will not be at practice today. We must take the time to honor this turning point in your young life."

Ari Ara did as Mahteni asked then listened as the desert woman spoke.

"If we were in our home," Mahteni began, graciously including Ari Ara as one of the Desert, exiled by fate as she was, "all the women of your family would gather, all of your aunts - "

"I have aunts?" Ari Ara asked in surprise.

"Didn't you know?" Mahteni replied with a blink of astonishment.

Ari Ara shook her head.

"Tahkan Shirar has an older sister, Moragh, who lives in the northern mountains, and a younger sister named Mirrin, but she was sent into hiding during the war and remains hidden still."

"Why?" Ari Ara asked.

"If you had not been found, she would have followed in

Tahkan Shirar's footsteps and continued the Shirar lineage. The king fears the Marianans might kill her or hold her hostage."

"Why didn't Moragh go into hiding?"

Mahteni's thin smile flashed.

"Moragh hides from no one. She is as fierce as the sand lioness. The Great Lady's army ran from her once."

"What?!"

Mahteni chuckled at the girl's shocked expression.

"Moragh is the commander of our army. We think she's half-mad, half-magic. But she cannot take over from the Desert King."

"Why can't she - "

"She cannot sing the old songs, though she manages the war cries and battle chants."

"But why - "

Mahteni held up her hand with a laugh.

"You'll understand in a minute. Let me finish the story I started."

Ari Ara bit back the questions brimming on the tip of her tongue. She had aunts! She could see why no one had told her about Mirrin; they probably didn't know. But why hadn't anyone mentioned Moragh? She had to be famous among the warriors. And why did singing matter?

In the Desert, Mahteni told her, aunts and grandmothers, cousins and female friends would gather when a young girl's monthly blood came for the first time. They would walk out under the stars and sing the song of wombs, praising the chain of life that brought each day out of yesterday, the same chain that linked the female lineage of the families. The young girl would say goodbye to her circle of child-friends who would remain behind in the village, and cross over to the women's circle.

"Thus, everyone crosses the threshold from child to adult," Mahteni said, her eyes distant as the scent of the dry night air brushed her memory. The girl would sing her song of becoming, having thought hard about the kind of woman she wanted to grow into. She would mention her mother's attributes, her aunts' strengths, and the qualities she admired in her grandmothers and the older women in her village. Through the coming years, the other women would remember the girl's song and help her grow into her ideals as she made the transition into womanhood.

"Do the boys do this?" Ari Ara asked.

"Yes, when their voices crack and begin to deepen."

"But I don't have a song," Ari Ara blurted out.

"I know," Mahteni answered easily. "That's why I told you to skip Azar practice. We are going to make one together."

She hummed a tune, simple and clear, and repeated it until Ari Ara caught it. Then she told her to think of the women she knew and the qualities she wished to embody someday. Ari Ara thought first of Alinore and the respect everyone had for her ability to make friends and find peace. She didn't know the name for that quality, it wasn't gentleness or diplomacy, but Mahteni suggested a word in Desert Speech: *corine-mettahl,* one who built peace among people. The Fanten Grandmother rose next in Ari Ara's mind, stern and mysterious. She immediately thought of the old woman's inner strength that ran like steel through her wiry body. As for Mahteni, Ari Ara shyly admired her quiet dignity.

"What about the Great Lady?" Mahteni asked. "It is traditional to include your living blood relatives, especially since you have so few."

Ari Ara made a face.

Mahteni chuckled.

"Think of her qualities in a different light," Mahteni suggested. "You see her as . . . what?"

"Bossy," Ari Ara said flatly.

Mahteni hid a smile.

"Her ability to give clear commands is a strength that is much praised by others," she pointed out diplomatically.

"It's not a strength I want," Ari Ara muttered. "You can be clear without telling everybody else what to do."

"So, do you think she has leadership?"

"Heap loads," Ari Ara sighed.

"Then let's put that in," Mahteni recommended, explaining softly that in the Desert, they learned to value each other's strengths. Everyone played a role and had something to offer the village. The most annoying quality of a person often proved useful to everyone in the end.

"What should I include about my aunts?" Ari Ara asked Mahteni.

Mahteni stared out the window, thoughtful.

"Include Moragh's fierceness - you have a bit of it already, and it will stand you in good stead in the life I suspect you will lead."

"What about Mirrin?" Ari Ara asked.

Mahteni sighed, a sense of sorrow weighing on her.

"No one knows much about her anymore."

"Maybe we could guess," Ari Ara suggested.

Mahteni sat still and silent for a long moment.

"Love for her people," she said finally. The sister of the Desert King had remained in hiding for most of her life, ready to serve her people if she had to.

Ari Ara agreed and Mahteni added it to the song. The desert woman hummed for a bit, fitting the words to the melody, translating it into Desert Speech.

"You will have to learn this in our language," Mahteni warned her. "If the whole song comes to life as you sing, you will know you have lived up to it. Otherwise, the words will be hollow in your throat."

Mahteni sang then, her voice clear and strong. Just like when Malak had sung the ballads about Alinore, the lyrics came alive. As each verse spoke a name, Ari Ara saw the woman rising in her eyes. Brinelle looked out over her city. The Fanten Grandmother slipped between the trees. Alinore and Rhianne walked together on the ancestor river. Moragh loomed, red hair like a mane, chainmail glinting under a fierce sun. Mahteni looked up from her stitching and smiled. Only Mirrin had no vision, the last image of Mahteni stitching faded into the real Mahteni singing. When the final note died away, Ari Ara remarked on it.

"Perhaps it is because so little is known about her," she answered.

Mahteni made her practice the song until the Desert Speech dried out her mouth like the dust of their lands. Then the older woman brought her a sip of water and told her to sing once more.

" . . . for our lives are the truth of dust and the sweetness of water. Sing and you will bring the song to life."

Ari Ara sang. The women rose, fainter than in Mahteni's rendering, but visible. Fierceness, peacebuilding, leadership, love of people, dignity, and strength: Ari Ara felt daunted and inspired as those qualities filled the room with the women's presence. To grow into those ideals was the task of a lifetime. And that, Mahteni told her, was the purpose of the song.

"You sing it each moon cycle when your blood comes. You can also sing just a single verse when you need your mother's peacebuilding skills, or Brinelle's leadership, or any of the other qualities. A woman never walks alone. We are always with you. And, perhaps someday, the young women of the Desert will invoke your name when they long for skill in the Way Between."

And as the Great Bell tolled across the city, Mahteni told her the answer to her question hours ago: the leaders of their people must be able to sing so they can bring the history, hopes, and honor of the Desert People alive, and hold them to their visions and dreams.

CHAPTER TWELVE

. . . . .

Minli of Monk's Hand

Cold winds howled around the edges of the House of Marin, rattling the shutters and sending flickering shivers through the candle flames. Ari Ara rubbed her eyes and read the sentence again. The dry language of the documents slipped out of her tired grasp. She propped her head in her hand and traced the words, willing them to straighten out like a row of soldiers standing to attention.

For the past six nights, she'd been staying up late searching for ways to end the Water Exchange. The urchins ran the streets with brilliant desert silk armbands, boldly calling for the return of the water - and the water workers - to the Desert. At Ari Ara and Rill's urging, the scrappy urchins had stopped pestering the water workers.

"Fight the problem, not each other," Rill urged. "We want the same things: Desert People back in the Desert, Marianans back to work, and urchins in apprenticeships. To make that happen, the water's got to go to the Desert."

Ari Ara did her part by scouring the records for how the Heir to Two Thrones - as some people were calling the Lost

Heir now that she was found - could help. She scanned the records on the powers of an heir apparent. She scoured the process of submitting a legal challenge to a law. She waded through the ways to break a state contract. Brinelle lent her stacks of books and scrolls, delighted - if mystified - by her sudden interest in her political and legal duties.

None of the answers had satisfied her. Ari Ara groaned and laid her forehead on the desk, hoping the solution would simply sink in through her skull. Thus far, her hours of searching had revealed only that she couldn't do anything until she was confirmed, and then not until she turned twenty-four and was crowned queen.

"There's no way I'll wait twelve years," she groaned. "That's as long as I've been alive!"

It would be quicker - and easier - to just win a Champion's Boon like Emir, Ari Ara thought in frustration, *and use that to end the Water Exchange.* She'd heard anyone could enter the annual Spring Trials. She stared at the spines on a stack of law books and pulled out the one on the Trials. She opened it up and tried not to groan at the convoluted language.

The door opened and Ari Ara turned to scold the interrupter.

"Never thought I'd see you disappointed to stop studying!" laughed a familiar voice, pushing back the hood of a traveling cloak.

"Minli!" she shrieked, leaping out of the chair and barreling around the desk to throw her arms around her one-legged friend from Monk's Hand Monastery.

The hardest thing to leave in the High Mountains had been her friend Minli. He'd stayed on to continue his studies, submitting his entrance exams for the Capital University in the early fall and passing with high marks just as she'd expected.

Minli was on the young side of the age range of the students at the rigorous Capital University, only twelve like her, but he would be housed in the Hall for Young Scholars, fussed over by the sisters, and put in introductory courses until his studious nature advanced him into the upper level classes. Weeks ago, he'd begun the long, winding descent down the mountains. He'd sent her a letter via messenger hawk, warning her that his progress would be slow; Scholar Monk insisted on stopping at every monastery along the way to look for more records on Alaren and the Way Between.

Ari Ara squeezed him happily, nearly knocking him off his good leg and sending his crutch banging into the wall, thrilled that he had finally arrived after what felt like an eternity of waiting. She could feel the cold air clinging to him.

"Just arrived off the road," he said. "Shulen met us at the bridge and brought me straight here, though I was supposed to go to the University."

Ari Ara stepped back, holding him at arm's length.

"You've grown!" she accused.

His bird's nest hair had been shaved clean in the custom of the monks' university students. He had shot up at least a hand and a half, and his wrists stuck out of the ends of his sleeves. She hurried to retrieve his crutch, apologizing for knocking it over, telling him to take off his cloak and stay if he wasn't too tired. Was he hungry? Thirsty?

"I'm fine," he answered with a laugh, "though a cup of hot tea would kick off the cold stretches of the road."

She swung the kettle back over the hearth as he settled into an armchair and warmed his hands. His brown eyes darted around the room with lively interest. A sudden flush of shyness struck her and she busied herself by collecting a second cup from the set she kept on a shelf. The months and miles since she had left Monk's Hand stretched between her and Minli. She could sense him measuring the changes in her, shifts more subtle than height. She poured out the old tea leaves and prepared a fresh pot, hoping she hadn't changed too much from the half-wild creature he once knew, an orphan with nothing more to her name than a cloak and a flock of black Fanten sheep. An intense surge of relief washed over her that Minli hadn't come a day earlier and caught her in one of the formal dresses and long gloves she had to wear for the evening banquets with the nobles. She'd have died of embarrassment.

"I'm not the only one who's grown," Minli remarked quietly as she handed him a cup of tea, "but I bet you'd still rather be on the training sands than reading whatever moldy old tome you've got on your desk."

She laughed, the tension broke, and she flung herself happily into the other armchair, asking him to tell her all the news.

"Monk's Hand Monastery has changed, Ari Ara," Minli told her enthusiastically. "You'd hardly recognize it outside the stones and sands."

For centuries, Monk's Hand Monastery had raised orphans and trained warriors, adhering to a routine older than the hills. The training sands had been filled with the cries of Attar since time immemorial. Orphans vied for the chance to become warriors and turn the nightmares of their pasts into dreams of glory on the battlefield. But last spring, the Head Monk had sworn the monastery to supporting the peaceful Way Between. The outraged nobles had cut off funding, but the Kitchen Monk negotiated with the villagers for supplies and they stayed firm on their new commitment. Monk's Hand Monastery was busier than ever. The villagers climbed up the long stairs to learn and practice. Orphans and warriors came from all over

Mariana to train in Azar, just as they used to train to become warriors.

"Even the Fanten come," Minli said.

"What?!" Ari Ara yelped in surprise, remembering how the violence-abhorring Fanten had shunned the war-obsessed monastery in disgust for all of the time she had lived there.

"The Fanten Grandmother oversees the practices," Minli explained. "After all, the Way Between was originally one of their Hundred Sacred Dances."

"But they haven't used it since Alaren's day."

"That doesn't stop her from bossing everyone around," Minli pointed out. "She perches on the side of the sands and corrects the warrior monks if they veer into Attar."

The whole monastery was alive with new interests and studies in the Way Between. The senior monks argued and debated the competing philosophies of Attar and Azar for hours. The Archivist turned the records inside out, looking for more references to the Third Brother. The orphans' classes were lively and unpredictable. Scholar Monk and Minli had been tasked with creating a new curriculum on the Way Between.

"I hope you brought me a copy," Ari Ara said.

She'd been waiting impatiently for months to see the teaching tool Minli and Scholar Monk had crafted from the *Stories of the Third Brother*. She'd received tantalizing letters from Minli over the summer, sharing the trials and successes of teaching inner and verbal Azar to the orphans in Scholar Monk's classroom.

Minli pointed to the satchel she'd knocked off his shoulder in her enthusiastic embrace. Ari Ara yelped and leapt for it, pulling a hand-bound book out of it and recognizing Minli's perfect script. Ari Ara turned the pages, awed.

As she looked through it, Minli told her that he and

Scholar Monk had visited dozens of monasteries as they traveled to Mariana Capital. During the slow journey down the Monk's Tears River, they'd stopped at each of the monasteries strung like pearls along the waterway. They'd spent days introducing the Way Between and the new curriculum to the monks. Some were curious, others skeptical. In a few places, the monks had refused to even consider the new ideas. Every monastery had been threatened with loss of funds, but the wealthy de Barres of the Southlands had offered support. As Scholar Monk had met with the senior monks at each stop, Minli's task had been to slip quietly over to the archivist and ask if there were any scraps or snippets of old scrolls on the subject of the Way Between. Most said no, everything had been destroyed in the Great Persecution, but a few archivists dusted off long-ignored records and pulled out secret chests of banned scrolls.

"We've found all sorts of new stories about the Way Between," Minli enthused. "The *Stories of the Third Brother* is just the beginning. The Way Between was really only in its infancy during Alaren's lifetime. The next hundred years of history hold incredible tales of mass action for peace. There's one I read about how the people of Mariana Capital linked arms together to stop their own army from attacking a group of Desert People who had come to make peace!"

Minli gestured with wild excitement, stories spilling out of him about students refusing to be conscripted into the army, farmers sending crops to refugee camps instead of military outposts, and merchants refusing to lend money to rulers until peace was established along their trade routes.

Ari Ara sat back and listened with a smile, soaking up the presence of her bookish friend. He and Scholar Monk had interviewed scores of people. New stories about Alaren were popping out of the woodwork. Ordinary people recounted hushed tales their grandparents had told them, their eyes bright with memories. Minli diligently wrote down the stories and kept notes for further research. A history of the Way Between was already underway.

"At the Capital University, there's a professor who's making a study of Alaren and the Way Between," Minli explained. "She wrote to Scholar Monk wanting to know everything we've found. I'm to be her student - she keeps saying assistant, but I can't believe she means that, it's far too important . . . "

"No, it's not!" Ari Ara interrupted loyally, congratulating her friend. "Look at me - they're trying to make me into a queen - that's even crazier than you being an assistant for a topic you actually know something about!"

They looked at each other for a moment and then burst into gales of laughter. For a pair of orphans from Monk's Hand, they'd certainly come up in the world!

"Now you," Minli urged. "Tell me everything that's happened. You're a terrible letter writer."

"I know," she groaned, burying her face in her hands. "Will you forgive me?"

"Maybe," he teased, "if you show me what's so interesting that you're still studying it at this hour of night."

She made a face.

"Old law records," she admitted with a moan, explaining in a rush of words that she was trying to find a way to end the Water Exchange.

Minli blinked. A grin burst across his features.

"Alaren's ear! I've missed your peculiar brand of trouble," he teased.

"Does that mean you'll help me?" Ari Ara asked, trying not to beg, but desperately hopeful.

Minli nodded. She cheered as he rose and peered over at her desk. If anyone could make sense of dry law documents, it was Minli. He leaned over the books and scanned the pages. After a moment shook his head.

"You're looking in the wrong place."

Ari Ara groaned, unsurprised.

Minli pointed to the page.

"This is about the Spring Trials and the Champion's Boon. Shouldn't you be looking at the rights and powers of the royal heir?"

"I did," Ari Ara answered grumpily. "It says I have to wait until I'm twenty-four."

Minli rolled his eyes. She'd never been good at patience.

"So, you thought you'd stand Trials and win a Boon?" Minli gave her a stern, monkish look and told her it was a bad idea.

"I've a fifty-fifty chance of beating Emir at the Trials," she objected.

"The Great Lady would figure out what you're up to and call upon Shulen to enter the Trials. He'd trounce you," he told her flatly.

"But if I won - "

"Have you ever beaten Shulen?" Minli asked pointedly.

Ari Ara made a face.

"I've got to do something," she grumbled. "It's terrible how they're working the Desert People to death for the water they need."

Minli said he'd look for other options . . . he was sure there were ways to file a petition with the Assembly of Nobles if you collected enough backing.

"I'll check in the Capital Library first thing," he said over a yawn, "but promise me something."

"What?" she asked cautiously.

"Try to stay out of trouble."

Ari Ara laughed. His warning came far too late.

CHAPTER THIRTEEN

. . . . .

The Capital University

In the morning, Minli crossed the cobbled streets of Mariana Capital in the graying light before dawn to attend Azar practice at the Training Yards. At first, the grizzled warriors laughed at the one-legged boy hobbling across the sands. Then the warrior monks from the High Mountains glided over quietly and their stern presence turned the guffaws into stony pity. When the training began, the condescension changed into grudging respect. Minli was not as uncannily skillful as either of Shulen's original apprentices, but he held his own against seasoned warriors with a summer of Azar practices under their leather belts. He won some matches, lost others, but the eyes that trailed him off the sands at the end of the morning's training did not see a crippled boy, but a youth of quiet dignity who worked hard and did not accept the limitations of others.

After practice, Minli breakfasted with Ari Ara, Emir, and Korin, then returned to the University. Ari Ara's eyes trailed him to the corner, wishing she could join him. University studies were not guided by the Four Arts like the Nobles Academy; they ranged over a wide array of subjects and the curriculum shifted each year. Students organized together to request certain courses. Professors offered their latest interests. Visiting researchers and resident artists taught their specialties. A scholar was expected to complete at least one independent study each year with an older student or professor as an advisor. Minli was researching the history of Azar with Professor Solange Bartou, a cultural studies researcher, and for once in her life, Ari Ara longed to pour over moldy records along with him.

The presentation ceremony of Minli's Way Between curriculum was scheduled to be held at the University, and after days of wrangling and a week of nearly perfect behavior, Brinelle gave Ari Ara permission to cross the city with Shulen and Emir to be a part of the official ceremony.

The Capital University clung to the east side of the island near the wide Middle Bridge. The buildings rose as crooked and eccentric as the rest of Marianan architecture, over five stories high with turrets and towers inhabited by the more reclusive scholars and professors. The walkways and bridges connecting the buildings reminded Ari Ara of the Urchins Nest, only more solid. Monks and sisters, students and secular professors crisscrossed the wide Common Yard that curved in a crescent between the halls. The immense Capital Library sat on the high side of the island, towering above the foot traffic, lifted on top of an enormous foundation of granite blocks that kept it out of range of the seasonal floods. Ari Ara blinked and squinted against the morning sun, shading her eyes to search the crowded steps. She could have sworn she had just seen Malak stalk out of the library then duck behind one of the columns along the stately entryway.

"Didn't you tell me that few of the Desert People read?" Ari Ara asked Shulen in a confused tone.

"They have an impressive oral tradition spanning millennia. They are trained to memorize spoken words instantly and accurately," Shulen informed her, "but yes, most prefer that tradition to the written one."

"But some read?"

"Oh yes," Shulen answered with a smile, "Tahkan Shirar reads in three languages. His spies know Marianan better than many of our own people."

Malak is a spy! Ari Ara thought as a thrill of excitement tingled from her toe tips to head top. Scraps of comments and bits of overheard conversations slid into place: Malak meant *Eyes of the King*, he did the King's bidding, he had offered aid on the first day they'd met . . . it all added up. She cast another glance and saw the dark-haired desert man watching her from the shadow of the column. She didn't wave. His secret was safe with her.

Streams of robed scholar monks and outlandishly attired students rushed across the footbridges as the bell tolled, loud and ponderous. She watched one boy dash madly through the moving crowds in the Common Yard, darting between bodies, slipping through openings, leaping sideways to avoid collisions, all the while racing toward his goal with an expression that suggested he was very, very late.

"He ought to study Azar," Ari Ara commented to Shulen, nudging him to look.

Shulen's eyes crinkled with mirth.

"He will be studying Azar. As soon as Minli's curriculum is implemented, Emir and I will hold practice sessions in the Common Yard until the snow comes. Then we will move into the University's Main Hall for the winter months."

The University students were welcome to train on certain days with the beginners at the Training Yards, but Emir had suggested holding training sessions here where it would be more accessible to the students. Ari Ara giggled as Shulen mentioned this.

"I bet he wants to show off for the girls," she said, hiding her laughter from Emir as he turned over his shoulder to glare at her.

The University was thick with young women wearing the latest styles. They made a colorful and vibrant contrast to the black-robed scholar monks and the white-cloaked sisters. Even the most serious student among them took care with her appearance and the young men were no less vain.

Shulen cleared the back of his throat.

"Emir takes his duties very seriously," he told his second apprentice, "as should you."

Ari Ara squawked in protest. *She* wouldn't be caught dead making eyes at the fancy peacocks of the Capital. She grumbled to Shulen that it was too easy for Emir to beat her if she got distracted like that.

The commotion in the yard rose as students gawked and turned, recognizing the Lost Heir. Two young lads crashed into each other, sending books and parchment flying. Heads stuck out of windows and people crowded in entryways. Bodies packed the steps of the Capital Library as the students poured out to catch a glimpse of the Lost Heir. The Head Monk came out of the Main Hall to greet them. Shulen kept one eye out for dangers as the solemn man offered formal words of welcome. The warrior surveyed the expressions of the students - interested, skeptical, wary, enthusiastic - and gathered that the general sentiment was curiosity rather than suspicion. It wasn't quite the same awe that young Alinore had inspired when she had convinced her reluctant parents to let her attend the University instead of receiving private tutoring. She'd caused quite a stir until her presence became ordinary and familiar. It had been a wise notion, ensuring that the populace saw Alinore as one of them, a queen who did not distance herself from her people. Shulen, assigned as her guard, acquired an unusual level of education for a warrior as he watched over the nation's heir apparent. His work had largely consisted of discouraging love-struck young men from pestering her.

The lecture hall where the curriculum presentation ceremony was to take place doubled as a theater and rose three stories tall, not counting the cavernous rafters full of pulleys that lifted and lowered set pieces and curtains. Students packed the benches of the raked floor seating. Scholars, researchers, monks, and sisters filled the first level boxes. Older students hung over the railings of the second and third floor balconies, hollering out to those below. In the wings of the stage, Ari Ara found Minli peering around one of the large stone columns that held up the building. He shot her a pale, nervous glance.

"It's a lot of people," he murmured, his voice squeaky.

Ari Ara nodded sympathetically. She'd felt the same way when she'd first arrived in the city. All those eyes, so many voices! There were more people in this room than in all of Monk's Hand - and that was including the Fanten.

"You'll be fine," she assured him as the Head Monk walked out to begin what she had learned to recognize as a long boring welcome speech.

It was a simple ceremony. They didn't have to speak much, just smile and nod and recite the basic formal phrases. Minli would give the new curriculum to her. She would then give it to the Head Monk, offering her official royal approval of the study and practice of Azar. Then they'd stand there looking polite while Minli's professor and Shulen gave a short introductory lecture on the Way Between.

"Wait 'til they make you give a dissertation on the development of the curriculum," she teased Minli.

"Oh, ancestors - "

He broke off as Shulen tapped their shoulders and raised his finger to his lips. A burst of applause lifted as the opening remarks concluded. The Head Monk turned expectantly toward the wings. Minli hooked his crutch under one arm and carried the new curriculum in his free hand. Ari Ara stepped out beside him. Emir and Shulen fell into their guard positions on either side of the pair. Ari Ara squeezed Minli's shoulder reassuringly as they moved into the glare of the lights. The audience rose to their feet as she entered.

"See?" she told him. "Standing ovations already and you haven't even opened your mouth."

"They're standing for you, silly," Minli muttered between his teeth.

Ari Ara thought the students could be standing for any of them; the followers of Alaren's Way Between were a distinguished lot. She smiled. She had no doubt Minli of Monk's Hand would outshine them all in the long run. The curriculum alone would make his name known in every village in the country.

She'd spent long evenings this week reading through the curriculum, neglecting her Academy assignments to pour over the pages of stories and lessons. She fell into the world of Alaren, a time almost beyond imagining, the dawn of their civilization. Nearly a year ago, she had read his stories while recovering from the beating a bully had pounded into her. It was the first book she had ever read, and Minli had taught her to read with it. She saw traces of their conversations in the lessons he had developed with Scholar Monk. The practices for calming anger and violence, negotiating an agreement, and holding difficult conversations had all been tested with the orphans at the monastery over the summer. The curriculum used Alaren's entertaining and often humorous folktales to teach students how to non-cooperate with violence and injustice. Theater and storytelling exercises engaged children in reenacting Alaren's blockades, marches, and protests, teaching the children the skills they would need to use those tactics in real life.

Ari Ara had paced her rooms one sleepless and inspired night after reading Minli's imaginative exercise on rebuilding Alaren's legendary thousand-person Peace Force. She'd tackled him the next morning at practice - voice raspy with exhaustion and her eyes blazing with ideas - ready to run away to the Border Mountains to revive the nonviolent army that waged peace instead of war. She'd been useless in practice, making so many mistakes that Shulen ordered her to the sidelines. She promptly fell asleep on a bench and dreamed of walking through the border passes with a winding march of thousands of people and Alaren, who looked strangely like Shulen.

A burst of applause and Minli's nudge startled her thoughts back to the present. She accepted the curriculum he handed to her. He thanked her for her vision of bringing back Azar from its centuries of secrecy. Ari Ara replied with equal gratitude and presented the book to the Head Monk. He, in turn, invited Shulen and Professor Solange Bartou to offer remarks on the Way Between.

Ari Ara squinted into the wings, eager for a glimpse of the woman who was Minli's mentor. Shulen had told her that she was a firm supporter of holding Azar practices at the University, and had been the first to sign up despite her notorious disinterest in any form of exercise outside of tromping around remote villages documenting subcultures. As she walked into the light, her frizzy brown hair illuminated in a halo around her plump cheeks. She lifted onto her tiptoes when excited - as she often was - and her half moon spectacles fell off her small and pointy nose. She wore the shabbiest clothes Ari Ara had ever seen in the Capital: a plain beige tunic and breeches with a long vest coat belted over. Solange Bartou gave the impression of a mad professor, but Shulen had seen the woman's wit and intelligence tie the Assembly of Nobles up in knots and out-debate the entire Society of Philosophy. She was a formidable intellectual presence steeping inside a cozy teapot of a woman. Students either adored or ignored her and she didn't go out of her way to court popularity or prestige.

"A treat, a rare treat," she enthused, "having four living practitioners of Alaren's Way Between standing right here in our very lecture hall. My word! The significance of this moment!"

"Yeah, not to mention she's the Heir to Two Thrones," an older student called out from the balcony. "You don't see that every day."

"Oh, indeed, right you are," Solange replied, blinking as if she'd overlooked that fact. "But, then again, we can't help the circumstances of our birth - "

"Solange!" the Head Monk spluttered.

"Oh goodness, I didn't mean any insult," she exclaimed, "only that the girl *chose* to follow and excel at the Way Between, whereas it was her parents' background that makes her a double heir. Earned merit must be commended, don't you think?"

Ari Ara grinned. She liked this woman whose hands fluttered about like a distraught hen while her mind thought with a hawk's sharp precision.

"Mark my words," Professor Solange told the students, "you will be telling your grandchildren about the day when you saw the Great Warrior Shulen and the Lost Heir come to revive the Way Between after centuries of persecution and secrecy."

She blinked back tears of emotion, and then launched into a talk on the history of Azar with the skill of a master storyteller. Ari Ara thought you could hear a pin drop in the round theater and was tempted to pull out one of her hairclips and try it. For several generations after Alaren's death, the Way Between had flourished . . . as did the world. The hundred years after Alaren's death were known as the Golden Years. With the wastefulness of war averted, both nations turned to other pursuits. Crafts abounded. New inventions emerged. The Capital University was founded. The Desert People's song cycle of the Elder Years was composed.

The followers of the Way Between grew into the thousands; Alaren's vision of a Peace Force recruited more youth to wage peace than either nation's army managed to train in warfare. When conflicts flared up, as was inevitable, the followers of the Way Between prevented violence and worked to find fair resolutions. There were factions, however, that eyed the border lands greedily, who craved the glory of war, or who nursed seething resentments toward their enemies over the mountains. The devotees of Attar, the Warrior's Way, viewed the Way Between as standing between them and the glory - and profits - of war.

Here, Professor Solange urged Shulen to speak up, adding his perspectives on what she was saying.

"In some ways," Shulen commented, "they were correct: the followers of the Way Between sought to end war and eliminate the need for warriors. Feeling threatened, a faction of the warriors attacked."

Shulen described how, during the Great Persecution, the warriors used a border skirmish as an excuse to build power.

151

The Way Between was scapegoated as weak and ineffective, and as the political climate turned fearful, the ruling king banned the Way Between and forced enlistment in Attar trainings. War broke out. When the followers of the Way Between tried to stop it, the warriors convinced the Marianan king to round up the peacebuilders as treasonous dissenters. As escalating resistance collided with fear of invasion, a terrifying campaign of extermination ensued and the Way Between went underground to survive, beginning a period of great darkness.

The century that followed the Great Persecution was called the Dark Passage, a time when scribes despaired and thought the end of the world drew near. War after war, one leading to another, created an epoch of endless hardship, plagues, famines, and poverty.

"The Dark Passage was a terrifying time," Shulen remarked. "Hiding the Way Between was like hiding the sun. Life grows from the ground of Azar and without it, when the only options are Attar's death and Anar's fear, the world grows dark and withers."

Yet, despite the laws banning it, the Way Between was never completely lost. For centuries, Shulen's father's lineage taught it to their children in secrecy, keeping the practices alive.

"Today," Professor Solange remarked in a proud and hopeful tone, rising onto her toes and flinging her arms wide in excitement, "we are being offered a unique opportunity to pick up this remarkable legacy and apply it in our lives. The landscape of our future may look vastly different than our bloody past. The practices of peace may supplant those of war. Someday, we may honor Shulen not as the Great Warrior, but rather as the Great Peacemaker."

Applause leapt up. A smile flitted across Shulen's face. Ari Ara and Minli exchanged grins. Professor Solange gestured for them to speak to the students. Minli flushed crimson and shook his head, but Ari Ara stepped forward.

"Death to Azar!"

A ragged voice rang out from the upper balcony. Metal glinted. Shulen dove toward Ari Ara. Emir yanked Minli out of the way. Professor Solange leapt back. A dagger hit the floorboards of the stage. Its hilt quivered in a deadly angle straight through the spot Ari Ara's heart would have been.

"Catch him," Shulen roared as a shadow darted through a flash of sunlight out through a balcony door on the third floor.

The older students in the upper balcony bolted after the assassin.

"The rooftops, the attics, the crawl spaces!" Solange shouted after them, gasping for breath.

The Head Monk thundered at the rest of the students to remain calm. Shulen hauled Ari Ara and Minli off the stage into the wings behind the wide stone column. Emir guarded them on one side, Shulen on the other. Ari Ara's limbs trembled with adrenaline, more shocked than scared. Beside her, Minli clutched her arm as he caught his breath. Ari Ara peered out toward the stage with a frown.

"Hiding in here isn't Azar," she blurted out. "It's showing all those students that Azar doesn't work, that we run from an attack. We should go back and show them our courage."

She started out from behind the pillar. Shulen lunged and hauled her back.

"You know what they're saying all over the city," she reminded the old warrior, twisting to get free. "Azar is the Weakling's Way. Azar makes us vulnerable. Azar is turning warriors into cowards."

She flung the words in Shulen's face, repeating phrases that Rill had reported to her. The old warrior must have heard them.

His face grew stony and troubled. Emir glanced at Shulen, nodding to confirm Ari Ara's points. Shulen's eyes lifted from one young face to the next, conflicted. Then Minli spoke up in his quiet, persuasive manner, acknowledging the dangers of going back out onto the stage.

"But, Shulen," he argued, "Ari Ara is right. Hiding isn't always the safest path, especially when it lets rumors like that multiply."

Minli went on, saying that the Way Between wasn't a delicate flower that bloomed only in rare times of peace; it was a tool for making the world safer.

"Please, Shulen," Ari Ara begged. "Let's set the rumors straight. Now, before they get worse."

The old warrior scowled in thought. Ari Ara held her breath, waiting for his response. Finally, he nodded in agreement.

"Be alert," Shulen warned them. "Take no chances. *Move* at the slightest sign of danger. *You*," he pointed at Ari Ara, "are to get off the stage if anything happens. No heroics. Leave the others to Emir's protection."

Shulen saw her nod, but sensed the agreement reached only to her eyes and not to her heart. She'd never preserve her skin at the cost of Minli's. She slung her arm under her friend's shoulders since his crutch lay on the stage. The hall fell silent as they entered. The babble of nervous talk died. A breathless suspense filled the rapidly-beating hearts of the students.

"Minli," Shulen ordered, "go pick up your crutch."

Minli let go of Ari Ara and hopped toward the wooden crutch.

"Ari Ara, stop him."

She bolted into motion. Minli leapt for the crutch, dropping and rolling. She blocked him. He rolled sideways, she moved between him and the crutch. He seized her legs and hooked her knees, knocking her off balance. She toppled and caught a glimpse of Minli's grin - he'd been practicing that move! She regained her footing just as Minli grasped his crutch.

"Try to tap her with your crutch," Shulen commanded. "Ari Ara, evade him."

The sounds of their feet on the wooden stage thundered in the absolute silence. The students watched every move, fascinated. Shulen began to speak about differences between inner and outer Azar. Professor Solange commented on the individual and collective uses of the Way Between. Ari Ara blessed Mahteni, whose fashions had her wearing trousers rather than full skirts as she evaded Minli's crutch.

Shulen drew close to Emir and murmured the next instruction to the youth. He obeyed swiftly, whirling and shouting in the tone of the assassin, "Death to Azar!" The audience gasped as the Mariana Champion launched a full-on assault of Attar at Ari Ara. She didn't hesitate. She moved. Any hits Emir thrust at her, she dodged. She grasped his limbs, cantilevered, and sent him diving, falling, rolling, and rebounding. Ari Ara heard a gasp of awe rise up from the students. Abruptly, Shulen halted them.

"The followers of the Way Between are not so easily killed," he said. "And, though some may call for death to Azar, all should know that Azar lives on so long as even one person dares to follow it."

Professor Solange waited for the cheer to quiet then made her announcement.

"My young assistant Minli and I will be here tomorrow at mid-break. Eat your lunch quickly and come learn more about the history and philosophy of the Way Between. The following day, Shulen and Emir Miresh will begin teaching in the

Common Yard until winter moves the practices into the Main Hall. Now, while we wait for that foolish person to be caught, are there any questions?"

Ari Ara snuck a look at Minli. He winked. As the questions shot out of the audience, the strategy of boldly standing up for the Way Between began to dispel rumors and lies, and to make the world safer for everyone.

CHAPTER FOURTEEN

. . . . .

Waterways and Maps

Mahteni and Malak were pacing the corridor outside her quarters when she returned. Mahteni looked white as a sheet and Malak's face was haggard with stress. His clothes were splattered with mud; he looked like he'd run the length of the island. Shulen took one look at them and shoved them inside her rooms, telling Emir to stand guard and admit no one.

Malak sank to his knees and held onto Ari Ara like she was in danger of disappearing. Mahteni patted her head over and over, clearly shocked by the news of the assassination attempt.

"I'm alright," Ari Ara repeated, touched by their concern.

"How could you let this happen?" Malak thundered at Shulen, shocking Ari Ara with his ferociousness.

"She's fine," Shulen replied softly.

"This changes everything," Malak swore. "She is not safe in this den of river dogs. I will take her to - "

"You will do nothing of the sort," Shulen cut in, gripping the Hawk Keeper's arm. "If you take her now, the Great Lady will launch the War of Reclamation she threatened last spring. Keep your head on!"

"Who did it?" Malak demanded to know.

"We've kept our eye on the House of Thorn," Mahteni reported, shaking her head as she confessed her suspicions, "but we heard nothing of this."

"Neither did the Royal Guard," Shulen admitted.

Voices sounded outside the door. Emir's firm tone replied to a messenger from Brinelle. Shulen sighed and reluctantly turned to leave.

"I must go report to the Great Lady. I will speak with you later. Put every water worker in the Capital on alert. Their eyes and ears will be needed to find the culprit," Shulen said to Malak as the two exchanged a long, somber look.

The warrior took his leave. Mahteni turned to Malak, pointing to the colorful silk that lined the cuffs and collar of a desert-style jacket.

"I think she should stop wearing our styles," she said sadly. "It's too dangerous. She must stop, at least until the confirmation. Between Azar and the water workers, she is making too many enemies."

"No!" Ari Ara exclaimed. That was Anar's Way, folding from fear, hiding. She wouldn't be like that.

"You will lose your bid for confirmation at this rate," Mahteni warned her.

"I don't care about the stupid confirmation!" she shouted. "I'd be doing exactly this - and probably a whole lot more - if I was just Ari Ara of the High Mountains. I won't turn my back on my father's people. There is no honor in being Queen of Mariana if it means hiding the truth of who I am."

She folded her arms across her chest. *Ari Ara* meant *not this, not that*, but it also meant *everything possible in between*. She refused to conceal parts of her identity to placate others.

Malak hid a laugh behind his hand. His eyes darted to

Mahteni. The woman stared at him and sighed. Her lips twitched. A chuckle broke loose between them.

"She is her father's daughter," she told the Hawk Keeper, giving up on trying to make Ari Ara stop wearing desert styles.

"Indeed," he laughed. "I sent the attacker's description to every water worker in the Capital. Our messengers are already spreading it throughout the valley. I gave chase, but - "

"You *were* there!" Ari Ara exclaimed. "I thought I saw you at the library. What were you doing?"

"Searching for something," he answered in a discouraged tone, "but I discovered only that water workers are not allowed in the library."

"What were you looking for?"

"An old record of sorts," he replied.

"I could help," Ari Ara offered. "My friend Minli is a student and has access to the library."

"I would not wish to bother you," he said stiffly.

"It's not a bother," Ari Ara answered. "Researching is what Minli loves best."

Malak hesitated then nodded his thanks, explaining that he was looking for a very old map.

"The Map of the World?" Ari Ara guessed. "The one that Marin and Shirar split? It's hanging in Brinelle's study."

Mahteni turned pale.

"That ought to be in storage, safely preserved in the archives, not exposed to light."

"Take it up with Brinelle," Ari Ara suggested in a joking tone.

"The copy in her study is not the original," Malak said, shaking his head. "It was made at the outset of the Hundred Years War. The real map was put in the Capital Library."

Ari Ara blinked. Was that what he was looking for?

"But, I don't need the Map of the World," Malak clarified. "Just a map of the Border Mountains before the Hundred Years War."

"Why?" Ari Ara asked, her curiosity rising like the itch welt from the needle flies that darted in blood-sucking swarms by the riverbanks.

"My king got into an argument with his sister over the size of the Goatherd Lake in olden times," Malak answered with a small gesture of respect. "Our library was destroyed in the Hundred Years War and our records of that time are lost, except for our songs."

Ari Ara slouched in disappointment. She'd half-hoped that he'd been looking for a way to free the water workers. An argument about an ancient lake was not nearly as interesting.

"Minli could certainly find you a map from before the war," Ari Ara answered. "He could even make a detailed copy of it for you."

"That would be very helpful," Malak said. "And please, be careful. We do not wish to lose you now that you have finally been found."

He gave her a quick embrace and studied her face for a long time before finally rising and leaving.

* * *

The world might be safer for Azar, Ari Ara thought grumpily the following week, but she certainly wasn't allowed to enjoy it.

Predictably, Brinelle curtailed everything fun in her life on the grounds of caution and safety. She was escorted straight to the Academy and back each day. Emir dogged her heels like a shadow. Guards trailed her around the House of Marin. Rill and Minli had to come visit her. She wasn't even permitted to go to Isa's house, let alone anywhere truly interesting. She was soon bored to the bone.

In the first few days, she wrote to the Desert King, receiving prompt replies that took her longer to answer than it took him to send. Nightfast flew swiftly on the East-West Winds that streamed like an invisible road over the Border Mountains. The Desert King was upset about the assassination attempt and told her that he, like Brinelle, was looking into the matter. Many people thought it was just a headstrong, angry student, but others suspected it was someone posing as a student. It had been a very accurate knife throw over a long distance, after all, and few students would have that ability. Rill offered her own theory: she suspected the House of Thorn had hired the attacker. Beyond Varina de Thorn's personal dislike of Ari Ara, the entire family had been grumbling about the urchins' armbands, the effort to end the Water Exchange, the Azar practices in the Training Yards, and the introduction of the Way Between curriculum at the Capital University. Huge numbers of messenger hawks winged northward between their house in the Capital and their ancestral home in the Orelands. Rill reported rumors that Rannor Thornmar, Lord of the Orelands, was planning to come south to the city.

"Probably to get the job done right," Rill complained. "He's a right nasty piece of work."

She slouched in Ari Ara's quarters, face still flushed from the morning Azar practice. She promised to gather more reports from the urchins, but warned that it would take time to track them all down.

"It's all chaos and madness in the streets right now what with the urchins scattering to winter posts and all. The Nest's empty 'til spring, mostwise."

"Winter posts?" Ari Ara asked.

During the snowy months, the urchins dispersed from the ramshackle nest at the South End, joining the orphans or seeking indoor employment.

"Minli got some of us urchins winter posts at the University," Rill explained. "And not a day too soon. Those of us who refuse to go stay with the sisters when the wind bites hard would've been solid icicles by next week!"

She stretched her roughened hands out to the fire. Desert silks continued to adorn the urchins' rags, stitched into hatbands, wrists of gloves, the ends of scarves, and collars of wool jackets. With the Mistress of Dress at the House of Marin setting a high bar of fashion from the Desert King's silks and Mahteni Duktar's styles being the talk of the town, the street urchins found their silk scraps to be precious treasures coveted by half the Capital. The fine fabrics turned into an unexpected windfall for the urchins as the dressiers and merchants started bartering other goods and services for the scraps. Because of this, Rill reported a shift of sentiment between the water workers and urchins from outright hate to uneasy tolerance.

On a brighter note, Minli was more than happy to research old maps. Before the week was out, he sidled up to Ari Ara after morning practice and pulled a bundle of papers out of his inner coat pocket. The Training Yards blew cold with the front edge of winter. The overcast sky threatened snow. Ari Ara pulled her cloak tighter and eyed the bundle curiously.

"Can you pass these on to Malak?" Minli asked, a troubled look on his face. "These are copies of the map records. They're accurate; I did them myself. I told the Archivist it was a surprise gift for you, so if you see him, mention how much you love old maps, would you?"

Ari Ara snorted as he handed her the packet.

"I like them a lot more than old records, that's for sure," she joked.

Minli nervously bit his lower lip, glancing over his shoulder to make sure they weren't being overheard. Shulen and Emir stood out of earshot, conferring about the practice. The warriors had moved onto other drills. The urchins had vanished; many of them hadn't come to the Training Yards this morning, choosing to train at the University with the students, where the practices were being held in the Main Hall as the weather grew colder.

"Don't get caught with these," he cautioned, "and tell Malak to be very, very careful with those maps. He'll know why."

Ari Ara eyed the package suspiciously.

"Are you going to tell me or do I have to open them myself?" she asked her friend.

Minli fidgeted. He'd hoped to deliver them directly and leave her out of it. Ari Ara glared and demanded an answer.

"It's the Mari River. It didn't used to be so big," he stammered. "Once, there were three passes through the Border Mountains to the Desert."

At her confused look, he lowered his voice even further.

"Three *river* passes," he emphasized. "The Marianans have blocked the two northern river passes and channeled them into the Mari River. They use the water in the northwest drylands and the mines, but that's not all."

During the Hundred Years War, Minli explained, the Marianans attacked the Desert People's records hall, burning it to the ground. Then they changed their own maps to show new river paths, stationing outposts on the dams to keep the Desert People from destroying them to get their water back. The records now said that the North Ravine was filled in by a rockslide that not even a miracle could budge, but Minli said he had also found references that indicated that a team of masons from the Stonelands had carved out the mountainside to collapse the slope.

"The southwest side of Goatherd's Lake should drain into the Desert," Minli explained, "but instead, it pours out the east side of the lake down into Mari Valley."

Ari Ara's eyebrows scrunched together.

"You mean, the Desert wasn't always a desert?"

Minli shrugged. It was hard to tell, but his sense of the references in the records was that the Desert had been dry, but not *this* dry. After all, everyone knew that Tobin's Battle had been fought in lush agricultural fields, not the sand dunes that were now in that region. He was unwilling to jump to conclusions, but there had definitely been revisions of the maps and tampering with the records.

"I'm going to keep researching," Minli promised, pulling the hood of his cloak up as the cold wind gusted. Ari Ara invited him to join her for breakfast, but he declined. He wanted to get back to his search.

As she walked him to the gates of the Training Yards, Minli caught her up on the murmurs of the rumor-river. The students gossiped about how the Desert King had sent a letter to the Great Lady threatening to seize his heir and keep her safe from the dangers of Mariana. The water workers, it was said, were scouring the city for clues to the assassin's identity, snooping in places they had no business being, huddling in small groups, and meeting clandestinely. Some warned that an uprising was imminent and that the Desert People would steal the Lost Heir. Ari Ara told Minli what Mahteni told her: the water workers were furious that someone had tried to murder their king's daughter and vowed to protect her from future attacks.

"With all this protection," Ari Ara complained, "the most likely thing to kill me is boredom."

As Minli departed, Ari Ara shaded her eyes and peered up at the Hawk's Keep, trying to decide if she should climb up to the tower in search of Malak. She had a letter to the Desert King in her pocket, a perfect excuse to go find Nightfast. A hawk's cry caught her attention. Ari Ara spotted a black speck wheeling high overhead. She whistled through her fingers, low then high. Nightfast shot downward. She held out her arm for the hawk to land.

Nightfast stretched out his talons . . . and zoomed past her.

She spun. The hawk settled on a surprised-looking Malak's arm. The man stood on the far edge of the Training Yard, returning from an errand.

"Naughty thing," Ari Ara scolded the bird, crossing toward him. "You're supposed to have better manners than that."

The hawk had been trained to come only to the girl and the Desert King. The black-bearded Hawk Keeper turned to Ari Ara with an embarrassed expression.

"Apologies, Young Queen, but I must have indulged him with too many treats," Malak confessed as he tried to hand the bird back to Ari Ara.

"Hold him for me," she requested. "I want to tie a letter to his leg. And here, hold these, too."

She passed him the maps.

"They're from Minli," she said quietly.

He smoothly tucked the papers into the inside pocket of his coat.

"In his last letter," Ari Ara mentioned as she tied the message scroll to the hawk's leg, "the Desert King asked for a copy of Minli's curriculum, but I don't know how to send it. Nightfast can't carry a book over the mountains."

She looked at the Hawk Keeper hopefully. She didn't want to ask the official mail carrier since she'd need to get Brinelle's approval. She wasn't certain that the Marianans would want to share Azar with their enemies, but her perspective was that two warring factions with knowledge of the Way Between could reach peace faster than just one.

"If something must reach the King," Malak offered softly, "you can entrust it to me."

"I'll bring it by the Keep later this week," she answered, stroking Nightfast's head feathers as she took him on her arm. "And you, naughty hawk, fly straight to my father with no side trips to Hawk Keepers who spoil you rotten."

She scolded the bird one last time and tossed him aloft. He spread his wings, flapped for a few moments then made for Malak again.

"No, no, bird, go on!" the water worker chided. "Don't get me in trouble for my kindness to you."

Nightfast flew off with an affronted screech. Malak rubbed the back of his neck.

"I won't give him any more treats, I promise," he said sheepishly to Ari Ara as Nightfast's shrinking form vanished into a speck in the sky.

A few days later, she headed for the Hawk's Keep with the curriculum and the *Stories of the Third Brother*. Emir glowered as she left without him. They'd had three knockdown, drag-out shouting matches this week over his duty to shadow her every move like an over-protective watchdog. Yesterday, Shulen had intervened just as they broke into a serious bout of the Way Between. Shulen had rubbed his temples over her hot-tempered frustration then worked out a compromise: she didn't need to have a guard within the House of Marin since the Royal Guard was posted all around the building. The Hawk's Keep sat in a gray-zone between the house and the Training Yards, but fortunately, Malak had somehow earned a spot on Shulen's extremely limited list of people whom he trusted with the Lost Heir's life. Otherwise, Emir would be dogging her steps all the way to the top.

The base of the tower spread as wide as Brinelle's smaller reception hall. The Marianan Hawk Keepers glanced up as she entered, respectfully bowed, then returned their eyes to their work of sorting the scrolls and sending out deliveries of messages. They managed the mail of the House of Marin and the Training Yards, including instructions from the commanders to the warriors.

She darted up the spiraling stone staircase before anyone stopped her. The climb wound around the Keep in a dizzying spiral. Rooms scarcely bigger than closets lined the core of the tower. The Marianan Hawk Keepers quartered here, senior staff in the larger bottom rooms, junior staff higher up the long climb, and apprentices higher still. Malak, as a water worker, lived at the very top in a small space on the north side of the Keep where he could be on hand to tend the hawks night or day. It was a long walk to anywhere and a steeper climb on the return.

Ari Ara reached the top landing breathless and with a spinning head. Korin had told her the tower was built tall enough to protect the messenger hawks from archers' arrows in times of siege. The circular room held crossbeams full of roosts. Water dishes and feed trays stood along the walls. Windows ringed the room, their shutters opened to allow the hawks to swoop in. The floor was strewn with clean straw and the east window was closed against the brunt of the wind that snapped its cold teeth around the Hawk's Keep. Malak was out, but from the rafters overhead, Nightfast winged to her and rapped her head reprovingly with his beak.

"Ouch," Ari Ara complained, stroking his puffed up chest feathers to settle him. "You're back quickly from the Desert. I hope you actually made it and didn't just turn back from blizzards over the Border Mountains."

Across the Keep, one of the heavy shutters banged, unlatched, held shut only by the blustering wind. Ari Ara put Nightfast down on the long wooden perch and set the books in Malak's quarters. She went to close the window and peered out. The wind stung her eyes, blurring the world. She blinked the moisture away, wiping the rims of her eyes with the back of her hand. Ari Ara was about to turn away when a flash of blue caught her eye. Shivering, she shaded the pale sunlight out of her gaze.

In a high-walled courtyard below, an Azar practice was underway. A flash of blue. A sweeping glimpse of movement. A hint of copper red. A frown deepened as she spotted water workers. They weren't allowed to study Azar, though she'd seen them surreptitiously watching the practices in the Yards. If anyone saw them actually training in the Way Between, they'd all be in a lot of trouble. She strained to make out the figures. There was Malak; she could see his dark beard. The short woman was probably Mahteni with her copper hair. A lean figure strode into the middle of the yard. The others stopped and turned to listen.

Shulen.

Ari Ara's mouth dropped open. What was Shulen doing teaching Azar to the water workers? *He'd best not get caught,* Ari Ara worried. She glanced around the Training Yards, but the drilling warriors couldn't see over the wall. The Hawk's

Keep was the only place where windows opened onto a view of the courtyard. She shut the window hastily and ran back down the spiral stairs.

CHAPTER FIFTEEN

. . . . .

The Art of War

A pool of gray, wintery light spilled through the skylight into the center of the Art of War classroom. Clouds swept in gray banks outside the windows. Three tiers of benches ringed the room, their polished wood gleaming darkly. Old armor and battle tapestries hung on the walls. In the center stood a large table with a contoured wooden map on top that displayed the geography of Mariana, the Border Mountains, and the eastern territories of the Desert. Every mountain, valley, hill, lake, river, marsh, city, and village was carved in exquisite detail. Tiny buildings were fitted into niches in the painted wood.

"It's updated each year," Korin had told Ari Ara on the first day. "If a village burns or is abandoned, the Map Table is altered. They carve new forests or clear fields according to reports sent in from all the different regions. They paint new trails onto the mountain passes as the traders and shepherds develop them. There are only three of these maps anywhere - the other two are at the University and in Mum's war room."

They'd never used it for anything more than geography references. Their Art of War instructor was a stodgy battle historian with a knack for putting Ari Ara in a stupor. Her mind was already wandering down more intriguing paths as she waited for class to start. Emir, still on guard duty, leaned his back against the wall, chatting with Korin.

One of her favorite ways to endure the Art of War's endless recitation of battles, victories, and defeats was to imagine how the Way Between might have avoided the whole war in the first place. As she leaned her elbows on the windowsill and stared out at the clouds racing over the rooftops, she pondered a story Shulen had told in training that morning. It was from the *Stories of the Third Brother.* Once, when a new war was brewing, Alaren has placed a thousand pairs of children's shoes on Marin's Way to remind his brother of the human toll of war and cool the populace's war fever.

"Some of the best examples of the Way Between are not fancy moves to fling aside an attacker," Shulen had told them, "but simple actions taken by large numbers of ordinary people to prevent the conflict from ever reaching the point of violence."

When people forgot their common humanity, Shulen had explained, they were more willing to harm each other. For centuries, war had kindled the Marianans' hatred of the Desert People and vice versa. Each victory for one was a bitter defeat for the other. Each body sprawled on a battlefield field sowed seething resentments in people for generations to come. Hate and violence chased each other in vicious cycles until the two sides stopped seeing each other's humanity. At the Academy, Ari Ara had overheard the noble youths telling nasty stories about the *desert demons,* as they called them. Many had never met a Desert person besides the water workers. Years of lies had turned ordinary people into enemies and enemies into monsters. Once people became monsters, folktales and hero stories about slaying desert demons rose up, valorizing violence and war.

"But don't you think the Desert People say the same things about us?" Ari Ara had protested to Korin over breakfast as they argued about whether or not her father's people actually hired real demons as mercenaries. "Somewhere, under the hot sun, they're probably telling their children stories about slaying, I don't know, river ogres or something."

"Dogs," Mahteni murmured, almost under her breath.

The two youths had startled. They hadn't noticed her as she slipped into Ari Ara's rooms with her usual silent tread to lay out the girl's garments.

"In our stories, we speak of a pack of red-eyed river dogs that breathe underwater and drink the blood of little children," she confessed. "We also have tales about the all-devouring dragon that lays waste to the land."

"That's nonsense," Korin scoffed.

"The emblem for the House of Marin, and the army it commands, is a coiling river dragon," Mahteni reminded him mildly. "I am not saying we are right to tell such tales, only that both sides of a war make monsters out of the people who attack them."

Later that afternoon, Ari Ara thought about that conversation and sighed. Her breath froze on the windowpane in the Art of War classroom. She traced the Mark of Peace onto the white circle made by her sigh. Minli's curriculum used the story about Alaren and the shoes to teach people to imagine war from the other side of the conflict, literally encouraging people to stand in each other's shoes. He'd tried it on the orphans at Monk's Hand, but his real dream was to test it on a group of Marianan and Desert youth in the Border Mountains someday.

Wish we could study Minli's curriculum instead of the Art of War, Ari Ara thought wistfully, resigning herself to another

173

boring afternoon of battle history and reciting the chronology of war.

The clomp of heavy boots broke through her thoughts.

"Seats."

The growl of a voice snapped through the room with the expectation of immediate obedience. The nobles scurried for the benches. Ari Ara turned to look at who had entered.

"I said, seats!" the man barked.

He towered over her, dark hair tied back in the warriors' style, leather vest weathered and black with age and oil, heavy boots tied mid-calf. His face was crisscrossed with scars, his nose broken. Beside her, she sensed Emir tense.

"What part of that word did you not understand?" he snapped at her.

"Sir, she's - " Isa called out.

The warrior wheeled. Ari Ara glanced at the benches where the others sat with mixed expressions of apprehension and awe.

"Isa de Barre, can a war be won by stupidity and ignorance?" the man asked in a deadly voice.

"No, sir," she answered meekly, blushing.

"Precisely. If I were as idiotic as your comment presumed, I would not have won the War of Retribution," he spun away from Isa in disdain and glared at the redheaded girl by the window. "Take your seat, Ari Ara of the High Mountains."

Ari Ara scowled. Shulen had never described the most recent war against the Desert as won or lost - only tragic and foolish. She shrugged and moved to the spot between Isa and Korin.

"In this class," the man was saying, "your titles and family fortunes mean nothing. Regardless of rank, you will *think* before you speak and do as you are told."

"Who is he?" Ari Ara whispered to Korin.

"Rannor Thornmar," he breathed back. "Varina's uncle . . . he's a war hero, Commander of the First Army, and the Lord of the Orelands. I'd heard he was returning to the Capital, but I thought it was to train warriors, not us - "

"Silence!" the commander ordered.

Korin shut up and sat stiff at attention.

"As your new instructor in the Art of War, I have the daunting task of preparing you to lead armies, win battles, and triumph over our enemies," he stated, clasping his hands behind his back and glaring around the room. "I have single-handedly faced hordes of desert demons with more hope than I have now."

He strode through the rows of benches, examining them with disgust twisted on his lips.

"You are weak. You are ignorant. You are coddled little darlings," he told them scornfully. "Out there, the enemy waits. Every choice is life or death. There can be no mistakes. If you err, brave men will die because of you. I demand discipline, determination, and dedication."

The nobles sat up straighter. Their eyes gleamed in anticipation of the challenge. Ari Ara stifled a sigh. She'd seen this strange blend of fear and worship before . . . the orphans and trainees had held Shulen in such awe, mimicking his stances, watching his practices, emulating his every gesture.

"There are some," Thornmar hissed, his gaze skewering Ari Ara as he returned to the front of the class, "who think that a time of peace is at hand."

He pounded the edge of the Map Table with his fist. The students flinched.

"They are wrong. A desert demon is crafty, wily. He has no morals. He has no scruples. He will stab you when your back is turned, use children as trap-bait, slaughter his own people to gain an advantage, send his daughter out to fight and prey on our sympathy - do not be fooled."

Thornmar's eyes swept the room, hard and unrelenting. They pinned Ari Ara as he growled his next words.

"A desert child is as dangerous as a full-grown warrior. They have no conscience. I saw good men die, fathers and citizens, at the hand of a desert demon not much older than this one here."

The others gasped. He crossed the room and stood over Ari Ara. Emir turned taut as a drawn bowstring.

"Don't think for a moment that I don't know what you are," he warned her. "You have undermined the dignity of the noble class, threatened our economy with collapse, and allied with the desert demons."

A flurry of whispers swept the room.

"You are either an imposter," he accused, "or you are the heart of our enemy lurking among us, waiting to attack."

Ari Ara glared back, furious beyond words.

"I will stop you," he warned in a hiss, "even if no one else in Mariana has the courage."

Thornmar straightened up.

"Gather around the Map Table," he barked to the class.

Isa's hand clenched her arm, trembling. Ari Ara was shaking, too, but from anger, not fear. The nobles gave her wide berth, clustering around the other three sides of the table, jostling for positions close to Thornmar, shooting nervous glances in her direction. Emir didn't relent in his wariness, hovering just behind her with his eyes fixed on Thornmar.

Korin threw his arm over her shoulders.

"I must be braver than Mum thinks, hanging out with this *enemy*," he joked, rolling his eyes to show that Thornmar's words hadn't frightened him.

The commander's lips thinned into a tight white line.

"The Great Lady has led our nation without misstep for many years . . . let us hope she continues in her wisdom," he said dryly.

Then he launched into an overview of geography, testing their strategic knowledge of the Border Mountain passes, the terrain of battle, and the desert lands. He grilled Ari Ara on the thirteen noblelands, hoping to expose her ignorance in front of the class, but Minli had just drilled her on them and she rattled them off.

The House of Marin's Riverlands ran in a serpentine ribbon between the other twelve lands. The narrow strip of the Monklands curved along the winding Monk's Tears River. The Craftlands bordered it to the north, a countryside of craft halls joined together in councils, the noble descendants serving as their spokespersons to the other nobles. The Fertilelands spread wide above them, a quiet plain of farms and fields. The Loomlands boasted a sprawling set of factory and mill towns. The pine barons of the forested Timberlands lay to the north. Southwest of them sat the Stonelands and Smithlands, and then the East-West Road through the Westlands where the army outposts maintained constant vigilance over the Middle Pass. The Sisterlands to the south raised many of the nation's war orphans. Below them, the hills of the Riderlands held numerous tribes of horsemen, rovers who gathered every three years to elect a delegate to the Assembly of Nobles. At the very bottom of the Map Table, near the High Mountains, lay Isa de Barre's home of the Southlands.

As Thornmar glowered at her, annoyed that she knew the answer, and then went on with the lesson, detailing the fortresses, army posts, and guard stations. Ari Ara began to wonder what lay beyond the edges of the Map Table, particularly to the west in the Desert lands. Beyond the first sliver of land next to the mountains, the Map Table was vague. The Desert People guarded their secrets fiercely and repelled invaders with swift determination. Ari Ara thought it was a shame that the wars had stopped the exchange of knowledge and learning. Maybe when she was confirmed, she could help change that. After all, peace could open doors that war had slammed shut.

Thornmar startled her with a growled comment that sent a cheer through the rest of the class. The young nobles leapt up with excitement as Ari Ara tried to figure out what she had missed. Thornmar pulled out a stack of painted boards - sections of the Map Table - and ordered them to pair up in teams of two, groups of four. With a look from Korin, Isa grabbed Ari Ara and Korin snagged a friend to make a fourth. Korin lined up to get a small box from the stacks on the shelves. Isa placed the board on one of the benches and whispered to Ari Ara that this was the Attar Game. The old instructor hadn't believed in letting them play it until they had memorized a thousand years of battle history. Korin removed the cover of the box. Inside were dozens of pieces with Marianan blue and Desert red symbols on them.

"Archers, warriors, soldiers, horsemen," Korin listed as he pulled each out and sorted them.

His friend picked up two and hid them in his fist for Isa to pick sides. She chose the red, putting the boys on Mariana's side.

"Today, you are low commanders," Thornmar instructed, "each seeking to win a limited victory over the enemy in your section of terrain."

He paced through the groups, hands clasped behind his back, listening to the discussions on how to lay out the pieces.

Each box contained a different mix and after each game, the pieces were jumbled together and scooped into new configurations for the next round.

Ari Ara held up a pair of white tiles with clouds and yellow lightning bolts painted on them.

"Weather pieces," Korin explained. "They have different symbols for heat waves, forest fires, snows, rains, floods, mud, and more. These are thunderstorms, leading to muddy slopes, delayed supply trains, low visibility, poor morale, and potential sickness."

As Korin and his friend conferred in low tones about the use of their troops, Isa set down a spy piece and claimed the right to adjust her plans according to Korin's. The boys had no spy information and had to remain with their first choices until the game began.

"We have plenty of horsemen - the Desert always does - but those mountainous slopes make them vulnerable. Wish we had more archers," Isa complained.

Ari Ara listened with a queasy sensation. Isa's voice was as calm and pragmatic as when they discussed the Art of Dress - but this wasn't clothes, this was war! Up until now, the dry professor had taught as dully as the dust that shook off the books he carried. Commander Thornmar's style of teaching evoked the screams and war cries of the battlefield. It thrilled the others; it made her sick.

Korin gestured impatiently for Isa to stop rearranging the horses.

"Get on with it," he said. "Desert always attacks first."

Ari Ara's face turned stony at the rule. She watched as the battle began. Isa loosed her archers onto Korin's leading soldiers - a set of marks on the edge of the piece determined the strength of their aim. Korin cleared a third of his front soldiers off the board and into the box while his friend set his archers on the opposite slope to take out Isa's. He picked out a few, but her terrain had piles of rocks to hide behind. That strategy slowed her assault slightly, but protected her precious archers. She sent a team of horsemen in and out like sword thrusts along the ravine bottom, drawing the opposing army into a more open spot where she could use her horses to the best advantage.

As the pieces piled up in the box, Ari Ara saw them for what they represented: mangled bodies on a battlefield, lives lost, children orphaned. She closed her eyes against tears, then swallowed and glanced around the room. The young nobles of the Academy bent over the boards, faces eager. Small cheers and groans shot out. Partners conferred in whispers. It was clear they saw the Attar Game as just that: a game. Ari Ara saw the blood and gore of a raging battlefield, endangered loved ones, and her two families slaughtering each other.

"What is the point of this?" she exclaimed, frustrated.

Korin looked up in concern.

"It's just a game, Ari Ara," he said soothingly.

"No, it's not," she argued back, scooping up a handful of pieces from the box and holding them in a trembling palm. "It's training for war. You'll be doing this same thing over Brinelle's Map Table in the war room someday . . . but it won't be little wooden pieces you throw in a box - it will be bodies thrown in graves."

"Exactly," Thornmar growled, crossing to them as the room fell quiet at her outburst. "So study hard. Kill them before they kill us."

"Or find out how to stop the war," Ari Ara retorted, pointing at the board. "Why is it happening in the first place? How can the problems be addressed? What would prevent each side from using violence to try to get what they want?"

Those were Alaren's questions from the *Stories of the Third Brother* and the discussion points in Minli's curriculum. The answers contained solutions that could save thousands of lives. There was no point in studying the bits and pieces of battles if there was a different way to address the issues that led people toward war.

"Your task is to win this battle," Thornmar stated coldly. "You are a low commander, not a queen."

His tone sent shivers down her spine. She straightened it stubbornly.

"But wouldn't ending the war count as a win?" she challenged.

"In the Attar Game," Korin answered in a worried voice, his eyes leaping from his cousin to Thornmar, "you have to send the enemy into retreat, take the territory, or have more soldiers standing than they do at the end."

"But those aren't the only options," Ari Ara countered. "They could stop fighting, make a truce, or work together to solve their differences."

"Your place is not to question, but to obey and learn," Thornmar thundered, his eyes hard.

Ari Ara bit her lower lip and took a breath. That would be true if she were just a noble - even if she were just the Lost Heir - but Alaren's spirit had told her to bring back the Way Between. She had to stand up for its principles, especially in the Art of War.

"It is always our place to question war," she answered back, ignoring Isa's warning nudge, "to challenge the reasons violence happens and to seek to end it."

Thornmar towered over her, cold and uncompromising.

"I do not tolerate insubordination from anyone, not even from the would-be heir."

"If the Young Queen doesn't have the courage to challenge the military, who will?" Ari Ara flung back.

"You are not the queen," Thornmar corrected sternly. "Not yet. Until the day you are confirmed, you are merely an impudent imposter in my eyes."

Then he spun away, snapping at the rest of the class to get their eyes on their Attar Boards where they belonged.

CHAPTER SIXTEEN

. . . . .

Azar vs. Attar

A cold, hard-edged blue sky had shoved the clouds aside by the time classes let out. Ari Ara's temper snapped and fizzled under her stony face as she, Emir, and Korin crossed through the gates of the Nobles Academy. Shulen waited for them at the entryway of the House of Marin. His gaze leapt to the stubborn set of Ari Ara's jaw and he steeled himself for a troubling report.

"What happened?" he asked as they neared.

"Commander Thornmar practically cut her beating desert heart out and threw it on the floor," Emir answered with disgust, stalking across the flagstones.

"What was Commander Thornmar doing at the Academy?" Shulen asked with a frown.

"He's the new Art of War instructor," Ari Ara answered sullenly.

"Thornmar?!" Shulen spat in shock. He picked up his pace. "Come with me. We must speak with the Great Lady at once."

Shulen tracked her down in her study, dragging Ari Ara and Emir behind him. The Great Lady looked up from the stack of reports; riots and fighting had broken out in the Loomlands between water workers and jobless millworkers. She ran her hand over her face, troubled. A crash of cold wind rattled the panes in the windows. The bare-branched trees across the river shivered.

"Did you know Rannor Thornmar is the new Art of War instructor?" Shulen cut in with an unusual abruptness.

Emir and Ari Ara exchanged glances at the bitter venom in Shulen's tone and quietly slipped over to a bench along the wall.

"I know," Brinelle replied, rubbing her temples. "There's nothing I can do. The Headmistress invited him and I have no authority over the Nobles Academy."

"You're the political commander of the army," Shulen pointed out. "Send him back to the front."

"I can't," Brinelle objected with a frustrated sigh. "You know Thornmar, he'll start a war if there isn't one underway. I need him as far from the border as possible. Even the Orelands are too close."

"So you want him here, teaching her?" Shulen snapped back, pointing at Ari Ara.

"At least I can keep an eye on him here," Brinelle said curtly.

"You know why he's come back," Shulen objected. "He's trying to finish what his niece started with that ill-planned knife throw at the University."

"Varina?" Ari Ara blurted out, shocked. She knew the noblegirl detested her, but to plan her murder? She gaped at the others.

Brinelle shot Shulen an annoyed look before turning to Emir and Ari Ara.

"Not a word from either of you."

"You can't just let her get away with this!" Ari Ara objected.

"She won't," Brinelle promised grimly. "I'll bring evidence against her after the confirmation hearing. Then, her attack will be judged as treason against the Heir to Two Thrones, not just a would-be heir. Until then, the last thing I need is a nobles' feud."

"You already have one," Shulen commented darkly.

"No," Brinelle countered, "what I have right now is widespread sympathy for Alinore's daughter who was nearly murdered - like her mother - for standing up for peace."

It was an ideal situation in Brinelle's estimation. She wouldn't risk ruining it by calling out the treachery of the House of Thorn. Commander Thornmar was as much of a war hero as Shulen. She couldn't afford to antagonize his faction.

"He will sabotage her chances of confirmation at every turn," Shulen warned, pacing the length of the room in frustration.

"I will not let him succeed," the Great Lady declared stoutly.

Shulen stilled and held her gaze.

"I hope you know what you are doing," he said softly.

"I do, Shulen. Trust me," Brinelle replied, inwardly hoping it was true.

"And if he murders her in class?" Shulen asked, pointing at Ari Ara.

"He won't," Brinelle said firmly, turning back to her work and dismissing them.

"How can she know?" Ari Ara asked Emir as they followed Shulen out the door.

"It's Thornmar," the youth answered with a scowl. "He'll wait until no one's looking then he'll stab you in the back."

Shulen told her to change into practice clothes and meet him and Emir in the walled courtyard on the north end of the house.

"If I can't get rid of Thornmar," Shulen grumbled, "I'll have to train you to survive him."

She obeyed swiftly, racing back to her rooms to change. Curiosity quickened her steps as she hurried through the corridors to the walled garden. High stone walls closed the garden off from view. No windows overlooked it from the buildings. Only the Hawk's Keep rose tall enough to look down into the enclosure. She ducked under the boughs of the tall willow writhing its bare braches in the wind. Beneath it, a shingled-roofed meditation hut overlooked an open, sandy area. Shrubs clung to the edges of the narrow garden beds. An old twisted pine stood in one corner. Brown, frostbitten moss clung to the cracks of the stone walkways.

"This is where Brinelle trains," Emir whispered to her as she joined him on the sands.

And the water workers, Ari Ara added silently, remembering what she had seen from the Hawk's Keep.

Shulen told them to stretch and warm up, his face drawn with memories, dark as the clouds overhead. In a hushed tone, Ari Ara asked Emir about the bad blood between Shulen and Thornmar. Emir pulled her to the far end of the garden and told her the history in snatches of words. Both youths cast nervous glances at Shulen, who stared moodily at the old pine as if he could read the book of his past in its twisting, wind-tossed boughs.

"Back in the day," Emir murmured, "Thornmar and Shulen were better friends than Korin and me."

As youths, the two warriors had trained together in the Yards, vying for the title of champion in the annual Spring Trials. Thornmar had visions of glory on the battlefield and dreamed of fighting back-to-back with his skilled friend, but

Shulen was tapped to serve in Queen Elsinore's Royal Guard and Thornmar was sent to the Academy with the nobles. The year Rhianne came down from the High Mountains, the frayed threads of their connection broke. Shulen fell in love with Rhianne and her influence revived the dormant seeds of the Way Between in his heart. He grew more interested in peace than war, love than hate, and the vision of a family than glory on the battlefield. When he and Thornmar faced off in the Spring Trials, Shulen beat him using the Way Between. Afterward, Thornmar confronted Shulen, furious that he had withheld these skills, but there was nothing Shulen could say: in those days, the Way Between had been a sworn secret of his family.

After their falling out, Thornmar's obsession with the Art of War strengthened. He poured his competitive thrust into the Attar Game, rising through the ranks of war strategists. When Queen Alinore died and it was thought that the Desert People had stolen the heir, Thornmar served as War Commander to the Great Lady in the War of Retribution.

"During the war," Emir murmured, "Thornmar's older brother Soldek - Varina's father - gave the order to attack a village of unarmed women and children. Shulen tried to stop the massacre."

"What?!" she yelped.

Emir shushed her as the stern man glanced in their direction. Ari Ara pictured one man against hundreds of warriors, frightened women and children behind him.

"Shulen invoked an ancient law," Emir whispered, "that says you can use a one-on-one match to settle a dispute and challenged Soldek and Rannor Thornmar."

"He lost?" Ari Ara breathed.

Emir shook his head.

"He won, but Thornmar and his brother broke their word. Their warriors overpowered Shulen and bound him as they massacred the village. Later, they tried to say he was a traitor who attempted to murder his commander, but it wasn't like that. Shulen never even used Attar. He won the challenge using only Azar."

"How do you know?" Ari Ara asked Emir.

The youth's dark eyes met hers.

"I was there."

"But you must have been - "

"Just a boy," he answered.

Emir had met Shulen as the warriors passed through the mountain village where he was born. Trailing after the warrior like a loyal puppy, he ran away with the army when it decamped. Shulen sent him back - he was only six - but he returned. Emir was put to work cleaning armor and helping the cooks, but he soon snuck into trainings to learn the skills of warriors.

Emir stopped talking as Shulen crossed the sands and stood close, speaking in a low voice.

"At the Capital University," Shulen said, looking at the two youths, "we showed the students a small demonstration of the uses of Azar against Attar. What we began as a demonstration, we shall now practice in earnest."

Emir and Ari Ara listened solemnly, struck by the seriousness of Shulen's tone.

"In Azar, you initiate by holding your center," Shulen told them, taking a calm, solid stance. "You stand between a person and their intention to cause harm, and offer them another way."

"But we can't just stand around waiting when harm's being done," Ari Ara objected.

"Trust me," Shulen replied knowingly, his eyes alight with

experience, "so long as your stance is correct, those who defend their injustices with Attar will attack you if you stand between them and their goals."

He gestured for Emir to demonstrate.

"Let's say your objective is to seize the Young Queen," Shulen told him, motioning for Ari Ara to stand behind him. "My task is to stop you."

Emir bolted into action. Shulen turned his attack aside, calmly, leisurely, like a cow swatting a fly with her tail. Emir circled. Shulen shifted position, calling out: *stance, stance!* Each time he slid between Emir and his target, he used the momentum of the youth's attacks to carry the boy further from his goal, flinging him across the sands, tumbling him in a new direction. Shulen moved effortlessly. By the time he called a halt, sweat beaded on Emir's brow, but the old warrior appeared as unruffled as when he stood guard, still and silent, during the Great Lady's formal banquets.

"Your stance is the starting point of Azar," he told them. "It is fluid, not static, and the banks of its river are justice and compassion. Those are the guiding principles. You find your Way Between two sides of a conflict by refusing to allow harm - *justice* - and refusing to do harm - *compassion*."

Ari Ara spoke up, twisting her face up over a memory of something Thornmar had said in class.

"In Attar," she repeated, "you bait, lure, and rile your enemy into attacking - "

" - when your strength is superior," Emir added, "or when you need to whittle down the enemy's forces through skirmishes, or when you need to draw the enemy into a trap."

Shulen shook his head.

"In Azar, you never need to trick your enemy. You don't even see enemies, merely humans in conflict, people in opposition to each other's views or goals."

Emir shot his teacher a doubtful look.

"It'd be hard to remember that on a battlefield," he confessed.

The old warrior sighed.

"When you live through as many battles as I have, it is sometimes all too easy."

There were two kinds of warriors, he told them quietly, the kind whose experiences broke their hearts and showed them that war was folly; and another kind whose hearts hardened into impenetrable armor as the world became a battlefield with enemies all around.

"That's Thornmar," Ari Ara gasped, recognizing the description.

"That was me, too," Shulen warned her. He had teetered on a knife's edge of the two paths, hardening his heart to keep it from breaking. In the end, it crumbled and his river of sorrow would have drowned him if not for the channel of the Way Between. For years, his secret study of waging peace sustained him through the nightmare of war. After Rhianne had been murdered, he allowed the mad fury of his grief and rage to carry him blindly into the War of Retribution. If not for Emir's arrival in his life, he suspected he would be dead, driven to madness on the battlefield. The boy, however, needed him to survive, to return each day, and to get up in the morning. He took Emir Miresh under his wing and trained him to be a Royal Guard, introducing him to the Way Between, and raising him like the son he would never have.

"Practice seeing people who oppose you as humans," Shulen instructed them, "and your heart will neither harden nor break, but will grow stronger than all the warriors in the world."

Then he set them to work, practicing their stances, showing

them firmness within fluidity and focused clarity in the midst of chaos. He drilled them on the ways to turn aside an attacker while holding one's position. He demonstrated how to maintain one's inner principles while adapting to an outer situation. He watched his two apprentices carefully as they practiced: Emir had to work on his flexibility - the girl's inventiveness kept catching him by surprise - but her temper flared along with her passion and her impatience weakened her.

"Don't give chase," Shulen warned Ari Ara. "Let his imbalance bring him to you."

"But what if he doesn't act?" she complained.

"He will," Shulen said with certainty. He had given Emir the goal of capturing a flag she was supposed to defend. "Until he releases his goal, he will always need to attack."

"I should get him to release it then," Ari Ara pointed out, "or we'll both be at this until we're dead."

Shulen chuckled.

"Very insightful, but I would call you off for dinner."

By the time Shulen stopped the match, both Ari Ara and Emir were breathless and tired. The slanted sunrays of evening pierced the top needles of the pine tree. The sunset turned the cold blue of the sky into a wash of reds and purples. Ari Ara's heart felt like the air, fresh and clean. She listened contentedly as Shulen explained that drills like this built both philosophic and practical skills for thwarting Attar with Azar.

"What about Anar?" Ari Ara asked, naming the third path, the Gentle Way.

Shulen smiled.

"What do you think?" he tested her.

Ari Ara frowned in thought. Anar avoided direct confrontation, retreating and circling, delaying and stalling. It was not aggressively violent - not in the way Attar was - but grave injustices occurred through Anar's avoidance of conflict. Shulen had told her once that followers of Azar and Attar could be found throughout Mariana and the Desert, while the elusive Fanten practiced Anar exclusively, retreating into the mists and refusing to get involved with the lowlanders' disputes even when they could have stopped the wars.

"You have to block Anar's retreat," Ari Ara said slowly, realizing another facet of the Way Between. "You have to choose your stance in a position that refuses to let the followers of Anar avoid dealing with the problem."

Her eyes shone as a surge of understanding opened up a new landscape of possibilities.

"Think on that," Shulen encouraged her with a chuckle. "We'll put the theory to the test tomorrow."

As he sent Emir off to the warriors' hall for dinner, Shulen held Ari Ara back.

"I want you to guard your tongue in Thornmar's class," he told her. "He - and all followers of Attar - will try to provoke you, to goad you into fighting. Do not be trapped. Use your inner and verbal Azar."

"Do I really have to study the Art of War?" she groaned. "I hate it. It's barbaric."

"You don't have to like it to learn it," Shulen told her. "If you wish to stop wars, you should know the thinking that gives rise to them."

Ari Ara sighed, but nodded in agreement. Shulen clapped her on the back and as they walked across the garden, the sun dove into the western mountains, flooding the dwindling day with gold. From the old twisted pine, a songbird sang out, hopeful despite the chill of winter.

CHAPTER SEVENTEEN

· · · · ·

Desert Speech

When she returned to her quarters, stiff and cold as the heat of practice cooled in her muscles, an anxious Malak waited for her, pacing the corridor outside her door. He handed her a letter from the Desert King. Then he paused, tilting his head at the guard by the door.

"Come in," Ari Ara said, guessing he wanted to say something. "I'll give you a reply letter."

No sooner had she shut the door then words burst out of him.

"I heard Rannor Thornmar is your instructor," Malak spat out. His jaw clenched beneath his black beard. "You must be very careful. He is dangerous. He has no *harrak*."

The word rang on the air, sharp and strong. A hint of bright desert light and scouring sands clung to the edges of the sound.

"What's that?" Ari Ara asked, edging closer to the crackling warmth of the fireplace to stretch her chilled fingers out toward the flames.

"Harrak?" he answered, stunned. "You don't know what harrak is? Hasn't the Great Lady taught you anything about my people?"

He snapped with an unexpected anger. Ari Ara winced at its ferocity.

"How dare she?" Malak growled, pacing the room. "These river dogs invade my country, kill my people, hide . . . hide our heir . . . and the Great Lady did not even have the decency to tell you our true name?"

"I'm sorry," Ari Ara whispered, taken aback by the outburst.

The fire extinguished in the Hawk Keeper's eyes.

"Don't be, *betta*," he answered, adding an endearment in his own language. "I am not mad at you. It is not your fault that you do not know your father's language."

"Perhaps you could teach me," Ari Ara suggested. "I'd like to learn."

Malak stared at her with a strange, sorrowful expression. His hand fell on her shoulder. He swallowed and nodded.

"It would be an honor," he answered. "I am a fool for not thinking of this months ago."

He pulled a pair of armchairs closer to the fire and sat down, gesturing for her to join him.

"The first word you must learn is *harrak*. It means honor," he told her, lacing his fingers together and leaning forward to place his elbows on his knees.

She repeated the word, but he shook his head.

"*Harrak!*" he said, rolling the r's and clacking the ending sharply across his tongue. He shone with ferocious pride, eyes fierce and blazing. "In our language, the sound and the spirit of the word must be spoken together. You must understand the meaning deeply in your marrow."

Harrak was a word of blood and bone, wind and sand. It

was the mineral and cultural integrity of the Desert. When they had nothing else, they had harrak. In times of famine, they gave the food to the children and lived on harrak alone. Facing hardship, they endured while their harrak burned as bright as a night-blazing fire. It was a way of life, a quality that meant survival through periods of drought and war.

"We are not a people of great riches," Malak remarked, gesturing to the opulence of Mariana Capital. "Hoarding jewels and silks while even one of our children hungers or thirsts diminishes our harrak. Our harrak - honor, dignity, integrity - is the true wealth of our people. All other riches can be stolen by thieves, but one's harrak cannot be taken away by others, only squandered through one's own folly."

Ari Ara thought about the Desert People she had met and seen throughout the Capital. Despite their lowly status as bonded workers, they held themselves tall and proud. When they bowed, it was with a dignity that had puzzled her, serving without being servile.

"Ah," Malak grinned when she asked, "that is harrak at work. The water worker does not see his master as his superior, but as a friend who has gone awry, one who has forgotten the basic truth of our equality and must be reminded of it."

Ari Ara wrinkled her brow.

"Then why do you put up with the Water Exchange? Why not confront the Marianans directly?"

"They did not see us as human," Malak said flatly, "so we have spent six years among them, attempting to show them that we are. As enemies on the battlefield, we could never do that. As embittered foes, we have had few opportunities to have our peoples meet face-to-face. The Water Exchange came about for terrible reasons, but we have used it to remind our brothers and sisters in the riverlands that we in the drylands are as human as they."

In the Desert, the people who became water workers were viewed as courageous protectors of families, people willing to sacrifice everything to save their family's lives. It was a fearsome prospect and so it was honored as an act of great fealty, a way of showing the highest love for one's family.

"That is why we act with dignity, no matter how the Marianans try to degrade us," Malak said.

To enter the land of rivers and live among the enemy in service of the people was considered a task worthy of a warrior. And for years, every water worker had also been a searcher for the Desert King, a pair of living eyes and ears scouring Mariana for a child who resembled Tahkan Shirar.

"We knew our heir was here somewhere," Malak told her gravely. "The Water Exchange gave us a chance to enter these lands to look for the child."

"But now that I'm found . . . " Ari Ara asked, trailing off suggestively.

"We will continue to watch over Tahkan Shirar's daughter and serve our people as eyes and ears among our enemy."

Ari Ara sat back, stunned, remembering what she had overheard on the night of the Urchins' Feast when Shulen had cautioned Malak not to unravel all the careful work that his people had done. The Desert King had hidden thousands of spies in plain sight. Every single water worker stood ready to do the king's command. He had placed an army inside the heart of Mariana . . . and during the years of rising dangers he had chosen not to unleash its force. She shivered. Malak saw.

"They will do no harm," he assured her. "We have no need to rise up, and far more to gain from watching, working, and waiting."

"But wouldn't you rather be free?" she asked.

"Ah," Malak reminded her, "it is a short-lived freedom if we do not get water for our crops and herds. We will endure through our harrak until the time is right for change."

There was more.

"Harrak," the desert man said softly, studying his worn hands, "is so integrally connected to the ways of our people that it is our name as well."

He glanced to the west, as if looking out to his distant burning lands.

"The Marianans call us the Desert People, but we call ourselves the *Harraken*, the People of Honor, Dignity, and Integrity."

Ari Ara watched the firelight bring a touch of sunset into the black twists of his beard, illuminating red undertones like a crackling ember. Honor and dignity were all a man of harrak had, the only possessions he needed. Ari Ara could see the Hawk Keeper was rich in these treasures, brimming with their strength and fire.

"Harrak," she murmured, practicing the rolling r's and clacking sounds. "Harrak."

The Harraken man shook his head, his lips pressing into a thin smile.

"You must feel the spirit of the word in your heart," he reminded her, "not just make the sounds with your lips. Tongue and teeth alone cannot make our language sing. Every word has spirit. Every sentence invokes it. We are a people of silence and intention. When we curse, it sticks. When we bless, it shines upon the person. That is why we must master our hot tempers early; our words have great power."

In Mariana, language poured like a river, rose like the fog, and showered like rain through every aspect of life. The streets brimmed with chatter. Gossip flowed and eddied. In the Desert, however, language was used with care. From words grew reality; the world could be changed by a song.

Ari Ara tried to wrap her mind around it, but it sounded like a winter's tale to her. The Desert was a world of wind, light, and sand, Malak explained. The workings of Desert Speech were wrought of poetry and sun. Magic clung to them. The desert language was an incantation, a weaving of realities. Few Marianans spoke even the outward sounds of Harrak-tala, Desert Speech, let alone the true spirit of the words. One could not tell lies in Harrak-tala, and the words one spoke often came true.

Ari Ara asked him the word for father, since she was about to write to the Desert King.

"Affanta, or Affa, as the small children say," Malak told her softly. Then, he fell silent, his taut skin stretching across high cheekbones and deepening into furrows of wrinkles by his eyes and mouth.

Ari Ara thought of the father she had never met. The word had little meaning to her, a hollow sound with no experience to back it up. She thought of Shulen, his patient teachings and stern rebukes. She remembered him carrying her back from the river after an exhausting test in Azar, and the sense of trust she had felt.

"Affanta," she murmured.

Malak jolted as if stung.

"Again!" he cried.

Ari Ara thought of the Desert King and the longing all orphans feel for family, the trepidation of finding it, the wild hope of being welcomed into a family, and the utter terror of rejection.

"Affanta," she repeated. The spirit of the word rippled

through the room, thickening the air with the energy-sparks of its presence. A shiver ran through Malak.

"Try mother, Ammanta," he whispered.

Ari Ara tried it, but the word remained empty. She thought of Mahteni, Brinelle, the Fanten Grandmother . . . nothing. She imagined Alinore, nothing. She desperately invoked the secret wishes in her head, nothing. She thought of the night in the High Mountains when Shulen had battled ghosts and, in her terror, she had shot a plea for her dead mother's protection.

"Ammanta," she said.

A tiny ripple shivered in the air; perhaps the spirit of the word, perhaps nothing more than a slight draft. Malak sighed and patted her shoulder.

"It is difficult to speak what you have never known," he stated. "A child who cannot remember rain cannot invoke its spirit."

"When I said father, it worked," she protested.

"Shulen," Malak sagely and sorrowfully, "must have given you a sense of the word. The Desert King is in his debt for that."

A thought shot through Ari Ara.

"What's the word for king?"

"*Harrak-Mettahl,*" Malak told her.

Concentrating on the concept, she spoke the word. Nothing happened. Malak chuckled.

"Are you thinking of a Harraken counterpart to the Great Lady, perhaps?" he guessed in a teasing note.

Ari Ara flushed.

"Our king is not the same as the word means here," Malak told her with a short laugh. "The Harrak-Mettahl is not a ruler like the Great Lady or Queen Alinore. Though he is widely respected and almost always listened to, the Marianans have no parallel concept. For convenience, we allow them to translate the word as king. It is simpler that way. They know what to do with a king. They cannot handle a Harrak-Mettahl."

A grin twitched under his beard.

"I will give you a hint and see if you can guess the true meaning," he told her. "Here, I am what we would call a Kyreeah-Mettahl."

Her eyes widened. The word *kyreeah* sounded like the cry of a swooping hawk and Malak nodded approvingly when she guessed the meaning.

"You're a hawk keeper, so a *mettahl* must be a keeper. Harrak is honor, so a harrak-mettahl is an honor keeper," she exclaimed in a burst of understanding. "That's what Tahkan Shirar is?"

Malak beamed. The Harrak-Mettahl was one who tended to the Harraken, the one who kept their honor and preserved their dignity and integrity.

"Tahkan Shirar is a descendant of Shirar," Malak told her. "His duty is to tend the Harraken as I watch these hawks, giving them food, water, shelter, healing, comfort, and training. He guides the people in maintaining our harrak and keeps our culture strong. Where the Great Lady rules, the Harrak-Mettahl serves. He is obeyed only if his suggestions maintain the people's honor."

"And, as his daughter, will I also carry that responsibility?" she dared to ask, a little overwhelmed.

"Perhaps, if you earn it," Malak replied softly, "but you must learn the ways of the Harraken, only then will the people accept you as the Harrak-Mettahl."

CHAPTER EIGHTEEN

. . . . .

Harrak

Harrak. The word echoed in her mind and straightened her spine. She thought about it as she watched the water workers from the corners of her eyes. She murmured it under her breath when she was annoyed with the subtle slights of the nobles. She gritted her teeth and clung to harrak when the noble youths whispered nasty gossip about her just loud enough to overhear. Thornmar's goading sneers continued. Varina's prickly jabs annoyed her so much that sometimes only her promise to Shulen kept her from bursting out in anger and frustration. The entire House of Thorn - all sixteen cousins, seven aunts, nine uncles, and uncountable in-laws and extended relations - seemed determined to sting her to death with a thousand barbs of insults. Shulen warned her that they were trying to find an excuse to deny her the confirmation. This made her stubbornly determined to succeed, if only to spite them.

The Art of War classes turned into an ongoing verbal sparring match. Every class, Thornmar tried to find an excuse to kick her out. Every class, she tried to use the Way Between to de-escalate the tension and remain. He growled at her for being lost in thought as she studied the Attar Board. He bit her head off for sneezing. He mocked her as ignorant for asking questions. Her answers, when called upon, were always wrong even when they were right. The others knew it wasn't fair, but few dared to stand up for her. Challenging the bristling Thornmar was like holding up a blade of grass against Attar personified. You'd be skewered before you stammered out your first words. She clung to her sense of harrak and tried to use the Way Between to survive.

Each time Malak delivered a letter, he taught her new words in Harrak-tala, the Desert Speech. Each time she dropped off a reply, he shared a new lesson in harrak.

"Your harrak cannot be diminished by others," Malak told her, "only by your own actions."

So, she lifted her head with the quiet dignity she saw in the water workers and refused to be goaded into anger. She learned that one's harrak was strengthened by treating others with respect, honoring the dignity of those around you, and reminding others of their integrity.

"That is why the Harrak-Mettahl is an honored position," Malak explained, "because he or she lifts up the harrak of others and calls us all back to what is right when we have lost our way."

She intervened when she saw the water workers being mistreated, telling the staff of the Academy and the House of Marin that beating a water worker for breaking a vase or forgetting a task diminished the honor of the beater, not the other way around. Korin overheard her arguing with Brinelle over the water workers' right to warm winter clothes and fuel for the fireplaces in their quarters. Surprisingly, he leapt in and took the side of harrak.

"She's right, Mum," he said with a look of distaste on his

face. "It looks bad on us if the water workers are mistreated, like we're stingy or cruel or something. The House of Marin is better than that. You ought to add a section to the contracts on the rights of water workers."

"Can she do that?" Ari Ara asked Korin later.

He shrugged.

"I don't see why not. The water workers are all wards of the House of Marin, technically. We write the contracts."

Ari Ara frowned.

"What do you mean?"

"The Water Exchange was negotiated between the heads of state midway through the War of Retribution," Korin explained. "The water workers are contracted directly between the Desert King and Mum. They sign up with him, and she holds them accountable to the conditions of their contracts using the Watch and our warriors. The water workers are all subcontracted from us to the dressiers, factories, noblehouses, or whoever uses them. It's a pretty lucrative situation for the House of Marin, as they all pay us a fee for the labor."

"Honor is more important than money," Ari Ara grumbled.

"Tell that to Mum," Korin suggested. "She sets the terms of the Water Exchange . . . on your behalf, actually."

"What?!" Ari Ara yelped, appalled.

"As regent, she acts in your stead," Korin pointed out.

"Then she can end the Water Exchange in my stead," Ari Ara argued.

"Not until you're confirmed," he reminded her.

Fine, Ari Ara noted silently, *the first thing I'll do after the confirmation is end it.* Improving the lives of the water workers was a decent thing to do, but until the water flowed freely into the Desert, she would always feel a sense of shame that one part of her family was exploiting the other. Malak had told her that

203

the hardest task of the Harrak-Mettahl was standing up to a friend, loved one, or family member when they were acting without honor. Ari Ara knew the feeling.

"The hardest and most loving thing we can do," Malak explained to her, "is to remind a beloved of his or her integrity when they have gone astray and behaved unjustly. Ask your father about it in your next letter. He has many stories to tell."

The Desert King wrote back swiftly to her questions.

There are two parts to my responsibilities, he wrote in his fine, decisive script. *The first is to teach my people to refuse to cooperate with anything demeaning or humiliating. The second is to refuse to demean or humiliate others. The second is, by far, the more difficult task.*

No one liked to be bullied, but Ari Ara knew from personal experience that some people found pleasure and power in lowering the dignity of others. Some, like Brol, the bully she'd encountered at Monk's Hand Monastery, thought that the only way to feel strong and powerful was to make others seem weak and powerless. Ari Ara disagreed. Helping others find their strength made everyone stronger together, a philosophy the Desert King shared. He was often called upon to visit people throughout the desert lands and remind them of harrak.

In the Desert, Tahkan Shirar told her, *it is the job of the Harrak-Mettahl to confront abusive leaders or bullying village lads. It is a powerful experience when the Harrak-Mettahl himself arrives in a boy's village and takes him for a walk. We do not punish the boy with beatings. Instead, I ask him: who is the most powerful man among the Harraken? You, he will say, for that is the truth. And then I ask him: what does the Harrak-Mettahl do? He lifts up the honor and dignity of others, the boy will reply. Now you know my secret, I tell him: treat everyone with dignity, raise the honor of everyone by acting honorably yourself, and build strength by strengthening others. That is the path of harrak; the way of being that maintains your own inner integrity.*

Ari Ara compared these ideas to what she knew of the Way Between and decided that Azar could be used to maintain harrak for one's self and for others. The Desert King wrote that they had stories and songs about Alaren and the Way Between. For her sake, he would ask his people to gather and resurrect them from the fading memories of the elders.

One morning, she heard voices arguing just outside her door. Mahteni was running late, and Ari Ara was hoping she could get out of going to her morning class due to having nothing to wear . . . an unlikely excuse, but she couldn't help but hope.

"Give her this and tell her that the Desert King wishes her to have it," a man's voice - Malak - was insisting.

"No, are you mad? That sash is too dangerous," Mahteni protested.

"Oh come, queens make rules, not bend to them," he answered with a hint of laughter and challenge in his tone.

"You're risking everything," Mahteni scolded in a fierce hush of a reprimand as she shouldered through the door.

Ari Ara waved to Malak, who winked as Mahteni shut the door on him.

"That man," she sighed, shaking her head and shoving a length of fabric in her apron pocket. She handed a set of garments to Ari Ara: a white blouse that tucked into dark pants and a short black jacket with embroidered cuffs. As Mahteni reached for the wide belt that went with it, the delicate gold silk fluttered out.

"What's this?" Ari Ara asked, fingers darting to catch the cloth.

"Nothing - "

Mahteni broke off as Ari Ara pulled the length free. Wonder flooded her face. A dark green pattern of ink was scrawled in long lines, interwoven with vines and tiny flowers.

"Do you like it?" Mahteni asked softly. "Malak says your father sent it."

Ari Ara nodded.

Mahteni hesitated for a moment. Then she nodded decisively and took the silk sash from the girl. She wrapped it around Ari Ara's waist, pulled it tight with a folding knot, and let the tasseled end hang down. She adjusted a fold and spun Ari Ara to the mirror, braiding and pinning up her red hair in a desert style that would appear charmingly unique to the Marianan nobles, and achingly familiar to Mahteni's people. It was the style of their daughters, as traditional as the songs with which their mothers rocked the children to sleep.

"You may run into some trouble over this," Mahteni murmured, looking at the girl in the mirror.

"I'll wear it anyway... for harrak," Ari Ara answered proudly.

The copper-haired seamstress flicked her fingers to the wind as a shiver of strange emotions ran under her skin. A blend of awe, hope, and trepidation tingled through her. Never before had she seen a Marianan speak the spirit of their words, never before had a child of the land of rivers stood shimmering with the intensity of harrak.

"Harrak en harrak," Mahteni whispered. "The honor in me recognizes the honor in you."

The desert woman could see Tahkan Shirar's blood in the proud lift of the girl's chin, the flash of fire and light in her eyes, and the way she stood with dignity in the garments of her father's people.

"This sash," she told the girl, "has a song inked into the silk

206

and, in the Desert, these are worn for important gatherings. Each family cherishes these song-sashes; they tell the stories of their ancestors."

"What is this story?" Ari Ara asked, fingering the material.

"It's - "

Korin burst in without knocking, interrupting whatever the desert woman was about to say.

"Aren't you ready yet? Emir's waiting by the gate and we're going to be late."

He didn't wait for her answer, but grabbed her by the hand so fast she barely had time to cram her feet into a pair of comfortable boots. Emir broke into a half-jog after them as Korin pulled her down the corridors. They were out the door and crossing the stone street before Korin slowed.

"Thanks," he said breathlessly. "Mum was about to find out where her book on *The Making of a Royal Heir* went and I didn't want to stick around for that lecture."

"There's a book on that?" she asked, incredulous.

"I'll let you borrow it when you're older," Korin replied pompously, patting her head.

She swatted at his hand. He darted to tug her sash.

"Don't!" she cried. "I'll never be able to retie it."

"I should think not. Mahteni's used some fancy desert twist," Korin laughed, squinting at the sash. "It looks like script."

"I think it might be the written form of the Desert Speech," Ari Ara guessed. She'd never actually seen it, but Minli told her once that it flowed in a line, each curl representing a sound, linking them together to phonetically spell out the words of the lyrical Desert Speech. She'd heard it was hard to learn to read; Mariana's writing was completely different, based on symbols and pictures.

"You're right," Korin exclaimed, wrinkling his nose. "I thought it reminded me of something. If I had paid more attention in class, I could read it."

Emir sighed and nudged him aside, picking up the end of the sash. He frowned in concentration as he deciphered it. A smile grew on his face. He chuckled.

"Fitting," he murmured. "It's part of a very famous story about a certain Desert King who fell in love with a certain foreign Queen."

"My parents?!" Ari Ara cried.

Emir nodded. A look of distant memory crossed Korin's features.

"Oh, I remember that. It's all metaphorical, flowery-poetry stuff – water in the desert, life returning, love like rain, that sort of thing. The song means a lot to the Desert People, at least, that's what Emir told me when he did my homework on it."

"There's more," Emir remarked, his face darkening with memories. "Remember what I told you about the massacre Shulen tried to stop? During the attack, the women of the undefended desert village joined hands and sang this song to the oncoming soldiers, desperately trying to stop them, to remind them of love and the reasons not to attack."

"What happened?" Ari Ara asked.

"They were slaughtered," Emir answered bluntly, "because Marianan soldiers aren't taught to communicate with their enemies."

Ari Ara fumbled with the sash, horrified, but Emir stopped her.

"Don't. The song is much more significant than that. It's . . . it's like a midnight promise that the sun will rise, or that spring follows winter, and that even between bitter enemies, the return of love and peace is possible."

He urged her to wear it proudly.

"It will mean a lot to the water workers to see you wearing this song-sash."

Ari Ara looked down at the words she could not read, thinking about the story of the women. She set her chin, determined. When she became queen, she would make everyone learn each other's languages.

"Come on," Korin urged, "we've got to hurry or we'll really be late."

As she passed through the gold-leafed doors of the Academy into the crowded front hall, surprised looks were thrown in her direction. Eyes narrowed at her sash. Fingers pointed. Whispers rose. Ari Ara lifted her head proudly and ignored the black glowers that the noble youths shot like arrows at her.

Nothing went terribly wrong until after lunch, when she, Korin, and Emir climbed the stairs to the Art of War classroom. She was crossing toward her usual place in the back - where Thornmar would hopefully ignore her - when a figure rose up from the benches with an outraged cry.

"*What* are you wearing?" a sharp, slightly shrill voice screeched.

Ari Ara glanced up to find herself nose-to-nose with a furious Varina, her painted nail trembling as she pointed to the song-sash around her waist.

CHAPTER NINETEEN

· · · · ·

High Attar

Varina's eyes narrowed into angry slits. Heads turned. Conversations faltered. The students stilled.

"How dare you!" she hissed.

"Wear the story of my parents?" Ari Ara shot back.

The older girl's hand rose as if to slap her. Ari Ara jumped back a pace. Emir leapt between them.

"Your parents?" the dark-haired noblegirl flung back, shouting over Emir's broad shoulder. "What about mine? My father was killed by a desert sorcerer, struck down by demon lightning, and you brazenly wear one of *their* sashes?"

She's crazy, Ari Ara thought wildly, trying to sort out the truth in Varina's tale.

"You're a traitor and an imposter," Varina accused, her voice ringing loudly.

Every eye in the room was pinned on them.

Ari Ara took a deep breath and reached for the Way Between as she answered.

"I can't be a traitor to the truth of my parents," she replied, choosing her words carefully as she drew upon her lessons from

Malak and Shulen. "And that's going to be hard for many people to swallow. I am sorry your father died."

She said the last in a whoosh, hoping to get it all out before Varina exploded. She'd made a promise months ago to start to apologize to both sides of the war for the deaths and pain caused by the War of Retribution. She hadn't thought it would start with Varina, but it had to start somewhere.

The older girl's eyes grew hot and shiny. Her lip quivered. Her jaw clenched as sorrow and rage competed for precedence.

"Take it off," she demanded.

"No," Ari Ara refused. Taking off the song-sash would be betraying one people for another.

"Get to your seats."

Thornmar's cold voice snapped through the tension. Like vines hit with frost, the young nobles wilted toward their places. Ari Ara and Varina didn't budge. Thornmar took three strides, grabbed Ari Ara by the back of her jacket and half-hauled her to a bench near the wall.

"I told you to sit," he thundered, slamming her down hard enough to make her wince.

Emir pulled Thornmar back. The commander whirled on him, eyes flashing dangerously.

"Do *not* presume to attack me, Emir Miresh."

"My duty is to protect the heir," Emir answered in a low warning tone.

The students backed up to the walls, eyes wide.

"If you dare challenge me again, boy, I will send you running back to Shulen with your tail between your legs like the dog that you are."

Emir stared him down, refusing to move an inch. He was the reigning Mariana Champion. Not even a bristling war hero could frighten him. The older warrior glared long and hard at the youth, the veins in his forehead lifting up the white streaks of his battle scars. No one breathed.

At last, Thornmar turned away, barking at the students to take their seats and launching into a lecture. Emir let the breath out of his chest. Korin scrubbed his white face with his palms. Varina smirked and swept to her place with an arrogant fling of her skirts. Ari Ara crossed her arms over her chest and leaned her shoulders against the hard wall, kicking her feet angrily. She glared at the noblegirl. Varina was a lying snake. If her father was struck by lightning, it probably had nothing to do with desert sorcery and everything to do with the idiocy of wearing an iron war helmet in a thunderstorm.

"What's she doing here, anyway?" Ari Ara muttered with a scowl, glaring at the noblegirl.

"Didn't you hear?" Korin whispered. "The Mistress of Dress is sick today. We've got double study with her second class."

Ari Ara groaned. A whole afternoon with Varina and Thornmar was her idea of a nightmare.

"Harrak," she murmured under her breath.

"Silence!" Thornmar barked, concluding his lecture. "You will split into two armies and gather on opposite sides of the Map Table."

"High Attar!" someone cried out in excitement.

"Indeed," Thornmar confirmed humorlessly. "Time to throw you into battle. Appoint high and low commanders, one king or queen for each side. The rest of you divide up as squadron leaders. No bickering. If you cannot sort it out, draw lots for a king or queen and let that person appoint the rest of the roles."

He pulled out the game pieces and flung them out on the Map Table. One of the students scurried around setting them upright as the others began to form teams. The Orelands youths and the Timberlands began to line up on one side. Thornmar halted near Ari Ara, lifting an eyebrow at her clothes.

"You will be on the Desert side, I presume," Thornmar sneered, his lips curling in distaste.

Harrak, she reminded herself.

"Thank you for the honor," she replied, rising and walking around to that side of the Map Table.

Korin and Isa exchanged anxious glances then hurried to join her. Emir ignored the dark look Thornmar shot at him and followed Ari Ara. Varina sauntered to the opposite side and declared herself Queen of Mariana. Ari Ara snorted under her breath. As the others shifted around the table, Varina began appointing her chain of command.

"You be queen," Korin urged Ari Ara with a wicked look, "and let's trounce her. I'm warning you, though, if you make us do anything stupid, we'll mutiny."

"Fair enough," Ari Ara answered as the rest of the group nodded along with his suggestion.

They sorted out the rest of the roles, Isa serving as High Commander, Korin as her general. As the lower ranks decided their positions by draw, Ari Ara offered to promote anyone who did well, rotating the higher command roles.

"That's not in the rules," said one boy with a frown.

Ari Ara shrugged.

"It's not forbidden either," she pointed out, "and this way, you'll be sure to pay attention to the whole board, not just your corner of it."

"Desert attacks first," Thornmar reminded them, pointing to the sites of three unguarded villages on the Marianan side of the Border Mountains, "here, here, and here."

"No," Ari Ara answered, lifting her chin. "They wouldn't do that."

The room stilled. Thornmar turned his stern fury on her. "What?"

Ari Ara swallowed. The rule had always bothered her and today she could no longer stomach the injustice of it.

"The Harraken would not attack those undefended villages. It serves no purpose and violates their sense of honor."

"Desert demons have no honor," Thornmar retorted flatly.

"That's not true," she answered stubbornly, ignoring Korin's kick under the Map Table. "Historically, the Harraken have not always attacked first."

"That's right," Korin chimed in. "We've loads of records about that."

"Silence," Thornmar ordered. "Do as you are told."

Korin scowled at the rebuke. The Marianans liked to claim that the Desert People started all the wars by invasions, attacks, or village raids, but he had his doubts. His mother had given him the secret books of Attar that instructed would-be rulers on how to use disguised raiders to rekindle national hatred of an enemy when war enthusiasm dwindled. It was common to invent reports of Desert aggression to foment a new war, or prevent a peace treaty from being signed (if the ruler did not wish to end the war), or agitate the populace when everyone was sick of fighting. He wondered if he should tell Ari Ara about the secret books. Korin decided against it for now; Brinelle would make her read them soon enough.

The war began. Varina rubbed her hands together, eyes narrowed at Ari Ara across the Map Table. The older girl snapped out orders, swift and vicious in her attacks, smiling at each defeat of her enemy. Isa and Korin made a powerfully strategic pair, countering her and exploiting her weaknesses. Varina waged a scorched earth campaign, exterminating entire villages and ordering her commanders to take no prisoners.

"The only good desert demon is a dead one," she cackled.

Ari Ara took a deep breath.

"Someday, I hope you have an opportunity to learn more about the Harraken," she said, mastering her surge of anger.

When Korin advised her to take an eye for an eye and execute Varina's captured soldiers, she shook her head.

"Two wrongs do not make a right," she answered, holding Varina's contemptuous gaze, "and if the Marianans forget honor, it is up to the Harraken to remind them of it even amidst their rage and bloodlust."

She put the captured soldiers to work rebuilding villages and resettled her fleeing refugees in them. Varina ordered her High Commander to destroy the villages and the noble youth objected.

"Our captured warriors are there," he protested.

"War requires sacrifice," Varina snapped at him.

A rumble of discontent rose from her teammates.

If this were real, Ari Ara thought, *I'd go among them like Alaren and undermine their support of her brutal style of warfare.*

Thornmar barked at Varina's teammates to follow commands and learn obedience if nothing else. He praised his niece's cutthroat tactics and mocked Ari Ara's compassion as she sent in her troops to rescue her cornered warriors.

"Your Way Between is weak," he sneered when Varina won a minor victory while the Desert's forces were split.

"Only if you're blind to its true strength," Ari Ara replied calmly, rallying the rescued squadron in a move that thwarted the bulk of Varina's southern flank. Half an hour later, Korin and Isa had squashed the core of Varina's army and scattered her flanks. Ari Ara expected Thornmar to call the game in their favor, but he said nothing.

"Send in a truce flag," Ari Ara suggested to the others.

Korin shook his head.

"The Desert People don't have a truce flag."

"Why not?" she demanded.

"Because it violates their sense of honor, no doubt," Thornmar sneered. "They never call off a war, the bloodthirsty savages. Regroup and continue, Varina. Marianans defend to the last."

She nodded and began to give out orders.

Ari Ara shook her head.

"That's not how it would be - " she started to say.

"Enough!" Thornmar snapped. "You are no expert in what the enemy will do, Ari Ara of the High Mountains. You will either play by the rules of Attar or you will leave immediately."

He pointed to the door.

Titters broke out from Varina's team. Noble youths snickered under their breaths. Ari Ara had no doubt she'd be the talk of the dinner tables tonight. She could hear them now: *she's not fit to be queen, can't even command an army at the Attar Game, a demon sympathizer, can't put her on the throne!* Ari Ara sighed. She'd been trying to avoid this situation for weeks, working hard to give Thornmar no excuse to throw her out. But she couldn't just stand back and let one part of her family insult and demonize the other. That was Anar's Way. The Way Between demanded that she take a stand, guided by a sense of justice and compassion.

A harrak-mettahl reminds people of their honor, she thought, *calling them to remember what is right.*

She made her choice.

"It's too bad your hatred blinds you," she told Thornmar, "because even the Great Lady respects your strategic ability. If you could see your enemy as people, you'd be even better at - "

Thornmar's face flushed with fury.

"Out."

Ari Ara sighed, turned on her heel, and left.

Trouble did not begin to describe the excruciatingly long, ear-splitting, coal-raking reaming out the Great Lady unleashed on her when she found out she'd been thrown out of class. Brinelle had just dismissed her high commanders from a military council session that left her with a heavy heart and a splitting headache. The reports from her warriors alarmed and saddened her. While her warriors in the Training Yards had seen the Way Between firsthand and learned of its strengths, suspicions and rumors grew like weeds in the military outposts throughout the country. At the army stations, the question was not *if* Ari Ara was an imposter, but *whose* imposter. The scuttlebutt pointed to the Fanten Grandmother, the Desert King, and worst of all, Shulen. Brinelle stared dolefully at the slender girl in front of her and wondered if she had any idea of the precariousness of her situation.

If the warriors gave credence to the rumors that Shulen was trying to gain power by putting his apprentice on the throne, Ari Ara would face distrust and mutiny her whole life even if she did manage to secure the confirmation. Brinelle rubbed her temples and paced the polished tiles of the meeting room, thumping her fist on the backs of the wooden chairs that circled the oval council table. She was certain Thornmar and his family were behind the suspicions. The commander's old grudge against Shulen, and especially the Way Between, had reached new heights of hatred. Brinelle came to stand near the girl, folding her arms across her chest. It was a shame that the sparks of animosity between the child and Thornmar served to fuel the fire of this political controversy, but Brinelle suspected it couldn't be avoided. Ari Ara was everything Thornmar detested: desert-blooded and Azar-following.

"Korin wasn't half the trouble you are, and he was famous for it," she complained. "Please tell me it isn't true that you told Thornmar that he was a pathetic disappointment to his ancestors."

"Stunning," Ari Ara sighed.

"What?"

"The exact phrase was that his ancestors would be stunningly disappointed in him," Ari Ara answered, regretting that she'd muttered it on the way out the door. She should have known the gossip would reach Brinelle before she did. "He was lowering his honor by insulting the Harraken."

"A barb for a sting leaves the whole world bleeding," Brinelle intoned, quoting Alaren.

"He keeps saying I'm an imposter!" Ari Ara protested.

"Are you?" Brinelle asked, lifting an eyebrow.

"No," Ari Ara replied, kicking the leg of a chair. "If I was, I'd have left for the High Mountains long ago."

Brinelle's mouth twitched. That was believable.

"Until you are confirmed as the heir, you cannot afford to antagonize any of the nobles," Brinelle admonished her, adding with a knowing glint in her eye, "and that includes Lady Varina and the other young nobles. You need their support."

"Varina's not even of age!" Ari Ara objected.

"No, but she, her cousins, and her seven aunts are all influential enough to sway the Orelands' vote."

"I hope they're smarter than she is," Ari Ara complained, "or this country's headed for trouble."

Brinelle hastily turned her laugh into a cough.

"There are many who will vote against your confirmation for reasons that have nothing to do with the veracity of the Mark of Peace on your back. People fear change and you force them to look at things differently. Some worry that practicing the Way Between will weaken us and leave us vulnerable to attack. Others dislike you for your desert blood. Many will fight tooth-and-nail against peace simply because they profit off of war. Be careful, Ari Ara, you cannot afford to make more enemies."

Ari Ara agreed. The ones she had were already dangerous enough.

The Great Lady dismissed her from attending the formal banquet that night, averting a confrontation with the Orelands nobles, and punished her with writing an essay on respecting her elders.

An hour later, Ari Ara angrily balled up her twelfth attempt after scribbling a line about how Thornmar was the one who needed to learn respect. Crumpled parchment surrounded her. She pounded her fist on the desk and flung back her chair. She grabbed her cloak and headed out the door.

"Where are you going?" Emir asked, standing on guard duty just outside her quarters.

"Nowhere. Anywhere," she fumed, scrambling for an answer. "The Hawk's Keep to see Malak. And you don't have to follow me!"

Emir sighed over her temper and left her alone.

Ari Ara was too mad to notice her friend's discretion. Heaps of snow dotted the edges of the Training Yards and she kicked the tops off them one by one. She scooped up a fistful of snow and packed it into a ball, hurling it out into the empty sands. How was she supposed to treat Thornmar with respect? Malak was right: he had no *harrak*, no honor. She'd been trying to use the Way Between on Thornmar, but it was hard to practice Azar with someone she disliked so much. She never had the urge to punch Emir even when he bested her in practice. With Thornmar, the burning scorch of her anger often threatened to flare out of control. Some days, her hands ached afterwards from clenching into fists.

All he loves is Attar, she thought bitterly. He hated everything else - especially her with her red desert demon hair.

She took the stairs of the Hawk's Keep two at a time and hurtled onto the top landing fast enough to alarm the birds. Malak turned in surprise.

"I hate him," she spat out.

"Who?" Malak asked carefully.

"Thornmar," Ari Ara answered, kicking the straw and blurting out the whole story. "I wish he'd jump off a cliff."

Malak shook his head.

"Don't wish such things even upon your enemies. Words are powerful. They can make curses fall like swords upon people's lives."

Ari Ara rolled her eyes.

"You don't believe me." Malak chuckled. "I will have to show you. This is the Harraken word for lightning."

Malak spoke a word and - despite the winter snows falling outside - lightning leapt out of the clouds and struck the flagpole atop the Hawk's Keep. Ari Ara shrieked - more from remembering Varina's story than from the thunder crack and sizzle of electric light.

"So, it's true?" she cried. "A desert sorcerer really *did* crack lightning down on Varina's father?"

Malak raised his eyebrows as he looked up at the hollow underside of the turret roof. The hawks screamed and fanned their wings in alarm. He called out to them soothingly until they settled back onto their roosts. Then, without meeting her eyes, he nodded.

"There are few who can call the lightning like a hawk, but Tahkan Shirar once dropped a bolt on Rannor Thornmar's brother for his atrocities. He struck Rannor once, too, but unfortunately, it did not kill him. It just made him crazier than before. Calling down lightning is not done lightly," he added sternly, seeing her smile at the idea of trying to hit her Art of War instructor with a lightning bolt. "It is always unwise to ask anyone - human, hawk, or lightning - to bend against their nature. I could not have called that bolt if it hadn't been hovering in the clouds. Even the Desert King could not have called the lightning that killed Varina's father out of a clear blue sky."

"Could I try it?" she asked Malak.

"Better to learn that word on a dry day, when you're less likely to hit someone with an unruly bolt," he told her firmly, lifting his eyebrows at her and adding, "a day when you aren't tempted to use it on people."

Ari Ara left that evening sobered by the power of Harraktala, Desert Speech, and wondering what other supernatural acts Tahkan Shirar might have done on the battlefield. Mahteni once said that his sister Moragh was half-mad, half-magic . . . did it run in the family? Ari Ara shivered and hoped she never wound up killing someone by losing her temper and saying the wrong thing.

"I won't be like that," she murmured, vowing to work on her temper and choose her words carefully. She was a follower of the Way Between.

"And I'll find a way to deal with Thornmar," she promised herself. It might not work; it might take years, but it was the only way forward. They had to find a way to live in peace.

And that, she decided, *was a task worthy of Alaren.*

CHAPTER TWENTY

. . . . .

The Great Feasts

The nights lengthened. The days dwindled. From autumn equinox to the Feast Days at solstice, the population of the island swelled as families gathered in the city. Merchants packed the streets. Goods and wares traded hands in a fevered rush, preparing for the long months when deep snows blocked the roads and froze the river ways. The nobles brought their entire families from their lands to their houses on Marin's Way, and Brinelle was not alone in using the flurry of the social season to reaffirm alliances, strengthen bonds, send warnings, and negotiate favors. The endless round of dinners, parties, dances, and celebrations laid the groundwork for the harder-edged political haggling of the winter council sessions of the Assembly of Nobles.

Upcoming heirs - like Korin, Isa, and most of all, Ari Ara - were presented and weighed on invisible scales of suitability and capacity. Ari Ara learned to be polite to everyone while promising nothing to anyone. When Brinelle told her to - for once in her life - just smile and be silent, Ari Ara sniffed and informed her aunt that she would simply pretend that the nobles were lumps of rock or woolly sheep. She'd had plenty of practice being silent around those.

She dined with ancient matriarchs who couldn't hear a word she said and kissed the newest baby in the enormous Stonelands clan. She picked up cues on flattery from Isa who navigated the treacherous shoals of society like a seasoned river sailor. She met with the Craftlands Council of artisans who came with their noble representatives. She greeted entourages of orphans from the Sisterlands. She endured the agonizing benefit soirees put on by noblehouses who used fundraisers for the orphans of war as an excuse for lavish festivities paid for by the spoils of war.

At these, Shulen watched her like a hawk, clearing his throat to cut off her stinging remarks about the practice of training orphans into warriors who waged wars that made more orphans who then made more wars. The time would come when she could change all that . . . but that day was not yet here. She needed to befriend nobles and court alliances and sway suspicious lords and ladies into supporting her bid for confirmation.

"Scholar Monk's long-winded lectures taught me one useful thing," she grumbled to Minli on a snowy morning after practice.

"What's that?" he asked, blinking in surprise - she'd been the worst student he'd ever seen at the orphans' class. He shook the snowflakes off the knitted cap that covered his shaved head.

"How to appear to be listening when you're not," she answered, grinning.

Twelve days before Marin's Feast Day, the Academy closed for the Great Feasts hosted by each of the noblehouses. The order of the celebrations was the result of a month of haggling. Each feast outspent the one before it, and the more lavish the party, the greater the standing of the noblehouse. The Great

Feasts escalated until the House of Marin put them all to shame on Marin's Feast Day, celebrating with a wild party and the annual renewal of fealty oaths. Ari Ara had thought the festivities for the Urchins' Feast were incredible, but they paled in comparison to the island-wide extravagance celebrating their founder. Bright banners strung between the houses, out the windows, down the facades of buildings, and over clotheslines; no two alike and all depicting scenes of Marin's life. Fir bough garlands with bright red berries, vivid orange flowers, and golden yellow wheat heads adorned the sills and railings, balconies and bridges, rain gutters and rooflines. Candles in paper sacks glowed, turning the long, dark nights into a scene of cheer and warmth. Merchant's Way burst into a frenzied bustle of activity as the city inhabitants scanned its carts and shelves for Marin's Feast Day gifts, feast-makings, decorations, and altar offerings. Inside the homes, small statues and paintings of Marin adorned the mantles over the fireplaces.

The noblehouses on Marin's Way strove to outshine each other's extravagant decorations. People strolled the street, bundled against the cold, admiring the beauty behind the windows and along the fronts of houses. The nobles had their servants stand on the front steps with packets of roasted nuts or dried sweet cherries. Special baskets offered wooden tokens carved to commemorate the year; people collected them and hung on home altars across the city. The House of Marin gave away a different treat each day to the children, offering paper ornaments and small clay-cast toys and whirling fans. No one thought to offer the heir such insignificant trinkets, but Shulen knew the austerity of the girl's life in the mountains, so he collected them for her. She set the clay figure of Marin on the mantle over her hearth and added his wife and children over the next few days. The light in her eyes gave Shulen joy to witness, though even he never guessed that these were the first toys she had ever received.

Not all were celebrating, however. The water workers, Ari Ara noticed, were grim-faced with exhaustion trying to keep up with the added demands of the season. They worked from dawn to midnight hanging decorations, tending to the swelling numbers of people in the noblehouses, scouring and polishing every inch of the homes, and cooking lavish feasts. Beneath their industrious obedience to the unending demands, chores, and errands, Ari Ara caught furtive glances as they took messages between houses. Quick whispers passed as they scoured the floors and hung the decorations. A certain tension rode their movements as they unloaded crates of supplies at the river docks below her window. Ari Ara uneasily wondered if the rumors of an uprising had any truth to them.

Mahteni seemed stressed and tired, but there was nothing suspicious about that. Each night of the Great Feasts required a different outfit for Ari Ara, Brinelle, and Korin, and she was stitching her fingers off.

"Thank the ancestors that the first two nights are the monks and sisters' celebrations, or we'll never finish on time," Mahteni exclaimed as she held out a simple white shift for Ari Ara to belt over warm leggings and long sleeves.

The Sisterlands and Monklands kicked off the Great Feasts with humility, fasting, and prayer. The first evening was spent in silence in the temple. Ari Ara poured the blessing wine on the altar stone and watched the incense curling in the flickering candlelight. The sisters sang of the turning seasons and the hope of light's return as the darkness gathered. The following evening, the monks chanted prayers in Old Tongue as the nobles coughed and shifted on the hard stone benches.

Along with Brinelle, she kept vigil on the first two nights of the Great Feasts. Korin scampered off, delighted to be relieved of the long, cold, and boring duty. Emir and Shulen kept watch. Ari Ara didn't mind. She had stamina and endurance from her training and was determined to be as still and silent as Brinelle. The Great Lady did not doze, did not speak, did not even shiver. Her prayers and thoughts were cloaked under her half-lidded eyes as the tingling energies of the night flowed past like a river. The second vigil was harder, but the two-day fast clawed the edges of Ari Ara's stomach and unlocked a surge of energy that carried her through the first half of the night. A few hours before dawn, as she struggled against exhaustion, strange half-dreams began to rise up like river fog around her. She saw a match between she and Shulen, and the tension on the old warrior's face hinted that it was not a practice session. She saw a river of people leaving the Capital. She saw the nobles shouting furiously at her and white flags with the Mark of Peace lifting above the heads of a crowd.

A crash of sound jolted her awake. The monks rang out the dawn with the rolling thunder of a Great Gong the size of the room. It reverberated in the stone walls, the hard benches, up her spine, and into her bones.

"You did well," Brinelle remarked as they walked tiredly back to the House of Marin.

"I fell asleep at the end," she confessed, her voice cracking with weariness.

"At least you didn't snore like Korin did," the Great Lady told her with a chuckle. "Did you dream?"

"Yes, I - "

"Don't tell me," Brinelle warned, raising a finger to her lips. "Visions and dreams at the Dark Times are not for sharing. They may or may not be true . . . often they are a warning so you can avert the nightmare from coming."

The real Feasts began with the Fertilelands this year and the farmers laid out a banquet that made the table groan. Even the richest nobles broke into smiles of delight as they spotted rare fruits and glasshouse treats. The noblehouse's Head Cook came out of the kitchen, red-faced, to accept the guests' admiration of her skillful work. Ari Ara complimented a particular dish with an unusual spice and the Head Cook beamed.

"That is *amanchi*, an herb of the Desert," she told the daughter of Tahkan Shirar.

A clink of a dropped spoon sounded. Ari Ara caught a glimpse of Varina spitting the dish out. *More for us,* Ari Ara thought, annoyed at the noblegirl. Korin distracted everyone by exclaiming over the novelty of the desert herbs and Isa switched the subject by admiring the ways in which Ari Ara's dress and the gown of the Lady of the Fertilelands complimented each other. The dresses both bore blue and green stripes embroidered and stitched into the waterways of irrigation that ensured good harvests in the bountiful fields of that area.

Ari Ara bit back a grin - if the negotiations for the order of the Feasts had taken a month, Mahteni and the Mistress of Dress had been working twice as long on the clothes she had to wear. Each dress bore a river dragon motif, the symbol of the House of Marin and its control over the winding rivers of Mariana. Tonight, the river dragon curled at the foot of her dress like a watchful and loyal dog guarding the green farms and orchards of the Fertilelands.

The next night at the Craftlands Feast, the dragon rode the waterwheels stitched into the pattern of her skirt, gleefully and happily turning the gears of the crafters' halls. The third night, the river dragon raced a herd of horses that thundered at the hem of her dress, telling the hosts of the Riderlands that the House of Marin supported their odd, but much-prized nomadic ways. The speaker for the tribes - for the Riders recognized no lords or ladies - presented her with a gleaming saddle, the leather worked with the same horses and dragon motif as her dress.

"Not much good without a horse," Thornmar commented in a sneer of a tone that cut the conversations short.

The speaker for the Riderlands drew herself up tall, affronted by the implied insult that her tribes would not bring the best of their fabled horses for the Lost Heir.

"It is not the place of a Rider to antagonize the Harraken. Among our heir's father's people, only a father chooses his daughter's first horse."

Ari Ara blinked in surprise before remembering that the Riderlands bordered the Desert. The tribes traded with the Harraken and shared bloodlines of horse lineages with the people the rest of their country saw only as enemies. She tucked the knowledge away for later and thanked the speaker for the gift.

The Stonelands Feast was held at the House of Mara, a fantastically-carved building with white marble lions at the front gate and imposing, two-story granite sentinels holding up the roof. Ari Ara realized with a start that her long, belted overcoat and trousers were a variation of the statues' garb. As they entered, Korin whispered to her that the sentinels were copies of the enormous carvings in the Stonelands' Valley of Statues. The originals were the size of mountains and made these look like Attar Game pieces in comparison. The two huge sentinels had been chiseled out of the cliffs by Marinmara's grandson; inside the helmet of each warrior was a lookout tower to watch for Desert attacks. The descendants of Marinmara seemed to interpret her clothes as an offer of shared vigilance and surprised even Brinelle with a promise to carve an ancestor statue of the Lost Heir this summer to add to the Wall of Ancestors.

"After the confirmation," Brinelle noted under her breath to Ari Ara. "They're hedging their bets, flattering us, but cautiously."

The celebration at the House of Barre was a welcome respite from the growing tensions and need for careful words. The Southlands was renowned for its grace and hospitality, and with all six of Lady de Barre's sisters and twenty of Isa's cousins in attendance, as well as a range of uncles, in-laws, and even her ancient great-grandmother, their feast was the first truly joyous celebration Ari Ara had seen.

Ari Ara held onto the memories of that night as she doggedly endured the snobbery of the rich merchants of the Westlands. A fleet of water workers served the richly sumptuous feast and Ari Ara caught them stealing glances at her dress all night. Mahteni had outdone herself using rare and expensive desert silks. Even the Marianans were impressed. One of the Westland lords told her that he would trade a whole caravan of goods for that dress.

The next night, the Lord of the Timberlands shocked her speechless by handing her a feast gift of a small carving of herself hewn from the heart of a Great Tree.

"Because I know the Fanten who raised you worship trees," he said in a smooth and oily voice as she struggled to control her dismay. Shulen came to her rescue with a quick phrase about the unusual gift, giving her time to swallow her fury. The Fanten would never - never! - cut down or carve up a Great Tree. Holding this carving was like holding a sculpture chiseled from Marin's bones. She had no doubt the lord's gift was done for malice and spite. The Timberlands faction thought Ari Ara was nothing more than a Fanten pawn, an imposter trying to gain the throne, manipulated by the Fanten Grandmother of the Monk's Hand Mountains.

"Someday," she replied to the Lord of the Timberlands, "I shall introduce you to the Fanten Grandmother and she will explain the full significance of this gift."

Then when a Great Tree smashes her boughs on this idiot's head, Ari Ara added silently, *he'll know what he did to infuriate the trees.* She privately suspected the Timberlands were losing equipment and woodcutters in the edges of the Fanten Forest. She sighed. Alaren and his Way Between would work to increase the respect and understanding between the Timberlands nobles and the local Fanten, resulting in saving the lives of the woodcutters and protecting the Great Trees. She made a silent vow to work on this when - or if - she were ever confirmed as the heir.

The next night's Great Feast was no easier, though the Loomlands lords and ladies fell over themselves trying to impress the Lost Heir. Their gift was bolts of fine cloth made and presented by water workers contracted through the House of Marin.

"With hundreds of nimble hands at the looms, we're producing fine weaves for practically nothing!" the chubby-cheeked Lady of the Loomlands enthused.

Ari Ara flushed beet red with shame as one of the water workers caught her eye then hastily looked away. There was no *harrak* in this gift, no honor. Later, Isa murmured that caravans of former Loomlanders were seeking refuge and employment in the Southlands.

"Mother says half the original factory workers have fled. We've so many begging for winter shelter that Mother's started a loomery. We won't be buying cloth made by water workers this year," she mentioned with a proud lift of her chin.

The Feasts went from bad to worse when, at the severe and hard hall of the Smithlands, the Battlelord and the Forgemaster together presented her with a finely wrought sword.

"Swords will be needed when the desert demons are upon us and you see the folly of Azar, the Weakling's Way," the Battlelord growled. The Forgemaster's mocking laughter thundered out and other nobles joined in.

"Perhaps," Korin commented brightly - and loudly - to Emir, "we should make a wager about how much dust that sword collects under the reign of the Lost Heir."

He picked up the sword on the pretext of testing its balance, thus sparing Ari Ara from having to grasp it.

"That's not a wager I would wish to make," the Mariana Champion stated to his friend, "since her Way Between already bests my Attar two times out of three."

At Emir's words, a shocked sizzle of murmurs whipped around the room. The gossip that the would-be heir could get the better of the tall, warrior-trained youth distracted everyone from the insinuations of the Smithlands' gift.

The Orelands' Great Feast came on the eve of Marin's Feast Day, the coveted last gathering of the twelve noblehouses' effort to outdo each other's splendor before the House of Marin's lavish festivities left them all in the dust. The House of Thorn's main hall was draped in glowing candles held by silver sconces. The sculpted ceiling gleamed with polish and dripped with filigree. Thornmar circulated among his guests in black velvet. Varina's gown rivaled Ari Ara's dress in expense. The wine flowed in silver and jewel-encrusted fountains. The feast made the tables groan under its weight. The Orelands' noble family circulated, handing out precious gems and promise notes for ores - a ruby wedding gift for the daughter of the Stonelands, a rare mineral contract for the Smithlands' forges, silver necklaces for the ladies of the houses, chalices for the sisters and monks' collections.

As the evening wore on, it became patently noticeable that none of the Orelands nobles had gifted anything to the House of Marin. Even Korin, who got along with everyone, was irritated by the slight. Ari Ara thought not having to talk with Varina or Thornmar was a gift in itself, but Brinelle's lips pressed together in cold fury at the insult. When the uncle and niece finally approached, she spoke to them in a sharp tone.

"I'd almost thought you had forgotten your duty to the House of Marin, Commander Thornmar."

"Indeed not, Great Lady," he said in a voice that caught the room's attention.

He gestured for Varina to bring forward a box. She smirked nastily and a cold dread sank into Ari Ara's heart. Varina opened the lid as she curtsied: a finely-wrought shirt of silver mail glistened. A collective gasp went around the room.

"Silverstar mail," someone breathed in awe.

"Yes," Thornmar affirmed, "strong enough to withstand even the blow of a sword such as the Smithlands gave this girl yesterday."

He gestured disdainfully to Ari Ara then continued in a hissing growl of a voice.

"And light enough to sleep in . . . so you'll be protected if - or when - the imposter tries to stab you in the back."

A deadly silence fell over the hall. Ari Ara's body clenched at the insult. Shulen took a step closer. Eyes leapt from the Great Lady to the commander to the Great Warrior, expecting blows at any moment.

Brinelle laughed coldly.

"With friends and allies such as you, Rannor Thornmar, I should hardly be worried about a mere girl."

Her tone froze the nobles in place as she swept out of the hall. Shulen nudged an astonished Ari Ara forward. Korin had already followed his mother. Emir slid like a shadow after them. They had left the House of Thorn and were crossing back over Marin's Way to their house when Shulen broke the silence.

"You should have let me call an Honor Challenge on him. Before I give up Attar entirely, I should like to - "

"Nonsense!" Brinelle snapped. "Show me how good your Azar is, Shulen. I want no fights between you two. Is that clear?"

She stopped suddenly and whirled on the youths.

"When the Academy resumes after the Feast Days, you are to apply your skills toward easing this tension amongst your peers. I want Varina de Thorn isolated in her animosity, understand? Make friends. Build alliances. Do not let this rude incident fester into larger problems down the road."

She whirled and stormed across the sands.

"Alaren's Ear!" Korin whistled in a low tone. "Who'd of thought Mum would be telling us to use the Way Between?"

CHAPTER TWENTY-ONE

. . . . .

Shirar's Feast Day

A hand shook her awake. Ari Ara groaned and rolled over. Yesteday had been miserable. Instead of being a celebration, Marin's Feast Day had been as somber as a funeral and ten times as tense. Walking out of the Orelands' Feast had thrown down the gauntlet between the two houses. The House of Thorn retaliated by refusing to come to the House of Marin's Feast Day celebration for the first time in Marianan history. Their official message claimed ill-health. Brinelle, bristling like a hedgehog, fired back a reply stating that unless Rannor Thornmar was dead by noon, she expected the war commander or his proxy to drag himself down the street in time for the annual renewal of fealty oaths. Otherwise, the Great Lady would interpret his absence as a declaration of civil war and act accordingly. She sent her warriors to line the street and surround the House of Thorn. She smiled her dragon-toothed smile and stated that it was simply to give him a proper military salute on his way over.

Rannor Thornmar appeared at noon sharp in a barely concealed fury and pledged his support along with the rest of the nobles - though he swore to defend Mariana rather than using the other formal vow that mentioned the House of Marin. Brinelle pursed her lips, but chose not to make an issue of the slight. She had Thornmar where she wanted him. The war commander departed after a scant half-hour, claiming poor health. The Great Lady graciously offered to send her royal physician to call upon the family. Thornmar turned pale and told her that wouldn't be necessary. Brinelle smiled toothily.

Ari Ara was thrilled that Varina, Thornmar and the rest of the House of Thorn weren't coming to the feast. Unfortunately, the tenor of the celebration remained subdued. Those that supported Thornmar eyed Ari Ara like wary chickens that spot a snake in the henhouse. Those who thought Thornmar and his family should be stripped of their nobility and shoved into the freezing river glared with equal hostility at the other faction. For the rest of the day, Ari Ara walked on pins and needles as she performed the obligatory small talk with the nobles. She wished they could just skip this part. She'd seen these nobles for twelve days straight and there were only so many polite remarks she could think up in such a short span.

By the end of the evening, Ari Ara had never been so grateful to strip off a fancy dress and sink into bed. She slept like stone until someone shook her awake at dawn.

"Go away," she mumbled into the pillow.

"Wake up," Mahteni's voice whispered in her ear in Desert Speech.

Ari Ara's eyes flew open. She cursed the power of the language and rubbed her face with her hand.

"What is it?" she asked Mahteni.

"Shhh," she hushed Ari Ara. "Do you want to come see something amazing?"

The desert woman was dressed for walking, heavy boots on her feet and a thick, hooded cloak over her layered trousers and thick sweater. Not a scrap of the water worker's blue sash adorned her. A rolling laundry cart sat behind her. Ari Ara scrambled out of bed. Mahteni held out a pair of dark wool pants. She handed the girl a tunic woven with handspun yarn in the natural cream and grays of undyed sheep's wool. A wide belt cinched the tunic at the waist and a pair of boots rose to her knees. Ari Ara's excitement quickened; any event that didn't require royal attire interested her.

"Is this a disguise?" she asked as Mahteni fastened a patterned scarf over her red hair.

"Not exactly," she answered, "but it will help us today when we need eyes to see a small Harraken tagging along with her aunt."

Ari Ara offered to wear a blue sash, but Mahteni shook her head.

"That won't be needed," she assured the girl.

The desert woman gestured for Ari Ara to hop into the laundry cart. She gathered up Ari Ara's Feast Day dress and piled the enormous gown with all its layers of tulle on top of the girl. Then Mahteni eased the cart out the door and thanked the guard on duty for letting her collect last night's garments. Swiftly and silently, Mahteni wheeled Ari Ara around the bend in the corridor, stopping only when the girl hissed to tell her about one of Korin's secret passageways. They squeezed through the narrow spaces and exited by way of the kitchen. The alleys of the city were buried in ankle-deep snow. The rooftops were blanketed with white. The hungry Mari River lapped up the pristine flakes. Except for the shush of falling snow, the Capital lay still and quiet.

As they turned down the street, Ari Ara began to glimpse other bundled, cloaked, and hooded figures. Malak appeared at their side, put a finger to his lips, and winked. Their path took them to the plaza where Ari Ara stopped and gawked in surprise.

Every water worker in the Capital must be here, she thought, staring at the size of the crowd. People greeted each other in the soft melodic tones of the Desert Speech, offering their blessings to one another on the Feast Day of their ancestor. On the far side of the plaza, heaps of snow piled up like strange white caps on the heads of the ancestor statues. The Harraken had cleared the snow off Shirar. Offerings of colored red cloth had been tied to his arms and legs until he looked like a festival dancer dressed in tasseled costume. The edge of the statue held gifts of small cakes, carved wooden cups of libations, coins, and polished river rocks. The crowd wove through one another, coming to Shirar's statue to lay out a gift, then backing away so others could approach.

A hum of sound lifted through the voices. One by one, people began to join in, until the hum swelled like a swarm of bees, circling and weaving into a simple, slow, three-note rise, haunting and beautiful. Ari Ara shivered as her hair stood on end.

"Today, on Shirar's Feast Day," Mahteni told her, "we gather to honor our ancestor. We begin at the beginning of our song sagas, the hum of existence that birthed the world from the black nothing. We sing to remind us of who we are and we lay out offerings to Shirar, asking his spirit to watch over us."

"We thought," Malak added, "that you might wish to see how your father's people honor their ancestor. And to be here in case - "

Mahteni cut him off with a jab of her elbow.

"In case what?" Ari Ara asked, alarmed and curious at once.

Malak cleared his throat. A silent exchange passed between him and Mahteni. A slight shrug lifted her shoulders.

"There are rumors that Shirar will appear today," Malak answered.

"The ancestor?" Ari Ara gasped. They shushed her.

"No, Tahkan Shirar," Malak clarifed. "He has been known, on Shirar's Day, to take on the spirit of our ancient founder and speak to his people across distances, generations, and time. It is an old tradition and the water workers think he will come here today."

"Why?" Ari Ara asked.

"Because you are here," Malak replied with a smile. "What father would not wish to see a daughter such as you? Tahkan Shirar would do far crazier things than fly with spirits to meet you."

"Enough," Mahteni snapped. "These stories are just foolish folktales."

Malak made a face back at her scowl. She rounded on him, shaking her finger.

"For the king to appear here at an illicit gathering would be deadly for many, including himself," Mahteni stated with a flush of irritation climbing her cheeks. "The Marianans would catch him and accuse him of inciting an uprising. Even to suggest such a thing is dangerous."

The tension between the two thickened. A question rose in Ari Ara's face. Malak saw it and answered.

"I am one of those who wishes the Harrak-Mettahl would appear today to give hope to his people."

Mahteni shook her head at such foolhardy dreams.

The humming gave way to a hushed song that slid like a wind through the crowd, waving from one side of the square to another and back again. Mahteni nudged them forward to lay out a gift at Shirar's statue. Malak pulled his hood tighter against the cold. They shuffled closer. The crosscurrents of song swayed around them. Ari Ara could feel the melody rumbling in her hands and through her chest, lifting her heart with its somber beauty. As they neared Shirar's statue, Mahteni tugged Ari Ara's kerchief back and snipped off a lock of her hair with her thread scissors.

"Climb up and place it in his hand," she told Ari Ara, boosting her elbow.

Watching the slick snow and mindful of icy patches, she climbed up and sat on Shirar's shoulder with her feet on his outstretched arm. From here, Alaren seemed to watch her with a bemused smile while Marin's serious expression frowned at her.

A murmur of surprise rippled through the crowd.

"It's her," Ari Ara heard someone say.

The song broke off as people turned in astonishment. Ari Ara laid the lock of hair in Shirar's stone hand.

"She's dressed for walking, Mahteni Duktar," a voice called out. "Is this it? Is this the day?"

Mahteni shook her head.

"Not today, but soon," she answered in a ringing voice. "That day will come as surely as the daughter of Tahkan Shirar just laid a lock of her hair in Shirar's hands."

A voice sung out a single line of a song.

"That's right," Mahteni affirmed, translating for Ari Ara's benefit. "Into Shirar's hands we place our lives; into the long lineage of the Harrak-Mettahl, we place our trust. One day, we will walk free and that day may be any time, so get ready!"

Eyes fixed on the girl perched on the statue. Ari Ara smiled back at them. For all that she had to learn, despite the truth that her family was as strangers to her, these were her people. One day, her two countries would live in peace. They would cross the borders as freely as her blood ran in her veins. The water would flow back into the desert, as it had in ancient times, as it had in her mother Alinore's times. She sensed the intense gaze of a pair of gray-green eyes and found Malak in the crowd. *He* believes I am my father's daughter, she thought, and suddenly, she felt the Desert Speech rolling off her tongue in a traditional greeting the Hawk Keeper had taught her.

"*In Shirar naht harrish,*" she said.

A cheer ran through the square at the familiar words.

"May the blessing of Shirar carry you.
May the sands settle at your feet.
May the water sing to greet you.
May the ancestor song praise your name."

Ari Ara remembered the ritual blessing and then added one more sentence before she exhausted her knowledge of Desert Speech.

"Thank you for welcoming me today."

The shrilling sound of the Honor Cry tore loose from a single throat and rose into a roar lifted by a thousand voices. Under the hawk's cry, a song threaded, swelled, and broke through the tumult. One by one, voices wove into it, layering the melody with the harmony of tribes and the counterpitches of each family clan. She saw Malak open his mouth then stop as Mahteni glared. Ari Ara hid a smile, suspecting he had started with the wrong notes for his clan. Then a new chant, a short phrase of words and notes, began to ripple through the crowd. Awe flickered in green eyes. Wonder spread across bronze faces. Ari Ara saw hands leap to cover trembling mouths and tears redden the edges of eyes.

Shirar en san. Shirar en san.
Shirar is here. Shirar is here.

The hairs rose up on Ari Ara's arms. She whirled to see.

"They mean you," Mahteni said, reaching up to touch her

241

knee with a shaking hand, "Shirar's descendant. Shirar is here in you, daughter of our Harrak-Mettahl."

Malak wept openly, his cheeks turning red as the tears stung and then froze in his beard, his breath puffing on the air, his strong arms clenched across his chest as if he would break to pieces without that grip.

"Mahteni, mir lanaan, I was right," he choked out, a laugh breaking through his emotion, "Shirar came!"

Mir lanann, Ari Ara thought, trying to place the meaning of the familiar phrase.

Suddenly, she noticed a ripple of movement snaking through the crowd. The Capital Watch! They had circled the fountain, blocking the streets and alleys out of the plaza. A few water workers struggled as the Watch grabbed ahold of them. The ring around the fountain took a protective stand. *They're trying to guard me,* Ari Ara realized. Mahteni cursed. The desert woman had suspected this might happen, though she had thought it would be later in the morning after the Watch's hangovers had worn off. She'd been hoping to have time to whisk Ari Ara back to the House of Marin, leaving only rumors and wild stories in her wake.

"You are ordered to disperse!" the Head of the Watch hollered. "Or you will be arrested and the conditions of your water contracts nullified."

Angry mutters swept the crowd. Ari Ara's eyes leapt to a man next to Malak, who cursed the Watchman next to him and spat in his face. The Watchman struck him. Malak grabbed the desert man before he was foolish enough to strike back, but even that flurry of motion triggered the Watch into action, beating the people nearest to them and seizing Malak.

"Mir talaar!" Mahteni screamed as the Watch began to haul him away.

Ari Ara jolted, suddenly understanding the meaning of the words that had eluded her earlier: *Mir lanann*, my sister; *mir talaar*, my brother.

"He cannot be caught. Not here," Mahteni murmured anxiously.

"He's your brother?" Ari Ara gasped, jumping down from the statue and threading through the crowd toward Malak.

"Shhh, no one knows," Mahteni answered swiftly, following on her heels. "Siblings are often used as hostages by Marianans."

"Young Queen - " a member of the Watch began, but Ari Ara cut him off.

"Release him," she commanded, hoping she sounded like Brinelle.

"Our orders are from the Great Lady - "

Ari Ara swung into motion, knowing the unconfirmed heir would never outrank the Great Lady. She leaned her weight across the fellow's arm, loosening his grip on Malak. He staggered and Malak tore to the side, wrenching free. The Watch lunged to grab him, but Ari Ara dove sideways and knocked several of them off balance. Malak struggled forward and broke loose. In an instant, the wiry desert man had vanished into the crowd. The water workers closed ranks, linking arms to form a solid wall as the Watch pushed to get through.

"We'll find him," the Head of the Watch swore, signalling to the others to circle around and comb the streets.

Ari Ara doubted it. In the center of the plaza was a drainage grate with loosened bolts that opened into the Under Way. With a lift and a slip, it was possible to trek beneath the city for the length of the island. Rill had told her about it and she'd mentioned it to Malak in the Hawk's Keep a few weeks ago.

She sent a silent prayer to the ancestor spirits to help guide Malak to safety.

The Head of the Watch asked her to return to the House of Marin.

"We'll let them disperse if you come," he said.

Ari Ara sighed and agreed. Mahteni was strong-armed into following.

As they turned down a side alley back toward Marin's Way, Mahteni spoke up.

"Remember, *betta*, we will not abandon you or our people. We are not gone, merely out of sight."

A chill shot through Ari Ara.

"Don't - " she cried, but the desert woman had burst into motion, flipping her Watchman with a move Shulen had taught her, spinning away from the next and breaking free. Ari Ara shifted into the path of the Watchman who started to charge after her. Pretending to stumble, she collided with another. By the time she looked up, Mahteni was gone.

"Sir?" a member of the Watch asked, moving to give chase.

"No!" the Head of the Watch barked. "Get the heir back before she is taken."

Ari Ara didn't tell them that no one could take her anywhere she didn't want to go, including them. If she wished to vanish like Mahteni and Malak, she would, but she knew that if the Marianans thought the Desert People had kidnapped her, every water worker in Mariana would be in danger.

Brinelle's deadly quiet stung worse than her towering rages. She ordered everyone but Shulen out of her study, her gaze fixed on the falling snow beyond the window. Her fist curled against her lips. Her eyes looked hard and worried. Without looking up, she spoke.

Tell me, Shulen," Brinelle pleaded in a low voice. "Tell me

that you had nothing to do with this. Tell me that the water workers who used the Way Between on the Watch know it from observation only."

"The water workers used Azar?" Shulen replied in a tone of surprise.

Ari Ara scowled as she studied the two. Some elaborate dance of words for spying ears was taking place. Brinelle had not questioned Shulen directly; she had commanded him to tell her that he had not taught the water workers. Likewise, Shulen had not answered, he had replied with another question. Ari Ara opened her mouth and two sets of steel-edged eyes shot her a stern warning to be silent. She closed her mouth.

"The rumor-river is flooding with stories I cannot believe," Brinelle growled, drumming her fingers on the arm of her chair.

The reports claimed that the water workers had launched an uprising. The Lost Heir had appeared to them on Shirar's Feast Day. Freedom had been promised.

"But worst of all," Brinelle said, tapping a report, "is the claim that the Desert King himself was there."

"That's just a rumor," Ari Ara blurted out.

Shulen's head whipped around to look at her.

"It's an old myth the Harraken have," she hastily explained, "that Shirar's descendant will appear as Shirar on his Feast Day. The water workers thought the Desert King would come because of the myth."

"Then *you*, daughter of Tahkan Shirar, showed up instead," Brinelle snapped, furious. "Do you have any idea what you have done?"

The Great Lady's tirade broke loose: she had fomented an uprising, incited the water workers, and offered them hope where there was none. Her reckless actions lent credence to the black rumors that she was the puppet of the Desert. Ari Ara hung her head and listened, hiding the hot flush of anger that climbed her cheeks. Stubborn frustration burned in her veins. She was sick of all the double meanings, the intrigues, and plots of Mariana Capital. She couldn't sneeze without someone taking it as a sign.

"I went because I thought *he'd* be there," she shot back, cutting Brinelle off mid-sentence. "I wanted to meet him. He's my father."

It wasn't exactly true, she didn't hear the legend until she was already on her way, but it would convince Brinelle - and the listening ears - that there was no plot, no uprising, no scheme with the Desert People. She had heard her father might be there, and, lonely orphan that she was, she snuck out.

"That was incredibly stupid," Brinelle stated flatly.

"I know," Ari Ara muttered.

"It will take me weeks to put out the fires of these rumors. You have done grave damage to your reputation and bid for confirmation."

Ari Ara rolled her eyes. She didn't give a broken thread for her reputation. Brinelle's mouth tightened at the reaction.

"This is not a game!" Brinelle snapped, losing all patience with the High Mountain girl. Ari Ara may not like the nobles, but their good opinion mattered to her survival. She did not have the same luxury of birth records and a lifetime in the Capital that allowed Korin de Marin to get away with scandalous mischief.

"Don't make me remind you that your position here is by no means secure," Brinelle informed her frostily. On the grounds of thorough investigation, she could delay the confirmation hearing until spring when the Fanten Grandmother could come to give her testimony about the girl's birth. Until that time, every untoward action weakened Ari Ara's position.

"If you fail," she warned Ari Ara, "the Assembly of Nobles will accuse you of treason for impersonating the Heir to Two Thrones. As a child, you will not be executed, but exile or imprisonment undoubtedly awaits."

She glared at the girl who sat stonily silent in the high-backed wooden chair across the desk. Shulen shifted his stance and shook his head imperceptibly. Brinelle held her tongue and did not spell out the dire consequences that the girl so obviously did not understand.

A child would not be killed, but her mentor would. If she did not recieve the confirmation, Shulen would be tried for treason and executed.

"As it is," Brinelle grumbled, "you have lost us Mahteni Duktar . . . and her wardrobe. There is no way you can wear her styles any more."

"What?" Ari Ara exclaimed. "Why not?"

"It smacks of conspiracy with the Desert. It's best not to remind everyone of your fondness for your father's people until this settles down. The Mistress of Dress will make you a new set of clothes in Marianan style. She just received some excellent new fabrics from the Loomlands - "

"I won't wear anything made by water workers," Ari Ara shot back.

"You'll wear what she makes," Brinelle insisted.

"No."

Brinelle stood and stared sternly down at her.

"You will wear exactly the styles of the Capital. You will blend in. You will look the part of the perfect, proper heir to the House of Marin."

"I won't!" Ari Ara shouted back. "I don't care what the nobles do to me, but I won't turn my back on the Harraken. I can't. I gave my word. The Water Exchange is shameful. It's horrid. I won't be part of it by wearing clothes made by bonded Harraken."

"Then you'll be confined to your quarters until you see reason," Brinelle thundered, slamming her hand down on her desk.

"Fine!" Ari Ara yelled, turning on her heel and storming out.

She'd stay in her room all winter if she had to.

CHAPTER TWENTY-TWO

· · · · ·

A Way Between

By midafternoon the next day, Ari Ara regretted her words. She paced the ten lengths of her bedroom feeling caged and suffocated by the press of walls and warmth. A flat cloak of snow plastered the windowpanes. The black river gulped the flakes as fast as they fell. Ice gnawed the banks like a row of teeth. The serving woman who brought her meals scowled, dour and silent. Ari Ara's questions went unanswered and the back of her neck tingled all day - a sure sign, Rill had told her, that someone was talking about her behind her back.

The whole Capital must be, she thought grumpily, needlessly poking the fire in the hearth.

Ari Ara wandered over to the wardrobe and pulled out the song-sash, missing Mahteni already. When she had stormed out of Brinelle's study, she'd hidden as many of Mahteni's clothes as she could, suspecting that the Mistress of Dress might destroy them, at least pull out the stitches and burn the desert silks in a show of opposition to the rumored conspiracies. Ari Ara had only a few in her wardrobe, the sash, a dressing gown, practice clothes with subtle edging in a slender band of desert red and gold, a few trousers, and a shirt she wore in the evenings while doing her Academy assignments. She hid them in different places, under the rug, between the mattresses, behind a painting, pinned to the bottom of a plump armchair, and in her bag of belongings from Monk's Hand. She tried on her old practice clothes, only to find that she'd outgrown them entirely. She realized sadly that while she was no longer a High Mountain shepherdess, she also didn't fit into the expectations of Mariana Capital either. She sighed. Ari Ara meant *not this, not that,* and she often wondered if she'd spend her entire life not fitting in anywhere.

Well, Alaren, she thought silently as she stared at the snow outside the window, *I belong with your Way Between, even if I've botched everything up royally.*

A tap on the door broke her thoughts. She glanced up as a snow-covered Rill shouldered in with Minli on her heels. Emir stood on guard duty outside, otherwise she doubted they would have been admitted. As it was, they said that they'd been turned away at the front door with a curt rejoinder that the Lost Heir wasn't accepting visitors.

"We had to come through Korin's passageways," Rill explained, shaking snow out of her hair onto the carpet as Minli nudged her toward the hearthstones. "A servant caught us coming down the hall, but Minli cleverly told him that he was just delivering an Alaren's Feast Day gift to Emir - no one'd let you have one, I'm sure."

Ari Ara winced at Rill's blunt honesty.

"I'm in more trouble than you can imagine," she groaned.

"Oh, we've an idea," Minli answered quickly.

The rumor-river gushed with gossip. The planned celebrations for Alaren's Feast Day had been cancelled - due to the weather, it was said, but everyone had heard the reports that two water workers had escaped the Watch using the Way Between, so . . . the rumors didn't quite finish the speculation, but left the thought hanging that the Way Between had become a method of resistance for the rumored water workers' uprising. The inhabitants of the island whispered feverish warnings to one another and the water workers had been locked in their quarters for the day.

"Good business for us urchins, though, just as we've always said," Rill commented. Her motley crew was crisscrossing the city running messages and errands for the noblehouses and everybody else. They hadn't abandoned their desert silk armbands; if anyone questioned them, Rill told her urchins to tell the Marianans to end the Water Exchange - obviously, it wasn't safe to have the enemy in their houses.

"Can't trust a desert demon," Rill quoted the common saying, rolling her eyes, "but you can trust an urchin - at least as far as you can throw us."

She made a wry face. Most of her lot were skinny as sticks these days. A good toss of wind could send the littlest ones clear across the river.

"Is it really that cold out?" Ari Ara interrupted as Rill stripped off her third shirt and heaped it onto the growing pile by the fire. The Urchin Queen had come in the door bundled round as a cloth merchant and proceeded to peel off two coats, four sweaters, three shirts, seven sets of trousers, six belts, and eight pairs of stockings. Rill shook the melted snow water out of her dark braids and emptied her satchel, turning out a pile of caps, finger gloves, bangles, head bands, scarves, necklaces, rings and wristbands. She laughed at Ari Ara's confused look and gestured for Minli to explain.

"All across the city," Minli said as he spread his fingers

toward the fire's warmth, "word has it that you told the Great Lady that you wouldn't wear a stitch of cloth made by the water workers. Rill tracked me down and hauled me out of class hollering about how you'd be stark naked since the Loomlands supplied everything the Mistress of Dress would use and - "

" - we thought you could wear our urchin's rags," Rill finished with a broad grin, yanking off a vest and tossing it to Ari Ara, "since they're antique, reclaimed, vintage fabrics already worn in opposition to the Water Exchange!"

Ari Ara felt a tickle of laughter rising in her chest as she looked from one friend to the other.

"These here came from every urchin I could track down," Rill explained, pointing to the pile. "Everybody wanted you to have something of theirs. Will you wear 'em?"

Ari Ara slipped the vest over her arms.

"Of course. It'd be an honor."

And, she thought with wicked delight, it'd put Brinelle in a tizzy to see her using the Way Between to neither concede to injustice nor stay sullenly in her room all winter. The Water Exchange was bad business for everyone except the nobles. She might lose the confirmation by angering them, but she'd keep her self-respect . . . and, she added, her *harrak*. She picked up a hat and tugged it on. By putting on urchin's rags, she could uphold the dignity of both her peoples, calling them all back to their honor by refusing to cooperate with injustice. Minli laughed to see her in the urchin's rags, but admitted it suited her better than fancy dresses. Ari Ara threatened to dress him like an urchin and he protested.

"The Capital University is having our class robes made by the Southlands looms. The Council voted on it months ago," he explained. "We're the largest employer in the Capital and we've never supported the Water Exchange. The Head Monk's always said he won't hire water workers in place of Marianans. So, when the Council members heard that the Loomlanders were losing their jobs to water workers, they decided to support the Southlands in re-employing them."

"I suppose that's an alternative if Brinelle locks me in a dungeon for these urchin's rags," Ari Ara mused, realizing that she, too, could wear Southlands cloth.

"Stick with the rags," Rill pleaded, "or nobody'll remember us urchins need employment, too."

Minli nodded in agreement.

The door opened behind them. They whirled. Shulen stepped in and raised an eyebrow at Ari Ara's attire. She held her breath. Silence lengthened. A crack of a smile formed on the warrior's lips.

"This will be interesting," Shulen commented.

"You're not against it?" Ari Ara asked anxiously, tugging on the flaps of the urchin's vest.

Shulen shook his head.

"It may be exactly what's needed," Shulen replied.

"There's going to be loads of trouble," she predicted.

"Trouble always heightens before injustice ends," he said implacably. "Don't mistake ease for peace. The Capital seemed peaceful on the surface when you first came, but the current roiled with injustice. You've just brought the tensions to the surface where they cannot be ignored."

"Do you support the end of the Water Exchange?" Ari Ara asked, curiously.

"It is wrong for the Marianans to deny the water where it wants to go," Shulen answered carefully, shaking his head.

In his view, the water belonged in the desert. Blocking it caused floods on one end, droughts on the other, and sorrow everywhere else.

"The Way Between isn't about avoiding conflict," he told the youths. "It's about dealing with it."

He took a small clay statue from his pocket.

"For you, for Alaren's Feast Day," he said, handing it to Ari Ara. "Since you seem to have found an unexpected Way Between your argument with Brinelle."

It was a statue of Alaren, his grin brimming with mischief over a long beard. He held a walking stick in one hand and stood light on his feet, poised on the verge of motion and laughter.

"I love it," she breathed. "Thank you!"

"I have something for you, too," Minli mentioned.

He brought out a package wrapped in oilskin to protect it from moisture. Ari Ara took it, though she hardly felt like she deserved gifts, especially on Alaren's Feast Day. Inside was a book - or rather, a copied manuscript of Professor Solange's unfinished *History of Azar* from Alaren's time to present. It told of the Golden Years, the Great Persecution, the Dark Passage, and onward to today. At the end, she saw her name, Minli's, Emir's, Korin's, and Shulen's.

"We're not done yet," Minli told her, sitting on the arm of the chair next to her and pointing to the last sections. "Shulen's promised to share his family's stories, but we haven't had time. Also, we think the Desert People have more stories in their songs, but Professor Solange says she can't get funding for research or permission to travel to the Desert."

"But," Shulen told Ari Ara gently, "you'd have use for what we know, even if it's incomplete."

Ari Ara had gifts for them, too. For Minli, she had a copy of a rare story about Alaren that Brinelle had found in her great-great-grandmother's diary. For Rill, she had extra lengths of the desert silks that had made her Feast Day dresses. She dug

Shulen's gift out from her hiding place in the bottom of the bag of Monk's Hand belongings. She shook the folded fabric out and held it up to the old warrior. A banner unfurled nearly as long as she stood tall, gleaming white with simple black ink brushstrokes forming the Mark of Peace.

"It's for you," she said shyly, "for when you retire, or stop teaching Attar and get to focus on Azar. I got it during the Urchins' Feast."

Shulen stretched out a hand and touched the brushstrokes.

"It's wonderful," Shulen said quietly. "I'm proud of you, Ari Ara."

"Are you?" she asked wistfully, thinking of all the trouble she'd gotten into.

Suddenly, Shulen crouched before her, looking up at her with compassion. He squeezed her arm gently.

"Of course. I am proud of the *harrak* of who you are."

It was odd to hear the Desert Speech coming from the old warrior, but he spoke it true, and the word rang on the air, straightening her spine and sending a glow of pride through her. Shulen took the banner from her and rose to standing, admiring it.

"I will hang it in my quarters, though I may not be able to fly this for some time," he warned her.

Rill nudged Minli.

"It might not be so long as he thinks, eh? Tell Shulen what we saw coming over."

"It's as good as a gift even if we can't wrap it up," Minli agreed excitedly.

While they were tracking down urchins, they'd passed the Wall of Ancestor Statues. As they walked by, a pair of urchins had approached and tied a set of twisted fabric charms to Alaren's stony wrist.

"But they weren't the only ones," Minli added.

Offerings had been piled at Alaren's feet. The snow had been falling swiftly, but they brushed it aside and found gifts of blue threads from the unraveled edges of the water workers' sashes. Merchants left small tokens of their trades. The scholars and monks had put little prayer notes on the base of the statue, weighed down with polished river stones. The orphans had come and gone, leaving their prized Feast Day trinkets in gratitude to Alaren. The warrior monks from the High Mountains had left traditional monastery offerings. Strips of warriors' tunics had been tied to Alaren's elbow.

Shulen turned away abruptly and looked out the window at the snow. He pressed his eyes briefly then spoke in a ragged voice.

"That has never happened before. Not in my lifetime. I never thought I would live to see this - to see people learning Azar, following the Way Between, honoring Alaren's Feast Day, reading his stories at the University."

He whirled back to the others and strode from one astonished youth to the next, placing his palm on Minli's shaved head, touching Rill's cheek, and finally coming to stand by Ari Ara, a blaze of light in his eyes.

"We have done what my father thought was impossible. We have broken the silence and secrecy, and brought Azar out of hiding. Thank you."

Ari Ara smiled for the first time all day.

CHAPTER TWENTY-THREE

. . . . .

The Flood

To no one's surprise, the Great Lady was not amused by the urchin's rags. Brinelle flatly forbade Ari Ara to leave her quarters until she was suitably attired to her rank and station. Winter snows and waggling tongues stormed the Capital while Ari Ara remained shuttered behind closed doors. She read the first chapters of the *History of Azar* and wrote to the Desert King, hiding the letters behind her wardrobe until the stormy weather of both people and politics cleared. She picked at her food as she grew increasingly restless. Korin came each afternoon and talked nonstop about the absurd stories racing the halls of the newly-reopened Nobles Academy.

"They honestly think Brinelle's got you locked in a dungeon for treason," Korin reported, flopping into a chair. "Varina's beaming like her birthday's come early."

The House of Marin's official story was that the Lost Heir had caught a cold over the Feast Days - which some people said served her right for traipsing out into the snow with the water workers - but the young nobles had also heard a strange and disturbing rumor that the Lost Heir was refusing to wear clothes.

"They think you've gone mad; plenty of Marins have, you know," Korin remarked with a grin, "so I told them the truth, which no one believed, of course."

Each day, the urchins brought new clothes for Ari Ara. At first, they left them at the gates of the House of Marin, but when the Mistress of Dress started confiscating them, the urchins schemed up clever ways to send clothes through sympathetic maids and warrior monks. A pair of finger gloves came tucked inside a book from Minli. A skirt was slipped inside her wardrobe while two maids cleaned her quarters. One shoe showed up under a covered dinner plate; the other arrived in the ashbin when the servants cleaned the fireplace. Shulen and Emir looked the other way as they stood guard outside her door. Once a week, Rill waltzed - or rather, waddled - in with layers of clothes wrapped around her like an onion.

Tension thickened in the city. The water workers were kept under tight watch, locked in their quarters at night, and confined to their workplaces during the day. They made no secret of their support for the young queen, boldly telling the Marianans that she was an heir they were proud to claim. Long into the evenings, the sound of their songs rose from their quarters, ballads about the Lost Heir who appeared to them as the rightful descendent of Shirar. Once, Ari Ara heard voices outside her window and flung back the curtains to see Mahteni and Malak rowing against the current of the ice-edged black river. They sang louder as they waved, awkwardly trying to navigate the shrinking tongue of open water as the snow fell all around them. The Royal Guard and the Capital Watch began to shout from the rooftop. Mahteni and Malak turned their oars downstream and sped away.

Frigid nights closed in. Ice shut the river until spring. One week dragged into the next. Ari Ara had just started to wonder if she'd be confined to her quarters for the next twelve years as the Invisible Heir when Brinelle paid her a visit.

"Did you put them up to this?" she demanded.

"Up to what? Who?" Ari Ara spluttered, hoping the water workers weren't putting themselves in danger.

Brinelle took her by the arm and brought her down the hall to a sitting room that overlooked the front gate. Beyond the courtyard wall, Ari Ara could see dozens of urchins holding up banners with the Mark of Peace and signs she couldn't quite read at this distance. Brinelle recited them for her.

Urchins have more freedom than the Young Queen.

Let her wear what she wants.

Queens aren't dolls. Don't play with us.

Ari Ara stifled a laugh. That sounded like Rill.

"The self-styled Urchin Queen, Everill Riverdon, demands an audience," Brinelle reported. "She is threatening an Urchins Unrest if we don't let you wear what you want."

Korin dropped by her quarters the following afternoon and reported on the fallout of the meeting: whatever Brinelle had said to Everill Riverdon unleashed a storm of urchin fury like nothing Mariana Capital had ever seen! Axle pins were pulled out of carts. Slop buckets were emptied on doorsteps. Barrels blocked the bridges. Draft horses were let loose from stalls. Awning strings were snipped. Snowballs shot in every direction. Messages went awry. Deliveries arrived at the wrong doors. The merchants tried to send water workers instead of hiring urchins, but the urchins cornered the blue-slashed workers and took their goods - or at least, that's the tale that was told. Korin said he couldn't fathom how even the urchins could make so much mischief and swore that the water workers had to be helping them.

After a week of mayhem, the merchants and tradesmen

began requesting that the Great Lady rein in the urchins. Brinelle sent out the Watch in response, but the urchins were slippery as eels. Minli managed to talk his way into visiting Ari Ara and confirmed Korin's suspicion that the water workers were supporting the Urchins Unrest.

Doors opened in alleyways in time for a racing urchin to duck away from the Watch. Water workers on the shipping docks toppled crates in front of the urchins' pursuers. In the Houses of Dress, desert seamstresses pointed irate Mistresses in the opposite direction when the urchins unraveled bolts of cloth and swapped the labels on boxes.

"Rill says locking the water workers up at night is backfiring on the nobles," Minli relayed to Ari Ara. "The Harraken spend half the night singing ballads about the Lost Heir and the other half plotting how to aid the urchins. There's no question in their minds that you're Tahkan Shirar's daughter. They say that only his daughter would be crazy enough to refuse to wear clothes in support of their water rights."

"I've heard madness runs in both sides of the family," Ari Ara answered with a grin.

The unrest swelled. Mice were let into storerooms. Floors were polished into sheets of slippery ice. A crate of hens, intended for a roast feast, were instead carried in live under lidded silver platters and released in a flurry of feathers and squawking. Storm windows were unlatched and snow plastered the carpets. Horses were turned out of stables and released into the Training Yards.

Rumors circulated that a man and a woman from the Desert were traveling between the water workers' quarters fomenting resistance. They masqueraded as bonded water workers during the day, but the nobles' spies claimed they were agents of Tahkan Shirar, spreading the unrest. Fears that the Urchins

Unrest would escalate into a violent bloodbath ran rampant. The Watch was ordered to interrogate the water workers one-by-one, but each Harraken said the same thing:

"If Ari Ara Shirar en Marin stands up for us, then harrak demands that we stand up for her."

After a month of mayhem, Mariana Capital was in a state of panic. The merchants and nobles demanded that the Great Lady put a stop to the chaos. The water workers quit working entirely, sitting at their benches and work stations humming one of their songs as their masters and mistresses threatened them with death, dismemberment, and other gruesome fates. When a gang of dockworkers shoved a water worker through an ice-fishing hole, the Great Lady put her foot down, forbidding murder or violence to the water workers, which were, after all, under her oversight. The violent edge of the seething animosity simmered, but did not break again. The Urchins Unrest, on the other hand, intensified by the hour until Mariana Capital came to a wailing halt one afternoon when the urchins occupied the waterworks in the Under Way and stopped the gears that powered the city.

"Let the Young Queen wear what she wants, it's not worth this," people moaned.

The Assembly of Nobles passed a resolution stating that the conflict had strangled the winter economy to the point of crisis and requesting that the Great Lady allow the Lost Heir to choose her own wardrobe.

At long last, as the edge of winter groaned and loosened its grip, Brinelle stormed into Ari Ara's rooms and tossed a newly-delivered urchin's vest at her.

"Enough of this," Brinelle snapped. "Tell those urchins to cease this mischief."

When the Lost Heir appeared on the front wall of the

House of Marin in urchin's rags, the mayhem halted instantly. In a show of magnanimity, the Urchin Queen told the astonished Capital that the urchins would repay any losses and repair any damages they'd caused. For the next two weeks, they ran messages perfectly and for free. They delivered packages at double speed. They helped the merchants set out their wares. They apologized to the Watch for giving them hard chases.

"Minli suggested it," Rill shrugged when Ari Ara was finally permitted to return to Azar practice and could bend her friend's ear for news. "He's really the best of us, you know."

"I do," Ari Ara agreed. Minli understood inner Azar in ways she couldn't even imagine. Only he would think to have the urchins repair the strained relationships all over the Capital.

Not everyone was pleased by the terms of the truce, however. The first day she returned to the Nobles Academy, she didn't last five minutes.

"What do you mean, you got thrown out?" Brinelle demanded, looking at the hall clock in astonishment. "You hadn't been there ten minutes. What could you possibly have done in that short amount of time?"

Ari Ara sighed and explained: the Headmistress of the Academy had instituted a dress code and the urchin's rags broke half the rules in the new book.

"She's just looking for an excuse to ban you," Brinelle commented acerbically, scowling in the direction of the Academy, "and to insult the House of Marin."

Ari Ara couldn't see the slight, but she didn't care to argue with her aunt while smoke practically curled out of her ears.

"It will be cold. It will be hard. But no doubt, you'll manage," Brinelle continued, talking half to herself. "I should have sent you there in the first place."

She's locking me in a tower, Ari Ara thought wildly.

"If Alinore went, I don't see why you can't cross the city to attend classes," Brinelle stated. "You'll be safe enough with Emir watching over your shoulder."

University?! Ari Ara realized that Brinelle was sending her to the Capital University.

"I expect you to study hard, do you hear?" Brinelle scolded.

"Yes, Lady-Aunt," Ari Ara promised with a thrilled expression.

"Go and get Shulen," she ordered a servant standing nearby. "I'm taking you myself. We'll pick up Korin on the way. No puffed-up pincushion of a Headmistress throws the Young Queen of Mariana out for wearing what she pleases. That sort of attitude simply won't be tolerated."

"But, Lady-Aunt, *you* opposed the urchin's rags," Ari Ara protested.

"That's different," Brinelle snapped. "I'm your aunt, the regent of the nation, and the head of the House of Marin. I have every right to argue with you over style and dress. *She* doesn't."

"But – "

"No buts," Brinelle said firmly, drawing herself up tall and imposing. "It's one thing for me to reprimand you; it's another for her to pull this stunt. No one - no one! - has the right to try to squelch the public statements of the Young Queen of Mariana, Heir to Two Thrones. You have a responsibility and a duty to *all* of your peoples, and if the Headmistress of the Academy does not understand that, then she isn't fit to be educating the heir to our throne."

Ari Ara stifled her groan. She would never understand the ways of the Capital, not if she lived here for a thousand years. She had to jog to keep up with the Great Lady's purposeful stride as she stormed from the house, calling for her coat, pausing only to check the angle of her hat at the front door mirror. She patted a tendril of brown hair into place and swept out to turn the Capital on its head.

The news that Brinelle had pulled the youths of the House of Marin out of the Nobles Academy set off a flashflood of gossip. Whole lengths of her tirade to the Headmistress were circulated verbatim: the water workers were the wards of the House of Marin and the urchins of the Mariana Capital were the business of the Lost Heir, and if she chose to call attention to the inherent injustice of this situation - with the express permission of the Great Lady - no person in the Capital had any ground to stand on if they tried to get in her way.

The southern nobles took Brinelle's fury as an opening to support the cause. They joined the boycott of cloth made by water workers, overhauling their wardrobes and branding their merchants' wares as Marianan-made. Isa and her mother hosted a series of Dressiers Parties featuring new fashions from the looms of the Southlands. Weavers, spinners, dyers, tailors, and seamstresses who had lost positions to the water workers quickly moved to gain employment with the Southlands Dressiers as the dispute split the fashion modes of the city.

The University students, always quick to adopt the latest fashions, began to wear Marianan-made garments from the Southlands. Some even mimicked the patched styles of the urchins, but Rill and company objected to the unearned adoption of their ways. Mobilizing swiftly, they went door-to-door among the students, explaining that their culture was built on giving, not selling, and no urchin's rags should be sold for coin. Professor Solange arranged a lecture for the Urchin Queen to explain the matter to the students, and fast as gossip travels, the faux urchin's rags vanished. Everill thanked the students for their support of Marianan-made styles and told them that the urchins would give swift and prompt priority service to those who bore the symbol of the Southlands, an ambling bear, on their makers' marks and labels. Merchants, too, began to hang the bear out of their neck collars. Soon, those who supported the cause of ending the Water Exchange gained a slight economic advantage over those who hadn't.

The ice around Mariana Capital began to moan in the night, cracking and breaking in explosions that woke Ari Ara up. The entire city seemed on edge; everyone looking over their shoulders, casting baleful and suspicious looks at the water workers. People openly called for the end of the Water Exchange, ready for the cursed desert demons to be sent back to their horrid desert to starve in the summer droughts.

"The end of the Water Exchange is no good to them without the water," Minli said to Ari Ara one afternoon. "Malak swears he'll find a way to get the water, too."

"You've seen Malak?" Ari Ara yelped.

Minli hastily shushed her.

"Yes, and Mahteni, too. Didn't you know?" he whispered.

The pair were moving through the Under Way and hiding with sympathizers throughout the city.

"Malak's had me researching water rights documentation all winter," Minli told her, his brow creased with worry. "I've been hiding records in Professor Solange's office."

"What?" Ari Ara gasped. The scholarly youth revered records ... he'd sooner tear out his eyebrows than steal a library book.

"I had to," Minli confessed, turning a shade of crimson. "Someone was taking them from the Capital Library and destroying them."

Ari Ara grimly told him to be careful ... people had died trying to end the Water Exchange before.

"It's worth the risk," Minli argued. "The Harraken might have a real claim. It looks like the free and open flow of the major rivers into the desert has been a part of every treaty ever signed . . . including the one at the end of the War of Retribution."

Ari Ara raised her eyebrows. A law that violated a treaty would be invalid; she had learned that much from her searches through the records. Minli's eyes shone with anticipation. Any day now, he told Ari Ara, the Desert King was expected to enter his official legal challenge to the Water Exchange. His eyes leapt to the winter sky outside the window as if expecting to see the messenger hawk soar past to deliver the documents.

Two weeks later, Tahkan Shirar's sealed documents arrived on a flawlessly blue day that sent trickles of snowmelt singing off the rooftops and through the gutters. One couldn't help but feel the surge of hope rising up with sun-streaming winds. The water workers went about the Capital humming at their tasks, unable to hide their grins.

It took the Assembly of Nobles fifteen short minutes to dash the hopes of thousands.

"We reject the spurious claims of the crafty Desert King," Thornmar declared, speaking as a representative of the Assembly of Nobles. "There is no documentation to back up his assertions about the water rights."

Minli was beside himself with fury and Brinelle stalked out of the Assembly session tight-lipped with anger.

"He's lying," she snapped to Shulen, "but he's got half the nobles tied around his little finger. Without the original records, there's little I can do to even investigate Tahkan Shirar's claims."

The next day, a white-knuckled, one-legged boy stood up at the Assembly of Nobles and held forth the stack of hidden books and scrolls that validated Tahkan Shirar's claim to the water rights. Minli's knees trembled as he spoke, but he refused to give up the records except to a task force made up of the Great Lady, the Harraken ambassador, and the Head of the Capital Library. The nobles threatened to have him expelled from the Capital University, but the Head Monk intervened, reminding them that the University stood autonomous from the nobles for a reason.

"You cannot punish children for speaking the truth," he coldly informed the nobles, glaring at Thornmar, "even if the truth inconveniences your plans."

When the task force wrote its report, it upheld the Desert King's views. Thornmar's faction of nobles barred it from being introduced on the Assembly floor, effectively relegating the report to the dust of forgotten archives.

"You will likely rue this decision," the Great Lady warned them.

Thornmar's faction scoffed, but all too soon, her words came back to haunt them.

At the tail end of winter, as the icicles dripped and smashed from the rooftops and patches of brown mud broke through the melting snow, a messenger hawk swooped into the Keep with an official seal and a message to the Great Lady requesting the aid of the warriors and squadrons of the Watch.

The Loomlands water workers had risen up.

A strange, dark-bearded fellow had been stalking the factory towns like an ill wind, the message reported. Crowds of water workers gathered wherever he went. He sang to his people in Desert Speech, telling them that the Water Exchange was a false deal: the water belonged in the desert and he had seen the Marianan records that proved it. The strange man called upon the water workers to shut down the factories and demand that the Assembly of Nobles honor the Desert King's claim. He was tricky, the spies reported, elusive and hard-to-catch, trained in the Way Between.

Malak, Ari Ara thought, a thrill of recognition surging through her heart.

The water workers revered this shadowy figure. At his behest, they shut down the factories like a row of candles being snuffed out. They stocked up on supplies then took over the factories and mills, barring themselves inside. The Loomlands Watch threatened to burn the buildings down on their heads. The Great Lady ordered them to do nothing of the sort; she wouldn't risk war with the Desert King over the treatment of his people. The Loomlands Lady eyed her precious factories and seethed. She wanted the water workers out, but she certainly didn't want her factories burned.

The water workers had timed the strike well. Snow still heaped in sullen piles across the countryside. The mountains rose stark and white above the valley. An edge of warmth struck the afternoons, but each night the day's melt froze into sheets of glistening ice. The Harraken did not yet need the water for their spring planting, but the factories needed the water workers' labor to produce the immense volumes of spring fabrics for the Houses of Dress. The water workers had the profits of the Loomlands by the neck, refusing to work just when the cloth merchants and dressiers demanded fabric shipments. The de Barre's business boomed. The Loomlands panicked. The Lady of the Loomlands demanded the Great Lady's military support to break the strikes. Brinelle asked Shulen for his advice.

"Just end the Water Exchange," he suggested, sighing as Brinelle's lips drew into a sour expression. "Don't even wait for the Assembly of Nobles. You know what the archives say . . . the water rights belong to the Desert. The South Dam should never have been blocked after the war."

"I know that," Brinelle snapped.

Shulen stopped. The Great Lady's countenance turned as dark and foreboding as a thunderstorm. Shulen knew she would not budge on this issue, not right now when Ari Ara's confirmation loomed so close. A move like ending the Water Exchange would send a lightning strike of fear through the nobles who would retaliate by rejecting her would-be heir.

"Send my Azar-trained warrior monks to keep the peace and prevent violence, then," he suggested. "I could go with them and - "

"You are needed here," the Great Lady reminded him curtly.

The Orelands youths' vehement dislike of Ari Ara cemented into an alliance with the alarmed Loomlands youths. Each day, packs of boys, joined by the Smithlands and Timberlands youths, heckled Ari Ara as she traversed Marin's Way to the University. Korin would have been bloodied and bruised in daily duels if Emir and Shulen hadn't been escorting them. Twice, they had thwarted the attacks of livid noble youths using the Way Between. Emir and Shulen stayed beside Ari Ara in class, taking no chances of another assassination attempt.

Day after day, Brinelle delayed making a decision about sending warriors to break the Loomlands strike. Ribbons of clear currents slid down the river. A seam opened in the swift section. The Assembly of Nobles raged. The animosity over the Lost Heir divided the nobles. The Southlands nobles refused to support the policies of the Loomlands. The Orelands fought the suggestions of the House of Marin. The other nobles picked sides and dug in their heels. Gridlock marked the sessions. The ice groaned, heaved, and finally flung itself forward, piling up in massive jaws of jutting chunks that the River Watch broke apart so the jam wouldn't tear the bridges off their pilings.

In the end, no warriors went to the Loomlands. The Mari River flooded, blocking the roads and turning the waterway into a roiling river dragon, curling and bucking in massive waves. The currents and undertows churned so dangerously that even the most seasoned river sailors refused to travel upriver. Rain fell in the north. The mountains unleashed more snow. The Mari broke her banks, angry and dark. The high stone buttresses of the North End sheltered the House of Marin, the Training Yards, and the noblehouses along Marin's Way, but the water flooded the shores of the rest of the island. The Common Yard of the University turned into a swirling lake. The urchins made a fortune poling students across in small boats. In the plaza, the smallest ancestor statues submerged and brown muddy water knocked against the Three Brothers' shins. The South End flooded miserably. The urchins took their boats through the streets or else traveled on the Urchin's Way across the rooftops. The rest of the lower city moved into the second stories of houses and put up with their neighbors tromping through their bedrooms to get to the next footbridge between buildings.

"It's crazy to hold back the river when the Desert needs the water and we need to get rid of it," Minli complained. "The river wouldn't flood so much if we opened the South Dam. As it is, it backs up and chokes around the island."

Rill's eyes blazed when she heard why the floods were climbing so high in the Urchins Nest. She'd spent days moving their kitchen and battening down the lower nests against the threat of the coursing waters. Last year, she'd lost an urchin when he slipped and fell in. She rallied the urchins to flood the rumor-river with the connection between the floodwaters and the Water Exchange.

As the information circulated around the city, every disgruntled family perched awkwardly in their upper rooms, every merchant losing wares and market days, and every dressier whose lower storage rooms leaked began to grumble against the folly of holding back the water. Only the nobles, high and dry in the North End, were profiting from the Water Exchange. The rest of them were paying hard for the price of cheap labor. With the water workers in the Loomlands on strike and the ones in the Capital acting mutinous, the scales had tipped on the profitability of the Water Exchange. More and more Marianans wished the Desert People would go back to where they'd come from ... and take some of these dratted floodwaters with them!

When the floods go down, they vowed, *we'll take the matter up with the House of Marin.*

And they watched the watermarks like a ticking clock.

CHAPTER TWENTY-FOUR

. . . . .

The Spring Gate

Ari Ara eyed the mountains, searching for the subtle hints of spring. The cold wind's crosscurrents still cuffed the heads of the peaks, but the fine snow dust had stopped wisping into the air. The knife-edges of the stark white drifts - almost invisible from the valley, but tall as houses up close - shifted and softened, settling in the warmth. The Mari River had been thundering, brown and colossal, for weeks when the messenger hawk finally winged into the House of Marin with the announcement: the Monk's Tears River wept. Today, the Spring Gate would officially open.

Just like the year before, when she thought war was about to break loose, Ari Ara's heart felt troubled and tumultuous. The Loomlands water workers were still on strike. The tension in Mariana Capital was thicker than a stone wall and just as painful each time she inadvertently walked into it. Half the Capital detested her, the other half worshipped her, and Ari Ara was on the verge of writing to the Desert King to ask if she could come live with him in the Desert after the confirmation hearing. Hot as those drylands were rumored to be, it couldn't be any more blistering than the scorching politics of Mariana Capital!

In anticipation of the Spring Gate opening, Brinelle had let Ari Ara and Korin stay home from class; the students would be distracted anyway, listening more for the distant rumble of the Great Gongs and the low moans of the Horns of Monk's Hand than to their teachers.

Just after noon, when Ari Ara's ears ached from straining in hope, they heard the moaning rumbles of the ritual. Ari Ara could hardly believe the faint sound was the same thing she had heard the year before. The five bronze gongs stood taller than the monks and the massive horns stretched the length of the roofs. When she had stood at the monastery, the deafening thunder had reverberated in her bones as the bowl of the mountains amplified its call.

A fierce yearning surged in her, pounding against the underside of her chest like a caged bird battering against the bars. She longed to fly with the messenger hawk back to the cold beauty of the High Mountains. The rumble of the Spring Gate opening reminded her painfully of how far the clear streams and shadowed forests and black rocks of her home were from the maze of streets on the island city of Mariana Capital. She missed the land of silence and wind song. A prickle of tears pooled in the bottom rims of her eyes. A hand fell on her shoulder.

"Listen," Shulen said gently, as if he had read her thoughts in the tightness of her shoulders.

"I am," she assured him, straining to catch the long echoes that drained out of the hills like waves.

"Not to that," Shulen said. He gestured to the Capital streets. "To that."

Silence. The entire city held its breath, bowed their heads, shushed children, stopped conversations, stilled carts, and ceased their work. People shaded their eyes and peered to the east with wistful expressions. A holiness washed over the city. A sense of aching love crashed in Ari Ara's heart for the Marianans. They were unruly, petty, gossipy, ridiculous - a thousand things - and yet, as the stillness and silence lengthened, she sensed their reverence, humility, and longing. Inside, each person yearned to quiet the storm of daily life, to remember or to dream of the High Mountains and clean air. And each year, the act of listening for the Spring Gate called them back to their hearts.

She and Shulen stood silently until the last hints of the gongs vanished. A child's laugh broke the quiet. The moment sped onward into the next, rushing eternally forward like the river. Korin ran up and shoved a parchment, ink, and brush at her. He breathlessly explained that she was to add her greetings to Brinelle's traditional annual reply to the Spring Gate's opening and send a messenger hawk back to Monk's Hand Monastery.

Ari Ara made her way up the winding staircase of the Hawk's Keep. She could have whistled for Nightfast or even just handed the message over to the Hawk Keepers, but she wanted the excuse to be by herself. The tower felt lonely without Malak. No one had taken the small, drafty room; the other Hawk Keepers preferred the quarters below.

She'd forgotten to bring a treat for Nightfast and he sulked, winging to the stand and screeching at her. Ari Ara searched the handlers' bins, but the tidbits of treats hadn't been replaced. She opened the door to Malak's old room and poked through the jars and drawers, certain she'd find something to tempt the hawk back to friendliness. Malak's clothes trunk had been removed, but the set of drawers built under the bed still held odds and ends. Reaching into the middle drawer, she yanked it out entirely, trying to see if the round objects just at the end of her fingertips were nuts. They weren't. She tossed the buttons back in and shoved the long drawer into place.

It struck something halfway. She jostled the drawer, but it wouldn't slide in. Ari Ara frowned and pulled it out again, lying flat on her belly and feeling into the darkness to see what was obstructing it.

Her fingers hit a bundle of papers and a stack of books. She drew them out. The parchment was creased and worn around the folds as if each had been read many times. She turned it over and the cord of rough string slipped its knot. The pile tumbled like autumn leaves off the tree branches of her fingers. The handwriting on the inside opened into view. She grabbed a letter. Then another. Her eyes widened in confusion and alarm.

Her letters to Tahkan Shirar!

She knelt amidst the scattered stack, reeling. Had Malak never sent them? No, that was wrong. She distinctly remembered sending them. She'd seen Nightfast winging out of sight as the bird carried the letters westward. Had Malak trained the hawk to return with them? If so, then . . . who was writing back?

She pawed the letters, searching for hints, but they were all hers. Her fingers hit the books and she lifted them. One was the Third Brother's Book. Another was Minli's curriculum book. The third was Malak's personal notebook on hawk ailments and care, filled with fine handwriting she recognized at once.

Malak was writing the letters from the Desert King.

Eyes of the King, she thought as bitterness rose inside her. Tahkan Shirar had not written to her - possibly ever and certainly not since she came to the Capital. All the kind words of the Desert King had been lies crafted by his spy. An ache squeezed her chest, stung all over again by the harsh loneliness of orphans. What good was it to have a father if he didn't care about her at all?

Ari Ara held back angry tears as she bound the coarse string around the stack again. She took the letters, the books, and the notebook, trying to decide whether to tell Brinelle or not. He had been her friend, after all, and kind . . . but how much of his kindness had been a lie, covering up the fact that Tahkan Shirar had no interest in her? Ari Ara set her jaw and began to scour the small room for other hidden things. She told herself it was for information about the spy, but her heart cried, *why? Why doesn't he like me? Why?* Why would Tahkan Shirar not write to her himself? Did he think she was an imposter?

Ari Ara yanked the drawer of the small desk out and felt in the back. Nothing. She could understand why the water workers wanted her to care for them - she was the best tool they had for ending the Water Exchange - maybe that's why Malak had lied. She slammed the drawer back in place, hurt at the thought of being used, even for such a just cause. Her search turned up nothing more. Her eyes fell on a jar of nuts and she remembered her task. Nightfast accepted her offering, nipped her ear in a gentle scold, and held out his leg for the message. She shook her head.

"I'm not sending you, you naughty bird. You took my letters to my father to Malak," she told him sternly.

She used another messenger hawk to send the letter to Monk's Hand Monastery then ran back to her quarters. She shoved the books and letters into the back of the wardrobe with her Monk's Hand bundle. When the maid came to bring her some tea, she snapped that she had a headache and wanted to be left alone. The maid scurried off and Ari Ara hurled a pillow at the door as she left. A fresh burst of tears broke loose. She wished she were back in Monk's Hand . . . or anywhere but here where the nobles were about to reject her and the Desert King didn't want her either.

"I should run away," she fumed, kicking the leg of her desk. When Alaren's family thought he was crazy, he just took off for the Border Mountains and proved them all wrong. He had crisscrossed the mountains all of his life, sleeping on trail sides and in villages, setting up peace communities and his Peace Force.

Ari Ara's eyes widened. That's what she'd do! She flung herself across the room to her bookcase and pulled out her books on Alaren and the Way Between. She'd once dreamed of running off to the Border Mountains to revive Alaren's Peace Force. What was stopping her? *Nothing,* she told herself. She might as well plan to run off before the nobles threw her out of Mariana Capital in disgrace. *Or before they imprison me for being an imposter,* she thought, remembering Brinelle's warning. Ari Ara grimaced and pulled out the *History of Azar,* intending to learn as much as she could about Alaren's Peace Force. As she flipped the pages, the words *Champion's Challenge* caught her eye.

The Champion's Challenge is an ancient law of single combat invented by Alaren to stop his brothers from sending whole armies into war to solve their personal disputes. The Champion's Challenge was used three times in the brothers' lives, and Marin and Shirar died of wounds they inflicted upon one another in the third battle. The Champion's Challenge remains one of the only laws the two nations hold in common, and it is still active to this day. The Champion's Challenge has been used throughout history, most recently when the Great Warrior Shulen tried to prevent a massacre led by Soldek and Rannor Thornmar.

Ari Ara sat up on her elbows. That's what Emir had told her about! Shulen had tried to use a Champion's Challenge to stop Thornmar's massacre. Ari Ara stilled as a realization struck her. Could she use it to end the Water Exchange?

She leapt off the bed and opened up the law books piled up on her desk, ignoring the call for dinner as she searched for references. She scoured her books until midnight, but the Champion's Challenge wasn't in them. Thwarted, she climbed back onto the bed to re-read the account of the duels in the *History of Azar*. She fell asleep over the book and her dreams shivered with battles and matches in which she desperately fought everything to save everyone.

CHAPTER TWENTY-FIVE

. . . . .

Fanten Dream

"Are you sure you want to do this?"

Ari Ara jolted awake. Her heart pounded in her throat. The sheets twisted around her legs. Darkness pooled outside the window. She shivered. The confirmation hearing had been set for tomorrow. The mountain passes were open and the Fanten Grandmother had sent word that she was coming. For the past three nights, Ari Ara had writhed in nightmares of standing on a mosaic tiled floor among a ring of Great Trees that wailed like lamenting bones as a crowd of nobles jeered and spat at her. Thornmar jabbed his sword at her throat, thundering out, "No one wants you, desert spawn, not even your demon father!"

This time, the nightmare had shifted into a series of Champion's Challenges where she fought Thornmar, then Varina, then the nobles one-by-one, then the Great Lady, the Desert King, until at last, as she reeled with exhaustion, Shulen stood up against her and she knew she would lose to the stern old warrior as he stared at her with sorrowful eyes. All the while, the Fanten Grandmother stood on the sidelines watching her silently, mysterious and foreboding.

Ari Ara had wrenched herself awake.

Or thought she had . . . but the Fanten Grandmother was still perched like a bird on the foot of her bed. She scrubbed her eyes with her fists. The woman cackled with a tiny smirk of a smile.

"Tomorrow marks a crossroad," the thin, silver-haired woman said, her wrinkles creasing like cracks in old stone. "What will you choose?"

The Fanten Grandmother watched Ari Ara with a strange look on her face - perhaps only strange because the girl had never seen the old woman appear the slightest bit uncertain, let alone anxious, and so it couldn't possibly be worry on her face as she crouched on her heels and balanced on the narrow footboard.

"Is this what you want? I pushed you into this, child, but I can pull you out again," the Fanten Grandmother said, her lined face creasing over the words, her wrinkled fingers drumming her knobby kneecaps.

Ari Ara struggled against the bonds of sleep that tied her tongue and weighted her eyelids.

"Don't squirm," the Fanten Grandmother scolded. "It makes this harder."

"Are you really there?" Ari Ara managed to choke out.

"Near enough," the old woman shrugged. "A bit real, a touch dream."

"Why - "

"The confirmation, silly. They've been waiting for me all winter. I told them I don't travel in snow. I'm old."

She flashed a toothy smile.

Ari Ara snorted. The Fanten Grandmother was lithe as a girl and twice as agile. She didn't travel in winter because, like all the Fanten, she rested in the half-sleep deep underground in the caves beneath the Great Trees.

"But tell me, girl, and tell me quick, do you want to be the heir?" the Fanten Grandmother asked her, rising to standing and peering curiously at Ari Ara's moonlit face.

"What would you do?" Ari Ara retorted. "Snap your fingers and take the Mark of Peace off my back?"

The Fanten Grandmother shot her a scowl of a glance.

"No. The Mark's there to stay. I don't do things by half measures. Alinore begged me to put it on the heir and so I did."

"So, how do you plan to get me out of this?"

The Fanten Grandmother didn't answer and an uneasy sensation squirmed in Ari Ara's stomach.

"It is true, isn't it? I am the heir, right?"

"Oh yes, child," the Fanten Grandmother assured her. "I'd never have marked you otherwise."

Ari Ara exhaled her relief in a whoosh. She wasn't an imposter. There was no conspiracy. If this was a dream, it was a Fanten dream and they weren't like ordinary dreams. A Fanten dream ran truer than truth. The dream was as real as day, even if hard to believe. And, it was impossible to lie.

The Fanten Grandmother looked at her quizzically, tilting her silver head and stroking the strand wrapped in a long blue thread.

"Think carefully. After tomorrow, there's no turning back."

"What choice do I have?" Ari Ara cried.

"You always have choices," the old woman reminded her sternly. "You could steal away tonight and live as a Fanten in the mists and shadows."

"And then the two nations would go to war trying to find a vanished heir," Ari Ara pointed out.

The Fanten Grandmother shrugged. All choices have consequences, some good, some bad.

"Why do you want to be the Heir to Two Thrones?"

"I don't," Ari Ara answered honestly. The whole job seemed like a lot of bother to her: too many rules, responsibilities, duties; too little freedom. She'd be out that window after the Fanten Grandmother in a flash, except . . . the faces of the water workers rose in her mind . . . the laughter of the urchins . . . the glow of respect in the warriors' faces in Azar practice . . . the wonder of the University students . . . the offerings at Alaren's statue on his Feast Day . . . Korin's good-humored teasing and staunch support . . . Isa's delicate shrewdness . . . Rill's bolstering confidence in her . . . Minli's steady friendship . . . Emir's respectful challenges.

She could vanish into the mists and live as the Fanten did, in the quiet and shadows, but she'd have to give them all up. Shulen's face rose in her thoughts. She couldn't leave him, couldn't disappoint him by running away.

"I can't," she murmured.

"What's that?" the Fanten Grandmother replied sharply, holding an ear Ari Ara knew was as sharp as a wolf's.

"I can't go with you. I won't."

"Why not?" the old woman challenged, arching an eyebrow.

"I love them all too much."

The Fanten Grandmother sighed. The girl was her mother's daughter, that one, pulled into danger and trouble for the love of her people.

"They don't deserve your love," the Fanten Grandmother said haughtily, stepping down from the footboard and circling to the side of the bed.

Ari Ara thought about Varina and Thornmar, the Mistress of Dress and the Headmistress of the Academy. A weight settled on her chest as she thought about the Desert King's silence and Malak's fake letters. She shook her head. Even if he didn't love her, that was no reason for her not to care about his people. *Her people,* she corrected.

"All the more reason to give it," Ari Ara replied, fighting the wave of sleepiness she was sure the old woman was laying on her as she put her hand on the girl's forehead.

"Sleep then, for tomorrow the day dawns long, and that hour is nearly here."

Ari Ara felt the warm comfort of sleep folding her in its arms. The last thing she remembered was the Fanten Grandmother's wise and secretive smile.

CHAPTER TWENTY-SIX

·····

The Confirmation Hearing

She woke to an uproar. The sound of voices, rough with emotion, rose over the thick grumbles of the bruised and muddy Mari River. Song lifted on a thousand throats and soared over the rooftops of the city. A maid frantically shook her awake, wild-eyed and trembling.

"They're here - it's happening - oh ancestors, preserve us!" the woman choked out, white as a sheet. "The Desert People are here!"

Ari Ara rolled out of bed as the maid blurted out the news. Frustrated by the Assembly of Nobles' refusal to hear Tahkan Shirar's case for the water rights, the Loomlands water workers had left the barricaded factories and marched to the river, singing about moving mountains. Yesterday, they had hopped on the empty factory barges and paid the idling river sailors to ferry them south to the Capital on the turbulent and treacherous waters. No one knew where they got the coin - like as not, they stole it, the maid accused breathlessly. The Capital water workers were singing about some black hawk that came like a prophet with the Desert King's word, telling the Desert

People to walk out of their worksites and assemble in the streets to protect the heir and demand an end to the Water Exchange.

"They're singing about peace and your Way Between," the maid gasped, "but those desert demons are back-stabbing monsters. They'll be slashing throats in an eyeblink and all the more so if the nobles refuse to confirm you today."

The maid flapped her hands to get the girl moving toward her clothes and snatched up the comb to yank out the tangles in the girl's hair, talking all the while.

The nobles were in a right tizzy, she reported. The rising sun had parted the river mists upon the shocking sight of the enemy standing on their doorsteps. The local water workers had walked off their posts in solidarity and now thousands of Harraken filled the streets of Mariana Capital. The stone houses echoed with their strange and eerie song-chants. The rooftops clattered with urchins' footsteps as they ran up and down the Urchin's Way, avoiding the crowded streets below. The noblehouses roared with panicked outrage.

With one last tug of the comb, the maid tied her hair back and shoved her out the door. Ari Ara wiped her clammy palms on the sides of her blue trousers. At least she had been allowed to wear a tunic and trousers like the ones Shulen had given her in Monk's Hand. The Mistress of Dress had threatened to quit, but the maid said that Brinelle had insisted that the Lost Heir was to come to her confirmation hearing as she had arrived in the Capital.

"Otherwise, they'll accuse the Great Lady of trying to sway the vote one way or another," the maid confided.

Ari Ara privately thought she could be holding the Sword of Marin dressed in a moth-eaten shroud cut from the Tomb of Queens and they'd still vote against her. Brinelle met her at the entrance of the tunnel that crossed under the street to the Hall of Assembly. The underground corridor had been built long ago to spare the royal family from getting caught in the crowds. As she half-jogged to keep up with the Great Lady's pounding stride, Ari Ara thought over all she had said and done since arriving in Mariana Capital. For a fleeting moment, she despaired. She should have obeyed more, played by the rules, worn the stupid cage-dresses of the Mistress of Dress, not challenged Thornmar in class, ignored the water workers, avoided the urchins.

She sighed. She'd done everything all wrong.

"Ari Ara," the Great Lady said, pausing and guessing the girl's thoughts from the look of distress on her face.

"I'm sorry," Ari Ara blurted out. "I should have - "

"No." Brinelle's voice was firm. She turned, placing her gloved fingers to her lips. "Don't ever say, *I should have behaved like a proper Marianan noblegirl.*"

"But, if I had been more like Isa - "

"Then you would have been a decent noblegirl, perhaps, but never a queen," Brinelle told her. The nobles would have a puppet on the throne, someone who behaved herself and did as she was told. That was not the hallmark of a great leader, but a weak one.

"A leader must do what is right," Brinelle said firmly, "not what is easy. And that is what you have done ever since you crossed the Mari River. I have not always agreed with your actions, but I understand why you pushed for the things you did."

Brinelle paused and hesitated. Then she took Ari Ara's shaking hand.

"If it helps," she offered, "Alinore was just like you. I have always believed you are your mother's daughter, no matter what the nobles say."

She patted the girl's shoulder.

"It does help," Ari Ara replied in a small voice. "Thank you."

The passageway under the street was long and dark. The scent of dampness and old stones clung to the air. Ari Ara was reminded of the Fanten caves beneath the Great Trees - a sensation that intensified with every step. A narrow stone staircase carved through the massive foundation of the building. They emerged in an anteroom designed to allow Brinelle to pause before making a sweeping entrance into the hall. Ari Ara rubbed the hairs on her neck, an uneasy tingling bothering her. A cold shiver rose on her spine.

Brinelle ushered her to the doorway and Ari Ara peered through the velour curtains that separated the anteroom from the main hall. A marble staircase descended to a black and white mosaic floor. The gold gilt ceiling reflected the light of high windows. A glass cupola poured a shaft of sunlight down like a glowing waterfall. Old carved chairs, black with age and oil, rose in tiers in an oval. The Lord or Lady of each nobleland sat in the front, their family members behind them. The upper balcony was packed with Marianans of all walks of life. Minli stood among a group of university students. Rill jostled shoulders with her urchins. The streets outside were crammed tight with water workers and Capital dwellers. A relay of whispers ran down from the upper balcony and out through the side door. The Capital Watch, the Royal Guard, and the warriors were all out in force, striving to maintain order in the crowded streets.

Brinelle nudged the girl to enter. Ari Ara would not move. Every muscle in her body tensed in rigid horror. Her mouth made silent gasping motions. Her fingernails broke the skin of her palms, clenched into bony fists in an effort to choke back the scream in her throat. Her body began to shake. She shook her head wildly. Tears slid out of her eyes.

"Get Shulen!" Brinelle cried.

"No need."

The man's voice cut like a sword, sharp with disapproval. The Great Lady whirled, consternation written across her features.

"I told you we should have brought her here earlier," he snapped at Brinelle.

He ignored her spluttered protest and crouched down by Ari Ara.

"Breathe," he commanded.

She struggled to speak, choking on the words, lifting a hand toward the massive pillars encircling the hall. Just like in her nightmare, the towering bodies of the Great Trees stood before her, wailing like lamenting bones.

"I know," Shulen affirmed gently. "Breathe."

The ring of ancestral Mother Trees, worshipped by the Fanten, rose almost where their original grove had once stood. Long ago, they had been severed at their feet and chopped down to hold up the arching ceiling of the Hall of Assembly. The king of that time had toppled them in a wanton act of destruction, cutting the heart out of the Fanten's way of life and murdering the Fanten Grandmothers who refused to leave the trees.

"The Fanten raised her to revere the Great Trees," he explained to Brinelle. "These trees, the Mother Grove, are seen as living ancestors from the dawn of time. To her, it is as if the grisly skeleton of Marin and your forefathers lifted their bones aloft to hoist up this ceiling."

"There is still a Great Mother Tree on the South End of the island," Brinelle hastened to point out.

Shulen stared at her reprovingly.

"Yes, but one mother standing alone at the South End cannot sing through the shared roots of her sisters. She is lonely and cut off from the other trees."

Ari Ara lifted her head. She had met the Mother Tree, laid her forehead on her bark, listened to her lonely song.

"How can you stand it?" she cried to Brinelle. "How can you meet in this hall?"

Her eyes pierced her aunt's.

"We do not sense the trees the same way that the Fanten do," she responded, shifting uncomfortably.

Shulen glanced at Ari Ara's strained face. Rhianne's reaction to the Hall of Assembly had been similar; he could still remember the eerie keening of the daughter of the Fanten Grandmother. When Rhianne had descended the mountain trails to serve as emissary for her people, the corpses of the Mother Trees had screamed to her like angry ghosts. She had danced the mourning dance to appease them; Shulen had watched along with Alinore, frozen in the back entrance by the sight of the writhing lamentation.

"Do you know the mourning dance?" he asked Ari Ara, thinking she could offer it to the trees.

The girl shook her head. She'd seen it, once, sneaking through the forest's shadows to glimpse it. She'd been permitted to learn the lesser dances with the other young Fanten daughters, but she had been barred from witnessing the high ritual dances of birth and death. The Fanten Grandmother had stood before her, stern and fierce, refusing to let her pass, pointing back to the hearth-caves under the old trees. She'd sat, cold and miserable, alone for hours, still young enough to fear the encroaching darkness. She'd been punished with a week of cold porridge and colder shoulders by the Fanten who refused to speak to her, teaching her not to meddle with forbidden rituals.

"Never mind, then," Shulen responded when it was clear she wouldn't dance the sacred dance. "The Fanten raised you to respect the Great Trees, but you must break that upbringing now. You must face them and the nobles."

Ari Ara took a ragged breath, wiped her face, and nodded, gripping her courage in the tight clench of her wildly beating heart. Shulen squeezed her shoulder encouragingly and rose to standing. She stepped through the curtains into the hall. A sudden hush fell.

From the far end of the room, a figure stepped forward in a black wool cloak. A surge of pride squeezed Ari Ara's chest for the cool dignity of the Fanten Grandmother as she entered the hall as regal as a queen. Mouths fell open. Many of the nobles had not laid eyes on a Fanten for over a decade. Most of the urchins and students in the upper balcony had never seen any of the elusive forest-dwelling people. The Fanten Grandmother wore her simple silver robes made from the oldest Fanten ewe's wool and made the Marianan nobles seem like overdressed peacocks by comparison. Ari Ara walked across the tiled floor to greet the silver-haired, sharp-eyed old woman.

If it was a dream last night, Ari Ara thought as they met under the pool of light pouring down from the cupola, *it was a startlingly exact dream, right down to the number of beads on the blue strand of the Fanten Grandmother's hair.*

"Pay your respects to the Mother Trees with me," the Fanten woman said in her native tongue, laying a wrinkled hand on the girl's head, seeing the shadows of fear haunting her eyes. "They will want to hear from you."

Ari Ara nodded shakily.

Together, they crossed the mosaic floor and laid their hands on the first of the thirteen mothers who stood bound in silence in the hall. Something changed in the air as the Fanten woman placed her wrinkled palm upon the wood. Tingles ran up Ari Ara's arms and down her back. The Fanten Grandmother spoke the words of mourning, keened in a breath of prayer, called out to the spirits of the trees, acknowledging the bones of loss. She called her ancestral mothers present, asking them to bear witness to the confirmation hearing, to uphold truth when lies were spoken, to stand firm among the descendants of murderers, and to help this girl pass this test, this girl who knew how to honor the Great Trees.

"For she is the heir of our heart, too," the Fanten Grandmother said in the language of the trees and her hidden people.

One by one, the silver-haired old woman guided the girl to each of the thirteen Mother Trees. Ari Ara laid her forehead on the uncanny smoothness of the oiled wood where the natural hairs of bark had been shaved and polished off. She breathed her words into the aching trunks and sensed a surge of energy revive in the wood. The spirits of the ancient trees awoke and stood like giants around the vaulted room. Ari Ara heard murmurs from the nobles full of fearful suspicions about the Fanten conspiracy to take the throne, and bits of disparaging comments about the primitive rituals of wild savages. She ignored the insults. Marianans never saw what was beneath their noses, after all, and the Fanten Grandmother was unlocking and unleashing a powerful magic in the hall, invoking an ancient bond of truth and oaths. Brinelle and Shulen felt it, Ari Ara could tell by the wary alertness in their eyes as they greeted the Fanten Grandmother.

The Fanten Grandmother began the confirmation hearing by retelling the story of the Battle of Shulen's Stand and the dream-call of distress from her daughter, Rhianne, that brought the old woman flying across the mountain in time to find Alinore in the Fanten cave, struggling to give birth. She could not save the queen's life, but she did as Alinore asked, placing the Mark of Peace upon the heir and hiding her from those who would war over her.

After her remarks, the nobles began to debate, picking at holes in the story, claiming the Fanten Grandmother lied. All the while, their eyes rolled uneasily to the heavy double doors, tall and dark with age, sensing the press of bodies in the streets, waiting in anxious expectation for the outcome of the hearing. Ari Ara stood in the center of the marble floor feeling small and miserable as they argued. Her position had always been tenuous at best, but with thousands of water workers on strike and amassed in the city, she doubted any of the nobles would support her.

Uniter, Divider, Liberator, Destroyer, Ari Ara thought bitterly, *I fit the prophecy of the Lost Heir even if they don't confirm me.*

The debate thundered around her, heated and sharp, lords and ladies interrupting each other, faces red with tension. At one point, one of the nobleladies told the Fanten Grandmother to sit down. The old woman's eyes flashed at the imperious command.

"I will stand by the girl, and by my claim that she is the true and rightful heir."

She set her thin and aged hand on Ari Ara's shoulder, giving her the strength of her support. Thornmar thundered about her dubious credentials and her appalling actions since the moment she set foot in Mariana Capital. He worked the nobles into a fury of fear and hatred, detailing his suspicious of the conspiracies to weaken and endanger the nation. Ari Ara clenched her hands into tight fists and glared at the warrior. The Lord of the Timberlands picked up where Thornmar left off and the barrage of accusations continued. An hour crept by, and then another, but still Brinelle did not cut off the long-winded blustering. Her eyes flicked to the door as if expecting someone, but, at last, she sighed and motioned for silence.

"The time for discussion has passed. Let us put it to a vote, for ill or for good. I say this girl is my family's heir. What say you?"

One by one, they spoke. Lady Ilsa of the Southlands declared her support. The Speaker of the Riderlands gave hers. The Lord of the Westlands cried that the desert demons were at their throats already and it was her fault; he voted nay. The Lord of the Timberlands echoed his words. The Orelands and Smithlands spoke with the same breath, claiming that her Way Between weakened the nation and left them vulnerable to attack - as the water worker uprising proved. The Head Monk gave the Monklands decision in her favor, mildly remarking to the other two lords that, thus far, the water workers had remained nonviolent, and they had the Way Between to thank for that. The Stonelands Lady said she could not tell if the Fanten Grandmother's story was true and refused to confirm a Fanten pawn. The Lord who served as the Craftlands Council's representative voted in Ari Ara's favor, arguing that the Water Exchange should be ended, citing the problem of unemployed workers. The Lady of the Loomlands rose on his heels and voted against Ari Ara, speaking of her empty mills, the riots, and the shock to the economy from the strike. The Lady of the Fertilelands scoffed quietly at this and surprised Ari Ara by voting for the girl.

Ari Ara was tallying the vote in her head as the Twins of the Sisterlands rose.

"The vote is tied, six for, six against, and alas, it comes down to us," said the warrior-sister who trained the orphans into soldiers.

"We cannot help you through the impasse," added the mother-sister who raised children for more peaceful pursuits. "We are not of one heart, my sister and I. She says the girl is a threat, and that her Azar will weaken us, yet I think a girl who seeks to make fewer orphans of war is good for our nation's children."

A burst of outrage and consternation lifted in the throats of nobles and spilled from the upper balcony. Officials scurried to consult the law records. The Twins split vote was unprecedented, a shocking indication of the depth of conflict among the nobles. The Twins stiffened like stone statues and clasped hands as each side hollered at one of them to change her vote. The ancient matriarch of the Timberlands clan fainted and had to be carried into an adjacent chamber. Ari Ara wanted to throw her hands over her ears at the harsh and bitter curses flinging left and right, over her head, across the room, and in her face.

Brinelle was calling for silence when a new commotion rose. A voice roared beyond the tall double doors. The sound of scuffling broke out. Brinelle ordered everyone to quiet down as a frantic guardsman ran up and whispered in her ear.

"He has a right," she answered. "Let him enter."

And the doors swung slowly open.

Rivera Sun

CHAPTER TWENTY-SEVEN

· · · · ·

Tahkan Shirar

A figure strode in, backlit by the sun, towering in the light. Behind him rose the song of the desert from the water workers in the street. The man stepped into the ring of chairs and the light from the cupola overhead illuminated his face.

Malak!

Just as swiftly as the thought struck, Ari Ara shook it from her head. This was not the water worker. Though the features were close to the twin of the Hawk Keeper, this man had a flame of dark copper hair. He was clean-shaven and his chin tilted upwards with a blend of stubbornness and audacity. His gray-green eyes held Brinelle's amidst the shocked silence that gripped the hall.

"Tahkan Shirar," the Great Lady drawled. "What a surprise."

Ari Ara whirled.

Tahkan smiled at her, a slow curl of a grin she knew all too well.

"Malak?" she whispered.

"Forgive my hidden ways," he said, "but how else could I see my daughter?"

A thousand bits and pieces fell into place: Mahteni cautioning against his recklessness, his search for the maps and water rights, the letters under the bed, Nightfast flying to him, his certainty that the Desert King would appear on Shirar's Feast Day, Mahteni's horror when he was nearly caught by the Watch, the reports of the man in the Loomlands drawing crowds.

For a long moment, Malak held her eyes. Then he straightened and in place of the quiet Hawk Keeper rose a tiger of a man, a king, a warrior, a Harrak-Mettahl. The room seemed full of his fire and light. When he spoke, his voice thundered and the nobles flinched at the sound.

"I heard through the rumor-river that the nobles were blind to the presence of my heir - and thus, your Queen's daughter - among them. So, I have come to set the record straight: this is Ari Ara Shirar en Marin, daughter of Alinore and myself, and should you be so foolish as to refuse this gift living among you, you will lose her to my people forever. For we already love her as our own, and the honor is ours to claim her."

The balcony erupted with cheers. Korin and Isa let out whoops of excitement on the same breath. Shulen's eyes crinkled over a hidden smile. Brinelle arched an eyebrow and addressed the nobles.

"Are there any who wish to recast their vote, in light of this . . . unexpected arrival?"

The silence thickened. No one stirred. Tahkan's gaze flicked around the room.

"Perhaps, Great Lady," he said in a soft but stern tone, "it would help them to know that my people and I will be leaving this city and your lands this evening. The terms of the Water Exchange are broken. We shall work for you no longer."

That caused a stir. The Lady of the Loomlands leapt to her

feet. The Lords of the Stonelands and Smithlands cried out. Tahkan Shirar eyed them knowingly - their objections to Ari Ara had been rooted in their purses, not in their concern for her legitimacy or bloodlines.

Thornmar rose in a quiver of hatred and rage.

"If you break the Water Exchange," he pointed out in a snarl, "the water of the South Branch will no longer flow to your lands."

"No," Tahkan agreed evenly, "it will flood yours. I have dwelled in your city for many months in disguise and I have seen the ravages of the Water Exchange on your people as much as on mine. It is time for this foolishness to end. We of the Desert will permit it no longer."

The water belonged in the Desert, Tahkan reminded the shocked nobles. Every treaty since the days of Marin and Shirar confirmed this. The Water Exchange violated the ancient water laws, upheld over centuries, which stated that the South Branch of the Mari River should flow through the Middle Pass into the Deep Sands Valley. He had scoured the old records, cross-referenced a dozen maps, and researched in their own archives with the aid of their own students. He had submitted these findings, only to have them ignored.

"The water is ours by right," he stated, citing the references. "Your laws and ours both decree it."

"We still control the dam," Thornmar bellowed.

"You may control the dam, but you do not control us," Tahkan replied in a deadly quiet voice.

"You will come back begging for the water in the heat of drought as famine strikes your land," Thornmar threatened.

Tahkan Shirar glared back.

"Then we will return armed and ferocious with death at our backs and only your pitiful hot air between us and our water."

"If it's war you want," Thornmar challenged in a roar, "it's war you'll get, Tahkan Shirar! That water is ours!"

He leapt from the row of chairs, hand reaching for his sword. Tahkan wheeled, ready to fight back.

"No!" Ari Ara cried. She leapt between the bristling men, hands raised. "I invoke the Champion's Challenge! I invoke the old law, still active in both of our lands, which says a match of single combat may settle this dispute and end the threat of war. I will stand against anyone - armed only with the Way Between - to defend the water rights of the Harraken."

"You have no authority," Thornmar reminded her with a sneer.

Ari Ara shook her head.

"I need none. Any person may call for a Champion's Challenge."

Thornmar's laughter rasped like a blade against the sheath.

"I will kill you as you stand, you impudent, treasonous imposter," he scoffed at her, towering over her with his hand on his hilt. "Your Way Between is a Weakling's Way, a peace through enslavement to our enemies. I will drive it into the ground along with your dead body."

"You will do nothing of the sort," Brinelle's clear, firm voice called out.

Thornmar spun.

"This is out of your hands, Great Lady. She stands as Champion for our enemies and openly so."

Brinelle looked mildly annoyed - as if a gnat circled her instead of a crisis - and, not for the first time in his stay in Mariana Capital, Tahkan Shirar felt a surge of respect for the iron-willed Great Lady. He knew her heart must be thundering as madly as his own, yet she merely pursed her lips.

"By the old laws of the Champion's Challenge," she

drawled, "the challenged party selects her champion. The dispute is over the water rights, and since the House of Marin controls the riverlands, then I have the right to select my defender."

She looked almost a mask of boredom as she waved her hand.

"I have a Great Champion - "

"Emir Miresh is her friend," Thornmar objected. "He cannot - "

"I call on Shulen," Brinelle finished.

"Shulen?!" Thornmar argued, furious. "He will not fight her, not fairly."

"Oh, he will," Brinelle answered with deadly certainty. "If she wins, she takes the water, but if Shulen loses, he dies. These are the rules of the Champion's Challenge. If Mariana's Champion fails, he or she is put to death."

The Great Lady rose and dismissed the Assembly. The nobles leapt up in shouts and arguments, but on this matter, the Great Lady's word was final. The Watch struggled to hold back the shocked fury of the people in the viewing balcony. The front doors were hastily barred against riot.

Ari Ara felt the floor drop out from under her. She hadn't known the penalty - the book hadn't mentioned that - it wasn't part of Alaren's original idea. The pillars of the hall spun. The mosaic tiles underfoot blurred. Her head reeled in confusion and panic. A roaring sound rose in her ears. For one terrifying moment, she thought she would pass out. Then Shulen gripped her shoulder painfully, breaking off the faint.

"I can't. I can't," she mumbled.

"You can . . . and you will," Shulen told her firmly. "They will kill you if you fail."

"But I can't let you be killed," she cried.

Shulen's stony face cracked a tiny, grim smile.

"We followers of the Way Between are not so easily killed. Just do your best . . . and let Alaren take care of the rest."

CHAPTER TWENTY-EIGHT

. . . . .

Champion's Challenge

The news spread like a forest fire through the island city. People poured out of houses and streamed toward the Training Yards, crowding in on the heels of the thousands who had packed the streets outside the Hall of Assembly. Bets and wagers traded hands as people climbed into the wooden stands that had been set up for the Spring Trials. The Loomlanders, the dressiers, and the warriors all bet on Shulen. The urchins, without exception, laid down their week's wages on the girl. In less than an hour, the entire city had crammed into the stands. Every shop on the island was closed up. Merchant's Way was littered with abandoned carts. The noblehouses stood empty as the servants locked the doors and joined the masses in the Training Yards. Every water worker in the city seemed to be crouched on their heels on the flat ground at the bottom of the tiered seats. The urchins lined the rows behind them. The students packed the benches just beyond.

Ari Ara peered out from the warriors' hall as she waited for the hour to turn, the messengers to return with all those who wished to witness, and the official invocation of the Champion's

Challenge to begin. Shulen sat quietly on a bench. Brinelle drummed her fingers on her crossed arms. Tahkan paced feverishly. If looks could kill, Emir would have murdered her on the spot.

"If he dies," he hissed to her from his place on the other side of Shulen, "I will never - ever - forgive you."

Tears stung her eyes.

"Leave her alone, Emir," Shulen ordered. "She feels bad enough already and she needs focus now."

Ari Ara looked up. Shulen seemed calm and at ease. Oddly . . . peaceful. Tahkan Shirar, on the other hand, strode back and forth across the room like he might explode with fury and concern.

"You do not have to do this," Tahkan Shirar told her.

"I can't ask anyone else to take my place," Ari Ara answered. "And I have to uphold harrak for both my people."

"For ancestors sake, Tahkan, stop that infernal pacing," Brinelle snapped at him.

"If she dies, my people will curse yours for a thousand years," Tahkan growled back.

"Then she'd best not lose," Brinelle answered stonily.

Ari Ara gulped. Shulen spoke quietly to Tahkan in Harraken. Ari Ara caught bits of phrases . . . water workers, dangers and protection, something about Azar and marches . . . it made little sense to her, but Tahkan's dark and glowering look lifted like storm clouds. He breathed deeply and a flash of relief shot across his features. Ari Ara wished she understood. Her tense anxiety whirled so tautly in her clenched stomach, she thought she would be sick.

Shulen laid a hand on her shoulder.

"Remember," he said to Ari Ara in Fanten Tongue, "you must not lose, Ari Ara, or we won't - "

"Places!" the Master of Matches called.

"Won't what?" Ari Ara cried.

"Just don't hold back," Shulen called urgently. "Trust in the Way Between."

"Silence!" the Master ordered, ushering them out.

Thousands of people rose in a teeming mass of faces, many flushed red with emotion. The stands ran the length of the Training Yards. A set of noble boxes with brightly colored awnings perched on one side. Brinelle and Tahkan took their places in the central box, their chairs edged as far apart as the space would allow, casting dark looks at one another. Korin stood behind the Great Lady's chair looking whiter than a sheet and on the verge of tears. The Fanten Grandmother sat next to him, wiry arms crossed over her chest, eyes glowering around at the seething crowds.

A primal roar lifted thunderously from the Marianans. Ari Ara flinched and stepped back a pace. Nauseous anxiety shuddered through her. She stumbled and a ripple of mocking laughter broke out.

The Desert King sprang to his feet in her defense and lifted the Honor Cry. The sound of hawks charged through the air. The Marianans roared back. The water workers started to chant: *harrak-mettahl, honor-keeper*. The words rang on the air, potent and strong. On the edges of the sands, a woman rose and began to sing.

There was once hope in the desert,
a green tendril snake of land,
the kindness of a cup of water,
the river people's daughter.

Mahteni . . . Ari Ara thought with a surge of joy at the familiar voice.

Others joined in, their voices lifting in the words from the

307

song-sash, a sweet gentle ballad of crossed lovers and immortal hope, peace and times of rain. The song of her mother and father rose in her heart like the surging floodwaters of a river, encouraging her. Mahteni's proud face and wide smile gave her courage. The chords of the Women's Song echoed in the melody. Ari Ara breathed deeply as her verses came back to her. One by one, Ari Ara invoked the women who inspired her: Mahteni's skillfulness, Alinore's peacebuilding, the Fanten Grandmother's strength. Moragh's fierceness roared in her blood. Mirrin's love of her people lengthened her stride. She glanced at the Great Lady sitting in the box, tall and stern. Leadership was her strength and Ari Ara borrowed that quality now.

I will win, Ari Ara vowed, stiffening her resolve, *and Shulen will not die.*

She wasn't sure how, but there was always a Way Between.

As she crossed the last steps to the center of the practice sands, she breathed the Harraken words invoking the grace, strength, and love of her women relatives and friends, sending those qualities flowing in her limbs, tingling in her blood, rising like fire in her eyes.

An urchin's rippling cheer pierced the air, then another. A flash of white caught her eye. In the lower stands just behind the water workers, the flag with the Mark of Peace rose. A second flag joined the first, and suddenly dozens had been raised by urchins and university students. Slowly, the stands quieted. The Training Yards sat in eerie silence as if a moment of sanity had broken like a ray of sunlight through a storm.

Shulen stood opposite her, light on his toes, calm and inscrutable, a trace of a smile hanging on his mouth.

The horn blew. The flag dropped. Shulen leapt.

And she had no more time to think.

"*Attar!*" Shulen roared.

The crowd bellowed the battle cry back.

Ari Ara dodged, backpedaling over the sand. Her mind refused to believe that Shulen would hurt her, but he advanced relentlessly. She dove out of the way, knowing that the Great Warrior could kill her with a single blow. Ari Ara pivoted, drawing on her training in thwarting Attar with Azar. She planted her stance and turned his momentum against him, sending him rolling across the sands. Shulen leapt, one foot raised in a kick. She ducked and knocked him off-balance in the air. She caught sight of a twitch of a smile on his lips. A burst of anger sparked like gold fire in her veins. All those countless hours of training, she'd thought it was to thwart Thornmar, but something gleamed under the fierce concentration on Shulen's face, and suddenly, she suspected him of planning - if not this, than something like it - a match of Attar against Azar before thousands of witnesses.

"Look out!" Emir shouted, his heart leaping in his chest for his young friend.

Her surprise had made her pause. Shulen had hurled his strength at her stillness. A collective gasp sounded from the stands. Ari Ara spun just far enough to deflect most of the blow. As he passed her, she gripped his forearm and leapt backwards, dragging Shulen off his stance with her weight. Then she dove to the ground and pulled him with her, giving Shulen no time to use his other limbs. She scrambled to find an opening, knowing that she would never beat him through strength alone. Shulen pivoted in close with a series of blows that would raise welts on her forearms as she turned them aside. A line of sweat broke out on her brow. He was twice her size and faster than lightning . . . but he was also her teacher and he'd shown her the weak spots of every move he was using.

He swung. She leapt. The old warrior dove like a cat, after her in a flash. She danced away, keeping warily out of reach. Their breaths rasped loud in the dead silence that had fallen. Ari Ara watched for an opening like a starving hawk searching for prey. Shulen's limbs blurred as he unleashed his force. Only the discipline of training kept her from turning tail and running. If any of his blows landed, they'd break her bones. She dove and wheeled, threading under and around the burst of Attar's violence, waiting and watching -

There!

Shulen flicked his fist into a hard palm, angling the edge in deadly move, but Ari Ara saw an opening. She dropped toward the earth, reached with her hand, and snatched his fingers out of the place her neck would have been. She trapped his wrist, curling it back behind him, immobilizing the arm and tugging him off balance. As he fell, she knelt on his back, pinning him.

"Yield?"

The word was out of her mouth before she remembered the consequences. She nearly leapt back, freeing him, but the eyes of the water workers bore into her. She froze, trapped between fight and flight, desperately scrambling for another option.

"Don't yield," she whispered to Shulen as the Master of Matches ran across the sands toward them.

"Take the match," he murmured, gasping for air.

"I can't," she said. "I won't. There must be another way. There's always a Way Between."

"Yield?" the Master asked Shulen.

"No!" Ari Ara cried as Shulen nodded.

The Master of Matches lifted her arm up and declared her the winner. Ari Ara saw the crowds rise to their feet with a bloodthirsty yell. The Watch charged across the Training Yards to seize the old warrior. Thornmar drew his sword and ran after them, ready to inflict the death penalty on his rival. Ari Ara dove toward Shulen, standing over him protectively. She couldn't let them take him away and sentence him to death.

"You cannot kill him!" she cried, exhausted and trembling, shouting to the stands and spinning to face Thornmar. "By Alaren, I will not let you!"

A flash of motion darted across the Training Yard. A figure raced toward her. She tensed, expecting an attack, but it was the lithe, dark Emir Miresh who skidded across the sands to stand beside her. The Watch froze. Thornmar raced forward.

"By Alaren, neither will I," he declared, glaring hotly at the enraged war commander, "and I am fresh and unwinded. Rannor Thornmar, stop where you are!"

The Lord of the Orelands hesitated, eyeing the powerful young warrior. He slowed his stride, weighing the situation.

A blue-sashed figure ran between Thornmar and the youths, then another and another. The water workers, unarmed and yet undaunted, moved to surround the trio. A mottled-colored streak shot forward with a white flag - Rill! - and the rest of the urchins followed close on her heels. The flags of peace soared across the Training Yard as Minli and the university students ran to join them. Minli, leaning on his crutch and holding a pole with a white banner in his hand, spoke up, addressing the stands in a clear voice.

"We are followers of the Way Between," he cried, lifting the flag high. "Since time immemorial, we have sought to stop violence and end wars. Ari Ara has won the water and ended the terms of the exchange. That is enough. Alaren's original Champion's Challenge included no death penalties. No one need die to settle this conflict, least of all the Great Warrior Shulen."

"He has lost the match," Thornmar growled, furious at the

turn of events.

"Yes," Minli answered evenly, staring down the lord, "but if you insist on trying to kill him, there seem to be a great many innocent people you'd have to kill first . . . to spare you the effort, I might suggest another option to the Great Lady."

Ari Ara heard Shulen chuckle. Thornmar shifted, uneasily sensing the balance of power slipping out of his control.

"Instead of death," Minli suggested, calling out to the special box stand where Brinelle and Tahkan sat, "banish Shulen for a year. Send him away until tempers cool off and we can assess this moment with greater wisdom."

"And if I do not agree?" Brinelle inquired archly, lifting her voice loud enough to be heard throughout the Training Yards.

"Then we will escort him out of the Capital and safely to the border," Minli countered.

"I see," Brinelle answered dryly, realizing they would leave her no choice.

Tahkan leaned over and murmured something to her. Silence fell while the two rulers conferred in terse, hushed tones. The teeming crowd held its breath. At last, the Great Lady nodded. She rose to a towering height and looked out over the water workers.

"Out," she commanded. "The terms of the Water Exchange are ended and the older laws on the water rights shall be upheld. I want every water worker out of the Capital immediately. And when you depart for your cursed desert, you will take Shulen with you. Ari Ara of the High Mountains, you have lost your bid for confirmation, and as penalty for standing as the Champion of the Harraken, you are hereby banished until such time as I see fit to revoke this order. As for Emir Miresh - "

"I'm going with Shulen," he declared hotly.

"Very well," Brinelle agreed with a flick of her fingers. She lifted her head to the stands. "No one shall hinder them. No one shall help them. Not one finger will rise against or for them . . . is that clear?"

A rumble of assent and unease rippled through the stands.

"Tahkan Shirar," Brinelle murmured in a fierce undertone, "go now, before trouble breaks loose. Take your daughter and your people."

"And the water," he reminded her with a mischievous grin. "I'll be taking that, too."

CHAPTER TWENTY-NINE

. . . . .

Song of the Desert

The stunned silence splintered into a wild bellow of objection from the Marianans. The Harraken exchanged grim looks. The urchins hollered back at their fellow city dwellers that rules were rules and Ari Ara had won the Champion's Challenge. Thornmar turned purple with anger. Just before he stalked away, he shot Ari Ara a glare of withering hatred. She shivered. The glower in his eyes stated that she hadn't seen the last of him.

Marianans began to shout for a re-match. The students shifted uneasily as they lifted the white flags of peace. The water workers hummed a song to try to quiet the rising tempers. Under the cacophony, Brinelle urged Tahkan to hurry before objection turned into outrage.

"You've prepared them to leave - don't think I don't know everything that sneezes in my city, Shirar. I've had my spies watching yours for years."

Tahkan did not argue. He'd worked night and day since Malak had vanished into the crowd, preparing for a spring exodus of his people. Suspecting the nobles would reject his daughter's bid for confirmation, he had timed the departure of the water workers with the confirmation hearing to provide a protective escort for Ari Ara out of the country. Shulen had been invaluable to his effort, sheltering him in a house of sympathetic friends in the South End, setting up way stations on the East-West Road under the auspices of bringing a camp of Azar-trained warrior monks out to the Border Stations. The old warrior had watched out for him from the day he had loosed the Honor Cry for his daughter. Shulen had recognized the Desert King at first sight, unfooled by the weathered lines of time and the black dye in his hair and beard.

Tahkan Shirar stepped out of the stands onto the sands and lifted his hands to silence the crowd. He wished he could speak in Desert Speech, where words could bind actions and forge truths, but the Marianans would not understand.

"It is time for the Harraken to leave your . . . memorable hospitality," the Desert King mocked his enemies with naked truth. He gestured to the white flags. "If you ever come to the Desert under the Mark of Peace, we shall have much to teach you about the ways of harrak: honor, dignity, and integrity. For now, we shall leave in peace. We have what we came for . . . my people, our water, and my daughter."

As he spoke, Tahkan Shirar realized with a sense of wonder that, indeed, those three unimaginable dreams had been achieved, and most miraculously of all, without bloodshed. The Way Between had delivered more than he had ever hoped . . . so long as they got out of the city alive.

He strode swiftly to Mahteni.

"Tell the others to start moving, sister."

Ari Ara whirled.

"Sister?! You mean - "

"Ah yes," Tahkan answered, "meet your aunt, *Mahteni*, a

name which means Hidden Spring. She is my younger sister
Mirrin whom no one has seen for years. She was the first to
hide in plain sight of our enemies, searching for her niece, and
serving as the eyes of our people."

Mahteni sighed.

"This is not the time for family stories, reckless brother of
mine," she reminded him. "Get us out of here. We can
reminiscence on the long walk home."

The Harrak-Mettahl signaled to his people and as one, they
began to walk across the sands toward the wide, heavy doors
that opened onto Marin's Way. Shulen gripped Ari Ara's
shoulder, his eyes alert and watchful. A low growl of anger rose
from the stands. A shoe flew and hit a water worker. People
began to clamber out of their seats, rolling back their sleeves.

"Urchins! To me!" Rill cried, and a hundred street orphans
linked arms in a chain between the furious Marianans and the
Harraken.

"Students, to me!" Minli called, mimicking the linked arms
on the other side of the line snaking toward the doors.

It was a story straight out of the Third Brother's Book, the
protective stance shielding the Harraken from the shocked
reactions of the Marianans. To Ari Ara's surprise, scores of
shopkeepers and ordinary Capital dwellers joined the urchins
and students until the lines of supporters outnumbered the
enraged sections of the crowd. She heard a noble order the
Watch to stop them, but the Capital Watch and the Royal
Guard both looked to the Great Lady.

"They won the Champion's Challenge," Brinelle said
sternly. "The House of Marin upholds its promises and its laws.
Your duty is to escort them out of the Capital."

Brinelle paused for a moment. A thin smile crossed her lips.
She set her chin.

"As is my duty," she said.

Amidst the startled gasps of the nobles, she stepped onto the sands to join the Desert King in leading his people out.

Ari Ara felt a tingle of tears press against her eyelids, moved by the Great Lady's act of the Way Between, choosing neither to fight nor to flee, but to take a stance guided by justice and compassion, doing what was right rather than what was easy. No one would dare move against them now, not with the Great Lady sanctioning the exodus.

Brinelle stood on one side of Ari Ara, Tahkan on the other, Shulen in front, and Emir on their heels. Three thousand hearts hammered in anxious chests. The water workers, flanked by students and urchins, filed between the gates out onto the cobblestones of Marin's Way. The Royal Guard ordered the Watch to join them in maintaining the Great Lady's command, ensuring the head and tail of the river dragon of marching water workers were equally protected from harm. Brinelle led them down a side street through the plaza and past the Wall of Ancestor Statues. The Harraken touched Shirar for luck, Marin in gratitude, and Alaren with great respect.

As they approached the East-West Bridge, Brinelle turned to Tahkan.

"Don't get too fond of her, Tahkan," Brinelle said in a low, bemused tone. "I suspect they'll want her back once they cool off a bit."

"If they were Harraken, they'd never cool off," Tahkan commented with a chuckle.

"Yes, well, we river-dogs are generally more sensible than desert demons," Brinelle retorted.

"Brinelle," Tahkan said hesitantly, "in the Hawk's Keep, under the bed, there are some items I would like returned."

"No, they're in my Monk's Hand bag along with my Fanten

cloak," Ari Ara corrected somewhat sheepishly. "I found them while looking for hawk treats."

"Didn't you guess I was your father when you saw the letters?" Tahkan asked her curiously.

Ari Ara blushed.

"I - I thought Malak was, um, writing them because the Desert King didn't really want to know me."

She blurted it all out in an embarrassed rush. It sounded foolish now, but all through her life, she'd been Ari Ara, *not this, not that,* the orphan no one wanted. It was easier to believe her father despised her than it was to suspect he loved her enough to go disguised into the heart of enemy territory to meet her.

"Never again, Ari Ara Shirar en Marin," Tahkan urged passionately as they halted at the foot of the East-West Bridge, "never again doubt that you are a beloved daughter."

"Or niece," Brinelle added, catching the girl's eyes, "and it's Ari Ara de Marin en Shirar. Even in the Desert, the mother's family name goes first."

She shot the Desert King a sharp look before holding Ari Ara's chin in her hand.

"I have not been easy on you, Ari Ara, but beneath what I had to do, I have cared for you deeply. I hope, at some point, you know that."

Ari Ara flung her arms around Brinelle.

"I know that, Lady-Aunt," she breathed. "I know."

Tahkan Shirar looked back at the city, searching the packed bodies in the winding street crowded with water workers, urchins, and students. Among a huddle of children carrying flags with the Mark of Peace, he spotted a certain skinny, fox-featured girl in brilliantly patched garments.

"Everill Riverdon, come here," he commanded.

Rill jolted at being singled out by the Desert King. Then she thrust her shoulders back and swaggered forward, noting her escape routes in case he tried to call lightning down on her head. Instead, the Desert King shocked her by formally thanking the Urchin Queen for the urchins' role in releasing his people from the Water Exchange.

"In our dry lands, the clouds gather and wait," he said, "until a single raindrop casts her weight downward and tugs open the seam of the storm. You were that raindrop, Everill Riverdon, Queen of Urchins."

Rill tried to dump the praise - and blame - on Ari Ara's shoulders, but the Desert King would have none of it.

"The urchins' call for apprenticeships tipped the clouds in our favor and gave the Marianans a reason to end the Water Exchange for the good of their own people. For as long as I am Harrak-Mettahl, the urchins will have gifts from our lands."

The urchins cheered wildly, their trills and whistles bouncing off the stone houses of the island and rippling across the river waters.

"Minli of Monk's Hand!" Tahkan called out next and waited with a smile as the boy came forward. "I believe you just saved the life of my old friend Shulen, on top of finding and safeguarding vital information about the history of water rights, and protecting my people. Ask a boon of the Harrak-Mettahl, and if it is in my power, I will grant it."

"I-I," Minli stuttered, caught by surprise. He swallowed hard and looked at the Great Lady. "It will have to come from her, too."

"State it and we shall see," Brinelle replied coolly. "I rather think giving up my water workers, my heir, my Mariana Champion, and my Great Warrior is already expecting too much of my magnanimity."

"Respectfully, Great Lady," Minli replied, "I also just saved all of those."

Brinelle looked bemused . . . and thoughtful. That one-legged boy was as clever as ten monks put together. She would have to keep a close eye on him.

"My request," Minli went on, "is for a formal academic exchange to be initiated between the two nations. There is far too much ignorance of one another, and it leads to fear, conflict, and war."

The two rulers exchanged surprised glances and looked at the shorn-headed, one-legged boy leaning on his crutch.

"It shall be done," the Desert King vowed as the Great Lady nodded.

Ari Ara whooped and threw her arms around Minli, telling him how brilliant he was.

"How else can I come visit you in exile?" he whispered.

"Oh," she answered in a small voice, suddenly realizing how much she was about to leave behind.

"Don't worry, you'll see me before you miss me," Minli assured her. Professor Solange had already drawn up the paperwork for a research trip. They had planned to make a formal request after Ari Ara's confirmation.

"Better tell that to Korin and invite him along," Ari Ara murmured back, giving Minli one last hug as she spotted her cousin trying to sneak into the crowd of water workers preparing to depart. She searched the faces for the Fanten Grandmother, but the old woman had already slipped away. Ari Ara sent her a silent thanks and hoped the spirits would deliver the message.

"Ready?" Tahkan Shirar called out to his people. "Are we ready to return to our beloved desert?!"

The Desert King reached for his daughter's hand and held

it aloft. The Harraken cheered and called out *harrak-mettahl,* *honor-keeper,* chanting for the girl whose Way Between had won them water, freedom, and upheld the honor, dignity, and integrity of all her peoples. Together, they stepped onto the bridge. The Honor Cry lifted and soared like a thousand hawks. The cry parted and wove into a tune, each Harraken breaking into song as they stepped westward. Like a wave, the melody washed over Ari Ara. She caught a word in the rippling strands of voices, then another.

River. Returning. Life.

"What are they singing?" she asked her father, whose eyes shone with tears.

"They are singing that they are returning to the desert like water and life, that they have become a river freed, and great hope follows in their footsteps."

Then he hushed her next question. He had to listen and then he had to sing. For this was a new song rising from their hearts. They would repeat and reweave the melody and chorus as they walked over the mountains. They would invent each new verse over the nightly fires. For this was the way of the desert, that they wove their stories, together. Later, he would explain all this to his daughter, but now, they had to sing!

The End

AUTHOR'S NOTE
by Rivera Sun

In Ari Ara's first story, *The Way Between,* she learns skills that help her stand up to a bully. In this novel, she learns that bullies aren't always people. Sometimes, they're systems, laws, and practices that cause harm, hurt people, and profit off injustice. To stop bullying systems like the Water Exchange, Ari Ara had to learn how to work with others to make change. Over the course of this book, Ari Ara discovers how the Way Between is more than a personal practice . . . it's also a way of taking collective action to challenge and transform injustice.

Like the Marianans, many of us live in a world where injustice is woven into the fabric of our lives: the clothes we wear are made in overseas sweatshops, the food we eat is grown with chemicals and harvested by underpaid farmworkers, our endless wars cause on-going harm around the world, economic injustices are built into every aspect of our daily lives. Like Ari Ara, many of us find that even something that seems simple - such as refusing to wear clothes made in unjust working conditions - can be difficult.

Challenging injustice can often get us into a lot of . . . but that doesn't mean we shouldn't do it! Learning to see injustice in the fabric of our lives can be hard, painful, and frightening. But it won't change unless we look at it honestly.

Mahatma Gandhi said, 'The first principle of non-violent action is that of non-cooperation with everything humiliating." This principle applies whether you're being forced to do something humiliating . . . or whether you're the one forcing others to do such tasks. While it sounds like a straightforward idea, non-cooperation with anything humiliating requires profound shifts in all of our lives.

If you resonate with the Way Between, remember that it's more than a set of fancy moves. It's a way of life, a way of looking at conflict, and a way of challenging and changing injustice in the world. Like Ari Ara, you can't always make these changes on your own . . . but neither can anyone else. We are all needed in the struggle to transform our world. We're in it together.

To follow the Way Between in real life, we all have to start taking steps in removing our participation from those systems that humiliate, demean, and degrade ourselves, other people, and the Earth. Changing unjust systems is the epic struggle of our times, the powerful story of our purpose in this world, and the context in which true heroes and sheroes arise.

Thank you for being part of this very large adventure along with me.

Yours,

Rivera Sun

Author Q & A with Rivera Sun

Where did the idea for this book come from?

Where does any story come from? It's a deep mystery. Mostly, I sit down and listen until an idea flashes past like a lightning bug on a dark night. Then I follow those little winking glimmers of inspiration until the dawn of a new novel arises.

The Lost Heir is a sequel, so I knew two things: Ari Ara would go to Mariana Capital . . . and she'd make trouble there! Beyond that, I was - and always am - fascinated by how people organize to transform injustice. As Ari Ara stepped into the world of the nobles, it was inevitable that she'd run into some issues around class, wealth, hierarchy, and exploitation. She'd be in a tricky position as the Heir to Two Thrones. Everyone would be both judging her and fighting to control her. But you know Ari Ara! She doesn't respond well to being controlled. The thread of the water workers was a surprise development in the writing process.

Why did you choose to make the water workers more like migrant laborers than slaves?

All forms of economic exploitation need to be critiqued, challenged, and transformed. In our contemporary times, we are grappling with the ways in which economic injustice propels immigration. Many are trying to turn back migrants at the borders without acknowledging or dealing with the systemic inequalities that fuel immigration. War, violence, and poverty are the drivers of immigration. Until we address those, people will always need to seek refuge in other countries than their original homes. By framing the water workers in the context of migrant laborers forced to exchange work for water, it helps us see the real life parallels that are happening in our world today. In the novel, the Marianan nobles sought to profit from cheap labor by forcing the Desert People to work for water. This, in turn, causes ripples of injustices that end up hurting the Marianan workers and fueling hatred and tension between the two groups. In order to resolve the conflict, both sets of workers have to understand the underlying causes of their conflict and find ways to address it, together.

The Water Exchange forces Desert People to work for water. Where did this idea come from?

Water privatization is a rising issue in our world. People around the earth are mobilizing to stop the extraction for profit, and to protect the water. I chose to weave this into the plot to highlight how water is a human right and it causes cascading injustices to try to profit off water while denying people access to it. So many courageous communities are standing up to remind us that water is life, *el agua es la vida, mni wiconi*. In this fictional story, I wanted to draw attention to the importance of water as a social justice issue.

In *The Lost Heir*, why is fashion such an important social justice issue?

Confession: I love movies with amazing costumes. But the fashion industry is full of sickening injustices. The ways our clothes are made are shocking. So, while I creatively invented a "language of fashion" for Mariana Capital, I also wanted to bring up some of the ways our love of clothing can create terrible working conditions for those who make our clothing. Ari Ara is a shero with a purpose, after all, and as she deepens her understanding of the Way Between, she discovers other ways to put it to use righting wrongs and ending injustice.

It's important to question where everything in our lives comes from. As much as possible, we should choose things that treat people and planet with respect and care. Making these changes is not easy, but it can be very powerful. When Gandhi was struggling for India's independence, the movement spun their own cotton, wove their own cloth, and wore it in a traditional style. This provided economic employment for poor people, built solidarity between the rich and poor, and deprived the British of a lot of tax money and profit they were making on imported cloth. Fashion is often full of injustices, but with some consciousness, it can also become a form of right livelihood for many. This is exactly the shift that Ari Ara and her friends encourage among the Marianans.

The concept of honor, called *harrak* by the Desert People, offers guidance to Ari Ara as she's navigating conflict. Will you explain that a bit more?

Yes. The Desert People have a word, *harrak*, that means honor, integrity, and dignity all rolled into one. To them, it is the most important thing to "have", far more important that riches or nice houses. It is a guiding principle for their culture. We all have core principles - things like courage, love, honesty, respect - and they can give us strength and purpose as we take a stand for change. As Ari Ara learns about harrak, she integrates it into her understanding of the Way Between. These ideas give her guidance on how and when to stand up for what's right even when it's hard or when doing what's right will get her into trouble. *Harrak* offers her a way to stay honest and humble while still lifting her head up with pride. It's a powerful idea for all of us. All core principles are.

Where did you get the idea for the tension between the street urchins and water workers?

Scapegoating is incredibly common in our world. We're taught to hate other groups of people rather than look for creative solutions to our conflicts. The street urchins and water workers are both suffering from the Water Exchange, but instead of understanding that the nobles' policy has driven the Desert People into Mariana, the street urchins fall into the trap of fighting with the water workers, who they see as having taken their jobs. Dr. King had a strong principle of nonviolence, *to fight injustice, not people.* I think it's an excellent reminder that our "enemy" isn't people, it's their actions, behaviors, beliefs, and policies that are terrible. In so many of our conflicts, if we can learn to see past our prejudices to the root problems, we can find ways to work with unlikely allies to resolve the conflict in a way that works for everyone.

Why do you feel it's so important to write about social justice issues?

All fiction deals with social justice issues. It's just a question of who the author is writing for: the status quo or the leading edge of change. We need to learn to read with a critical gaze and to recognize that all stories are teaching us lessons. Those lessons may lead toward the exploitation of others; or they may lead us into action on behalf of equality, justice, and peace. A novel about a handsome prince is about class issues; generally, it tells the story that inequality is acceptable, even praiseworthy. I choose to challenge notions like that. Any time I set up an inequality in my books, you can almost count on the characters challenging those structures and world views.

Which leads us to the last question: what's coming next for Ari Ara?

No spoilers! I can only say that her adventure continues - and that she turns thirteen in the desert. Democracy, cultural understanding, women's rights, and warrior cultures vs. peace cultures all show up as themes in her next book. (Wink)

If you enjoyed *The Lost Heir*, spread the word!
Most of Ari Ara's readers find her stories through word-of-mouth. You can help friends and new readers connect to these great books in these ways:

Tell your friends.
Post about it on social media.
Review the book on your blog, book review site,
or favorite online bookstore.
Write a blog post about it.
Recommend it to your book group.
Suggest it to teachers and students.

Thank you!

ABOUT THE AUTHOR

Rivera Sun is the author of *The Way Between, Billionaire Buddha, The Dandelion Insurrection* and *Steam Drills, Treadmills, and Shooting Stars,* as well as theatrical plays, a study guide to nonviolent action, three volumes of poetry, and numerous articles. She has red hair, a twin sister, and a fondness for esoteric mystics. She went to Bennington College to study writing as a Harcourt Scholar and graduated with a degree in dance. She lives in an earthship house in New Mexico, where she writes essays and novels. She is a trainer in strategy for nonviolent movements and an activist. Rivera has been an aerial dancer, a bike messenger, and a gung-fu style tea server. Everything else about her - except her writing - is perfectly ordinary.

Rivera Sun also loves hearing from her readers:
Email: info@riverasun.com
Facebook: Rivera Sun
Twitter: @RiveraSunAuthor
Website: www.riverasun.com

Praise for *The Way Between*
by Rivera Sun

Between flight and fight lies a mysterious third path called *The Way Between*, and young shepherdess and orphan Ari Ara must master it ... before war destroys everything she loves! She begins training as the apprentice of the great warrior Shulen, and enters a world of warriors and secrets, swords and magic, friendship and mystery. She uncovers forbidden prophecies, searches for the lost heir to two thrones, and chases the elusive forest-dwelling Fanten to unravel their hidden knowledge. Full of twists and turns and surprises, *The Way Between* is bound to carve out a niche on your bookshelves and a place in your heart!

"This novel should be read aloud to everyone, by everyone, from childhood onward. Rivera Sun writes in a style as magical as Tolkien and as authentic as Twain."
- Tom Hastings, Director of PeaceVoice

"Rivera Sun has, once again, used her passion for nonviolence and her talent for putting thoughts into powerful words."
-Robin Wildman, Fifth Grade Teacher, Nonviolent Schools Movement, and Nonviolence Trainer

"A wonderful book! It is so rare to find exciting fiction for young people and adults that shows creative solutions to conflict, and challenges violence with active nonviolence and peace. Ari Ara is a delightful character and this story is a gem."
- Heart Phoenix, River Phoenix Center for Peacebuilding

Praise for Rivera Sun's
The Dandelion Insurrection

A rare gem of a book, a must read, it charts the way forward in this time of turmoil and transformation." - Velcrow Ripper, director Occupy Love, Genie Award Winner

"When fear is used to control us, love is how we rebel!" Under a

gathering storm of tyranny, Zadie Byrd Gray whirls into the life of Charlie Rider and asks him to become the voice of the Dandelion Insurrection. With the rallying cry of life, liberty, and love, Zadie and Charlie fly across America leaving a wake of revolution in their path. Passion erupts. Danger abounds. The lives of millions hang by a thin thread of courage, but in the midst of the madness, the golden soul of humanity blossoms . . . and miracles start to unfold!

"This novel will not only make you want to change the world, it will remind you that you can." - Gayle Brandeis, author of *The Book of Dead Birds*, winner of the Bellwether Prize for Socially Engaged Fiction

"Close your eyes and imagine the force of the people and the power of love overcoming the force of greed and the love of power. Then read *The Dandelion Insurrection*. In a world where despair has deep roots, *The Dandelion Insurrection* bursts forth with joyful abandon." - Medea Benjamin, Co-founder of CodePink

"THE handbook for the coming revolution!" - Lo Daniels, Editor of Dandelion Salad

"*The Dandelion Insurrection* is an updated, more accurate, less fantastical *Brave New World* or *1984*." - David Swanson, author, peace and democracy activist

". . . a beautifully written book just like the dandelion plant itself, punching holes through the concept of corporate terror and inviting all to join in the insurrection." - Keith McHenry, Co-founder of the Food Not Bombs Movement

"Rivera Sun's *The Dandelion Insurrection* takes place in a dystopia just a hop, skip and jump away from today's society. A fundamentally political book with vivid characters and heart stopping action. It's a must and a great read." - Judy Rebick, activist and author of *Occupy This!*

Also Available!
The Dandelion Insurrection Study Guide
to Making Change Through Nonviolent Action

You'll love this lively, engaging journey into the heart of The
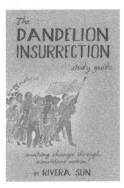
Dandelion Insurrection's story of nonviolent action! Taking lessons off the page and into our lives, author Rivera Sun guides us through the skills and strategies that created the thrilling adventure of The Dandelion Insurrection. Using your favorite scenes from the book and also drawing on historical examples of nonviolent struggles, this study guide brings the story to life in an exciting way.

You're in for an exciting ride as incendiary writer Charlie Rider and the unforgettable Zadie Byrd Gray rise to meet the political challenges flung at them from all sides. Freedom and equality loom just out of reach as the outraged corporate oligarchy scrambles to take back power after the Dandelion Insurrection's successful nonviolent revolution. Everyone from schoolteachers to whistleblowers leaps into action to help them confront the forces of corrupt politics. But the struggle turns volatile when an armed group called the Roots shows up. They claim to be protecting the movement . . . but who do they really serve?

"If you loved Starhawk's *Fifth Sacred Thing*, if you loved recently-departed Ursula K. LeGuin's *The Dispossessed*, if you admire the spirit of the Standing Rock Water Protectors, you will drink in this must-read page-turner . . . an epic story that will move your spirit, bringing tears to your eyes and healing to your soul." – Rosa Zubizarreta, Author of *From Conflict to Creative Collaboration*

"Rivera Sun always gifts us with usefully creative fiction. Her *Roots of Resistance* – the second novel of her Dandelion Trilogy – offers an inspiring story to help guide love-based strategic change efforts . . . . It takes a storyteller like Rivera Sun who inspires us to rise to the challenge as her characters do, because her stories tell us how." – Tom Atlee, Co-Intelligence Institute.

Reader Praise for Rivera Sun's
Steam Drills, Treadmills, and Shooting Stars

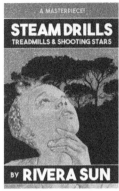

Steam Drills, Treadmills, and Shooting Stars is a story about people just like you, filled with the audacity of hope and fueled by the passion of unstoppable love. The ghost of folk hero John Henry haunts Jack Dalton, a corporate lawyer for Standard Coal as Henrietta Owens, activist and mother, wakes up the nation with some tough-loving truth about the environment, the economy, justice, and hope. Pressures mount as John Henry challenges Jack to stand up to the steam drills of contemporary America . . . before it's too late.

"This book is a gem and I'm going to put it in my jewelry box!"

"It 'dips your head in a bucket of truth'."

"This is not a page turner . . . it stops you in your tracks and makes you revel in the beauty of the written word."

"Epic, mythic . . . it's like going to church and praying for the salvation of yourself and your people and your country."

"Controversial, political, and so full of love."

"Partway through reading, I realized I was participating in a historical event. This book has changed me and will change everyone who reads it."

"I am sixty-two years old, and I cried for myself, my neighbors, our country and the earth. I cried and am so much better for it. I would recommend this book to everyone."

Praise for Rivera Sun's *Billionaire Buddha*

From fabulous wealth to unlimited blessings, the price of enlightenment may bankrupt billionaire Dave Grant. Emotionally destitute in the prime of his career, he searches for love and collides with Joan Hathaway. The encounter rattles his soul and unravels his world. Capitalism, property, wealth, mansions: his notions of success crumble into dust. From toasting champagne on top of the world to swigging whiskey with bums in the gutter, Dave Grant's journey is an unforgettable ride that leaves you cheering!

". . . inspirational and transformational! An enjoyable read for one's heart and soul."
-Chuck Collins, senior scholar, Institute for Policy Studies; co-author with Bill Gates Sr. of 'Wealth and Our Commonwealth'

". . . inspiring a skeptic is no easy task and Rivera Sun manages to do so, gracefully, convincingly, and admirably."
- Casey Dorman, Editor-in-Chief, Lost Coast Review

"People, if you haven't gotten your copy of *Billionaire Buddha* yet, you are letting a rare opportunity slip through your fingers. It's that good."
- Burt Kempner, screenwriter, producer and author of children's books

"This is the kind of book that hits you in the gut and makes you stop and think about what you just read."
- Rob Garvey, reader

"A clear and conscious look at our times and the dire need for a real change to heart based living."
- Carol Ranellone, reader

9 781948 016063